DATE DUE

MAR 3 0 2017	
	PRINTED IN U.S.A.

IN A LAND OF PAPER GODS

IN A LAND OF PAPER GODS

REBECCA MACKENZIE

TINDER
PRESS

First published in Great Britain in 2016 by Tinder Press
An imprint of HEADLINE PUBLISHING GROUP

1

Cataloguing in Publication Data is available from the British Library

Hardback ISBN 978 1 4722 2419 4
Trade paperback ISBN 978 1 4722 2420 0

Typeset in Sabon by Avon DataSet Ltd, Bidford-on-Avon, Warwickshire

Printed in Great Britain by Clays Ltd, St Ives plc

Headline's policy is to use papers that are natural, renewable and recyclable
products and made from wood grown in well-managed forests and other
controlled sources. The logging and manufacturing processes are expected to
conform to the environmental regulations of the country of origin.

HEADLINE PUBLISHING GROUP
An Hachette UK Company
Carmelite House
50 Victoria Embankment
London EC4Y 0DZ

www.tinderpress.co.uk
www.headline.co.uk
www.hachette.co.uk

For my family

My name is Henrietta S. Robertson. That's my English name. It is the name on my name tags, my holiday suitcase and on my cabin-trunk. It is the name written by my mother on the first page of my Bible. My Chinese name is Ming-Mei, which means Bright and Beautiful. It isn't labelled anywhere. It's just a name I carry in my thoughts, a name that echoes when I try to remember Mother's voice.

Growing up in China, we missionary children have two names. We are called by our Chinese name every day until we are six, when we're sent to the mission's school, high up on a mountain peak. There, answering roll call and following the trail of labels above sinks and hooks and beds, we become our English name. Our Chinese name, like the sound of our mothers' voices, fades.

I was born in the winter of 1930 in Shanxi Province, born blonde and pale as can be. The third of my mother's children, I was the only one to survive. When I grew sturdy enough, Mother took me on her gospel-telling trips. She'd place me upon Good News, our family mule, while she, dressed in her blue peasant's tunic, her dark hair coiled in a bun at the nape of her neck, walked along the red dust road, shading us both under a great oiled paper umbrella. Mother's work was to visit the women of our village and those in the villages nearby, squatting with them by their black-sooted stoves, or sipping tea on a warm brick kang. As she spoke, Mother gripped the back of my tunic with one hand, and in the other she held her gospel. Mother's gospel wasn't a Bible or a tract. It was a glove. Each finger was a different colour: black for sin, red for blood, white for holiness, yellow for heaven, each telling a different part of the story.

'Women of Pingxia village,' said Mother, wiggling a finger, 'do you remember what red is for?' But the women of Pingxia were more interested in pinching my white skin pink than remembering the blood of Jesus. As I squirmed across the kang, tiger-faced slippers kicking furiously, Mother would say, 'Please, ladies, listen to this gospel. It's a matter of eternal life.' She'd wiggle the yellow finger and add, carelessly, for that's how best to begin a bargain, 'Look, Celestial Heaven.' But the ladies would not look, for tug, tug, tug, they wished to pull my strange white hair. 'It's a ghost-girl,' they said, shuddering, before reaching out their hands to touch me once again.

These women know ghost-girls well for they are what float beyond the outer wall of every Chinese village. Some nights, when undressing me by the flicker of the oil lamp, Mother would find tangles of string, peach stones and paper gods in my pockets. They'd been placed by the women to protect me from becoming such a creature.

Set in the dusty loess hills of Shanxi Province, Pingxia village overlooked the mighty Huang Ho, a river made yellow from loess sediment, made cold from the melting ice of the Tibetan Plateau, a curving river, riddled with rapids and currents, which travelled nine provinces before casting itself into the Yellow Sea. The Huang Ho was called China's Sorrow, for it flooded the plains and its violent currents sucked travellers down, sending them to heaven in a swirl of yellow silt. From the village temple, incense rose each day, burnt to appease the River God from any sorrow he might send.

The Interior Alliance Mission had two thousand workers and a vision for taking the gospel inland by wheelbarrow, boat and mule to places of cholera, bandits and famine, for these were places where no gospel had been heard before. Just days after they'd been married in Shanghai Cathedral, Mother holding chrysanthemums, Father in a borrowed suit, their wedding rings moulded by a dentist from Tibetan gold, my parents sailed on goat-hide rafts up this river of sorrows towards their new post. That year the Huang Ho was full of boil and rage, and at the Taoping Rapids, my parents had to throw everything overboard just to stay afloat. The river ate up all their wedding gifts: the dishes, tablecloths, the framed wedding photograph, Mother's harmonium, the boxes of tracts, and the tin bath they'd stored them all in. When they appeared at the gates of Pingxia, barefoot and clutching only their Bibles, the villagers ran to their houses for they were afraid of my father, who had yellow hair and was as tall as a door. But moments later, it was the women of the village who, curious, emerged, sashaying over on their bound feet to touch Mother to see if she was real. They looked at her big feet, ugly and unlike their own, which were as dainty as the lotus flower, and gave scornful laughs. But they approved of her round face, and her hair, dark and glossy like theirs.

Soon the women began to invite Mother into their kitchens,

where she sat and preached, beginning with the very first gospel. The women asked to hear again the first stories of the venerable lineage of Abraham the ancestor, the evil emperor Herod, warnings in dreams and a family fleeing to a foreign land. In turn for these stories, they brought Mother red tea and herbs to heal her from her dead babies and to pity her when finally it was a girl and not a son that thrived.

Our house was like the others in the village, with a series of rooms built around a courtyard, but it was the only house without a paper god in the kitchen, and instead of paper gods above the entrance, we had a small wooden cross, which Father had cut, varnished and nailed to the wall. While a few were cautious to step inside, the children of the village were not, and we spent hours playing amongst Mother's pot plants and climbing the golden scholar tree. But on some afternoons, having tired of these games, my Chinese friends and I would go out beyond the walls and wander the dry fields, and up on the hillside to the caves where it was said the ghost girls lived.

Sleeping at a height too steep for my short legs to climb were the graves of my brother and sister, both buried in a tin suitcase, both mounds marked by a small stone. Aware of them up above me, I played lower down on the grassy slopes, finding on some days the bones of the baby girls who had no graves. Even at that young age, I knew to bury these bones in the soft earth, to decorate the mounds with feather, shell and twig, to weave over a litany of prayers, calling to Jesus, the River God, the wind.

On the eve of my departure from Pingxia village, we had Family Prayers, Mother and Father sitting on the kang, Father with his leather-bound Bible, heavy as a baby, resting on his lap. The light of the oil lamp flickered across the room. Pinned on the wall above the kang was a cotton sheet. Mother had drawn a map of China on it. There were black dots for mission stations, blue dots for villages visited, red dots for the Catholics. Father closed the Bible and looked at Mother. She dipped her head. Then Father raised his hands in a blessing over us. He said, 'Just like Abraham and Moses, we are a pilgrim people. We are called across the face of the earth. And now, Ming-Mei, you are six, and it is time to begin your own journey.' I looked up at the map. Day and night a trail of ants worked their way across it.

Later that evening, while Mother packed into my trunk the last items on the school's list, Father read from the school's prospectus. He read to me in his bedtime story voice. The first words were: 'Lushan School has been established so that parents can pursue their calling uninterrupted.' As he read, I leant near, and looked at the pictures. There was a school – white buildings above a black ravine – and next to it, a picture of a great bell. A pale girl with blond pigtails was ringing it. The bell was calling us children to the mountain of Lushan, and from all the corners of China we would come.

But that night, while Mother stood in the courtyard unable to sleep, Japanese troops gathered south-east of Peking, and just before dawn on the day of my leaving, a shot was fired by Marco Polo Bridge. A day later, as Chiang Kai-shek gathered his generals, preparing to declare war against Japan, I and twenty-seven other children of the mission's Northern Provinces gathered on the pier of Yuncheng Port. Here, knowing nothing of the disturbances further east, we waved goodbye to our parents, and boarded a boat upon the Huang Ho, river of China's Sorrow. Together we would travel for three weeks, by boat, by truck, on foot, towards Lushan, a land of mist and ravines, and into the darkness of war.

Part I

Lushan School, Jiangxi Province, China, 1941

Four years into the Second Sino-Japanese War

EACH MORNING, THE MIRROR BOBBED WITH FACES, PONYTAILS, and plaits. Faces peeked, puckered and frowned. A tall girl pouted, a short girl strained on tiptoes, all chin, trying to peer higher. The girl who could not bear to look at herself made gargoyle faces to hide behind. Wisps were tucked away, hairpins asserted control. Then the faces disappeared and the mirror rested calmly, for Muriel MacKay had rung the bell.

The bell resounded throughout the room, clear and sharp, calling all the girls of Dormitory A towards it. It was time for breakfast, and to get to the dining hall a single line had to be made. Muriel MacKay liked her lines to be straight.

When the line was to Muriel MacKay's satisfaction, it filed out of the Girls' Building and marched towards the dining hall. Sixteen legs, with seven pairs of socks pulled to the knee, one pair drooping to the ankle, marched clip clop, clip clop, clip clop. They passed over Celestial Stream (which had been renamed Livingstone Stream by the missionaries), across Drill Court and on to the dining hall, a narrow building at the far edge of the school. From here the neighbouring peaks, Old Man, Lily Lotus and Lion's Leap, could be seen across the gully. On a ridge above, the White Pagoda gleamed in the pale daylight.

The mountain was believed to be a sacred mountain and so far its inhabitants – the monks in the temple, the teachers and children in the missionary school, the villagers of Woosung, a hamlet in the valley below and the mountain-chair men who threaded their way up the winding paths – had all been left in peace while the Reds stormed north, and the Japanese came inland along the Yangtze, Shanghai, Nanjing and Wuhan burning behind them. Once, for days, there had been a terrible smell of sulphur and rot, and when the mountain's mist fell it was black. A year ago, for seven nights, there had been the steady drone of planes, heading west to Chongqing at nightfall and returning east to Wuhan at dawn. And then there was silence. Nothing. The air cleared and the mist drifted as white as before. In Woosung, the shutters of the noodle shop and rice merchants clattered open and the mountain-chair men took up their poles and once again brought baskets of vegetables and visitors, and news of refugees returning home, of troops regrouping on the other side of the Yangtze. But how long could this lull last? There was still a Japanese battleship in Poyang Lake. How long would they be protected? Of course, this question was not discussed with the children. It was left for the staff prayer meeting and the Lord.

In the dining hall there were six long tables of a dark, polished wood, with a napkin marking out each place. There were large windows down the sides of the room. On the far wall, an enormous painting showed a tiger lurking in a bamboo thicket.

'It's always watching us,' whispered Philip Hill.

'Just like Jesus is,' his friend replied. Then both boys turned their eyes from the painted sinews and claws to the dark pines that grew beyond the window.

The hall slowly filled with wave upon wave of children in single file, as Mr Dalrymple rang his gong. Each adult seemed to have a bell of some sort, each with a different ding, calling everyone to come along. Then all stood to sing the grace, 'Jehovah-Jireh is his name, he will provide'. When the 'Amen' had been sung in a three part harmony, napkins were pulled out of their holders, smoothed over laps and Wednesday's breakfast of hard-boiled egg was ready to be gobbled.

That day the sun did not seem to appear, but a cadaverous gloom hung over the valley. Muriel MacKay felt as if it was lodged inside her, a strange melancholy that put her off her breakfast. The dining hall was always chilly in the morning and Muriel MacKay nestled her chin into the scarf she had knitted on the voyage from Southampton. The clacking of the needles had kept her company throughout the five-week journey, each line of knitting marking off a distance covered. Muriel MacKay sometimes felt she had stitched her way to China, a knitted sea unravelling behind her.

China. The word had once rung in her mind, clear and bright. Yet now as she sat here in the dining hall, high up a Lushan peak, she struggled to remember her reasons for coming. All around her, children chattered, they boasted, they whispered, glared, twitched and fiddled. Muriel MacKay felt like a tree covered by incessantly chirping black birds.

'Etta, eat up your egg – it's good for you. Egg and

marmalade – really, Edith, that concoction might make you sick. Hilary, eat more slowly or you will be hungry before break.' As she dusted the crumbs off her skirt, Muriel MacKay wondered how she could sit here and be these two people at once. She looked at Mr Dalrymple, who was sitting at the next table. The bald patch on his head reminded her of a hole in a sock that just keeps getting bigger until, one day, the whole toe pops out. She looked at Maureen Baxter. She was a huge boulder of a woman whom the boys called Aunt Nebuchadnezzar because they said when she got mad she really would feed you to a lion. At that moment she could be heard across the dining hall, saying, 'Philip, where are napkins to be kept? Yes, laps! Laps!' And Miss Preedy, the Head of the Prep School, for whom everything jiggled: the wobble of skin under her neck, the bunch of keys around her middle, her nerves, which were intolerably jangled by reports of socks that had not been paired before the wash.

Muriel MacKay felt a cool hand on her shoulder. She turned and came face to face with Mr Dalrymple. He gave her a smile, neat-toothed as a pocket comb, and whispered, 'Miss MacKay.' Addressing her as 'Miss MacKay' was a formality from which he never wavered, even when there were no children present.

She returned like with like: 'Mr Dalrymple.'

'Miss MacKay, there has been an . . .' He raised his eyebrows then released them on the word 'incident'.

She mouthed back, 'Jap . . . ?' Her heart pounded.

He shook his head. No, not the Japanese. His eyes went to the girls at her table. He came closer to her ear and lowered his voice. 'A school matter. We need to rule out any cause for concern.'

Mr Dalrymple smiled his pocket-comb smile. 'After breakfast there will be a meeting at the Headmaster's Cottage.'

For the rest of breakfast, the tickle of Mr Dalrymple's breath was in Muriel MacKay's ear. Secrets, they tickle you so, she thought, watching her girls carefully.

Attached by golden pins to every dormitory and classroom door is a sign. It was drawn up as a precaution in the days that the Japanese pressed inland from Shanghai along the Yangtze and it lists the school's out-of-bounds areas, parameters that no child should be found beyond:

1. The Great Steps
2. Livingstone Stream
3. The laundry
4. The kitchens
5. The bank behind the Girls' Building
6. The arbour unless accompanied
7. The steps up to the pagoda
8. Memorial Hall unless on piano practice
9. The Headmaster's Cottage
10. Gardener Chen's Nissen hut

After breakfast, when the girls had been ushered to their classrooms by the big school bell in the playground, Muriel MacKay walked through the empty dormitory. The dormitory was set out in lines of bunks; each bed had a doll resting on its pillow and a dressing gown draped across the end. Beside each bunk there was a bedside cabinet with a family photograph on it. There were parents in Chinese dress outside mud-hut churches, Bibles in hand; brothers and sisters in wheelbarrows; a family sitting by their courtyard pond, a girl's hand trailing in the water.

Muriel MacKay inspected each bed's hospital corners. Tuesday nights were bed-making nights, which meant that Wednesday mornings were bed inspection mornings. She marked every girl's attempt with a score from nought to ten. One girl would have to be the best and get an eight. (It was helpful for there always to be room for improvement and Muriel MacKay had promised herself that she would not give anyone a ten until the last week of the school year.) As usual, that top-scoring girl was Florence, and, as usual, the girl with the lowest mark and bedspread a-drooping was Henrietta.

After she had finished the inspection, Muriel MacKay stood in front of the dormitory mirror, tidied her red hair and straightened her bun. She gave herself a mark of four out of ten. She tested a polite smile, reassessed her score at five, then unwrapped and redraped her scarf, and improved that to a mark of six. With the necessary adjustments made, Muriel MacKay headed to the out-of-bounds Headmaster's Cottage.

The Calling

Two Months Earlier

THE BATHROOM WAS FILLED WITH ITS VERY OWN STEAM CLOUD AND the green tiled floor was slippery underfoot. It was Saturday night, and Saturday night was bath night. All twelve of us girls wore dressing gowns, towel turbans, or pranced naked. There were two sinks in the middle of the bathroom, each with its own mirror, now blinded by the steam. All about there were sounds of water: a tap dripping, a plughole glugging, a girl gargling to the tune of 'Jesus, Thy Robe of Righteousness'.

I had to share a bath with Big Bum Eileen. The water was a murky yellow because the previous night it had rained so hard that the stream was flooded with mud. Rain droplets were still sliding off the forest's rubbery leaves that morning, and the afternoon had been spent playing in a world that could flip you upside down in an instant. We'd all got some small souvenir from the day: a rosy bump, a blue bruise, a pair of muddy-bottomed knickerbockers.

Big Bum Eileen settled into the bath first and took the

tapless end. I got in at the tap end, easing in a toe, then a foot. The water was still deliciously hot, and I stood gasping for a moment. My legs looked like they were wearing pink knee-high socks. Big Bum Eileen had her shower cap on, its lovely little strawberries beautifully embroidered with three brown seeds on every berry. My shower cap was red and had begun to grow mould around the edges. Florence said that I shouldn't be sad about the mould because the green edging made the shower cap look like a very big strawberry. Big Bum Eileen leant back in the bath and sighed as if she was an elegant lady looking out of a train window. Then she started talking about her boobies.

This term Big Bum Eileen's boobies had become the thing to talk about at bath time. And morning wash time. And dressing for games, and undressing for bed. In fact, they were talked about any time that there was nakedness. Big Bum Eileen came back from her summer holiday and there they were, nestling on her chest. She was the only one so far to get them. We all thought that Kathryn might have them too, but Kathryn hated being inspected. She wrapped her towel tightly around her, giving a look nastier than off breakfast milk.

Big Bum Eileen had stolen a measuring tape from the dormitory sewing kit and stuffed it in her toothbrush cup. Every Saturday bath time, we went through the ceremony of measuring her chest. We would do this when Aunty Muriel was at the other end of the dormitory, inspecting our wardrobes for dangly buttons, holes through which toes might pop, and ripped knickerbocker bottoms.

Big Bum Eileen stretched out her legs in the bath. Her toes reached into my bit of water and prodded my leg. Because of her breast status, it was difficult to complain as I usually would. 'Eileen,' I muttered, as I floated myself an inch towards the taps. But she didn't notice because she was too busy looking at her boobies.

'They have definitely grown. Wouldn't you say, Etta?' she said, her gaze fixed firmly on her chest.

I was fed up of hearing about her boobies. They were getting too much attention. They were putting her and the other girls in danger of committing idolatry. For it is written, 'Thou shalt have no other God but me.'

I gave them a good look anyway. They seemed pretty much the same as last week. I screwed up my whole face as I inspected them, to prove that I was really, really looking. I said, 'The right one has certainly grown. Yes, it has. My, my, it's quite enormous.' I peered at them again and sighed, 'Eileen, your right breast is truly blessed.'

Horror flashed across Big Bum Eileen's face, a moment that was unto me as short but as delicious as scoffing a candied crab apple. Then I made a splashing cacophony with my hands and started singing 'Onward, Christian Soldiers' so that I wouldn't have to talk about them any more. Marching as to war, splash, splash.

As I sang the school's favourite war-time hymn, Big Bum Eileen rammed her feet even further into my territory. She lazily slopped her flannel over herself and then stood up in the bath, a pink-bottomed, pink-socked statue.

She got out and glided through the steam cloud towards the sinks where the other girls awaited her arrival. I lay down in the bath with my eyes just above its edge, watching them like an old crocodile floating near the banks of the murky Nile, camouflaged by a very big strawberry.

Once Hilary had given the all clear on Aunty Muriel, they got on with the measurement.

'Do they hurt?' asked Edith, as concerned as a Good Samaritan.

'Have they grown since last week?' asked Sarah, double-checking the measurement again.

'When will the milk come out?' asked Hilary.

Even Flo, who is my best friend, was entranced. 'Do they wobble yet?'

Big Bum Eileen dismissed her disciples with a shrug. 'It is just part of becoming a woman.'

I thought her boobies were stupid. I was cross, cross, cross to see all the other girls measuring and questioning and committing idolatry. I could bite them all. I flung off my shower cap and disappeared under the yellow water where all I could hear was my blood pounding and the water-warped murmuring of the outside world. My hair swilled behind me as I thrashed around like a mean mermaid.

Then, clear as a bell, the Lord spoke to me. I surged out of the bath, gasping for air. A revelation had been born! It was: YOU MUST TEACH THE OTHERS TO BE PROPHETESSES.

I hunched over and listened to the words echoing within me. They were crisp and light and true. The Lord's words had opened up a path for me. I would follow.

Less than two weeks ago, the Lord himself had called me to be a prophetess. This meant spending many hours on my own, for in that time I had obeyed my calling by going on secret journeys in search of signs from which to prophesy. Along the school's twisting paths, I prowled, I snooped and then I ventured further. Just the previous day, I had stood on the cusp of out of bounds, listening to the howling dogs of Woosung. Afraid of what those hobbling dogs might summon, I clapped my hands over my ears and fled back to the dormitory, where the girls were helping Aunty Muriel make the first fire of autumn, where voices spoke only of cross-stitch, wart cream and Aunty Muriel's watercolours.

It was lonesome being a prophetess, so now God had asked that they be called, too. Yes, God had given an answer. I would follow.

I looked around. The girls were at the far end of the bathroom, trying to get Kathryn to let down her towel. I got out of the bath, tiptoed up across the wet floor to a steamed-up mirror and wrote:

TONIGHT.
YOU WILL ALL BE CALLED.

I wrote this on Big Bum Eileen's mirror because she would make the biggest fuss on finding it, and a big fat fuss was what I needed.

Then I turned and ran naked through the dorm, shouting 'Heavens above, Heavens above . . .' before flinging myself face down on my bunk and going silent for authenticity. For before Zacharias revealed his prophecy, he was struck dumb.

My silence didn't last long. 'For goodness' sake, Henrietta Robertson, what is all this commotion?' said Aunty Muriel, drumming her fingers on my head.

'I'm having a prophecy,' I said into my pillow.

'Well, you had better have it with some clothes on,' said Aunty Muriel. I slipped my fingers under the pillow and pulled out my white nightie. It is a sin to be naked for too long.

After lights out, I risked two points off my Goodness Card by getting out of bed and slinking up to each girl's bunk, whispering, 'You,' followed by their name as written on their name tags. 'You . . . Edith W. Crickmay . . . are called to become . . . a prophetess.' Not every girl was awake to receive her visitation. That didn't matter. Those who had been left out would be even more dizzy to be part of it.

When I had visited each girl, I climbed back into my own bunk and shivered. I wasn't sure if I was shivering because I was cold, or because I was bad. I drew my blankets up to my eyeballs and smelt the musty hand-me-down smell of the children before me.

Then, as most nights, I worried about the state of my soul. I lay very still and tried to feel if the Lord was alive within me. But I felt nothing, just the bang-bang of my wicked heart.

The First Prophecy

IT WAS ON A WEDNESDAY, TWO WEEKS EARLIER, THAT I'D MADE MY first prophecy. That Wednesday was Aunty Muriel's half-day off and so Miss Preedy looked after us. It was a terrible day for my Goodness Card. I already had two order marks, and I was going to get a third, but it didn't take the gift of prophecy to know that.

We were brushing our teeth before assembly, six girls to a sink. Above each, the mirror was busy with faces. Our mirror showed: in the back row, Kathryn, tossing her brown mane; Big Bum, her eyes green and slithering. In the middle row, Florence and Hilary, mouths open like good choir girls, singing 'aah' as they brushed, and at the front, Edith and me, short and barging.

Flo stopped brushing and wobbled a tooth.

'Let me have a look,' I said. Flo opened her mouth. I peered inside. Flo's tongue was pink and at the back were little bluey-pink folds of flesh and a pink hanging thing. Flo was made of meat and wobble and bone. She was an animal. We were all just animals, like chickens ready to be roasted.

'I have seen mortality,' I said. The words just popped out.

The girls turned to look at me. They kept on brushing.

'We are all going to die. All of us!' I yelled, staggering about.

The girls calmly foamed at the mouth.

'Someone here is going to die very soon.'

'The Japanese,' said Hilary. The others stopped brushing. I could see that I had their attention, that they were thinking of bayonets, of warships, or mustard gas.

I narrowed my eyes. 'Who will it be . . . ?' My toothbrush wand pointed at each one of them in turn. Edith started to turn away. 'Edith!' I pounced. 'You are going to die first.'

Edith screamed and ran into the dormitory. Moments later Miss Preedy appeared at the bathroom door. She was sniffing, as if sniffing out a sin. 'What is this noise for? Why is Edith crying on her bed?'

One by one the toothbrushes pointed at me, but it was Big Bum who spoke.

'Etta told her she is going to die. Very soon, in fact.'

'Henrietta Robertson,' said Miss Preedy. She looked suddenly ravenous. 'I should have known.'

Edith dragged herself back into the bathroom, flung her arms around Miss Preedy and gave her beggar-girl wail. From her cuff, Miss Preedy took a handkerchief embroidered with the word 'Wednesday' and gave it to Edith.

As Edith blew her nose, Big Bum Eileen said, 'But, Miss Preedy, I look forward to dying, because then I will be with the Lord. My heart,' she spread her arms out, 'longs for the Lord.'

'Well, that is very nice, Eileen,' said Miss Preedy, patting Big Bum Eileen's shoulder. Big Bum Eileen is clever. She knows that the Second Coming is Miss Preedy's favourite topic, especially when there has been any mention of war.

But despite Miss Preedy's talk of angels thronging above the Dormitory A bathroom, Edith could not be consoled. Death lingered and no amount of brushing or celestial visions helped. The bell went for assembly, which reminded Miss Preedy to say, 'That is an order mark for you, Henrietta Robertson.'

The girls finished brushing, leant over their basins and spat.

The Girls' Building used to be a hotel for foreigners and had been sold to the mission for just one dollar. It was covered in a tumble of passion flowers. It was large and leaky, and I had lived in its dormitories since I was six. Whenever I stood on the balcony of the Girls' Building and looked out over the school, I would be reminded of standing on the deck of a ship. And whenever I thought of ships, I'd remember saying goodbye to my parents for the first time at Yuncheng harbour. As the twenty-seven of us from the Northern Provinces gathered with our suitcases and trunks, knapsacks, dolls and slingshots, between the ship and the land ran many strands of red string. Mother and Father gave me a red string and said, 'Don't let go.'

I followed the big children up the gangplank holding my string. The red string was a goodbye tradition. We children on deck held one end, and our mothers and fathers on the cobbled quayside held the other. Each child had his or her own string. The Gable parents held three strings, one for each of their daughters. Then I felt my whole self joggle and shake, my legs, my arms, my teeth. 'Mother!' I called. 'Father!' I clung to Mary Gable. I hadn't realised that I couldn't come back down.

Underneath us the brown water churned, a terrible smell of fish and sludge rose, and the ship shuddered out of the harbour. Holding my string, I couldn't see Mother's face properly because of her sunhat; just her mouth, which was stretched wide, and both hands waving. I watched her and Father shrink. I felt the red thread in my fingers pull, pull, pull until it snapped and went slack. Down the Huang Ho we tumbled and out into the North China Sea.

We sailed south for three days, then travelled up the Yangtze in a creaking river boat. Both starboard and port-side, the paddy fields glittered with sky. At Jiujiang we got off into a hubbub of noodle men, were loaded on to a lorry, which rolled along pock-marked roads into the green hills, where we edged hairpin bends until the road became a steep paving-stone path, and the journey was continued by mountain chair. The mountain-chair men sang their famous song, 'The lonely pines of Lushan, the rock is their mother, the mist is their milk', as we made our way through the many strangely shaped pines. Each pine had a name, and the Gable sisters, who'd been up this mountain many times before, called out to them like old friends – 'Tortoiseshell Pine', 'Ink Pot Pine', 'Scissor Pine' – as we swayed up the mountain. Around the peaks we spiralled, until we came up to a flat path that headed along a ridge. There, up at the top of one hundred steps carved through a ridge of black rock, was Lushan School. White buildings in a scoop of land, surrounded by dark peaks, twisted pines and clouds. Then into the Girls' Building I was taken, given a glass of milk and put into a bunk bed, my sheets tucked tight as a pinch.

And it was here, on the balcony of the Girls' Building, that I now stood having Miss Preedy's punishment. She had not liked my prophecy about Edith that morning, especially because Edith had cried all breakfast and refused to eat.

'What lives inside you? Will it grow good fruit? Or wicked fruit? You, Henrietta Robertson, must make a choice.' Miss Preedy placed my Bible on the railing, drummed its cover to emphasise her point, then slip-slopped along the balcony and down the stairs. The front door closed with a bang.

All the school could see me. I wanted to run away but I couldn't because I was standing on a wooden stool, my hands gripping the railing. It is difficult to consider the state of your soul when a whole playground is looking up at you, and also, I was scared of falling.

Below, on Drill Court, Amah Liu was sweeping pine needles with her bamboo broom, her bound feet tiny as gazelle hoofs, her long black plait swinging. Beyond her was the playing field, where boys in white ran back and forth on the scorched grass. I couldn't see the girls, but every now and then I heard 'Leviticus, Numbers, Deuteronomy' and the tsk-tsk of the skipping rope. They were tucked around the corner of the Girls' Building in the dormitory garden, memorising Bible Class prep as they leapt. At the top of the Great Steps, a file of mountain men arrived with baskets of pak choi and cucumbers. They put their green burdens down by the Guest Welcoming Arbour. They were naked apart from trousers, which is a sin unless you're a mountain-chair man.

The Sons of Thunder got up from the sandpit where they'd drawn a map of China and placed battalions of marbles, and began to march in formation across Drill Court ready to begin one of their rounds of the perimeter of the school, which they had taken upon themselves to do daily. Sons of Thunder was the name Jesus gave his friends James and John, and those boys had decided to call themselves that when the Japanese ran reconnaissance flights the year before. But that afternoon, their military discipline quickly vanished, for they had seen Gardener Chen.

The boys began to holler and leap after Gardener Chen, for he carried a large glass jar and they were very interested in its contents. When they got to the bank by the Livingstone Stream, which is out of bounds, Gardener Chen jogged down the steps to his Nissen, Aunt Neb leapt up from the bench, waving her hands in alarm, and the Sons of Thunder booed because they were not allowed to follow. They made a new marching formation, and strode back, hup, two, three, four.

As they passed the Girls' Building they talked about killing snakes. 'Bash its head,' said Roland, 'bang, bang, smash.' His fist punched the air. Then he looked up at the balcony. 'What are you doing up there, Etta?'

'Oh, nothing, just standing and looking,' I said.

'You're in trouble,' said his friend Nigel Pinsent.

'No, I'm not.'

'She is,' Nigel Pinsent said to the boys. Rather than lie and bear a bad fruit, I pretended not to hear. A stone whizzed past my cheek and landed on the wall behind. Nigel Pinsent had flicked it.

'You, you . . . just you wait . . . I'll put you in a jar and pickle you alive.' I shook my fists. The boys skedaddled across Drill Court, laughing.

Oh, stupid Miss Preedy, stupid Nigel Pinsent. Stupid everyone. I shook with a terrible rage, then began to sob. I let go of the railing, opened my Bible and tumbled in. I landed at the foot of Jesus. He was eating an olive.

'Etta,' he said.

'Hello, Jesus,' I said, resting my head upon his knee.

'Etta, Etta,' he said.

I sighed.

'Etta, Etta.' Someone was calling my name. But it wasn't Jesus, it was Flo, standing below the balcony, her hands cupped around her mouth.

'Guess what!' Flo shouted up, 'Edith's in Sick Bay!'

I nearly fell two floors.

At the table, Dormitory A's dinner talk was all about mumps. The girls looked inside each other's mouths for signs of sickness. Edith had been first. Who would be next?

Hilary leant over. 'Etta, you knew Edith was sick. You feel my throat.' I stretched my arm across the table and placed my hand on her throat. She gulped. I could feel her gulp in the palm of my hand. It felt like holding a baby swallow just fallen from the nest. 'I think you're going to be okay,' I said, wiping my hand on my skirt.

'And me?' said Sarah. I felt her throat. She held her breath and blinked. I could feel her jugular pulsing, boom, boom, and I felt my own blood thump in time with hers. It gave me a giddy feeling. Something inside was trying to get out. My hand went clammy.

'You'll be okay,' I said, but this time there was no chance to wipe away the feeling, for Kathryn and Fiona put their forks to their plates and asked to be next. Big Bum Eileen shoved in. 'And me?' she said, leaning over, her thick plait tumbling on to the table. I stretched my arm across.

'Rears on seats, girls,' said Aunty Muriel, ringing her 'Rs' like a bell. 'And not a peep until you've eaten your meat.' Aunty Muriel knows rules are easier to keep when they rhyme. You just can't get them out of your head.

As I chewed the squiggle of liver, twenty chews per mouthful, I looked at Edith's empty chair. Edith was a gap between

Big Bum Eileen and Kathryn. Thin air. The knife and fork were laid out ready, but there was no Edith to raise them up. Edith had vanished and I had prophesied it.

As I chewed in silence, I slowly looked at the other girls. Watching each one of them, the feeling came, light and bright and clear. I could see things others could not see. The Lord had chosen me.

At first I felt scared. Then I felt powerful. Soon I wielded my toothbrush meanly morning, noon and night. I draped my towel biblically, and annoyed everyone. I swooned at my reflection in the bathroom mirror for I was the Lord's handiwork and most beautifully made. There and then I named myself Samantha, the girl version of Samuel, and a most beautiful name for a prophetess.

'For goodness' sake, stop mooning in the mirror and get on with your teeth,' said Aunty Muriel.

'I prophesy, I prophesy . . .' I said, shaking myself down the dormitory.

When Aunty Muriel helped the girls with long hair do their hair before breakfast, I joined the queue. 'Aunty Muriel, please may I have the white ribbon in my hair? White for holiness.'

'Etta, your hair is now too short for a ribbon of any colour,' said Aunty Muriel. But because people feel sorry for girls with short hair, she looped it around my head and, with what was left, tied a tiny bow.

'Oh, Aunty Muriel, thank you, thank you, now I'm holy-looking.' I hugged her.

Aunty Muriel pulled my arms from around her neck. 'You can only be holy-looking if you think holy thoughts,' she said.

I thought holy thoughts loudly. During Quiet Time, our morning daily devotion, I sat on my bunk and coughed until the girls looked at me. I closed my eyes and tittered like a lady having tea at Headmaster's Cottage. Flo, on the bunk below, thumped my bed slats. But I couldn't stop. Then straight after Quiet Time, when we were shining our black school shoes by the shoe rack on the balcony, I shook my head and said, 'Deary goodness me, how I love speaking with our Lord Jesus every day.'

'What did he say?' asked Edith, who, fortunately, had not died.

'A funny joke.'

'What joke?' asked Edith.

'The one about the pencil.'

'They didn't have pencils in the Bible,' said Big Bum Eileen.

'But he is alive today. And so he has pencils,' said Flo.

'Yes, and so he knows jokes about pencils,' I said. 'Someone prayed it to him.'

'Who prayed him a joke about pencils?' asked Edith.

I had a think. 'Mr Dalrymple.'

That afternoon, Big Bum, who is not afraid of male authority, put her hand up and asked Mr Dalrymple if he knew any jokes. As we'd all done well in the arithmetic test, except Edith, whose place at the bottom of the class I had prophesied, Mr Dalrymple stretched his long legs forward, leant backwards, waggled his knees, tapped his bald patch with his yellow pencil, and finally said, 'Yes.' And that's how we heard the one about the chalk. During Quiet Time the next morning I told it to Jesus, who laughed so hard I nearly fell out of my bunk.

'Will you be quiet, Etta, I'm trying to pray,' hissed Flo

from the bottom bunk. Of course I couldn't reply to her for I answered not unto my old name but only to my prophetess name, Samantha.

Flo and the other girls kept forgetting to call me Samantha and over the next few weeks, they forgot to call me at all. I spent more and more time on my own in search of signs. A bird's nest, a broken jar, a snake's skin. Further and further I went, until in the fourth week, I was wandering up by the laundry. That's when I first saw her. Our daughter.

The laundry is the highest building in the school. It's above the kitchens and the Boys' Building. Practically built into the rock. There are rows and rows of sheets, billowing. Like a cloud factory. I loved the smell of cleanness, the bright white sheets, the escaped bubbles drifting.

The laundry is out of bounds, a place you could only go if you had a task, such as nit combing, or to get a box of soap for a dorm aunty. It wasn't a place to be aimless as a bubble. I had a feeling that there was something waiting to be discovered in the laundry but what it was I wasn't sure. I gave my scalp a scratch and imagined lots of little black dots crawling over it and made my way slowly for a nit combing, looking carefully about me as I went.

Making my way to the middle of the sheets, I let them billow around me for a while, and leant back on a washing line, bending as far as it would go, feeling sun-warmed like a sheet. These sheets would make a wonderful costume for a prophetess, I thought. Then, on I went to the laundry room to look at the laundry ladies.

It was a dark, hot room. It smelt of ironing and carbolic. The floor was slippy and wet. From beside the piles of washing by the door, I noted the hoses, strangled in a knot, buckets, Quaker Oats tins filled with odd socks, pegs galore, scrubbing boards ribbed like chests, and wooden brushes that were, I noted, the size of small slippers. In the corner, on a bamboo mat, sat Amah Liu and Amah Wei, folding a pile of shirts. I noted with interest the small lacquer tray filled with nuts between them.

I went over. '*Ni hao.*' Imagining the dirty little lice running with dirty little feet, I itched my head once more. Amah Liu gestured for me to sit down, found her nit comb and started working on my hair. Tug, yank, ow, ow, tug. Tug, ow, ow, yank. Ow.

The terrible combing done, I stood up, my scalp and conscience cleaned. Amah Liu gave me three nuts, then wiped the nit comb on her blue cotton trousers. I looked at her tiny bound feet in their black silk slippers. Even through the carbolic, they stank.

I wandered out of the hot laundry room and through the washing lines. The littlest ones were being done today. Sheets, tiny pants, tiny socks, little dresses and shorts. They were so small. Soon the magical world would be unpegged, the clouds folded away and put back in the laundry basket.

The sky was blue, the pillowcases billowed. I sat down in between two rows of sheets and ate the first nut. Then I heard soft footsteps. I froze. They were getting nearer. A small ghost shape formed in the sheet ahead of me. Small hands, face, knees pressing into a sheet. Then, pop, through the sheet, the ghost became a girl. A small Chinese girl. I followed her through the washing.

The girl ran to the steps that led from the back of the school up the mountain to the temple. There were wooden posts at either side of the path. Each post was carved with a dragon's head, and its tail was the railings that led up to the temple. Its eyes were bulging and its tongue stuck out.

Standing on the bottom step was a stooped old lady. She wore a grey peasant's tunic and carried a basket with a few eggs in it. The old lady tipped her head to the sky and called, 'Shi'Er', which means, 'Twelve.' When the girl reached the bottom step, the old lady touched her face and they turned, heading up the path to the temple.

After weeks of my prophetessing, Aunty Muriel had had her last straw. We were on our way to Friday Evening Prayers. There was a beautiful sunset with a pink peony sky. The White Pagoda glowed rose and we all dawdled on the Red Step to admire it.

To show Aunty Muriel how much I appreciated the works of the Lord, I placed my hand upon my heart and let out a yelp. I staggered, saying, 'The Beauty of the Lord, I am quite overcome.' Then I collapsed, grabbing Flo and Edith's arms on the way.

'Aunty Muriel, wait,' said Hilary. 'Etta's been overcome and taken Flo and Edith with her.'

'My name's Samantha,' I called from the fifty-seventh step.

Edith began her beggar-girl wail. Flo brushed the gravel off her elbows and knees, saying, 'I am so sick of you, Etta.'

'My name's Samantha,' I said.

Someone kneeled by me and took my hand. 'Leave her,' said Aunty Muriel to them.

'But I'm overcome,' I said. The person let go. My hand flopped to the ground. There was the sound of many departing footsteps, then silence. I opened mine eyes. Above a blade of grass, I watched them leave.

When they disappeared into Memorial Hall, I sat up and looked around at the empty playing fields, the sunset turning the world violet and ash. I wanted to show them that I was special, but being a prophetess on my own was lonely. Sitting there, looking at the pink pagoda, I saw a cloud of black fly out of the pagoda, a screeching, rising flurry of bats. *Bats, black and wicked from upside-down sleeping.* I picked myself up and ran after the girls for I was afraid that the bats were a sign, or worse, that my wicked spirit had called them into being.

The First Meeting of the Prophetess Club

THE FIRST MEETING OF THE PROPHETESS CLUB WAS A GREAT SUCCESS. After Sunday lunch we sat under The Beard, the pine tree at the centre of our dormitory garden. The feathery canopy of The Beard was to be our Tent of Meeting. Everything smelt earthy and wonderfully fertile after the rainstorm. Ferns glistened with droplets, the black soil wriggled with worms. On the East Steps that led from Headmaster's Cottage to our garden, a green frog croaked.

I had decreed that anyone with little brothers and sisters was allowed to bring them to the garden. I did this because on Sundays it is loving for families to be together. Sarah said that the children could be our Temple Children. Hilary chopped down big ferns with her penknife and the Temple Children got to work fanning us as we sat around in a circle. Flo's little brother, Peter, found some monkey cups, which he filled with water from the muddy Livingstone Stream and we pretended to drink from them. We sent away Peter's friend Philip because he didn't belong to anyone. Hilary's little sister, Emma, brought slugs on moss platters, which we passed around, everyone minding their Ps and Qs, for it had been agreed that Prophetesses were to have etiquette most exquisite.

First of all everyone received their Prophetess name. There is a shortage of lady prophets in the Bible to choose from. But this hindered us not for there are many ways to make men's names more ladylike. Simply add 'ine', 'ina', or 'ella', or indeed 'etta' to the end of the name. So, Big Bum Eileen became Elijine. Edith became Elishella. Florence became Habakkukina. Sarah became Baptistina, although she said her family was Methodist and would be upset about it. Hilary, who was taken captive for five days in the Haicheng piracy, and has since been obsessed by ships, was named after Jonah and so became Joan. Fiona became Isaihette. Isobel became Zephanella and Kathryn, who is mostly focused on being a horse, we gave the name Jere-Neigh.

We were all there.

'Now what?' said Big Bum Eileen. She was sat with her back against The Beard's trunk, the best spot. She tossed a tumble of pale, slinky hair over her shoulder. Big Bum Eileen grew up in a mission home. It had banisters, which is where she learnt to glide. It also meant that somehow she always got the best spot, such as sitting next to Aunty Muriel at dormitory prayers, or being at the head of the glossy dining table.

Everyone was looking at me. Even the Temple Children stopped fanning. Oh dear, they wanted a speech. I stood up. A beat thrummed through my chest. I began. 'From this afternoon onward we are no longer just girls of Dormitory A, we are children of the Prophetess Club. We have been

35

chosen, each one of us, and soon signs and wonders shall be revealed. Of course, there will be sacrifices, but these will be as nothing to us. We shall grow in height, strength and breast, we shall prophesy, we shall preach, and there will be miracles. This is the promise of the Prophetess Club.' I sat down, red as a burning bush.

'Are prophetesses Christian?' asked Sarah, her brown hair lifting in a breeze made by a Temple Child.

'Of course they're Christians,' I said.

'Is it the same as being a Christian but more fun?' asked Edith.

'It's more fun,' I said, 'and more dangerous.'

'I don't want to do anything dangerous,' said Sarah.

'It's dangerous, but remember, we will never be left alone,' said Big Bum Eileen. She blinked her straw-coloured eyelashes, and her green eyes slid to the sky. We knew she was gazing at the Lord.

'It's fun because we'll go hunting for prophecies,' I said.

'But how will you know when you've found one?' All the girls were looking at me. I'd had a prophecy, so I should know.

I said, 'A strange tickling feeling comes over you and you see pictures, and you feel a bit sick as if you might fall over, and you want to say . . . "hark" a lot.'

'Hark,' said the girls, trying on the word for size: slowly at first, then louder, and a bit shrill, then a whole chorus of harks. The Headmaster, Mr Lammemuir, went past, jogging up the East Steps to his cottage high up the hill. We held our harks.

'We shall have to learn the Scriptures off by heart,' said Florence when he'd passed.

'And be very good.'

36

'And be very kind.'

'Just like our mothers,' said Sarah. There was a silence while we thought of our mothers. Then we began our list of commandments.

The Commandments of the Prophetess Club

1. A prophetess must have a prophetess name. She must answer only to this name at all times, except when Aunty Muriel is nearby, or in the classroom, or when the Sons of Thunder are near.
2. She must be charitable. She must donate to the Prophetess Club fund, Save Poor and Lost Chinese (S.P.A.L.C.). Donations are to be in the form of one afternoon break biscuit per week.
3. She must have exquisite manners.
4. She must look for prophecies.
5. She must look out for others.
6. She must be overcome by the beauty of the Lord.
7. She must sing beautifully, for time and time again it is written, 'Sing, O Daughter of Zion'.

'And the eighth commandment?' I asked as Flo scribbled into the back of her prayer diary.

'There shalt be no false prophecies.' That was Big Bum Eileen. Her head was resting peacefully against The Beard's trunk but her eyes slid around each of us.

'False prophecies?' the girls murmured.

'Yes, if you make a false prophecy you become a false prophetess,' said Big Bum Eileen, hissing the Ss of 'prophetess'.

'But, what if you're just learning and you couldn't help making a mistake?' (That was Edith.)

'It should take at least two false prophecies for you to become a false prophetess and . . .' I said.

'. . . And then you're expelled from the Prophetess Club,' said Big Bum Eileen.

There was a silence.

'You become an F.P.,' said Big Bum Eileen.

We took a shocked breath. All at once 'F.P.' were initials to be despised.

'But . . . but . . . I'm F.P.,' said Fiona Pinder quietly.

'F.P. are your worldly initials,' I said. 'Your prophetess initials are "I.P." for Isaihette Pinder.'

'No, not Pinder; we can't use our worldly surnames.' That was Big Bum Eileen. She liked to say no.

'We no longer belong to parents,' said Florence, who knows her Bible and could recite her catechism backwards if it wasn't a devilish thing to do. 'For cast off thy mother and brother.'

Sarah told her Temple Child to go. He put down his fern-fan and tiptoed away. The other Temple Children followed.

'We belong to the Lord,' said Big Bum Eileen, her green eyes sliding heavenward.

'How about Care of the Lord? Like a suitcase, c/o the Lord,' I said. We all had a trunk and a holiday suitcase. Our trunks were stored in great Nissen huts down by Carey Stream. There since we were six years old, they were getting old and growing cobweb beards. Because of the great distance between Lushan and Shanxi Province, and the ever-changing territory of the war, my holiday suitcase had only been used on two occasions: once when I was seven and once again when I was nine. For some, like Kathryn, whose parents were always on the go across the plain, the holiday suitcases had not yet left the hut.

'Okay, we're c/o the Lord,' said Big Bum Eileen. And with that we all shared the same surname. We looked at each other. We were a family. We were all c/o the Lord. I felt so moved by this togetherness that I found myself making up a chant.

I stood up in the middle of the prophetess circle and remembered the faces on the family photographs that sat on top of each dormitory locker. I began to speak on a beat, with a deep voice.

'Elijine, daughter of Mr and Mrs Cuthbert of the Shanghai mission home, a home with banisters, she is called. She is c/o the Lord.'

The girls joined in, '*She is called. She is c/o the Lord.*'

'Elishella, daughter of Mr and Mrs Crickmay of Lijiashan village, who live in a house-cave and once gave communion to Mrs Chiang Kai-shek . . .'

'*She is called. She is c/o the Lord.*'

'Habakkukina, daughter of Dr and Mrs Templeton, of Qingdao Hospital, where opium addicts are healed . . .'

'*She is called. She is c/o the Lord.*'

'Baptistina, daughter of Mrs and Mr Charleston, who are Methodists and translating a gospel for the singing hill tribes of Yunnan . . .'

'*She is called. She is c/o the Lord.*'

'Zephanella, daughter of Mr and Mrs Enkel, whose uncle and aunt were massacred by the Boxers but whose parents still came to witness to those that had slaughtered their own . . .'

'*She is called. She is c/o the Lord.*'

'Jere-Neigh, daughter of the Reverend and Mrs Singleton, who live in a tent and gallop bareback across the desert plain with the descendants of Kubla Kahn . . .'

'*She is called. She is c/o the Lord.*'

'Joan, daughter of Mr and Mrs Hodgkins, whose parents are currently on furlough in Perth, Australia, and hope to return to a new calling probably in Peking, Lord willing, war willing . . .'

'*She is called. She is c/o the Lord.*'

'Isaihette, daughter of Mr and Mrs Pinder, whose parents play tennis at the Shanghai British Club and who are sadly not missionaries but merchants, for whose conversion we pray . . .'

'*She is called. She is c/o the Lord.*'

'And I, Samantha, daughter of Mr and Mrs Robertson, Pingxia village of Shanxi Province, whose mother sits upon the kang preaching to the women with her finger gospel and whose father hands out tracts in the market square . . .'

'*She is called. She is c/o the Lord,*' chanted the prophetesses.

'Now, let's go down the stream and get anointed!' Hilary yelled.

We prophetesses arose, brushed pine needles from our skirts and skedaddled down the hill, or, in the case of Kathryn, trotted. We took our shoes and socks off and waded in. The stream was toe-pinking cold. Slicks of underwater grasses sucked at our legs, waving like the palm leaves.

'We'll baptise each other,' I said. I turned to Florence, my bottom bunker and my best friend. 'Florence, you are now prophetess Habakkukina.' I dribbled some water over her hair.

The other prophetesses baptised each other. There was much splashing and harking.

We climbed up the bank of the stream, newly anointed. Everything seemed clearer, brighter. The bubble of the stream, The Beard glowing green, the afternoon air sprinkled with bird notes. Everything was potentially a sign.

'Let's find a prophecy,' called Hilary.

In silence, with water dribbling down our faces, we looked. We read the shapes of the boughs, we counted the steps, we watched the ferns shiver in the wind. We listened to the birds, the crickets, the stream. There was a holy quiet over us. Then faster than an Abyssinian's chariot, a mist descended.

It was one of the great mists of Lushan. A mist that starts by wiping out the white finger of the Pagoda and then the ridge of the mountain until the school is a pale cluster of buildings floating on a cloud, and then it too disappears. Teachers' House dismissed herself, all that could be seen of The Beard was its trunk floating in mid-air, then nothing. There were no signs to be read in a vanished world, unless of course you counted the mist as a sign.

'But what about the ninth and tenth commandment?' a prophetess called out.

'We will have to do them another time,' called Florence. 'I can't even see my pencil to write them down.'

We were girls floating. We were skirts, legs, arms, plimsolls, floating in mid-air. Soon all that was left of us was harks and hot breath and the sound of footsteps, running, running, as we scrabbled up the green bank towards the Girls' Building. We'd disappeared.

The dinner bell rang out, urgently, which meant, TO YOUR DORMITORIES! A dorm aunty was clanging it, like a dreadful wail. It was calling us away from the mountain, away from the stream, away from the grass and ferns and trees. The school dogs yapped and circled, chasing ankles. Everyone was making a run for indoors. There was a holy migration. From all sorts of cubbyholes, boulders and trees, children came.

Run, run. But be careful of what you step on in the mist: a yellow belly, a viper, a child, afraid and crouching. Be careful not to lose your footing and fall, not to twist, not to topple, not to spin down the mountain.

When we entered the dormitory we became girls once again. We had disappeared, and now we'd appeared, out of breath, panting. I looked at myself in the mirror. Yes, I was here. It was a miracle. Nothing could ever take away the surprise of having vanished and returned.

Aunty Muriel appeared, with a touch of the mist about her, her red hair all a-frizz. She began to count us, saying our English names, Eileen, Edith, Hilary, Florence, Etta, Sarah . . . She touched us on the head, a tap on the tip of the skull. Yes, you're here, the tap on the head said. This is how the lovely shepherdess counted her sheep. No one had gone missing today.

We wetted our fringes and wiped our faces with our flannels and when Aunty Muriel said, 'Chop chop,' we filed into line for our walk to the dining hall. I flashed myself a glance in the mirror. I looked at my prophetess self. She shimmered there just under the girl I was leaving behind.

That night, after lights out, I let my hand down and Flo put her hand up to meet it. A stripe of moonlight ran through the dormitory. Edith had opened the curtain. She must be seeing her parents, Mr and Mrs Crickmay. That's how she did it, by imagining them sliding from the moon.

Lying there, I thought about Mr and Mrs Robertson. I remembered a man covered in dust, galloping down from the hills, the gospel flag streaming behind him, a ripple of brightness on the wind. I remembered a mother on some villager's kang, preaching with her gospel glove, black, red, yellow, white. I remember, I remember, you cannot reach out and touch an I remember.

Then I slipped my other hand under my pillow, pulled out my Bible and tumbled on to a Psalm. I flew out of the window and above the school. Up, up over the black peaks I sailed, over the hungry-mouthed ravines, over the paddy fields glinting in the moonlight, over the Japanese gunboat in Poyang Lake, over the Reds in their mountain barricades, over the Yellow River and loess plains, further north to Free China, towards the village of my birth with its watchtower and guarded gates, its temple and ancestral hall. I flew to the north of the village and hovered over our grey brick courtyard. There was Mother watering her peonies, and there, Father dusting down our mule Good News. I waved to them with both hands from my flying Bible but they could not see me. I watched them for a while, then flew back over lights out China, back to my bunk, where I toppled out of my Psalm.

Psalms hold you, our Headmaster said. They carry you through life.

I lay in my little bed watching Edith's stripe of moonlight. I wondered if it had worked for her. Slowly, I felt Flo's hand fall away into the black of lights out.

The Ninth Commandment

FOR A WHOLE WEEK THE MIST SWIRLED. ON THE SATURDAY WE TRIED to go on an outing. Aunty Muriel led the way along the old priests' trails that crisscrossed up the eastern peak behind the school. We followed, our water bottles slung over our shoulders, walking single file along that path that led us between boulders, over streams, to paths that clung along the side of the mountain, then deep into the forest itself. The trees were green-tinged silhouettes. The mist crept around us. It was as if the Lord had put his face to the mountain, and was breathing.

We all stopped for Aunty Muriel had stopped. We were in a clearing with a white tree in it. White as bone, leafless. It was as if it had experienced a great shock. What had it seen? Hidden above us, a bird scribbled a thin song. Aunty Muriel placed her rucksack down. The mist lowered and thickened. We watched it without moving, as if listening to a prayer.

Aunty Muriel put her hands on her hips and breathed in. 'Smell that, girls,' she said. 'We are deep in the forest. Oh, China. She is a land of such great beauty. Her forests and her mountains are a song of praise to God.' Her face was turned up to the vanished canopy many, many feet above.

'Smell that, Dorm A.' We girls smelt the air, putting our hands on our hips as we breathed in.

'This is a thin place, Dorm A,' she said.

'Hmm, very thin,' said Edith, closing her eyes and taking a snort of air.

'What *is* a thin place?' asked Florence. The girls looked around the forest and then at Aunty Muriel.

'A thin place is where the gap between you and the spiritual realm' (Aunty Muriel said realm with such a rolling 'r' you got celestial shivers) 'is very thin. You can almost feel it like something pressing at you from behind a fabric.' Aunty Muriel rubbed her fingers together as if between them there was a cloth of divine making. 'There are many in Scotland, and many here, too.' Her voice trailed off and the mist curled closer.

After a while Aunty Muriel said, 'Well, girls, I don't think we'll be going much further today. We'll have to have our packed lunches here and try a trip to the Boiling House another day.'

As we sat down on fallen trees and took out our triangle sandwiches and our apples, Big Bum said, 'All prophetesses shall seek out thin places.'

'Prophetesses are small enough to slip through,' said Sarah.

Together we listed all the thin places that we knew. Down by the stream, under the bridge, the back of the laundry, the Great Steps. The strange thing was the thin places were all out of bounds.

'The prophets of the Bible wandered in the deserts and lived outside the city gates,' said Flo, crunching her apple.

'Then so must we,' said Big Bum Eileen. And so there, under the white tree, surrounded by swirling mist, we discovered the ninth commandment of the Prophetess Club: you must go out of bounds.

The Sign

ALTHOUGH THAT WEEK THE SCHOOL LOOKED AS IF IT WAS FLOATING, things carried on just the same. There was History and Arithmetic, English and Scripture, Geography and French. We went to piano practice and learnt our Bible verses. On Monday we wrote our letters home. On Tuesday afternoon during recitation, Amah Liu shuffled from chair to chair on her tiny bound feet, giving our nails their weekly clip. On Wednesday there was mending class and a black mark for me from Miss Preedy. Everything went on as normal, until Thursday afternoon.

'Let's hunt another prophecy,' said Hilary. It was afternoon playtime and the mist was the thickest it had been. It was hard to see anything, never mind a sign.

Big Bum Eileen said straight away, 'Maybe we'll find one out of bounds.'

And so we prophetesses gathered in a cluster at the top of the bank behind the dining hall, just above Livingstone Stream, where the edge of the school met the forest. We stood on the edge of the bank just inside the out-of-bounds boundary. The mist swirled.

Edith was first. She raised her leg over out of bounds and held it there, one elephant, two elephant, three elephant, four. Then she snatched it back and shivered. Then Hilary did it. She managed five elephants before the fear of being wicked made her stop. Then I did it: six! Then we all did it, standing in a line, facing Livingstone Stream. We counted in a low unison. I bent my foot in such a way that I could barely see my wrongdoing.

It was Edith who fell, at the fifteenth elephant, headfirst down the bank, arms, legs, plimsolls into whiteness. Her voice floated up. 'Someone pushed me.'

'Pull your socks up, Prophetess Elishella,' said Big Bum. She turned to us. 'I suppose someone will have to fetch her.'

'We'll all have to go,' said Florence. 'To keep it fair.'

'Hark,' the girls said, and we tumbled down the bank to rescue the fallen prophetess.

Edith had landed in a clump of forget-me-nots and moss. Her dress was stained green, her hair was stuck to her face where she'd been crying. We crouched around her. The stream twisted and flowed loudly beyond us.

'Elishella, can you stand?' asked Flo. She crouched down next to Edith, put her hands under Edith's armpits, and helped her up.

'Thank you, Habakkukina,' said Edith, obeying the third commandment of the Prophetess Club.

We went along the riverbank, slowly, gently with our fallen prophetess. We were heading towards the steps that led up from Gardener Chen's hut, up the bank and back to within bounds. We listened to the stream flowing, purposeful and unseen to our left. Above us, the trees played Chinese whispers in the wind.

'Stop,' I said after a couple of minutes. We all gathered in a close Prophetess Circle so we could see each other's faces. 'We're nearly at Gardener Chen's Nissen hut.' My head nodded in its direction. The mist swirled around the edge of a grey building. The girls' eyes went wide.

'The fall of Elishella . . .' I continued.

'It was an actual fall, not a spiritual one,' corrected Edith.

I started my announcement again. 'The actual fall of Elishella was a call . . . we've been led to Gardener Chen's Nissen hut.' We edged closer to the building and came to the steps that led up to it.

'Go and take a look,' said Big Bum Eileen.

'You go,' I said, for we all knew what was kept in there, what was held in Gardener Chen's glass jars.

'I can't, I'm helping Elishella.' And to demonstrate, Big Bum let go of Edith, who staggered a step.

'Oh, all right then,' I said, and tiptoed up the steps to the hut. I pressed my face against the glass. It was covered in cobwebs where spiders had spun themselves to sleep, old webs, once sticky and tight, now dust.

'Samantha,' said Big Bum, 'what can you see?' The cobwebs were thicker than mist so I tried the door. With a sharp shove, it let me in and I tumbled forward into the hut.

I had heard what was in the hut, but I'd never been inside. Along each side, from the wooden floor to the tin ceiling, there were stacks of shelves crammed full of jars of pickled snakes. Yellow bellies. Vipers. A baby python. A cobra. All asleep in acid. There were stacks and stacks of snakes in jars. My skin turned cold. Curled up snakes. Pale bellies, pink tongues. I wandered the length of the Nissen hut, looking at those tongues, those faces, jaws as delicate as a wishbone, pressed up against the glass, with a throat that goes on and on, until it becomes tail.

I came out and ran down the steps, clattering the door shut behind me. I pushed myself into the circle of girls, 'Snakes,' I said. The girls gulped mist. 'Not alive. Sleeping. Thousands of snakes.' I clutched my breast, as if bitten.

'Go back there,' said Big Bum Eileen. 'Bring us something.' She narrowed her green eyes. 'Bring us a sign.' I had to go. The big boob had spoken. I ran up the steps again and walked deeper down the corridor of snakes. Curled snakes, swirled snake, snakes asleep. White, soft, plump, they looked so easy to kill. But it takes skill and bravery to kill a snake. Never look at its eyes. It might beguile you. You bash a spade over its head. Then you watch its body thrash and coil, until it comes to stillness. The boys, who like to watch these killings, say Gardener Chen makes sure it is completely dead before he puts it in the jar for the school's snake collection.

Then I heard a jangle. My heart thumped.

It was nothing. Just the wind, puffing the door open and closed. I moved towards the door. The mist lifted a moment. I saw the stream, the forest beyond it, and further upstream, in the side of the bank, I saw a great hole. It was a large dark circle, as if the mountain had a mouth. I had never seen the hole before. Then the mist blew down again and it was gone.

Then, I heard singing. 'Immortal, invisible . . .'. No school-boy would be happily singing hymns out of bounds. It could only be Gardener Chen. Although he'd been converted twenty-two years before, he'd kept all the joy of his baptismal day, which Headmaster said was a lesson to us all. Knowing he wouldn't be joyful to find me in his hut, I leapt from the top step down to the bank and rolled underneath the steps. I curled up tight as a knot in a thread and held my breath. From there I could see the joyful jog of Gardener Chen go up the steps into the hut. 'Immortal, invisible . . .' If he'd been a lady I'd have seen right up his skirt.

I came running out of the mist to join the dinner line.

'Samantha, you didn't get caught?' said Flo, giving my hand a squeeze. 'Sorry, we saw him and ran.'

'And you didn't get bitten?' asked Sarah.

'But do you have a sign?' said Edith.

I nodded.

'Well, show us then, Samantha,' said Eileen.

'It's not a thing, it's something I saw, but just for a moment. The mist lifted and I saw . . .' I was on tiptoe with excitement, but before I could finish my sentence Aunty Muriel swooped in. She was having a strict day. You could tell from her bun.

'Today's line shall be done according to height, tallest at the top, shortest at the bottom. Arrange yourselves quietly and quickly, Dormitory A. Chop chop,' said Aunty Muriel. She tugged sharply at her sleeves so they covered her wrists.

'You saw a what?' said Big Bum Eileen, heading up the queue.

I was at the back of the line, so I had to finish my sentence by sending a whisper all the way up, girl by girl, until it reached Big Bum. It passed like a Chinese whisper. Everyone heard something different.

She saw *a foal*,
a fool,
a pool,
a mule,
a mole,
a tadpole . . .

'A flagpole?' snorted Big Bum Eileen. We'd entered the dining hall by the time the whisper reached her. We stood behind our chairs waiting for all the dormitories to file in. Instead of telling us to be quiet, Aunty Muriel closed her eyes and lifted her head to the ceiling. While she silently prayed for divine patience, I smiled at Big Bum Eileen, saintly as a dove.

It wasn't until nearly bedtime that I had a chance to explain the sign. I sat with Flo on her bed while we brushed our hair. We were counting together, her odds, me evens. Counting with a friend is a most pleasant way to get to a hundred.

'Tell us what you saw,' said Hilary. She was standing at the end of our bunk.

Edith, Kathryn and Fiona sat down on Flo's bed. 'Tell us, tell us.' Big Bum sat down, too. She leant on the bedpost and watched her hair shimmer gold as the black brush tore through it.

Flo took up counting my even numbers, 'Seventy-four, seventy-five . . .' To the sound of brushing and Flo's count, I began to speak on a beat.

'I saw something, a place, a doorway to a place, in the mountain, but it is so out of bounds I'm not sure . . .' My voice trailed off.

Flo counted steadily on. 'Eighty-one, eighty-two . . .'

'What I saw was the mouth of the mountain,' I said.

'It was shown to her,' said the girls to each other.

'What does it mean, this mouth?' said Kathryn.

'I feel . . . it is calling us,' I said. There was silence apart from the steady brushing and Flo, who was on ninety. 'I'll need to wait. For my eyes to be tested.'

'You'll have to go to Shanghai for that,' said Edith.

'No, not my real eyes. My prophetess eyes.' Again there was silence. My prophetess eyes. What had they seen?

'Ninety-nine, a hundred.' Flo pulled the hair from her brush and rubbed it into a ball. 'Do what Gideon did with his fleece. Take your dressing gown and put it on the end of your bed, pray over it, if it gets wet the next morning, then it's a sign.'

'A sign to what?' said Edith to Flo, who'd walked to the bin at the end of the row of beds.

'To go,' said Big Bum Eileen, 'inside.'

Flo threw the ball of hair in the bin, walked back, got out of her slippers, placed them neatly by her bed, pulled down the covers and slid in.

'That's right,' she said. 'If the dressing gown is wet it means we have been called to walk into the mountain. Now will you lot all get off my bed?'

No one moved while we thought about the call of the dressing gown.

'Lights out,' said Aunty Muriel from the dormitory door. There was a furious rush of slippers and creak of bunks. 'Hurry up, Etta. I didn't say on to bed, I said into bed.' I finished laying my dressing gown neatly across the end of my bunk. I didn't want God to find it all lopsided.

'Good night, Dormitory A,' said Aunty Muriel from the doorway as I hurried myself under the covers.

'Good night, Aunty Muriel,' we sang.

'Did you pray, Prophetess Samantha?' said the girls as Aunty Muriel's footsteps disappeared down the corridor.

Into the darkness, I prayed. 'Lord, give me the sign. As you dampened Gideon's fleece, so let your dew tell me what to do.'

'Amen,' said the girls of Dormitory A.

Muriel's Diary

10 October 1941

IT'S LATE. I'M SITTING AT MY DESK AFTER THE STAFF PRAYER MEETING and have been searching through the Chinese dictionary that Mr Dalrymple lent me. After flicking through the pages of characters for more than half an hour, I finally found it. *Shanshui*. It is a composite character of mountain and water and means landscape. With that in mind, I used up the last of the week's oil rations to have another look at yesterday's paintings, the quick watercolours that are mine, and the one, in a scrawl of ink, that belongs to another hand.

Earlier this week, on my morning off, I went again to the waterfall. It was such a misty start to the day and I wanted to capture the mist over the pool, its loose wandering over the jagged rocks, how it creeps through the pines' twisted boughs. I am falling in love with Lushan. I can feel it undoing some sadness in me. I sat down on a smooth, broad rock and set up as I normally do, clipping my paper to the board, filling a cup with some stream water, and began. I worked for a while creating a wash across the page, an outline for dense granite over which the water falls. Then, I sensed a presence. I turned round and saw a monk. I jumped a little in surprise and my mixing cup spilt.

The monk had lively brown eyes and his lips were twitching with a smile. Beside him was a boy. Both had shaved heads, both were dressed in grey robes. A monk and his novice. They'd come from the temple above the school and they smelt of fires and incense. I had turned to right the mixing cup when I felt the monk's presence at my shoulder. He sucked in a whistle of air – disapproval, I think. He kneeled beside me and ripped the top sheet of paper off. He took his own brush from his tunic, dipped it in an indigo rinse and drew a line. And there it was: the waterfall in a few brush strokes. The essence of it. '*Shanshui*,' he said, pointing to the water and to the forest around us, and drew the character in the corner. Then he did something strange. He thrust his hands out to the whole forest around him. Then back at me, jabbing his fingers towards me. The forest is you, he seemed to be saying. He drew a little more with the brush. Then he stood, and he and his novice walked along the path, disappearing into the trees with soundless footsteps.

Right now I am looking at the figure he drew. A woman surrounded by mist.

Into the Forest

THAT SATURDAY AFTERNOON THE MIST LIFTED AND WE WERE ABLE
to go on our Saturday outing properly. Once again, Aunty
Muriel led the way through the forest, up along the old
priests' trail. As we walked, we sang. This is the Christian
song we smuggled deep into the forest:

> Jesus, Thy robe of righteousness
> My beauty is my glorious dress
> 'Midst flaming worlds in this arrayed
> With joy shall I lift up my head.

Our voices coiled up, up, up and into the forest's great
canopy. The light floated down. It danced. It dappled the
earth with leaf-shaped shade. All about us the ancient trees
were alive with twitching and scurries. Here and there little
streams spilt over the path. We trod over layers of rotting
leaves, over black clods of earth strung together with fine
white roots.

On we sang. When it got to the fifth verse, I added a few
Chinese opera warbles to the three-part harmony. The dan

part is my favourite, for it belongs to the leading lady. To sing like a dan you make your voice go duckling crossed with bluebottle. It's a sound others want to swat.

'F.P.,' said Big Bum Eileen. Kathryn whinnied. Flo, who was just ahead of me, went silent with crossness. As soon as I stopped, Flo began to sing again.

I hopped over a root that didn't need hopping over at all. I felt as playful as light. Shining, peeking, flooding everywhere. I loved walking through the forest on days like these. Sniffing the green air. Nuzzling it with my thoughts. With Aunty Muriel ahead, we were striding deeper and deeper into the forest. I felt so fresh and free and fertile. It was the sort of day when a prophecy might happen.

Aunty Muriel's voice broke out somewhere above us, clear as a bell: 'We're at the waterfall.' The waterfall's Chinese name had been Celestial Fall but it was renamed Thomas Falls after the founder of the mission, which I wasn't sure was godly.

Steps had been cut into the bank of Thomas Falls. They were steep and slippy. 'Watch out for each other!' called Aunty Muriel over the rush of the waterfall. Then, later, we heard her voice again: 'Girls, be careful, especially Edith.'

'They could call it Edith Falls,' said Kathryn. We sniggered. Even Edith. She didn't mind as long as it was an actual and not a spiritual fall.

'They should have called it Headmaster's Wife Falls,' said Hilary. 'This is where she fell. My brother said. Twenty steps up. She slipped and fell, spinning like a rag doll, thump-thump arms and legs, down the side of the cliff.' Hilary's hands circled each other, violent and fast.

Although we didn't know the exact step, we all knew the story. Fifteen years ago, in the month of the great mist,

Headmaster had taken up his post at the school, accompanied by his wife. In the first week, on a wander up the mountain paths, whilst searching for shortcuts to the Western Ridge, Headmaster's wife had slipped and fallen. She could not move. They carried her down the mountain to Poyang City Hospital for treatment, but despite three operations to her spine she had never recovered the use of her legs. She was brought back to Lushan several months later and there she lay in the cottage ever since. She always reminded me of a mother in a dream, up on the hillside above us, beautiful in a yellow dress, with yellow hair and sad eyes. There, among the big red and white roses of her garden, she was a sort of Lushan angel watching over us, busying her hands with crochet, and her heart with prayers for our safety.

Which was the twentieth step, we all wondered. Hilary went down the bottom and came up, counting. 'Sarah's on the eighteenth, Flo's on the nineteenth.' She stopped next to me. I was standing on the twentieth step.

I looked down the bank, through the trees to where the water tumbled into the frothy pool. And I saw her there, right below us, her body flung upon the black rocks. There she lay, twisted, her arms and legs bent in ways they should not be. My mind began to spin. My heart began to pound. I looked again. She was no longer there. Instead, all through my body galloped a tumbling feeling, just as Headmaster's wife would have felt. A prophecy was stirring.

But it was stuttering Kathryn who began to prophesy first. The prophetesses shushed each other: 'Jere-Neigh is about to say something.'

Kathryn was staring at me, her eyes wide as Balaam's donkey. All the girls were staring at Kathryn waiting for the stuttering to become words, for the words to be a prophecy, a terrible prophecy about how I would crash through the trees, called by the song of the rocks, falling, falling, with nothing to cling to. I did not want to hear it. The only way out was to prophesy first.

'Prophetesses, I prophesy,' I said, then declared the first thing that came into my head. 'Aunty Muriel, Aunty Muriel, we have to save her from her funeral . . . We have to save her! Run!' I charged up the steps, pushing past Edith, past Florence, past Big Bum Eileen and yelling 'Hark' so loud that two birds shot out of the canopy and into the silent sky.

By the law of forest walks, if one person runs and yells, everyone runs and yells. And all the girls of Dormitory A ran and yelled. We reached the clearing, bashing into each other as we stopped. There, sitting on a root, was Aunty Muriel, unharmed and tapping something out of her brown leather shoe.

'Girls, whatever took you so long?' said Aunty Muriel.

We stared at her, astonished.

Kathryn picked up Aunty Muriel's shoe and looked in it. Edith flung her arms around Aunty Muriel's shoulders.

'Come on now,' said Aunty Muriel, who doesn't go in for hugs, 'a sip from your water bottles and then let us press ahead or we'll never get there.' The girls spread out across the clearing, making chairs of tree-trunks, thick twists of roots or padded mounds of moss.

I sat next to Aunty Muriel. I still felt the tumbling feeling of the twentieth step. I was hovering on the brink of a discovery. I stood up, tiptoeing with a thought. Then I sat down again. I edged closer to Aunty Muriel. As she picked up her other shoe I asked, 'Aunty Muriel, when a terrible thing happens does the place where it happens become a thin place? A place where you can poke through to the other realm?' I rolled the 'r' of realm. 'Like pressing through a sheet from one world into the other?'

Aunty Muriel looked inside the shoe. 'Yes, perhaps.'

'Like the waterfall, where Headmaster's wife fell, that feels . . . thin. Perhaps it has been made thin because a terrible thing happened there. Like when you get a cut or a bruise, like a scar that still hurts.'

Aunty Muriel put her shoe on and stood up in a column of light that had broken through the sky of leaves. Golden dust shimmered around her. Aunty Muriel shone. She answered me but spoke to all, 'Now, girls, what I said about thin places. It's not strictly evangelical. Remember what Miss Preedy says: that we are protected by a throng of angels.' She wanted us to feel safe. She gave a sweep of her hands above her head. We looked up to the canopy, at the branches stretched out like wings over us. A leaf fell through the stripe of light. Aunty Muriel checked her wristwatch, a tiny face on thin leather straps, and turned back into a dorm aunty again. 'Come on, chop chop, quick march to the Boiling House.' Aunty Muriel picked up her knapsack and we did the same. On through the forest we went.

As we began to sing, I warbled more loudly. I was scared. I wanted the girls to know that I was there, bringing up the rear. What if I slipped? What if no one saw? I warbled like mad, even when I heard Aunty Muriel's voice, higher up the trail, calling out, 'Etta, be quiet.' I could feel the hurt of the place all over me. So I sang like that, like a crazed dan, screeching, 'With joy shall I lift up my head' until we were out of the forest, to drown out the black song of the rocks.

Beyond the trees, the sun was bright and the peaks dazzled. We walked across a scrub of yellow grass until we came to the Boiling House, a small cottage at the edge of a view that made you wish for wings. While we girls ran to the mountain's edge and felt the giddy rush the Lord felt upon Sinai, the Boiling House woman took the pennies from Aunty Muriel and bellowed the stove under the black kettle.

'Sixth commandment,' shouted Hilary, for the sight was beautiful and a prophetess must be overcome by the beauty of the Lord. The girls began to spin. I hung back at first, but soon I joined in, near the edge of the cliff, looking at the rising peaks, at the clouds below us.

'It's too wonderful,' said Big Bum, placing her hand on her chest.

The other girls put their hands to their chests too, and grimaced in pain, just like Big Bum. 'Oh, Elijine, you're so moved,' said Edith, 'you might faint.' But Big Bum didn't faint.

'Elijine,' I said, 'you're so moved, I think you should have a prophecy.' But Big Bum didn't prophesy. She's too clever to be flattered into that.

'F.P.' she said instead, spinning past me.

'What?' I said, spinning myself nearer to her.

'False prophetess,' she said, spinning away.

'Am not,' I said, spinning after her.

She stopped. I stopped. We watched each other through dizziness. Big Bum Eileen is strong. Her teeth are big and white. Too big. Teeth that show how strong her bones are. She's got a big skull, that Big Bum Eileen. Everything about her is big. Even when she's quietly crossing her arms or turning in her bed, you know what Big Bum Eileen is doing, is thinking. The kneecaps of Big Bum Eileen! Big as a baby's skull. To think I have to share a bath with all that.

'You made a false prophecy,' she said, then turned and pushed against the wind towards the Boiling House. The other girls were not interested in the glories of the Lord without the glory of Big Bum Eileen so they followed. As did I for I didn't want to be the last upon the cliff.

'Goodness, girls,' said Aunty Muriel as we staggered into the shade of the Boiling House. All that being overcome had frizzed our hair in a thousand directions. Aunty Muriel made us have a sit down and a cup of tea. There were three benches. I sat down. Kathryn, Edith and Big Bum Eileen got up and moved over to the other bench. I got up and moved over to the other bench too. They all got up and moved away. I followed them. They moved back to the first bench.

'Sit down, girls,' said Aunty Muriel. 'It's unbecoming to have tea and gallivant.'

Kathryn, Edith and Big Bum Eileen sat down on the furthest bench and the girls that had to be on my bench squeezed up to the other end. Even Florence.

I was alone at the end of the bench. The tea was too hot to drink. I blew on it. I looked at the Boiling House lady who was turning over the coals under the kettle. She smiled at me and there were no teeth.

The wind calmed down and we went back outside. We were going to sit on the big boulder to have our picnic, lichen-covered, grey, sparkly and rough. I was the last one to climb up, but Edith said there was no room. They all had their legs stretched out, hogging all the boulder. No one, not even Flo, was bunching up to make space. I slid back down the boulder and sat at the bottom. I felt sad in its shade. Then Kathryn came and joined me. She'd decided there wasn't enough room on the boulder for both her and her horse. There she sat, with her sandwich in one hand and a scrunch of yellow grass in the other. A hawk swooped in the gully. Strangely shaped pines clung to the rock face. And it was here, on the cusp of an astonishing view, that Aunty Muriel painted us.

I balanced my apple on my knee to remind me to keep still. I looked at that apple and thought about how I wouldn't eat it, but give it to the S.P.A.L.C. fund instead. A trail of mountain porters moved along the path that wound the mountain's edge. They carried poles with weights of water-melons and spinach at each end. They sang as they walked, 'The lonely pines of Lushan, the rock is their mother, the mist is their milk.' A tear slid down my cheek. I wiped it away. I didn't want Aunty Muriel to paint me crying.

When we got back to the school that evening, things were strangely quiet. There was no whack of the cricket bat, no children calling from trees, nor the tsk-tsk of skipping ropes. Everyone had gone indoors, apart from Mr Dalrymple, who was at the other end of Drill Court, waving a piano book.

'Miss MacKay.'

'Girls, clean up for supper,' she said to us, then, calling to him, 'Mr Dalrymple.'

As Aunty Muriel walked into Teachers' House with Mr Dalrymple, a few Sons of Thunder stepped out of a classroom. When they saw us standing by the sandpit, they hurried over.

They looked worried and for once were not pretending to be soldiers. 'Where have you been?' they asked. 'Haven't you heard?' Then they began to explain what had occurred while we had wandered in the forest paths above the school.

'Japanese soldiers came. A small band of them. They were armed with guns, bayonets and swords.' Roland made a big cut through the air. 'They requested a meeting with Headmaster.'

Then Nigel Pinsent spoke. 'Over here, everyone.' We turned our gaze to where he stood at the other end of the sandpit. We crowded around him. There in the sand was a footprint made by a boot with the toe separated out.

'Actual Japanese footprints,' said Nigel before Roland continued with the rest of the story.

Headmaster had told everyone not to worry, for the Japanese were not at war with us, but also, to go indoors. The soldiers could be seen walking around, counting the number of buildings and Nissen huts. According to the boys, by the look of these soldiers the Japanese army was so much better equipped and organised than Chiang Kai-shek's, and in their opinion it would be only a matter of months before China fell. The soldiers had come through the forest from the White Pagoda, had made their inspections, drunk lemonade in Headmaster's office and then left an hour later, down the Great Steps.

'No prophetess foresaw that,' said Hilary as the bell rang for dinner. And we looked at the soldier's footprint stamped in our sandpit and worried for the days left on Lushan.

False Prophetess

'OF COURSE, A MEETING OF THE PROPHETESS CLUB HAS TO BE CALLED,' said Big Bum Eileen, and so that Tuesday afternoon, we prophetesses gathered in the shelter of The Beard. We all wore our padded jackets for there was a chill in the breeze. It was a crisp autumn day and the air smelt of jewelled pine gum. Big Bum had her usual spot resting back on The Beard.

'Prophetesses,' she said, 'we all know, two wrong prophecies and you're a false prophetess. It's the rule. We all know that Prophetess Samantha has made a false prophecy.'

'A false prophecy,' said Edith, who liked to say what Big Bum Eileen had said. I thought back to the moment on the twentieth step, the giddy dread rising up through me.

Kathryn repeated the false prophecy. 'Prophetess Samantha said, "Aunty Muriel, Aunty Muriel, we must save her from her funeral."'

'It was just a joke,' I said.

'But it wasn't funny.'

Flo defended me: 'Her jokes mostly aren't funny.'

'Exactly,' I said.

'But you got it wrong. Aunty Muriel was in no danger;

64

there was nothing to save her from. She didn't need us to rescue her at all,' said Kathryn.

'It's easy to get frightened in the forest,' said Flo. 'Prophetess Samantha got frightened and made a mistake.'

I looked up at The Beard and trembled, to show my fear of trees.

'And I was going to make a prophecy and then Etta made all that fuss and the prophecy went,' added Kathryn.

'Let's take a vote,' said Big Bum Eileen.

Edith stood up. 'Members of the Prophetess Club, who votes that Samantha has given a false prophecy?'

All the hands shot up but mine and Flo's so that was that. I had become half false prophetess.

'Well, prophetesses, I shall prophesy something very important. I can feel it . . . yes, it will be soon. And you'll be wishing you believed me,' I said.

'But which part of you will be prophesying? Your good part or your false part? Which are we to believe?' said Big Bum.

'Which part?' said Edith.

'I think she should sit outside the prophetess circle until we can trust her,' said Kathryn.

'Yes, sit over there,' said Big Bum Eileen, pointing to a stump of wood at the edge of the flowerbed. I sat down there. 'Now, what about the Japanese?'

As the prophetess circle talked about cutlery, trowels and Eileen being a booby trap, a tear slid down my face. I gazed into the distance and pretended that I wasn't there. Then through a blur of sorrow I saw something on the slope above us. It was wheeled slowly out on to the green. There, in the chair, was a long, pale figure.

Headmaster's wife had been brought to her wicker rest

chair by Amah Liu, where she might feel the autumn breeze. Watching her lying there, a figure high above us, I was seized with the longing to be closer. For her not just to be a lady floating above on a lawn of green while she hummed Psalms and prayed for us children below but to be within touching distance. Someone whose hand you could reach out and hold. I held my breath and imagined sitting, not here on this lonely log, but by her side. How I would tell her my sorrows, how she would tilt her head and watch me kindly, and then, with the afternoon breeze fluttering through the grasses and over our faces, she would sing a little. But for now, she was so far away. A woman whose face watched not mine, but looked at the sky, the peaks and that unseen world. She was as reachable as a mother in a photograph and quite, quite out of bounds.

'Girls, mine good eye is seeing something.' I spoke quietly. 'Over yonder.'

'Headmaster's wife,' said Edith. We watched from The Beard.

Then it began to rain. The girls clucked about, the meeting was drawn to a close, but no one came to get Headmaster's wife.

'She'll get soaked,' said Flo.

At last Amah Liu came out and wheeled her back in.

Then it struck me that perhaps Headmaster's wife was not just the lady praying for our protection, but that she needed ours. For how would she stand up, how would she run, should the Japanese come? Who was there to help her to safety?

We Shall Enter Canaan

ON THE SATURDAY OF THE FOLLOWING WEEKEND, WE MADE THE journey to the bank by the East Steps. Hilary carried Edith's kite on her back. Edith's kite was our excuse. Kites so easily float out of bounds. They can't help themselves, it's in their nature. And if we needed to rescue it, we'd have to go out of bounds, too.

'Prophetesses, we have arrived in the land of Canaan,' said Big Bum Eileen.

'Canaan,' we whispered to each other. 'Our Promised Land.' We formed a line and edged in for a closer look. We were standing at the top of the bank, out of breath and almost out of bounds. Below was a steep drop of rock, crisscrossed by blocks of concrete to keep the mountainside in, to stop it from falling down. We'd just climbed up, hands red, knees scraped pink.

Headmaster's Cottage was at the highest point in the school. Inside the white fence was a rectangle of lawn and roses. Yellow, orange, white roses. Deep red roses, the colour of love. Then we saw her. There, on the rolling lawn in her wicker chair, lay Headmaster's wife.

'Did you know, her children are grown-ups in England? Mabel types letters in London and Vincent is a chemist. She used to be a wonderful singer,' said Hilary, who knows many things from her big brothers.

'Do you think she'll sing today?' asked Edith.

It was a sunshine afternoon and Headmaster's wife lay under a lemony blanket, her chest rising and falling. It did not look like she would sing. Her hands were placed across her chest in prayer. She had holy silence. Those fingers, long, conical-tipped with shiny nails, were purple tinged. A breeze of a smile drifted across her face.

I wondered what her favourite Bible verse was. I love to know people's favourite Bible verses. It's like tiptoeing across their soul.

'Do you think she might be taller than Headmaster?' asked Sarah. We all had a guess, a bit like that half-term game, guess how many boiled sweets are in the jar. A little bit taller was the agreement. I had never seen a wife taller than her husband. It didn't seem decent somehow. Even a lying-down wife.

'He's coming! Kill the kite,' someone said.

Headmaster was heading up the steps. Hark! We grabbed about for the kite, all hands pushing and pulling, looking busy, earnest and helpful. It was Hilary who shoved it in a rose bush.

'My kite,' said Edith. 'My birthday kite.' Headmaster was coming nearer when there was a scream from the playground down below. We all turned to look.

By the arbour at the top of the Great Steps there was a boy. His arms were around a lady's waist, gripping her as if she was a piece of driftwood upon the Yangtze rapids. The lady was his mother. Mrs Hill, a lady with a great green hat, had been visiting for some mountain air and was now leaving. She had a little girl, a baby, that she held over her hip.

The boy lifted his arms up to her as if to say, 'Pull me up, Mummy; carry me, too.' The lady was stepping backwards. Her arms were full. Aunt Nebuchadnezzar went to them. She said some words to the boy, who only clung tighter to his mother. She tried to get him to let go. He wouldn't. So Aunt Neb picked him up and swung him over her shoulder, then began to march across Drill Court. The boy kicked her tummy, thumped her back. Then he broke free, leapt off Aunt Neb, and ran to his mother.

Aunt Nebuchadnezzar bolted across Drill Court like a buffalo on loess plains. She was surprisingly graceful at full speed. She scooped up the boy, flinging him over her shoulder, light as a tea towel, and took him away.

The games had stopped, the children stood still. Even Sun the dog stood frozen from tail to nose. Headmaster rushed down the steps and across Drill Court to Mrs Hill. He put his arm around her.

'Is he allowed to do that?' said Edith.

'I don't know,' I replied.

The little girl around the lady's hip was bawling now. 'It's not fair of her to come and visit him,' said Kathryn. She was sat curled up at the base of a yellow-headed rose bush. Her chin was puckered like a peach stone.

'If only she'd let him get on with it. Coming here made him remember her,' said Hilary.

'Remembering makes you sad,' said Sarah.

'What's his name?' asked Isobel. But no one knew the boy's name. We tried, but remembering the names of children without a bigger brother or sister always takes longer.

I heard a sniff behind me. I turned. It was Big Bum. Eyes

red as a rabbit. Then, beyond her, I caught a movement from the garden. In between the roses, I could see Headmaster's wife. It looked as if she was caught in a bad dream. Her head was shifting from side to side. Her Bible had fallen to the ground.

'Oh, oh, his mother's leaving,' said Sarah. I turned back towards the school. The mountain chair was raised. We watched as the lady with her baby and hat box were carried away.

Headmaster's wife was moaning now. I could just catch bits of it on the breeze.

'She's singing,' said Edith.

I listened closer. It was the sound of a coolie after being beaten into a heap.

'That's not singing,' I said. 'She saw what happened.'

'Let us leave Canaan,' said Big Bum Eileen. Hilary pulled the kite out of the rose bush while Edith gasped at the sight of it. We went down the long way, sliding green-bottomed towards the stream. Edith held the kite to her chest as if her heart had been ripped out.

Everyone has their own aloneness. This is different from prayer time when you are with the Lord. This is when you are simply with your thoughts that aren't prayers. Often when you are alone, these are sad thoughts. For us, usually our sad thoughts were because our parents were far away.

To have your aloneness, you need an alone-time place. The dormitories were out of bounds during the day, so you couldn't go and bury your head in your doll's hair, or lie on your bed, with your family photograph turned so you could see it and trace over the grey shapes that are mother, father, brother, sister. You had to be outside with your sadness.

You didn't tell anyone that you were going to be alone. You just slipped away. We all did it. And that afternoon, after Mrs Hill left, all the prophetesses slipped away.

Kathryn watered her feet and her horse down by Livingstone Stream. Hilary went to the boating pond where she sailed her balsawood ships. Florence went to the library where she lay on her tummy, looking at an atlas on the floor, her chin rising up out of the South Pacific. Big Bum went to the games box, picked up a rope, skipped furiously until sweat and a small crowd appeared. Then letting the rope drop, she stepped over it like a towel on the bathroom floor and stormed off, leaving the little ones to squabble over who got the rope, at last agreeing to share it, three girls skipping hopelessly side by side. Sarah, who never goes far on her own, weeded the dormitory garden, piling up the little weeds in her skirt and burying any worms she'd disturbed. Edith headed up to Sick Bay with her broken kite in hand, for nurse to put ointment on an ache that shifted from her left to her right leg and back again.

I had two alone places. When it was raining my alone place was the gap in the bank underneath the tree house. I liked it under there, listening to the rain on the wooden house above. Sometimes a drip dropped through but mostly it was dry. I liked looking at the bank where the roots stretched out. I pretended they were shelves. I set out imaginary glasses and cutlery and bowls and plates. There was space for medicines, tea towels, tins of tea, carbolic soap. I inspected them like a dorm aunty. The thunder passed above as I played. The mountain was washed with sounds. The splat of rain on the East Steps. The soft, wet drip from the leaves long after the rain itself had been.

As it was a sunny day, I headed to my rock. It was on the other side of the Livingstone Stream. I would lie upon it and stare up at the pines. Then where the branches met, making a patch of sky shaped like a heart, I would imagine Mother and Father.

Crossing the Livingstone Stream bridge, I passed three little girls. They were huddled around a hymn. They were singing the chorus over and over again. Singing in a group is another way of being alone with your thoughts without anyone knowing. Underneath us, Livingstone Stream rushed, escaping the mountain.

'Girls, what was the name of that boy?' I said.

The singing stopped.

'Philip Hill,' the blonde one replied. 'He's in our class.'

They'd been crying. I sat down with them. Everyone has their own way of being cheered up. You poke around a bit and you find it. 'Would you like to learn my happy song? The song I sing when I'm sad?' The girls curled nearer to me. 'I made it up myself.'

I shake my bum, shake-shake, wobble-wobble, just for fun,
Then I shake out my hair, shake-shake, like a snake,
And I stick out my tongue, poo-poo, to you,
And I shake my bum and my hair and my arms all at once,
And I kick my legs, left then right,
And I jump up and down with all my might,
Shake-shake, happy-happy, wobble-wobble goes my bum.

I hopped up. 'But, of course, remember when you're sad it is Jesus you must tell. He is our Comforter,' I said, and skipped off down to the stream. All missionary children learn this.

You can do it any time, any place through prayer. At the stream, I climbed up the bank to my rock.

Imagining is a bit like praying. You make your thoughts only one thing. You concentrate very hard and don't think about other things. But that day it was difficult because of Mrs Hill's leaving. I gave up and went back over the bridge, past the singing girls, and headed up the secret path behind the Girls' Building towards the laundry.

I was standing among the sheets when I heard Miss Preedy. 'He bit me,' she said to someone. 'Bit me. He'll have to learn some Christian manners. I've sent him to The Wall.' There by the outdoor sink Miss Preedy was running her hand under a tap. I didn't want her to see me out of bounds. I crept through the sheets towards the steps that led behind the kitchen, then ducked around the corner. There right in front of me was the boy.

He was punching the gritty, stone laundry wall. Philip Hill in his cricket shorts and cricket shirt. He had to keep punching until his fists bled. That was the punishment. His knuckles whacked the grey stone. I wondered what sounds Headmaster's wife would be making now, for surely she could feel this too. Then Philip looked up at me, his face creased with pain, and I fled.

The Tenth Commandment

OVER THE REST OF THE WEEKEND, I COULD NOT HELP BUT THINK OF Philip Hill. His limp hair, his snub nose, and his missing front teeth. His hands, which were fists, red, the skin broken, the streaks of blood on the wall. It made everything different.

That Sunday night at Evening Prayers, when Headmaster stood to tell the story of the parting of the Red Sea, I could see it clearer than ever before. The runaway slaves carrying their runaway suitcases. How the Egyptians charged upon wooden chariots pulled by snorting horses, until, halfway across, they were sunk. The crashing waters came. Sea spray, saltiness, crabs big as dinner plates plonking on their heads. The water was a sinew of the Lord, crushing, bending, snapping. The men spat out the salty water and gasped for air. They yelled with a great rage, a bellow that says: I will not be destroyed! The horses reared and whinnied. But struggle as they might, man, boy and beast were swallowed up, and the surface of the Red Sea was still. Passing on a fishing boat, you'd find nothing that would seem strange. But that did not mean the calamity had not happened.

Then came Tuesday, which was letter writing day. Miss

Otis clapped the duster on the edge of the blackboard and the sunlight fizzed. Then, she rubbed out the 20th and wrote the 21st on the blackboard so that the date read 21st October 1941. I liked the blackboard when it had been given a good mopping and shone slick as liquid. But that day it was grey and swirly, and in a moment any difficult words that might go into our parents' letters were printed in Miss Otis' curly writing, which ran in a straight line from left to right. By 'difficult' I don't mean things that were hard to say, but things that were hard to spell. These weren't always the same thing. I could spell 'punch' and 'wall' and 'little boy' but I wouldn't put them in a letter for it was too hard to say.

That day we were going to write about baptism. The baptisms had been announced by Headmaster in church. It was a yearly event, one that usually coincided with a visit from the Duo, two famous lady missionaries who worked in the plains below Lushan.

To get to the church we trooped down the Great Steps and along the path to the edge of the village. The whole school went every week, all wearing white boaters, brothers and sisters holding hands. White is, of course, for holiness, but to the Chinese it is the sign of mourning and the villagers of Woosung never got used to the sight of a mountain path flooded with children dressed for death. At the edge of the village we crossed a small stone bridge, dipped under an old scholar tree that arched over the path, and entered the cool, dank church. It was made from stone the colour of rain cloud.

Headmaster peered from the pulpit. 'Boys and girls over the age of ten can apply to be baptised,' he said. 'To be accepted for baptism you need your parents' permission and also to pass the Baptism Preparation Course. Your teachers will write to the parents of every eligible child.'

His announcement caused great excitement amongst the dormitory, and after church we ran to the Tent of Meeting. There, under The Beard, it was declared that every prophetess must be baptised. 'It shall be,' said Big Bum, 'the tenth and last commandment.' Flo wrote it down in her neatest writing. Then we pointed at the page in the back of Flo's prayer book and said in growly voices, 'For it is written, "Thou shalt be baptised". This is the tenth commandment of the Prophetess Club.' And the way we said it, the last commandment sounded very ancient.

So that Mother and Father would agree to me being baptised, I made sure signs of faith could be detected in my letter to them. I underlined 'will', which shows Christian conviction. I wrote 'Him' with a capital H. I couldn't wait to sit in Sun the dog's kennel, my letter-reading place, and read their reply.

I waited and waited.

Florence received her letter. Letters arrived for Big Bum, Fiona, Hilary and Isobel. I had no letter. I was worried about Mother and Father. They were in Free China but maybe they'd been got by the Japanese, or worse, the Reds. Every time I thought of them I felt a tumbling sickness, like looking over the edge into which I'd fall.

Finally a letter came. I sat in the flea stink of Sun's kennel and ripped open the envelope. Inside was a photograph, taken in Yuncheng port last summer holiday. I'd been dressed up in a silk tunic and told to hold a chrysanthemum. My yellow hair was so bright that, captured in black and white, it shone like a halo. Perhaps this would have been a sign to Mother that I was ready. Perhaps the photograph would say, 'Yes, you may be baptised' on the back. I turned it over. All that was written was my name. Not Samantha, Prophetess but just plain old Henrietta S. Robertson. The same as it was spelled on my name tags, as it was written on the first page of my Bible.

The letter was dated three months before. Many things could have happened in that time. The letter shook in my hands and I was unable to make the words still on the page and become sentences. Then I calmed, and read from beginning to the end.

Reconnaissance ships had come up the Huang Ho, Mother wrote, and Japanese Zeroes flew overhead. The people from the village hid in the loess caves, but Hequ village in the neighbouring district had been bombed and three ladies from the Norwegian mission were killed, for they could not run from the village square quickly enough; their old bound feet could not flee their market stalls. Mother and Father would stay with the Christians in Pingxia village. They would not leave their flock. God had placed the caves so close, and there they would hide, trusting in him for protection.

I ate this news like Gobi dust.

In the end it was just Edith, Kathryn and I who awaited a reply, for Sarah's answer arrived in person.

Mrs Charleston Arrives

IT'S REALLY STRANGE, WHEN YOU'RE THE WRONG SIZE FOR YOUR mother. You expect to be little, to be flung up in the air. But you're not. You're all the wrong size. And you don't know what to do. That's just how it was with Sarah and her mother, Mrs Charleston.

It was Saturday playtime and we were awaiting the arrival of Sarah's mother. She was coming for a visit. We'd picked passion flowers from the tumble of vine that covered the Girls' Building and were helping each other put them in our hair, poking hairpins through their pale green stems. We were sitting on the benches at the far end of Drill Court. This gave us a good view of the top of the Great Steps and of the arbour where Mrs Charleston would arrive, having travelled from the nearby mission post of Fengxin and up the Western Pass where it was said no troops had yet gathered.

'What does your mother look like?' we'd asked Sarah. Of course, we already knew. We'd studied her family photograph.

'But tell us again.'

'She's got blond hair and she's tall.'

'All mothers are tall. How tall?'

A woman with an enormous mound of curly hair stood at the top of the Great Steps. It's your mum, Sarah! She's arrived safe and sound. We watched as Sarah ran across Drill Court to her. In her grey dress, Sarah looked like a goose running to take off. But she didn't fly into her mother's arms as you'd expect. She pulled up short by a yard or so, put her hands behind her back and went shy.

Mrs Charleston kneeled down on one knee and cocked her head. Then she put her arms out. Lovely arms, elegant like a swan. Hug me, said the arms. Sarah stood there. Move, go to her, we hissed. Why isn't she going? Maybe she's having a prophecy? What had she foreseen?

Slowly Sarah started towards her mother. The lady smiled and seemed to talk about the passion flower in Sarah's hair. Sarah pointed at the Girls' Building, and then at us. We were something to talk about in a time of trouble. The lady looked. We checked our flowers, we sat straight. It was far away, but we wanted to make a good first impression for Sarah's mother. Then Mrs Charleston stood up. She had bags and things that needed fussing over. It was so much easier, fussing and faffing. Easier than standing in front of each other, gawk, gulp. Looking at your blood, your flesh.

'Bazooka boobs.'

I was shocked. It was Edith talking about Mrs Charleston's boobs. That didn't seem becoming for a welcoming party, no matter how far away we were. I gave Mrs Charleston's boobs a good look. I could see what Edith meant.

Then Freddie, Sarah's big sister, appeared by the arbour. She had her mother's tumble of hair but underneath it a pale, sour face with dark circles under her eyes. She gave Mrs Charleston a light, quick hug. Then she pushed Sarah into her mother's arms. The girls were awkward. All the wrong size. We could tell, but still we watched them jealously.

Then Mrs Charleston did a big laugh and brought out presents. They were wrapped in bright green paper, as bright as tree frogs. She kept brushing out flops of hair from her face. She needs a hairpin, I thought. Aunty Muriel would make her have a hairpin. The girls sat down in the arbour with their mother. We could tell that they were talking about the journey and the steps. I could tell because Mrs Charleston was doing an impression of being in a mountain chair. The one guests often do, leaning back, looking down at one side, and suddenly frightened. Sarah and Freddie were watching her, watching her arm movements. They were watching her speaking, soaking her up, her body, her voice, rather than listening to what she was saying. Then Aunty Muriel strode, bounce, bounce across the Drill Court to the arbour where she shook hands with Mrs Charleston. Mrs Charleston did the mountain chair story again, and this time, everyone laughed.

That evening we got to meet her close up. She sat down at dinner with us. We were all on our best behaviour. Ps and Qs. Elbows off the table. Twenty chews per mouthful. Mrs Charleston sat at the top of the table, squished in, too big for the chair. She talked with her head at the side, her voice soft and breathy, in an American accent that was quite different from Sarah's British one. Her face was gentle. She had big blue eyes. Periwinkle. Cornflower, Himalayan poppy, we threw the words around the table in a secret game of colours. We couldn't decide. She wore a tawny coloured linen dress, shapeless as a hammock, with a lace collar and a string of long jade beads. She had freckles everywhere. On her hands, her arms, her neck. Just before dessert, I swung my head under the table and looked down at her sandals. Yes, there were even freckles on her ankles. I swung back up. 'Bazooka!' said Edith, stabbing her fork into the bread and butter pudding. Sarah glared.

We went to Celestial Waterfall Pool for our outing the following Saturday. Sunhats and bathers. A scorcher, a corker of a day. We all rushed to Mrs Charleston's hand. Even Sarah had to wait her turn. Flo and I took turns holding her left hand all the way up the short cut. Her hand was so lovely and freckly and she smiled down at us, her face patterned under the sunhat. It was so lovely to be smiled at by a real live mother. I felt as if I was tilting my head to the sunlight. I think I grew an inch.

When we got to Celestial Waterfall we shimmied and fiddled under towels, and emerged with bathers on. Then to the pool. Turquoise waters, just like Aunty Muriel was painting from a rock at the water's edge.

We dived – Mrs Charleston, look at me! We bombed – Mrs Charleston, watch this! We roly-polied underwater – Mrs Charleston, did you see that? We swung on the vine, out over the pool – Mrs Charleston, look, I'm a monkey! Mrs Charleston's name rang across the forest. Even Sarah leapt up on the vine shouting, 'Look at me, Mrs Charleston!' When she caught what she said, a look of pain crossed her face, and she fell into the pool. Mrs Charleston clapped and exclaimed and was very nice about everybody, not just Sarah, as she sat and watched.

I felt so happy. The strange darkness of the last few weeks, waiting to hear from Mother and Father, had gone and I was beautifully happy and peaceful. Warm water all around, slopping at my sides. I floated myself in the shallows, near Aunty Muriel and Mrs Charleston.

Mrs Charleston was saying, 'It grew a whole inch.'

'A whole inch?' said Aunty Muriel. 'Now that is a work of faith. What a powerful ministry Miss Kingsley and Miss Tippet have on the Women's River. I do wish to see it someday. Perhaps I will ask Miss Kingsley when she comes for her annual visit. But back to that leg. A whole inch, you say? Now, was it the man's left leg or his right?'

Where was this Women's River? I looked at my toes, at my whole body stretching out in front of me. Thigh, knees, calves. Ten toes, peaks on a mountain range. I wiggled them; faith moves mountains. Then I felt a ripple of something, not water, but fear. It wriggled slowly up my legs, then punched me in the heart, squished me in the lungs, and I found myself standing at the water's edge, shivering and gawping at the pool.

'Everyone out!' I yelled. 'Out.'

Everyone stopped. 'What is it, for goodness' sake,' said Aunty Muriel.

'This is the baptism pool, you can't go in here unless . . . won't it make the water dirty if we're not baptised?' I was shivering with cold.

'It's symbolic,' said Aunty Muriel. 'When you perform a baptism, it has a meaning, but for now it's just a pool of water.' The girls had stopped what they were doing. They were staring at me. My feet were in mud, soggy and dirty. I'd been in the water so long, the skin on my fingers had puffed up. I could see the shape of my fingerprints. Like the insides of a tree.

'Dry yourself off and sit down. Have a sandwich,' said Aunty Muriel. I sat beside her and took a bite of the sandwich. The bread tasted of petrol fumes. The girls started laughing and playing again. I watched Aunty Muriel paint her watercolour pool, blues, greens, swirling, little flicks for leaves, a long swoosh for the vine, pinky yellow for us girls, bathing.

'Are you okay, Henrietta?' asked Mrs Charleston.

But before I had the chance to answer, Big Bum Eileen, who was floating nearby, said, 'Oh, that's just Etta being Etta.'

'She's always like that,' said Kathryn.

From behind a rock in the water, I heard Edith shout, 'Bazooka.'

I bowed my head. The girls were as one inside the baptism pool.

Gideon's Fleece

I WAS TURNING INTO A DRAGON. I COULD FEEL IT, NOSTRILS FLARING, eyes wide, hot breath. Hands becoming claws. God make me less angry, I breathed. After the afternoon in the pool, I felt sensitive to everything. I was angry, the sort of angry that makes you want to cry. Everything was annoying me. The way Big Bum sat around the dormitory as if she were lying in a waterfall pool. The length of Kathryn's mane. Flo's perfection. I stomped from the bathroom through the dormitory to my bed. I heaved my dressing gown on the bed and leant my face on it. I rolled my head around for a moment. Firm towelling like crisp grass. A laundry lady had gone to town with the ironing.

Flo came along, tip, tap, in her slippers. She laid her dressing gown at the end of her bed and sat down. She eased her feet out of her slippers and placed the slippers side by side and exactly perpendicular to the bed. Then she climbed into her sheets, which were taut, smooth and hospital cornered. Oh, 10 out of 10. I wanted to applaud her excellence. If I went to bed like her, I would feel calm, neat, nice. But when I went to bed, I felt like a shovelling, thumping, porridge-bedded Barabbas, a bad-mood bandit. Perhaps Samantha, prophetess needed to improve on her hospital corners.

I jumped into bed, kicked my blankets about me, threw my dressing gown across my feet. Mrs Charleston and Aunty Muriel were talking directions to the Happy House Hotel, a half-hour mountain chair ride away, tucked into the cliff on the other side of Woosung. A trip to the hotel was the most popular treat from visiting parents. And the next afternoon, in the Happy House Hotel's dining room, which was furnished with carved wood tables and chairs, and had a chandelier under which General Chiang Kai-shek and his beautiful wife once ate dumplings, Mrs Charleston, Sarah and one of Sarah's friends, would sit down to eat ice cream from glass goblets.

Who would Sarah choose to go with her? Who? Who? That's all we'd talked about on the way down from the waterfall.

Mrs Charleston was sitting on Sarah's bed, with Sarah next to her trying to decide who should come. Her hands played on her lips. Me, me! I sat up in bed and smiled like an enormous animal on a Chinese wedding kite. Who would be Sarah's friend tomorrow?

I leant out over the bed and kow-towed my arms like a peasant with the mandarin. 'Mrs Charleston,' I hissed, 'me! Me!'

Then Sarah turned to her mother and mouthed, 'Is-o-bel.'

I flumped back in bed and let out a big fat tsss like a silk merchant who's just lost a customer. I listened to Mrs Charleston and Aunty Muriel discuss the journey. Mrs Charleston sounded like a schoolgirl as she talked to Aunty Muriel, but perhaps everyone sounds like that when they speak to her.

Just before it was lights out, Mrs Charleston came to each bed and gave us a good night hug. All freckly hands and looking at you kindly. I did wish I had been chosen.

Muriel's Diary

8th November 1941

SITTING DOWN THIS EVENING, I AM FULL WITH THE MEMORY OF MY arrival in China, of standing on the ship, watching Shanghai's bay full of winged junks and hundreds of sampan and ferry-boats, weaving back and forth from the shore. The stench of fish heads, floating coffins and, as we stepped on to the land, walking through the pier, the dark shops aglow with their candlelit idols. I was twenty-three years old, the prime age for candidates. It was 1937 and I felt such purpose.

And yet, ascending this mountain in my tea dress, wool coat and Dornoch boots, I was disappointed with my appointment to Lushan. I had wanted to go to the field after training. I wanted to evangelise at the side of senior missionaries, not teach their children. Yet I remained sure of my calling to China, confident in my ability to win people over, my administrative excellence, and my sense of what prayer was and how it worked in our lives.

I believe I will now leave this mountain, to the Lord's next calling or at the bidding of the Japanese emperor, unsure, unsettled.

Arise, Samantha

LATER THAT NIGHT, I WAS SLIPPING INTO SLEEP, WHEN I HEARD A voice.

'Samantha,' said the voice. 'Are you awake? It's God.' I sat bolt upright. It was a good thing I wasn't on the bottom bunk or such visitations from the Lord would be painful.

'Samantha.'

'Yes,' I said into the blackness.

'What?' said God. 'Speak up.'

'Yes,' I said more loudly.

'Yes, God,' corrected God.

'Yes, God,' I said.

'Stand up, Samantha,' said God.

'But we're not allowed, not on our beds.'

'Arise, Samantha,' said God.

'Okay, God.'

'Now, Samantha, shout Bazooka.'

'Bazooka.'

'Give it more oomph and you'll get on the baptism list.'

'Bazooka!'

Throughout the dorm there was wild and silent laughing.

Bunk beds shook. There were a number of snorts. Then the dormitory door was yanked open.

'What is this nonsense?' said Aunty Muriel. The hallway light showed her face, meaner than a gorse bush. I was red with shame. Stupid girls. Snorting pigs, pigs you all. There was only one thing for it. To carry on, louder.

Arms up in front of me like a ghost, I yelled, 'Bazooka. Bazooka.' The girls stopped laughing.

'Etta, Etta.' Aunty Muriel's voice was soft as a dandelion's face. She touched my arm. I burst into tears. 'There, there. Get down from your bed.'

The dormitory was wild shapes in the light of her candle. She led me out on to the balcony. 'Shouting like that, even the monks up above will hear you.'

'Aunty Muriel, do you think God heard me?'

'I very much hope not, Etta,' she said, and gave me a hanky. We were outside her door. 'Come in,' she said. Of course I had been inside Aunty Muriel's room before, but I never got used to it, like your favourite hymn. It was warm and yellow and it didn't smell of us. There was a narrow bed, a desk, a small wardrobe, a sink, a shelf with five books. There was a stove and an orange rug and a large, red paper lantern. There was a window at either end. Along both windowsills were spider plants. Miss Preedy had given her a sucker when she joined and now they'd bred. There was even one on the bookcase with little babies sprouting from it.

'Take a seat. How about the rocking chair?' she said. 'The cushion was made by my mother. She sent it all the way from Scotland.' The cushion had a huge purple thistle cross-stitched on to it. I didn't think a thistle was a good thing to place your bottom on, but perhaps it reminded Aunty Muriel of home. I sat down on the chair and began to rock while she made me a hot cocoa on her little stove.

On Aunty Muriel's desk were photographs of her mother and father and a book that said 'Missionary's Diary'. Hanging along the wall was a row of watercolours. There was one of the forest and one of a monk. There was the one of us from the outing to the Boiling House. I looked at us on the mountainside, the pines, great peaks and huge ravine behind us. Edith was squinting at the sun. Big Bum basked. Sarah plaited Flo's hair. I was sat on the ground with an apple on my knee. We were girls caught in Aunty Muriel's painting.

'You're all growing up,' said Aunty Muriel, looking at the picture. 'Sometimes growing up can be difficult.'

'Yes,' I said. I sighed. Having problems to sigh over made me feel grown up.

'Let me tell you a story,' she said, leaning back in her chair, her hands warming around a cup of cocoa. 'A famous missionary called Shanghai Gunn came to our village and gave a talk in the Fishermen's Hall one Friday night. She spoke about serving God in China. She told us there was a great darkness of the soul across China, and that workers were needed. I knew there and then that God was calling me to China. I ran all the way home through the rain without a bonnet or a brolly and told Mother and Father.

'I thought they'd be so happy, but Father's face went white. No. No. No. He was very against it. He didn't speak to me for three months. As we lived in the same house this was difficult for both my mother and me. He knew how to make you feel you weren't there. He has his reasons, my mother would say. He doesn't want any harm to come to you, you're his only daughter. But I was a stubborn lassie. I think you know some of what that feels like. I decided to go. God had called me and to ignore his call to serve him in China was a sin worse than ignoring my father's wishes. I travelled down to London and stayed in the Wimbledon compound along with the other women candidates, and after six months' candidate training I was ready to go.

'The journey was a long one, starting with the train from Waterloo to Southampton and then by liner to the docks of Shanghai. Well, can you guess who was there at Waterloo Station to wave me off? My dad. He'd travelled down on the *Flying Scotsman*, which is a train, from Inverness. And there on the platform he told me that when I was born, he'd dedicated me for the mission to God in China. And as I grew up he hoped that vow would just be the noise and pomp of a young man, but no, the night I came to the door, hair soaked and without a brolly, there to announce my good news, he knew God was making him honour his promise.'

Aunty Muriel stopped speaking. She didn't know she'd stopped. She was still seeing Waterloo Station, the puffing steam train, her father. She'd forgotten that I was in the room. Then she sighed and checked her tiny wristwatch. 'Time for bed. Go quietly. Chop chop.'

'How old are you, Aunty Muriel?' I asked as I reached the door.

'I'm twenty-seven.'

'Aunty Muriel, was it a calling or a sending?'

Aunty Muriel crossed her ankles and leant back in the chair, resting her head on the wall. The front legs of the chair were off the ground. She could have given herself an order mark.

'Were you called or sent, Aunty Muriel?' I asked as I stepped out on to the balcony. I never heard her reply.

*

I dreamt I was in one of Aunty Muriel's watercolour paintings. The forest, cool, dark, shafts of light ahead. I pushed forward into the deep, whispering green. Then I heard a waterfall. Leaping over tree roots, I ran towards the pool, I would jump right into the crystal waters, but someone was there in the frothing pool, a small child drowning.

I awoke, sweating, thrashing my sheets.

Cloud god, River god, Rain god. God is everywhere. The next morning I sat up soaked but it wasn't me who'd wet my bed. It was the Lord.

It was about a quarter to seven when I seized the sodden dressing gown, stood on my bed and because people are more likely to take note, I began to speak King James. 'Arise, O prophetesses, I hath received a sign, my robe hath been soaked.' The girls turned over and looked. Even Big Bum Eileen was smiling, propped up in bed on her elbows. The rain banged on the roof like a dragon trying to get in.

'Hark,' they said, 'now what?'

'It means that today we face our biggest trial of faith.' I leant over and picked up Flo's glasses from the side cabinet. It gave me a more serious air. I pushed them up and down my nose. I paced my bed. It is hard to look definite on something so springy.

'Today we are to enter—' I began.

'Ssh,' said the girls all at once, for Aunty Muriel had run into the room with stacks of Quaker Oats tins in her arms.

She yelled, 'Glory, glory be.' And then, 'Henrietta, do not stand on your bed. Get down at once.'

We all leapt out of bed to help Aunty Muriel catch the drips, even Big Bum Eileen. The drops ticking into the tins made the dormitory sound like a clock shop, each tin ticking a different time.

'Enter what?' said the girls as they searched the floor for wet spots.

I placed a tin down by the wardrobes where the final drip was. Drops pinged brightly. 'The time has come. During the night it was revealed. We've been called to enter the mouth of the mountain.'

The Tunnel

WE STOOD IN THE STREAM WEARING ONLY OUR PANTS AND VESTS. WE looked towards the dark mouth of the tunnel that gaped in the green bank ahead. The stream bubbled around our calves. It was Sunday afternoon and the sun was shining. All of us except Sarah and Isobel, who were at the Happy House Hotel, followed the stream to the furthest reaches of the school. We were on the edge of out of bounds and we were, if I could persuade everyone, about to smuggle ourselves right off the school map.

'It looks dark in there,' said Hilary.

'And echoey,' said Edith, testing out a hoot.

'Elishella, ssh,' I hissed, calling her by her prophetess name to remind her that this was no time for casual hooting.

Edith stepped away from the mouth of the tunnel and we fell silent again.

We were having a rest before going into the tunnel, and now that we had stopped, our excitement had disappeared. I wondered if the girls were grumpy because they had to sacrifice their Sunday cake. After we had neatly folded and hidden our dresses, each girl had laid her slice of Sunday cake, raspberry sponge with pink icing, on the bank by the side of the tunnel. The Sunday cake sacrifice was to protect us as we disappeared into the mountainside. The cakes were sweating in the sunshine. The prophetesses hadn't noticed that my cake wasn't next to theirs. I had kept it in my napkin and when no one was looking, popped it in my pocket.

Hilary stood on guard by the bank in case boys or Japanese soldiers came in sight. Big Bum Eileen plopped herself down on a broad boulder in the middle of the stream, where she sat like a sulky Miss Muffet. She scooped a handful of water over her face, a droplet trickled its way down her throat. The prophetesses watched the black mouth ahead of them. It didn't look like we would ever climb inside it. I had to do something.

I leapt on to the boulder by the mouth of the tunnel. 'Prophetesses! The time has come for us to enter the tunnel,' I said, trying to make my voice boom over the jibber-jabber of the water. The girls looked from me to the tunnel, then back at me again. Apart from their eyes, my words hadn't moved them.

'Prophetess Samantha, what is it like again, the place on the other side of the tunnel?' asked Fiona, shielding her eyes from the sun. They waited for my answer. I couldn't get away with hints any longer, I had to say something. I looked at the stream. It had passed through the tunnel. It knew what was on the other side.

'Waiting at the end of the tunnel are . . .' I had to be careful, I didn't want another prophetic mistake or else I'd be condemned as a false prophetess. I turned my thoughts inside myself. What did the Lord want to reveal to me? All I could see was Mrs Charleston and her freckly hands. I tried making a prophecy again, 'Waiting at the end of the tunnel are . . . mothers.'

'You've seen them? Our mothers?' The prophetesses chitter-chattered over each other.

'Each person can only see their own mother,' I said.

'I don't believe there are mothers,' said Big Bum Eileen. 'I can't be bothered with this game, I'm going back.' She stood up from the rock, grabbed her stick and leapt to the bank. Edith got up too. Soon everyone would go; they all did what Big Bum Eileen did. I'd be all on my own and we'd never know what was at the other end of the tunnel. There might even be mothers. Then I surprised myself. I leapt from the boulder and on to the tunnel's ledge.

Turning to the prophetesses, I shouted, 'O ye of little faith.'

It was a shock when the tunnel then spoke. 'Faith, faith,' said the tunnel.

Encouraged, I said, 'Yes, you must have more faith.'

The word 'faith' echoed out again. This got the girls bustling into action.

'Maybe our mothers will give us ice cream,' said Fiona, grabbing her shoes. We all did the same.

'Let's pick them a posy of flowers,' said Edith, snatching a handful of clovers as she clambered back down the bank.

I turned away from the school playground and faced the tunnel. I took a deep breath and stepped inside.

The tunnel was dark and cool. The water was strangely quiet, unlike the giddy stream outside. It was smooth and strong around my shins. If you had been a teacher or dorm aunty, you couldn't have stood up straight for the tunnel wasn't very high. But it was just the right size for a prophetess. My feet were firm on the concrete floor. I stretched out my arms to either side of the tunnel. The walls were coated in spongy green moss. A droplet broke free from the ceiling, and with a plink, became part of the stream.

One by one the girls clambered on to the ledge and once we were all in line, we started to move through the tunnel. There was a heavy, tangy smell in the air. The prophetesses in the tunnel made a gentle sloshing sound. We were walking deeper into the darkness. The tunnel was a long throat and we were being swallowed alive.

After a good three or four minutes, the tunnel veered sharply to the right and a circle of brightness appeared. With each step, the circle got bigger. Being in the tunnel reminded me of being underwater in the bath. That is where my prophecies come, I thought. I felt a tingle. Maybe my prophecy would come true. I hoped so or that would be the end of the Prophetess Club.

I imagined Mother. She would be standing in the stream at the other end of the tunnel, the water playing about her ankles. She would be dressed in a blue tunic and trousers with an oiled paper umbrella to protect herself from the sun. She'd be calling out to me, 'Ming-Mei, Ming-Mei.'

The gloom of the tunnel began to lift. The tunnel is taking me to the outside world, and Mother will be there, I said to myself. She will be carrying a goblet of vanilla ice cream.

With two more steps, I was standing on the concrete shelf at the other end of the tunnel. I was in bright sunshine. Ahead lay a long, deep pool of water. Red dragonflies zipped in between the reeds, water spiders scooted busily. I quickly surveyed the scene with my clever prophetess eyes. I knew exactly where we were. I turned to Hilary and whispered in her ear, 'Welcome to the Pool of Mothers.' She smiled at me, her eyes widening. 'Pass it on,' I added, before leaping on to the grassy bank. Hilary then turned, whispered into Big Bum Eileen's ear and jumped to the bank. And Big Bum Eileen turned to Flo and so on, until each prophetess had been welcomed to the Pool of Mothers.

I gazed around. The tunnel had smuggled us deep into the forest. High trees stood around the pool, the leafy fingers of a vine trailed in the water. There were cushions of bright green moss and clumps of forget-me-nots. Hidden birds sang in the tree tops. In the distance, temple chimes chinked. There were butterflies galore. Long grasses grew up, up, up, untouched by Gardener Chen's mower. It looked like no one had played there before. It was our very own.

We quickly put on our white plimsolls, for as everyone knows there can be yellow bellies and centipedes in grass that has not been clipped by Gardener Chen.

'This beats the Happy House Hotel,' said Hilary.

'Now let us see, who can be the first to spot a mother?' I said. We stood still for many minutes, watching the forest, listening to the bubble of the pool, the trink-trink of the temple chimes.

The first person to speak was Hilary. 'I can see my mother,' she said. She had kneeled down and was peering into the pool. 'Hello,' she said to the water. We crept over on tiptoe as we didn't want to frighten her mother away. Would our mothers be there, too? We crouched down at the edge of the pool and looked. Staring back were six peering girls. I searched the mirror of the pool for my mother. I looked for her high up in the trees, in the twists of the vines. I looked in the clouds that floated across the water. She wasn't there.

I heard Fiona say, 'Hello, Mummy.'

And Kathryn say, 'Hello, Mum. It's me!'

I concentrated harder and looked at the pool's surface again. I wanted to see Mother. Where is she? I thought. I scrunched my eyes tight and hoped as hard as I could, then slowly opened them again. I looked at the face of the girl in the water. Her forehead was wrinkly and her eyes squinty with all that hoping.

Edith started to sob. The clover posy she had gathered flopped over her fingers. 'I can't see anyone,' she said. The posy dropped into the water and was sucked towards the tunnel and back to the school.

The pool's surface shattered. Eyes and lips fled in a thousand flashes of colour. Big Bum Eileen had thrown a rock, and with a plunk, we had vanished. 'This is stupid,' she said. 'No one can see their mothers. And now Edith is crying and we'll have to explain her red face to Aunty Muriel.'

I drew myself up as tall as I could, but I was still a head shorter than Big Bum Eileen. 'The mothers will come. We just need to wait,' I whispered, like how Aunty Muriel tells us off when we're holding our hymn books upside down in church.

'Who can see their mother?' Big Bum Eileen asked. Her toe tapped like a cat's tail.

No one raised their hand or nodded.

'See,' she said. 'It's just a silly game.'

I jumped on to the grey rock, for talking from a rock always gives you strength, and said, 'Elijine, you are a false prophetess.'

Big Bum Eileen laughed. 'No, Samantha, you are the false prophetess. You said our mothers would be here, but they are nowhere to be seen.'

'Hark, hark,' said the girls. They stood up and gathered

98

around Big Bum Eileen. Everyone, that is, apart from Flo, who stayed looking at the pool.

'Etta made us sacrifice our cake,' said Edith, not even using my prophetess name.

'Our dresses have probably got centipedes crawling on them,' said Kathryn.

'Hark, hark,' said the girls.

Big Bum Eileen jumped up on to the rock, too. There wasn't enough room for both of us to stand. I felt the curve of the rock under my feet; I was dangerously near the edge. She might shove me right into the pool.

Then, Flo, who is the most sensible of us, said, 'Ssh.' She watched the forest, her hands at her mouth.

'What, Habakkukina?' I said. Flo's whole body was listening, watching.

'I saw something,' she said, her voice slipping from her as smooth as fish meat from the bone.

'Our mothers . . . ?' said Hilary, looking to Big Bum Eileen.

The temple bells rang. Were they calling us to them? A gust of wind shuddered through the trees and the sun had disappeared behind a cloud. Everything became a shade darker. We were standing in the cooling afternoon, in pants, vests and goose bumps.

There was a crack of branches. We clung to each other. Up on the rock, even Big Bum Eileen and I clung to each other. It could be a Japanese soldier.

Then out of the jungle, a white chicken bolted. It squawked and squawked. Chasing after the chicken was a child. Edith squealed. We all squealed. The chicken and child hurtled towards us, and landed together in a heap on the grass. The child thrust out its arms and snatched the dazed chicken.

Black eyes glinting, ugly feet scratching, the chicken tried to flap its way free.

I looked at the child. She was a girl of about four or five, a little younger than we were when we came here. She wore ragged cotton trousers and a top. Her feet were covered in grey cotton and tied with straw. There were cotton strings with an amulet of peach stone around her wrists, to protect her from evil spirits.

I looked at the clasping hands. An extra little finger grew out of the knuckle of each pinkie. A slender finger with a tiny nail. It was then that I knew who she was. She was the child who had run through the sheets in the laundry.

The girl buried her head into the back of the chicken. '*Guimei*,' she said. Ghost girls. We were so pale and strange to her. Flo kneeled down and went to stroke her but the girl shrunk back and let out a high-pitched 'eeeeee', like a tiny boiling kettle.

I shook my head and said, '*Bu shi guimei*.' Not ghost girl. We were not allowed to speak Chinese, but the words 'not ghost girl' came out so easily, for I had said them many times playing on the red dust roads near my home.

The girl stared at me, for ghosts don't normally talk, and the chicken ran off as she let go her grip.

From my pocket I brought out the slice of Sunday cake. Eating is what Jesus did after he was risen to show the disciples he was really alive. But there was no time to explain that. I unwrapped the napkin and kneeled beside the girl. I rubbed my tummy to show her that I was very hungry and this cake was going to be very tasty indeed, and took a vast bite.

'Hark!' said Hilary.

'*Bu shi guimei*,' I said again to the little Chinese girl, my cheeks puffed up with cake, my hands out in the shape of ta-dah. I repeated my words: '*Bu shi guimei.*' Now she knew I couldn't be a ghost girl. Then I offered her a bite. She looked wary but bit.

Big Bum Eileen cottoned on. She pointed at herself and the other girls. '*Bu shi guimei.*' The prophetesses nodded, they were not ghosts either.

I scraped the pink icing from the roof my mouth with my tongue and said to the prophetesses, 'So you see, there *are* mothers at the other end of the tunnel.'

They looked at me blankly.

'We are the mothers,' I pointed to the girl, 'and this is our very own child.'

In the distance the dinner bell rang. It sounded so very far away, just a tickle in the ear. I would come back to tend our child. I stared at those two extra fingers. They had a cleverness of their own.

'Prophetesses,' said Big Bum Eileen as we finished dressing on the other side of the tunnel. We made a prophetess circle. There was much white in our eyes, for we had been greatly astonished. 'It is decreed, we have a daughter.'

'A dormitory daughter.'

'A secret daughter.'

'It is decreed!'

Then we ran like the Psalmist's gazelles, free and light and strong. We leapt across the stream to the far bank, back in bounds, and ran along the curve of the stream, over the wooden bridge and then up the steps towards the playing fields. The world was bubbling and gurgling. It was covered in a pink light.

*

After washing our hands and faces, we ran from the dormitory to the dining hall. The walls were rose with sunset. The serving spoons shone. Then through the glow came Mrs Charleston. 'Mrs Charleston,' we said, 'where are you going?'

'To have a lie-down,' she called behind her. But I could see she was upset and Headmaster could, too. He stopped her at the dining-room door and there they stood, Mrs Charleston speaking quickly, her face flaring with many expressions of anxiety while Headmaster drummed his fingers behind his back. Then Mrs Charleston stopped talking and stared at the forest. I saw her gulp. Headmaster steered her towards the door and together they left.

But there was not time to think of what had troubled Mrs Charleston, for in arriving at the table I saw that in her place was another woman.

'Miss Kingsley,' we whispered to each other as we found our seats. Miss Preedy made an announcement introducing Miss Kingsley to the dining hall, but we girls of Dormitory A all knew the story. Miss Kingsley was one half of the famous Duo, who had preached up and down on the Women's River for more than thirty years, who ran Agape House, a school for abandoned girls, and who, annually, would take turns to visit Lushan, to give encouragement to the staff and instruction to we children on spiritual matters, such as baptism. Miss Kingsley was a woman with great ministry and neither she nor her other half, Miss Tippet, had sat at our table before.

We acknowledged this sign with knowing looks, then sang grace with good-girl gusto, and in the 'Amen' Edith did not mouth 'Bazoooka-ka-ka', for there was nothing bazooka about Miss Kingsley. This was a woman of bone and shadow and, as Kathryn pointed out, of clavicle.

The dinner was meatballs. They were sweet, sour and chewy, and they took up much of our attention until the moment Miss Kingsley began to speak.

Through chews of gristle she was trying to tell Aunty Muriel something. '. . . Trenches are being built . . . Garrisons . . . the Japanese . . . Inland . . . Agape House is in the march . . . My visit can't be . . . need to get back . . . keep them safe.'

'Ah,' said Aunty Muriel. She saw how we'd stopped chewing and were staring at Miss Kingsley. She smiled briskly and tried to change the subject from girls in danger. 'Has the Women's River – Edith, don't chase your meatball like that – seen many conversions recently?'

Miss Kingsley chewed for some time, then gave up on the piece of fat, hooked it out of her mouth with her finger and answered. 'Many of our congregation have fled to the refugee camps or have been commandeered into digging those trenches. It's not much better in the towns. Just last week a new missionary couple, the Watsons, had their church burnt down in a bombing raid.'

Aunty Muriel gave Miss Kingsley a pointed look, and hurried to say, 'But the Japanese regard Lushan as a sacred mountain. They will not wish to see it come to any harm.'

'Indeed,' said Miss Kingsley, looking at each one of us.

Aunty Muriel turned to Sarah. 'Now, girls, what ice cream did you have?' She pushed the meatball around the plate.

'We didn't have ice cream. The Happy House Hotel was shut,' said Sarah. 'A band of Japanese lookout soldiers came to the village this morning and they put a big sign up that ran all the way from the second floor to the ground saying it was closed. All the Chinese had disappeared. Then one of the soldiers took us into the tailors and locked us up there for nearly an hour while he took our details: age, nationality, name.'

'Is that why your mother was so upset?' said Edith.

'That's enough about soldiers for dinnertime,' said Aunty Muriel. Now we all chased our meatballs round our plates. They were slippy in the sauce and difficult to capture.

Sarah went on with the story, but without soldiers. 'Afterwards, we walked past all the closed shops and a man in an oily apron came running up the alley and grabbed us. I thought this time we really were going to be caught. He took us into his noodle shop, which had swallows in the ceiling, and served us tofu dumplings. Isobel ate six of them, which cost Mother a lot.'

At the mention of the dumplings Isobel leant back on her chair and groaned.

'Sit up straight,' said Aunty Muriel. Then she and Miss Kingsley shared a look. Quiet alarm passed through us and I noticed no one was eating their meatballs. They sat on our plates pink and fatty. There was worse that the Japanese could do than steal our appetites, and we all knew it.

The Eleventh Commandment

AFTER SUNSET, WHEN THE SKY WAS BLACK AND SPLASHED WITH STARS, we sat in the beeswax smell of Memorial Hall in our dressing gowns. My dressing gown had dried from its night-time soaking on the outside but was still damp inside. It clung to me through my nightdress.

Just in front of the stage, Aunt Nebuchadnezzar thumped out a tune on the shiny black piano. Her eyebrows zinked and zoinked. Aunt Neb played with such gusto that you felt you'd done a sprint across Drill Court. We sang out into the mountains of Lushan a song that must have been strange to its immortal self. Our hymn marched forth, bright and strong. Singing together, we were a powerful arm, and I did not feel afraid of the Japanese, or anyone.

After clapping a warm welcome until our palms stung, we sat down, caught our breath and watched Miss Kingsley walk to the stage. She had a sad slow way about her. The pace of a slow-moving river.

'She's ugly,' Edith had said. 'She's not as fun as Mrs Charleston,' said Hilary. It was true. But Miss Kingsley had something. She had ministry.

I couldn't wait to hear about it. She'd sailed the Women's River up and down for thirty-two years, preaching with her gospel glove, converting the wives in their courtyards, going from fishing village to fishing village, baptising the women and their children in the mud-swollen waters. I watched Miss Kingsley through a rockery of heads.

When she reached the stage Miss Kingsley said nothing. Instead, she dipped a calligrapher's brush into a pot of ink. Then she went to a large piece of paper on the board behind her. She stood looking at it. Even though I could see only her back, I knew she was praying because a quietness came over her body. Then she raised up her right arm and drew, very slowly, a Chinese character. The character filled the whole paper: Miss Kingsley was used to being seen by big crowds.

'What does this character mean?' she finally said. Her voice was low and shimmery. Like the bellow of a water buffalo.

Her eyes searched us for a child that would answer. No answer came. We hadn't been allowed to speak Chinese for many years, never mind write it. Chinese makes children's hearts crooked. Whenever we called each other or ourselves by our Chinese names, or shouted at dorm aunties the words muleteers used for the donkeys, we were spanked. Although I do still keep some words. They won't go away.

We sat still in our dressing gowns and were embarrassed because we couldn't answer her question. After a long silence, while the staff had crossed and uncrossed their legs a lot, Miss Kingsley said, 'Surely you remember some Chinese?'

I shot my hand up.

'Yes?' said Miss Kingsley.

'My Chinese name is Ming-Mei. Ming-Mei means Bright and Beautiful.'

There was a titter from the school. Staff shook their heads.

'My mum called me that because that's what she thought when she looked at me.'

The laughter got louder. Aunt Neb snorted.

But I went on, saying in Chinese, '*Ni hao Kingsley. Wo jiao Ming-Mei. Ni chi fan le mei you?*' Hello Miss Kingsley. My name is Ming-Mei. Have you eaten yet?

Miss Kingsley replied, '*Ni hao Ming-Mei. Wo chi fan le.*' Hello Ming-Mei. Yes, I've eaten.

'Sit down, Etta,' said Miss Preedy.

And I sat down happy because Miss Kingsley and I understood each other.

'Now back to the word "*Ai*", what does it mean?' Miss Kingsley's gaze drifted to a point several rows behind ours. 'Yes?' One of the Sons of Thunder had his hand up.

'It means . . . love,' said Bertie Ducat. Love, love. Bertie Ducat had said love. I looked at Flo; her cheeks were pink for she rather loved Bertie Ducat. He was the only Son of Thunder to have glasses.

'That's correct. Love,' said Miss Kingsley. She wasn't at all embarrassed. She even said it in Chinese. '*Ai*.' Love.

We watched as she turned once again to the board and started to draw another shape inside the big Chinese character. The shape she drew was a woman. And then the Chinese character for Love became a picture of a woman in a shed looking over a manger. Miss Kingsley drew another shape in the manger. A wiggle with eyes. It was a baby.

'This is love.'

Oh, that love. I knew all about that love. For Mary loved

her son. For Jesus loved the world. For God so loved the world he gave his only son. It was a less embarrassing love. She said love again in Chinese. When she spoke Chinese, Miss Kingsley had another voice, not the voice of an English woman speaking Chinese, but the voice of a Chinese woman.

'God loves China and that's why he called your parents here. Your parents love God and that is why they listened to his calling them to work and win souls for his Kingdom. They obeyed. Whatever our calling, we are all called to love one another. God loved us and we show his love to others.'

I knew that too. I looked down the row of girls, belts of their dressing gowns tied tight, hymn books in their laps. Then I felt a chill up my spine. I had thought there were only ten commandments in the Prophetess Club, but as I sat in the cling of my damp dressing gown listening to the ministry of Miss Kingsley, it was revealed to me there was to be an eleventh. I whispered it to Flo and Hilary, who were sitting at my left and right hand: 'This is the eleventh commandment of the Prophetess Club: we are called to love our daughter.'

'Our daughter, our daughter . . .' echoed down the row.

I imagined loving our daughter. I'd give her a toothbrush and help her brush her teeth. I'd dress her in her nightdress, which would be white with pink stripes through it and a name tag in the collar, stitched in my best stitching. I'd help her into bed, which would be on a bottom bunk for she was a little child, as little as we were when we first came here. And I would say good night and tell her to go to sleep and she would turn on to her side and fall asleep with a smile on her face. And I would sit by her for a while as she slept, pulling the covers up to her neck, smoothing away any bad dreams with my kind hands. I would love her in English and Chinese.

Part II

The Baptism Girls

IN THE STEAM OF THE BATHROOM, I DISCOVERED THE PROPHETESS Club had been disbanded. That was the truth of it. They all wanted to be baptised, which was more grown up.

'No one had any real prophecies anyway,' said Hilary, drying a leg.

'I did,' I said, stepping out from the bath where Big Bum Eileen now stretched full length, crowned by her strawberry shower cap. Recently, she'd not just been taking up more bath space, but more bath time. I left the bath cubicle and joined the girls by the sinks.

'We should never have gone out of bounds,' said Flo. Her head was bent and she was combing her wet hair briskly.

'But, Habakkukina, we prophetesses found a daughter. Habakkukina, we've been told to love. The eleventh commandment.'

'Well, we shouldn't have gone,' said Flo.

'And *we* can't go again,' said Hilary.

'What exactly will you do in *your* baptism class?' Edith asked the baptism girls.

Hilary shrugged. Flo combed her hair with fast, firm strokes. Sarah, Fiona and Isobel, who had also been invited into Aunty Muriel's room that afternoon for an announcement of their baptism date, patted themselves down in a cloud of white talc.

'Elijine?' I called, high and hopeful. From the bath cubicle where Big Bum lay there was a violent swirling. 'Elijine?'

'She no longer answers to that name,' hissed Edith to me, and then to the cubicle, 'Are you ready, Eileen?'

'Coming.' There was an upheaval of water. The girls hopped to. Big Bum entered, walked to her sink and let down her towel.

'I was just imagining being baptised,' she said, her voice low. 'I dipped under the water and imagined Headmaster lifting me out, anointed.'

'Every time we have a bath we can practise,' said Sarah. 'That's what me and Fiona did.'

Hilary unravelled the tape measure and Flo did the measuring because she was the most accurate. 'Gosh,' she said, 'I think they might have grown since last week.'

'I certainly feel more womanly,' said Eileen as Flo marked the measurement in the back of her prayer diary.

'In what way womanly?' asked Edith, taking the measuring tape and wrapping it around her own chest.

'Well, for one thing, I don't want to play any silly games,' said Big Bum, turning to face me.

'Measuring your boobies is a silly game.'

'My breasts are a fact,' she said, turning back to the sink, 'Unlike the Prophetess Club.'

'Our daughter is a fact,' I said to her reflection.

'She's not our daughter, Etta. She's someone else's daughter.'

'My name is not Etta. It's Samantha.'

'Is that so, Etta?' said Big Bum Eileen.

'Yes it is, Big Boob.'

The girls gasped. I snatched Flo's diary and shouted out the measurements: '24¾ inches, 26⅛ inches, 27¼ inches. A thousand big-boob inches.' Then I ran through the dormitory, yelling, 'Big Boob, Big Boob. Stupid Big Boob.' The girls chased me through the room.

'Give that back,' yelled Big Bum Eileen, clutching her towel about her. She was fast but I was faster. I climbed up my bunk, threw off my towel and danced naked shouting, 'Big Boob, Big Boob, Stupid Big Boob.'

Aunty Muriel shot into the room, paint on her hands. 'Girls, silence. I am shocked. This is a disgrace. Henrietta Robertson, get down off your bed this instant. I want you dressed and in my room in the next minute. Girls, you will dress and get into bed in silence by the time I count to twenty. One, two . . .'

Flo took back her prayer diary. The girls moved to their own beds. 'To think you want to be a baptism girl,' said Hilary. I didn't care. I put on my nightdress and slid down my bunk.

'Explain yourself,' said Aunty Muriel when we were in her room. On her desk next to a jam jar of murky water was a painting of a waterfall with a monk watching the pool. Next to it were our letters home, which she had to read through before sending.

Mine was addressed to Mr & Mrs Robertson of Pingxia village. I wondered if they'd already moved to the caves above the village and if this letter would find them there. The one I wrote about the baptism had had a long journey across China, and a dangerous one. The letter might have been blown up in one of the railway bombings that were happening north of the Yangtze Delta, or intercepted by General Chiang

Kai-shek's spies while travelling by mule towards Pingxia. It could have been captured by roaming communist soldiers, or drowned in the rapids of the Huang Ho. But perhaps that letter had not been answered for another reason. I could see it now, resting by the chopstick holders on the dining-room table, the jagged edges of the opened envelope, the read letter tucked back inside, unanswered, for Mother and Father did not think I was ready for baptism. I must show everyone that I was ready. I must make a better effort to improve my spirit and show a willingness to learn.

'I am waiting.' Aunty Muriel's fingers drummed the side of her desk. 'One point off your Goodness Card, two points off your Goodness Card, three points . . .'

I flung myself at her feet. 'Please can I join the baptism girls?'

'Henrietta, you know that's not possible.'

'But I have faith, I have zeal.'

'Well your zeal shall have to last another year.'

For the first ten minutes no one had known I was in Miss Kingsley's baptism class. I was crouching under the arbour table looking at the swinging legs of the baptism girls and Miss Kingsley's big old feet, in her big old sandals, firmly planted on the pine-needle-scattered floor. Miss Kingsley had asked, 'If John baptised the people with water, what would Jesus baptise with?' and Hilary, who gets very fidgety when thinking, kicked. I howled. All the legs froze and Miss Kingsley said, 'What was that?'

'The Holy Spirit,' I said from under the table, 'Mark, chapter one, verse eight.' But I was wrong, very wrong. Miss Kingsley ordered me to get out, and I sat outside for a few minutes, before Eileen said, 'She's still here,' and Miss Kingsley looked out from the arbour and told me not to bother the baptism lesson any further.

I climbed The Beard. It was a sunny, blustery day. I went higher than I'd ever climbed before. The rough red bark scraped my hands and knees but still higher I went. I climbed up past the initials carved into the bark, faint scars from the cuts of boys. But perhaps L.S. 1921 and T.J.M. 1924 and O.T. 1931 were girls, with knives. Below, through blusters of green, children played on the field. Boys in batsman whites, girls on wooden stilts. The Chinese and British flags whipped and strained. And by the Great Steps, the girls in the arbour, ponytails blowing, chanted their catechism. I saw how they shared their favourite Bible verses, how Flo tipped her head back and laughed with Big Bum Eileen, how they all cocked their fingers with their glasses of milk. They were changing.

Where the branches began to bend, I stopped and sat cradled in a crook. There, as the wind chanted, *Get out, get out, Etta*, I swayed and cried. When I opened my eyes, I saw a tiny white spider crawling along the branch towards me. I'm so big I could flatten you, I said to it. It kept coming anyway. I squashed it, under my fist, feeling its insides spread across the bark. It disgusted me how its legs twitched. How easily it had been killed. But as I brushed the smear of its body from my palm, I began to feel so sad. The white spider had been going somewhere, perhaps to its shimmering web, and then because of my anger, I'd stopped its life. Gone. Squish. Dead. All with a grind of the hand.

Just then I heard more voices. It was Kathryn and Edith. They walked below in the garden carrying the rusty dormitory trowels. They'd spent the afternoon being useful. Edith bent down and pulled something from the earth. 'Look, a worm. We could put it in Etta's bed.'

'Or those snails, we could put them on her plant,' said

Kathryn. The wind lulled, then roared again. Then Kathryn and Edith started gathering snails and placed them at the bottom of my tuberose.

Bad, wicked, nasty girls. My sadness turned to rage. I imagined leaping out of the tree, like an enormous locust to plague them, flinging my arms in the air like crazy antennae. I imagined it, then I did it. Flinging myself at them, shouting, 'I hate you, nasty girls.' Then I ran helter-skelter, hating, hurt, sobbing, the wind howling, *get out, get out, Etta.*

I ran down the West Steps, along Livingstone Stream and up to my rock. I looked into the heart-shaped space where the trees met. I tried to imagine my mother and father, but they would not appear. I imagined hard, hard as when you're praying. Nothing happened. I sat up and spat. A big hoiking bit of gob. I was foul and stinking as an old amah's bound foot. It was a bad, mad day. I stomped through the long grass. It itched about my ankles. The world was falling apart. No one wanted to be a prophetess. There were Japanese soldiers. I could feel the calamity. I realised I was stamping my way towards the tunnel. My wicked feet were carrying me there. There was the mouth of the tunnel right ahead. I kicked off my plimsolls, tied them around my neck and stepped up on to the ledge. Quickly I darted inside.

It was cool and dark. I felt calm and the bad mood had disappeared. I was being drawn further and further down the tunnel towards the light, towards the Pool of Mothers.

Mother, perhaps she would be there. I stumbled towards the light. Mother, are you there? I imagined her in her blue tunic, with a goblet of ice cream.

I stood in the mouth of the tunnel. Mother? She was not there, but playing with a stick, digging up the dirt, was my child. We had found each other.

Twelve

THE GIRL WAS SQUATTING AT THE EDGE OF THE POOL. SHE WAS jabbing a twig into the mud. I stood in the mouth of the tunnel with my feet on the edge of the sill. There, in the tunnel's lip, I spoke. The tunnel echoed my words. They were friendly words.

'Hello, daughter.'

The girl looked up, startled.

I leapt from the tunnel to the bank and went to where she was playing. I squatted next to her. She had a scared look but she didn't run away. The first thing was to do names. I wanted to call myself by my prophetess name, but Samantha was a bit long. I kept to 'Etta'. I patted myself on my chest, 'Etta', then pointed at her and made my face a question. The girl waved the mud clogged twig. I looked at her.

I did it again, patting my hand on my chest and then at her, who was she? She turned away, and gouged a big glob of mud. 'Shi'Er,' she said. That meant twelve. I looked at her fingers. Yes. Twelve. The dragonflies zigged and zagged across the pool; the water was darker than I remembered.

I turned to Twelve and patted her head. It seemed a friendly thing to do. The sort of thing my father did when he went around the villages telling stories of the Jesus King. I patted my head to show her that she could pat my head if she liked. She reached up and patted my head, and I saw again the peach stone amulet she wore around her wrist. Peach stones were what protected children from being stolen. I always remember that once they were converted, Mother and Father asked the villagers to burn their idols, which meant taking the paper gods from above the stove, and above their doors and setting them on the fire, and taking from about their body any charms or amulets and casting them into the flames. The amulet, I knew, must be cut from Twelve's wrist.

But for now we would play. I patted her head again and she patted mine. I laughed. She smiled. Then she went back to gouging a line in the thick mud at the pool's edge. I shuddered because the finger had touched me.

I started playing my own game. That's the best way to get someone to play: make your game very interesting. I walked away from the pool, across the long grass, towards the bank that led up the hill. There was a large tree with its roots showing. It was the perfect place for a little home. The roots could be shelves. The canopy could be the ceiling.

I marked out the area of our house. Marched around the inside of the walls. Marched so that I could see the walls clearly in my mind's eye. And the door. Pulled it open and closed. Went in and out. In the middle of the room I placed a beautiful paper lantern with such long yellow tassels that you had to duck. There were four windows, each with paper panes. I added a bunk bed and a lacquer chest of drawers, a stove and, in the middle of the room, a dining table. There were many shelves with big tin pans, cups, saucers, napkin holders and a thermometer for when we got sick.

I called to Twelve. She lifted her head, then came running up to me. She ran right through the wall.

'Sit,' I said, and pointed to a large bare root in the bank. Twelve sat and swung her feet.

'Mamma, mamma.' I pointed to myself. She was ours to love. I went to pick her up. She didn't want to be picked up. I wished she was smaller, that she was a child that wanted to be picked up.

I imagined taking her back to the dormitory. Saying, look, girls, here is our daughter.

I looked at our little girl. Now she was sitting on the stove. 'I am your mother,' I said to her patiently.

She started dancing. She hadn't understood the importance of what I'd told her. I grabbed her wrist and made her look at me. 'I'm your mummy.' She was so small, so thin. 'This will be our house,' I said. She was too young. She didn't know how to imagine walls.

I let go. I'd left a red mark around her wrist. I felt frightened. I looked at those fingers and felt a queasy disgust. Then the bell for supper went. I could hear it, distant as calling from a dream, and beyond, the strange tinkling of the temple bells. The thought of girls lining up, and straight sock inspections, the singing of 'Jehovah-Jireh is His name', seemed so far away.

Wading through the tunnel, I felt relieved as the school began to appear, neat grass, friendly stream and a group of Sons of Thunder running across the bridge towards the dining hall. I stepped out of the tunnel and did my laces up tight. I began to run, fast, faster. I wanted to get away from the tunnel, to see Aunty Muriel, even to confess that I had led myself astray. I wished I hadn't crept to the Pool of Mothers on my own. *But, oh, oh, I have heard the child in the bulrushes, I have wandered through the waters, and found it. I am its mother and it is my secret.*

I could not stop what had been started. I hoarded biscuits, toast, Sunday cake, I slipped useful things such as a comb into my pocket, and as soon as playtime began I flew off down to the stream, clattering over the bridge, past the Nissen hut towards the tunnel. I no longer felt so alone, for I had the company of a secret, and from time to time, when she came to play by the pool, a daughter. And so this world, with its vines, trees and darting reflections, fuelled my every daydream.

A Haunting

SURROUNDED BY TREES, THICK CREEPERS AND UNMOWN GRASS, I SAT on the rock by the Pool of Mothers. I had tiptoed through the tunnel, with its recital of drips, and was here in the blue sky, green quiet of the pool. The sounds of the school were far away. You had to concentrate to hear them. Even though Twelve was not here today, I was happy. My eyes were closed, my face was tipped to the blue sky. My hand dangled down and tugged at a clump of long grass and I pulled off the little seeds with a clean swipe. The dragonflies buzzed low and slow, the water splashed over the rocks. The trees moved as if settling feathers.

As I gazed at the surface of the pool, memories came, quietly, gliding as if from a deep watery world. Her, on the yellow dust track, pale blue eyes bright with the glare of the sun. Her, whisking me in a waltz around our courtyard, the smell of a camphor dress and a sour desert breeze. Her cross-legged on a kang, preaching, her round face furrowed to show Mary's grief to the villagers. With each memory, her presence became more real. I leant over the pool and opened my eyes. The water showed my reflection, serious, alive to every flinch and ripple, but she, my mother, was not there. She had not come. I lay back on the rock, felt the sun-warmed solidity of it, and then sliding towards me, smooth as a junk, came the memory of a holiday. I had had just two holidays in the time I'd been at Lushan and I thought of these times over and over. They were strange remembrances. Sometimes they frightened me. I called them my holiday hauntings.

The boat is juddering. The engine is spluttering. We are waving in the Yuncheng sunshine. Ten girls and thirteen boys on a boat. With boxes, suitcases, a portmanteau, several baskets of pears, and a queasy dorm mistress called Miss Otis, whose merry chuckle was drowned at some point over the East China Sea. We have eaten all the oranges and ham sandwiches and dumplings. We are hungry to be held.

This morning Mary Gable, who is sixteen, helped me with my hair, weaving a green ribbon into my plait. Now I look like the most wonderful daughter you could imagine. And now that we are all here jerking about on the top deck, I am wondering if my parents would not rather prefer one of the other girls. But I am sure that when they get to know me, they'll like me very much.

As we approach the jetty, Miss Otis, says, 'Hold on, children!' It's hard to look for your mother and father when you are being shaken around so much, the blustery wind flicking your plait this way and that. But I know my parents off by heart. They are black and white, always wearing the same clothes, and looking straight at me. I try to remember some colour. The jetty is packed. Chinese men carry luggage and ladies on their backs. Stalls are bursting with watermelons. Eels squirm in buckets. A man is selling cigarettes from an upturned crate. A sheet is laid out on the ground with a handful of dried out fishes. There are some white-faced mothers and fathers looking up. They do not belong to me. But don't you worry, Mummy and Daddy, I will find you!

The boat clangs against the side of the jetty, which sets the sailors and the men from the pier yelling and throwing ropes at each other. And then, in the middle of the crowd, I see them. My parents! I am waving, I am smiling. Look at me, look at me!

The gangway is wheeled out and clatters to the pier. My mummy and daddy are looking and looking, but they cannot see me. It is like hide-and-seek! I start walking down the gangplank. My mouth is dry and my hands are shaking. We are all full of jangling excitement, we make a run for it down the gangplank. My parents crane their necks, but they are looking in the wrong direction. It makes me feel very clever that I know where I am and they don't!

The jetty is full of Chinese market men, rickshaw men, and grannies chewing betel nut. I run helter-skelter through them, my ribboned pigtail going boing, boing out to the side. I'm out of breath and they still haven't seen me. Their faces are confused. As I get nearer, I shout out, 'Mother,' and when she doesn't look I call more loudly, 'Father.' But he doesn't answer. I run up to them, abruptly halting by their sides. I am shy. I am not sure if I am allowed to touch my parents. I do a sort of star jump. They don't seem to notice. I look up to double check that I have found the right parents. They aren't how I imagined. It's not that they look different. It's that I forgot that they might have voices and move. I forgot to imagine that bit.

The pier is full of hugs from mothers, and fathers' cheerful back pats. Slowly the families leave, and it is just me and my parents standing there, the last white people on the pier. They look so sad. My father holds my mother's shoulder. She is crying. I stand next to them. 'But I am here,' I say, beginning to doubt myself. Hide-and-seek is no fun if you're not found.

Then off they walk, my mother's head is crooked into my father's neck. My mother is wearing her dough-coloured coat. Now that I have seen it again, I remember it. It is the one she'd only wear on special days, like dining with the Governor of Hequ. There is a peony blossom in her hair. My father wears a neat suit. I follow them at a pace behind. Then I remember my suitcase!

There it is, alone on the pier. It has a tag with 'HENRIETTA S. ROBERTSON' on it. Perhaps if I could show this label to my parents, they would realise it was me. I run up to it and drag it along the gritty pier, trying to catch up with them. The suitcase is heavy. I pull. I heave.

My parents, they turn the corner into the market. Quick, I must not lose sight of them, I must not let them disappear. A Chinese man comes towards me, his face riddled with wrinkles and his mouth empty of teeth. I try to tell him to go away, but the Chinese words that I used to speak as easily as English have vanished. People stop to grab me and rub my pale cheeks, Ah, a foreign devil child. I am alone on the pier with just my suitcase.

The dinner bell rang. I looked at the pool one last time. Neither the child nor my mother came. Other than the water, all is quiet. No dragonflies buzz and the air has thickened with dusk. The pool's quiet seems to speak sadness. Maybe tomorrow they will come.

*

I long to run to the pool during assembly and evening prayers when the baptism girls sit together and Edith and Kathryn hold hands, leaving me alone at the end of the row. I long to go when we do Drill and Aunt Neb shouts, 'Left, *right*, Henrietta, left, *right*,' across Drill Court so everyone can hear. I long as Mr Dalrymple's wooden globe spins at the front of our classroom and I wonder where in the globe my parents are. I long as the girls measure Big Bum Eileen and write down the results on a piece of paper that they keep hidden from me. I long to be found.

The Gospel Glove

THE FOLLOWING MORNING, ALL, THE BAPTISED AND THE UNBAPTISED, were to attend Miss Kingsley's Dawn Service for Girls. At six o'clock we were woken by Aunty Muriel, who didn't ring her brass bell but walked by each bed and shook us gently, pressing an arm, a forehead, with her cool hand. We dressed by candlelight and in silence. Flannel skirts and woollen cardigans put on at this strange hour, the hour before waking, felt new. Shadow arms and hands swooped across walls and ceiling. Vast shadow faces bent forward as, button by button, hands crept up the chest, like butterflies walking.

With soft steps, we followed Aunty Muriel and her lantern into the dormitory garden. Past the dahlias, the chrysanthemums, the orange tree with its leaves of dark bitter. There, under The Beard, ready for the sermon, sat Miss Kingsley. Her Bible was in her lap and on it lay a glove. We sat cross-legged in a circle around her, the pale grey of day creeping from behind the black peaks. A dormitory of older girls joined, making a circle around us. The service started with a prayer, heads bowed.

As Miss Kingsley began to speak in her watery voice, the

world changed about us. Slowly and without pause. The white blooms raised their heads and let out thin threads of scent, the trees changed from black to grey to green, the morning glory clinging to the wall opened her face to the light in the east, where the red paw prints across the sky marked the coming of the sun. Then Miss Kingsley held up the glove. She explained the gospel our mothers knew.

Black is for sin. Red is for blood. White for holiness. Yellow for heaven.

The glove was worn. Miss Kingsley had preached from it for nearly twenty years. It was her second one. The first she lost three years into her work when a court official in Nanchang confiscated it for fear his Concubine Number Two might convert. As I looked at the glove, I thought of my mother's own gospel glove. She held it in one hand, and in the other she held me as she preached the Good News. All our mothers had gospel gloves. Our fathers didn't. The glove was for telling stories to the women. I looked around at the girls. Held in the hands of our mothers as they'd preached, were we, too, our mothers' gospels?

As Miss Kingsley spoke I imagined our mothers and their days of ministry. This is what I saw. A missionary woman picks her way through the narrow alley of houses that cling to the bank, propped on thin bamboo legs over the brown river. Dressed in an indigo tunic and trousers, she enters one of the shacks, and squats down. There, by the stove, she tells a Chinese mother about the gospel while the water flows fast below. The river carries all sorts of rubbish, vines, vegetable peel, bloated cats, tin cans, all out towards the sea. As she preaches from her gospel glove, she raises her voice over the clang of a neighbour's wok and the husband yelling from the veranda where he smokes and mends an old fishing net.

The lady's baby, a little boy with his head shaved except for a tail of black hair, squeals. He clambers towards his mother, then is off again. He is in his first days of walking. Through the door comes a granny. She sits close by, holds the missionary's hand, strokes the missionary's white arm. Her feet are small, her legs and arms as thin as twigs, and her face is wide, moon-shaped. The missionary talks, God loves you, and God loves you. God so loved the world he gave his only son. The stink of the rubbish rises from the river. The baby boy cries out, stumbling forward, his mamma catches him.

Miss Kingsley laid the glove flat on her Bible and closed the dawn sermon with a prayer. As we raised our heads, I noticed the White Pagoda, a glimmer of pale stone on the peak above. Her finely carved verandas, her roof like a pointed hat, how she teetered. How could something heathen be so beautiful? I imagined her straight, tried to fix her straight, but she never would be. As we brushed off pine needles from our skirts, the golden clang of the school bell rang across Drill Court, shaking out all the children from their dormitories, and into lines.

And that afternoon I strode right into the tunnel without even taking off my dress. I marched through, stomp, stomp, kicking up the white stream, whistling. Just before I reached the tunnel's end, I closed my eyes, put my arms out, one elephant, two elephants, three, I opened my eyes.

Mother was not there but the girl was. She was sitting on the rock by the pool, gathering pebbles around her. I went up to her slowly so that I wouldn't scare her away. After we patted each other's heads hello, I led her up to our house.

I opened the door, told her to mind the stove and led her to the chairs, which were a row of roots in the clay bank.

'Time for supper,' I said, and took the Rich Tea biscuit from my dress pocket.

I laid the biscuit on a thick leaf. I folded my hands neatly together. 'Let us pray.' I felt like Aunty Muriel praying over a Saturday picnic. I closed my eyes. 'Thank you, Father, for this delicious provision of food.' When I'd opened my eyes the biscuit had gone. Twelve was eating it. I waggled my finger at her, 'Thou must obey thy father and mother.' Twelve was not familiar with the Ten Commandments. She flung herself backwards right into the stove.

As she lay there chewing, her head in the fire, burning away like a heretic, I thought I could make my own gospel glove. I could get two pieces of paper and glue them together and colour them. I could convert her.

The next afternoon I borrowed some of Aunty Muriel's paper and watercolours. I sat under The Beard and made the glove. I made it to fit my hand, tracing my fingers and then cutting it out with the dormitory scissors. I glued it together carefully with the dormitory glue and when it felt firm, I began to paint. So that the jam jar of water didn't get dirty straight away, I did the white finger first, then the yellow, then red, and last of all the black. As I finished the black finger it began to rain. I ran inside, hunching over the glove to protect it.

Kathryn Goes Genghis

THAT EVENING I WAS INSPECTING THE GLOVE, OPENING MY BEDSIDE cabinet and blowing mysteriously into it, when Kathryn climbed up on to her bunk without taking off her slippers and yelled, 'It seems to me that's all we do,' into her pillow. 'Give. Give your time, give your things, give your parents. I don't want to give any more.'

Miss Kingsley had led Evening Prayers and said that when it came to giving, the question was not 'What could we give?' But rather 'What should we keep?' On returning to the dormitory, we'd gone to our shelves and found things to put into the S.P.A.L.C. fund. Two Danish stamps, seven boiled sweets, an odd and much handed-down sock plus Edith's ripped kite had been placed on the dormitory table.

Kathryn's feet bashed up and down on the mattress. 'I'm sick of giving. Who's giving to me?' The feet flopped.

Aunty Muriel came in with some extra wood for the stove.

'Kathryn is upset at God,' said Edith straight away.

Rather than tell Kathryn off, Aunty Muriel came over to the bed, and removed Kathryn's left slipper and said, 'Sometimes people do get upset with God.'

That was the first that I'd heard of it. I couldn't imagine Mother or Father or Miss Kingsley or any other Christian I knew get angry with God. I felt anxious that Aunty Muriel might be trying to change things.

'Think of King David. Some of his Psalms are cries out to the Lord for deliverance,' Aunty Muriel said, removing the right slipper.

'God's given you so much, Kathryn,' someone cried.

'And he's still giving to you.'

'He's going to keep on giving to you for ever and ever.' We stood on Fiona's bottom bunk and looked on to Kathryn's top bunk, clinging to the wooden railings that kept her in.

'If God is so good, then why do I feel so lonely?'

We began one of our lists. 'You're not lonely, you've got us.' We all piled on to her bed now. We spoke as one. 'You've got God, your mother and father who are Christians, a school with Aunty Muriel and us.'

'And a brassiere,' said Fiona, who would know because they shared a cupboard.

'And your flock of horses,' said Sarah.

'That's a lot God has given you,' we said.

'It feels so little.'

Kathryn was not playing the game of pretending things were okay. She shook, silent tears under our touch. We laid our hands upon her. Along her limp brown arms, her spine, her shoulders, her ankles and her now unslippered feet.

'What's that?' said Big Bum Eileen. Her hairbrush was pointing. My Bible had fallen from my cabinet and lay on the floor. The glove's black forefinger poked out of the Good Book.

'It's nothing, Eileen,' I said. I snatched the Bible off the floor and slipped it back into my cabinet. The glove wasn't fully dry yet. A light imprint of fingers – red, black, white and yellow – had been left within the Psalms. Like a ghost, or a memory of a hand.

The next day, as soon as the play bell rang, I went to the Pool of Mothers. Twelve was there expecting a biscuit. We sat on the rock. I gave her a tuck box crumb. Then I held out my hand again. This time it was wearing the gospel glove. I had kept the glove spatter-free the whole way through the tunnel.

'Listen, Twelve,' I said. 'Black. Are you listening? Sit still. Black is for sin. Red is for the blood that Jesus spilt to save us. White. Ssh. I am your mother. Listen. White is for holiness. White is the opposite of black. Holiness is the opposite of sin. Don't move. And yellow, which is meant to be gold, is heaven. Heaven is where we will all go because that is where Jesus, who is our heavenly father, lives. Apart from when he's in our heart.' I looked at her pinkie, the extra finger. What was the gospel for that? It didn't have a part in the gospel story, as far as I knew. And it made me shudder, that same feeling of being in a shrine room, the wooden and clay figures with grinning faces staring at you.

The little girl squeezed her arms together and stuck her tongue out the side of her mouth. It didn't look like conversion. But I'd done my best. Then we played mud pies, me and the girl, but those extra fingers did not touch the mud.

Edith and Kathryn Join

THE AFTERNOON WENT BY TO THE SOFT SOUND OF RIPPING WEEDS. Squatting down by the roses, Kathryn, Edith and I worked quietly in a line. We dug the weeds of the dormitory garden and placed them in our skirts. Aunty Muriel had given us jobs to make us feel useful while the baptism girls prepared their hearts in the arbour. 'I want this whole lot cleared,' she said, pointing to the rose bed. She spoke sternly to make the task sound more important than it was. All Christians are useful. Our parents are useful, the staff are useful. Weeding the garden was useful.

Above us, a glossy crow strutted about The Beard. Below, with weeds in our skirts, we girls were useful but sad. Kathryn, Edith and I were sad not just because it was too late for us to be included in the baptism, but because our parents' silence made us worry for their safety. We wanted to see them. Even if it was just a glimpse.

As we tugged up the weeds, we placed the pale green stems and their fine white roots in the lap of our skirts, to make a sort of skirt bucket. We were carrying the weeds along the row of rose bushes, to the weed pile on the far edge of the garden, when Edith asked, 'Bet you wish you were at the Pool of Mothers.'

'What?' I said, nearly dropping my weeds.

'Kathryn and I have followed you. We've seen you climb into the tunnel,' said Edith.

'Do you see her there?' asked Kathryn. 'Your mother? Do you see her?'

I looked at Kathryn, her skirt full of ripped roots, her toes poking out over her leather sandals, which bought by her parents from a goat herder in an Urumqi stall, were posted only to arrive already outgrown.

'It's not like that,' I said, tipping the weeds from my skirt into the pile. 'Being part of the Prophetess Club isn't about imagining things. It's real. There aren't mothers. But there is a real child who eats biscuits, who cries when you comb her hair, who splashes mud everywhere, whose snot you have to wipe away.'

'But we could help you look after her, couldn't we Kathryn, I mean Jere-Neigh?' said Edith, to which Kathryn gave a sad, 'Hark.'

Beyond us in the arbour, the baptism girls, in three-part harmony sang, 'Amen.'

'We'd like to have a real daughter to care for,' said Edith.

'Hark,' said Kathryn again.

The next afternoon, before Aunty Muriel could give us any jobs, Kathryn, Edith and I ran out of bounds. We entered through the tunnel's lip, sloshing along until we came to the Pool of Mothers. There we put our plimsolls on and wandered around, hugging ourselves as it was cold. The Pool of Mothers wasn't at her best. The sky was dull, the trees were dark, close. The water glittered black.

We walked around for a while. Then there was a scuff of earth and dust and Twelve came skipping down the path, her hair more tangled than ever, her legs scabbed with cuts and bruises from her days of play within the forest's twisted roots, streams and winding paths. She stopped when she saw Edith and Kathryn.

'Stay back,' I said. 'You might scare her off.'

'We don't want to scare her, Samantha,' they said.

'Promise,' I said.

They promised.

I sat down on the rock and brought out a piece of biscuit from my pocket. The girl came over and took it. After she'd eaten the piece, small as a fingernail, I called behind me, 'You come now. Slowly. And with your biscuit gifts.'

There we sat, the four of us. While our daughter ate the biscuits, I told Edith and Kathryn about the house. 'And there . . . Elishella, Jere-Neigh, just where the roots to that tree are, that's our shelves for our things and there is a window, there and there, with lattice blinds and a veranda is just there.'

'A house for mothers,' said Edith.

'Yes, but she's too young to imagine,' I said, pointing at Twelve, who was squatting in the grass next to us. There was so much to do. We had to comb her hair, we had to properly convert her, and before we did that, we had to remove the amulet.

'Miss Kingsley says that amulets are like an invitation to the evil spirit to enter your body,' said Edith.

We watched Twelve walk along the edge of the pool poking her stick deep in the mud.

'Perhaps an evil spirit has already entered her,' said Kathryn. Then she began to tell her story of evil possession.

'My mother once met a lady who had long tangled hair past her waist and wailed words neither she nor anyone else understood: one day in Italian about the best shop for silks, the next day commenting on the weather in Russian, the next discussing different cuts of pig in French. She was totally fluent even though she'd never left Mongolia at all. Of course, when Mother expelled the spirit, the woman's family were spitting mad, for the woman could no longer read fortunes, and the family had lost their income.'

We all had such stories of evil possession, and these we'd swap at nights when the wind was at its strongest, when no one could sleep, and the windows rattled and the trees swayed so loudly that Aunty Muriel, in her iron bedstead, could not overhear. What we did not know, however, was how these castings-out were done. What intricate prayers, what holy words, persuaded these spirits to up and leave?

I went to the water's edge and grabbed the amulet string that hung around Twelve's wrist with both my hands. Twelve squirmed, cross that I'd stopped her mud-poking game. I held her even more firmly than when I'd tried to comb her hair, and pulled the string. It snapped. The peach stone spun into the pool. We watched it bob into the tunnel and back towards the school.

'You're free, little baby, from that evil, evil amulet,' said Edith in a lovely sing-song voice that stilled Twelve's crying. Twelve pushed herself free from Edith's hug and began wandering through the grass with her stick.

'I think she will be safer now,' said Kathryn.

Twelve was whispering to herself as she whacked the long grass. I called her name. She did not turn. She was too busy swiping the long grass. Good. When a child is playing, it's the perfect time for a mother to sneak away, just as Flo's mother did when she was first sent here. Mrs Templeton told Flo to play with her dolly and when Flo turned round to show the doll's stuffing was springing from the doll's neck, she saw her mother had vanished from the Hequ mission home, and only Miss Otis remained to escort her for the rest of the journey to Lushan.

So while Twelve skipped through the long grass, spanking the world with her stick, Kathryn, Edith and I slipped through the tunnel and ran up towards the school, our three shadows chasing us through the dusk towards the great bell that rang out over the mountain.

As the three of us approached the dinner lines, we could see the school had just received more news about the war. I felt relieved that this was the case for it can be difficult to hide your thoughts and feelings after an afternoon on the other side of the tunnel, and I was worried that with all the excitement Edith might blurt.

Children stood closer together than usual, their voices were hushed yet urgent, the smallest ones holding hands as if a 'Ring a Ring o'Roses' might protect against soldier, gun, sword. When we joined the queue of baptism girls, Edith, Kathryn and I discovered that not only was there a second Japanese gunboat in Poyang Lake, but Sarah and Mrs Charleston were leaving.

'But what will you *do* in America?' Hilary was asking Sarah as we fell into line.

Sarah shook her head, unable to imagine herself on the other side of the world.

'America! America!' called Edith, and flung herself at Sarah.

'Mrs Charleston got a letter this afternoon with news from

the American Government. They say China has become too dangerous,' explained Flo, while Edith sobbed into Sarah's neck. 'All Americans have been asked to leave. Mrs Charleston doesn't feel safe in China any more.'

Aunty Muriel came over, separated Sarah and Edith, told us there would be plenty of time for goodbyes, and asked us to line up as first shall be last and last shall be first, to get a bit of commotion going and distract us from the awful news.

As I stood at the front of the line, I thought of all I knew of America, Stars and Stripes, seminaries, prairies, chewing gum, and imagined Sarah and Mrs Charleston in each of these situations. Then I thought of Sarah and Mrs Charleston and me in these situations. We'd be happy and safe, far, far away. And then I felt bad, so I added in Mother and Father. We'd all be with Mrs Charleston, happy and safe, chewing gum and far, far away from the Japanese.

Despite the war tightening around us, school carried on. Ticks, corrections, repetitions and Amah Liu's weekly clip. The wintery mountain wind blew through the classroom's loose windows and we sat on our hands to keep them warm. One afternoon it was my turn to recite 'Hedge Sparrow'. I stood at the front of the class, the blackboard behind me, Mr Dalrymple to the side with his feet on the desk.

'"The tame hedge sparrow in its russet dress",' I said, and on I went, stumbling over words, blathering through the giggles of all the girls except Kathryn and Edith, and Mr Dalrymple's rolling eyes. '"It makes a nest of moss and hair and lays . . . Its eggs . . ."' And while I recited I watched the little wooden globe on the edge of Mr Dalrymple's desk. His foot was turning it slowly. As one part of the world entered light, another entered night. Where were Mother and Father?

In China? Or, as some parents had, escaped on a P&O cruiser? To Sydney, to San Francisco, to Southampton. Were they on a P&O cruiser heading up the Adriatic Coast, or perhaps turning the corner at Portugal? And the Japanese soldiers? They could be anywhere. During break-time I had seen five little boys playing soldiers, shooting each other's heads off with a stick – '"Bright beautiful and glossy shining shells"' – Dead, then resurrected over and over. In the evenings, the big boys, including the Sons of Thunder, were now to patrol the school. Above, the monks prayed at all hours, they drummed, let off firecrackers, they rang their temple bells. The mountain was turning burning red as autumn came. And it was cold, pinching cold. Cardigans and jackets, gloves and scarves – '"Much like the firetails but of brighter hue"' – I was so worried so very worried. For Mother and Father – '"Yet in her garden home . . . Yet in her"' – I was so worried for our dormitory daughter – '"Yet in her garden home much . . . much . . ."'

'Henrietta Robertson, concentrate.' The foot whizzed the globe.

'Sorry, sir – '"much danger dwells"' – Our dormitory daughter upon the mountain without her peach amulet – '"Where skulking cat with mischief in its breast"' – What evil might get her as she waded through the grasses, as she made her filthy mud pies, what evil – '"Catches their young before they leave the nest."'

The Knives

THE KNIVES GLINTED IN THE BUCKET. WE'D FINISHED OUR SUPPER OF bread and Sunday lunch leftovers and were now in the large, grey-walled kitchen drying cutlery. It was our dormitory's turn to be on Sunday night wash-up and set-up. Sunday night was the Chinese staff's night off. There were black scorch-marks streaking up the back of the chimney and pots so big that they could cook a crouching child. The cutlery clanged. My hands were withered from dipping into the water. The tea towel was more wet than dry. It was the sort of thing bad boys make weapons out of. I picked out some cabbage from a fork. The bucket was full of drowned stew, all bloated and pale. At the bottom of the bucket a sharp knife glinted. The tea towel was so wet, there was no point drying it. I picked it up by its wooden handle and held it for a moment. Hot metal. Droplets of water. Steam. I leant down and slipped it into my sock. I could feel it pressed against my calf, a burning against my skin.

We walked along that night, from the kitchen to the dormitory, accompanied by a guard of the Sons of Thunder. They had a lantern each and we heard them arrive because one of them was shouting out, 'Hup, two, three, four.'

Everything had become a sign of military excellence: beds shipshape, blazer and shorts soldier neat, yes, sir, they said to every member of staff, especially when it was Commander Neb. The Sons of Thunder were very interested in protecting us from a Japanese invasion, I could see that. Just look at how Roland Kai-shek Blatts marched next to Big Bum Eileen, how Bertie Mao Ducat reconnaissanced Flo, how John Cheng Jones leapt in to protect Hilary so enthusiastically from an azalea, I was shoved to the back.

The lovers, the stupid lovers, I thought. Everyone is growing up and going off, and here I am in the dark, alone. Then, there at my elbow, was Nigel General Fu Pinsent. Him all glum with his lamp. I hated him. The moon that night was so big, yellow and low. The pagoda stuck out like a finger pointing up to touch it. Then I felt Nigel Pinsent's hand in mine. I took a sharp breath. I had a knife in my sock and a boy's finger in the palm of my hand.

I slipped the knife behind my family photograph, the one which had somewhere on the journey to Lushan gained a gash in the glass that ran across Mother's face. Where the potted plants are in bloom, where my father stands with his hands on Mother's shoulder and I rest my arm on her lap. We are in Chinese dress. We stare at the camera.

Headmaster's Wife

THAT MONDAY AFTERNOON, KATHRYN, EDITH AND I TRIED TO GO TO the Pool of Mothers but Aunty Muriel had seen us without jobs. 'Girls, look. The tuberose bed needs a good sorting from useful girls like you.' She was wearing a pretty shawl the colour of heather.

Minutes later, Edith and Kathryn were weeding and I was up The Beard. I could see the baptism girls across Drill Court, sitting in pairs, ponytails bobbing, one interrogating, the other reciting the articles of faith.

'Come and help,' said Edith, shoving her trowel into the ground.

'Oh, Martha, Martha,' I said from my branch. Calling someone Martha is a good way of not helping. Even Jesus did it. Then underneath The Beard passed Mrs Charleston, Aunty Muriel and Miss Kingsley. They had their Bibles in their hands. After they passed, I called out to Edith and Kathryn, 'Girls. There's a procession of women. They've got their Bibles.' Mrs Charleston, Aunty Muriel and Miss Kingsley began heading up the path towards Headmaster's Cottage. 'And guess what . . .' I stood up on the branch, which bent wildly. 'Headmaster's wife is in her garden.' I swung out of The Beard. 'Girls, we've weeded the whole garden. Now to Canaan.' Kathryn and Edith dropped their trowels and followed.

We crept on tiptoes, down to Livingstone Stream and then up the bank. I could feel the girls' breath behind me. The bank was no longer green with grass as it had been on our last visit. It was prickly with yellow stubble; it was rough with dead leaves.

It felt giddy to be so high up. 'Be careful. Especially you, Edith,' I said over my shoulder. Then we edged along the bank, ducking between the rose bushes, until we found the spot from which we could spy into the garden. There, surrounded by Mrs Charleston, Aunty Muriel and Miss Kingsley, was Headmaster's wife, the mother among the roses.

But today was different. There were no roses on the bushes, the petals lay dead on the ground. I felt queasy.

'Are you okay, Etta?' said Edith.

I sat down. Yes, yes, I said. I took my hand away from my mouth. Something was going to happen today. I could just feel it.

Headmaster's wife was propped up on pillows and she was wrapped in a yellow blanket. She was smiling at her guests and speaking. She did not look frightened. I began to relax a little. 'Edith,' I said, 'do you know, I think she might sing.' Edith wriggled closer. We three girls squashed together. Unbaptised but cosy.

Through the rose bushes we saw the ladies – our teachers. How different they seemed when there were no children around. We noticed how they sat in their striped deck chairs. Look at Aunty Muriel. She was laughing.

'So elegant,' said Kathryn. Elegant. Yes, it was true. Ankles crossed, faces smiling, hands nicely upon laps. There was nothing to worry about. Mrs Charleston was nodding and giggling. Even Miss Kingsley smiled, but gently, as if partly listening to the ladies, whilst mainly being in conversation with the Lord.

Amah Liu swayed over with her tray. 'Scones! Red jam!' we whispered as the tea towel was whisked off it. The tea set clattered. Spoons rattled inside the cups. I couldn't wait to be a grown-up and have a prayer meeting.

While the ladies chattered, Miss Kingsley opened her Bible. When she found her page, she raised her head. That was the sign. Tea cups were placed on the grass, crumbs brushed away and hands placed in laps. Then, Miss Kingsley read something from the middle of the Bible, which meant it was probably a Psalm. This was followed with a prayer. The ladies shifted in their deck chairs and found the pose from which they pray. Chin tucked in, slightly hunched. This is a good shape to pray in, as they listen for God, whose voice is heard from deep within. Lovely looks came across their faces. Soft, as if all the wrinkles had been smoothed away. Headmaster's wife could not sit and bow her head like them. Instead, she closed her eyes, her mouth a little open; her face, so pale, was lifted to the sky.

Miss Kingsley finished her prayer, saying 'Amen' and shutting her Bible. The ladies murmured 'Amen' and kept their eyes closed for a few more moments as if still enjoying the taste of pudding just eaten. 'Savouring,' I said to Kathryn. She looked at me sidelong and nodded. Yes, this is what it was like to be a woman. Then the missionary women opened their eyes and blinked as if astonished to find themselves in this world.

They all turned to Miss Kingsley. She leant forward over Headmaster's wife. My chest tightened. This was it. This was the moment. Miss Kingsley put her hand on her shoulder and began to speak. This time, however, she did not speak in English, nor the Chinese of the Women's River. This was a strange language, sharp with lots of 'shak' and 'taks'. It went fast then slow, loud then whispery. I didn't like the sound of it, the rhythm of it. I felt frightened. The ladies were speaking under their breath. Their eyes were open.

'She's praying in tongues,' said Kathryn.

'Hark,' said Edith.

Something felt wrong. I reached for Kathryn and Edith's hands. Surely it wasn't good to pray without closing your eyes, and all together, at once.

'Sha weh de, sha weh de cooom.' Miss Kingsley began praying more urgently, keeping her hands on Headmaster's wife. Miss Kingsley's face reddened, her voice shook. The women called after her. They raised their arms to the heavens. They chanted. Their faces gripped, set, eyes closed, as if cheering something on. Like boys wanting to see the contents of the glass jar. They were excited, flustered. Blinking quickly, looking up to the sky, chanting non-stop. How long had the chanting possessed them, five, ten, fifteen minutes? We watched.

'Fill us, Lord!'

'Yes, Jesus!'

'Yes, Lord!'

This was not elegant, this was not savouring, it was something else and it frightened me.

Then Headmaster's wife gripped the edge of the chair, her hands mottled purple-pink. Her spine stiffened and straightened. She jerked forward and pulled herself to sitting.

We didn't gasp or cheer, we watched in perfect silence for we knew more miracle was to come. Then Aunty Muriel and Mrs Charleston put a shoulder under her arms and with their help she was raised up. She swayed between them, and then steadied herself. The ladies stepped aside. Miss Kingsley's praying stilled.

Headmaster's wife stood, panting. A sheen of sweat covered her whole body. There were damp patches under her arms. The yellow blanket fell, her Bible fell, but she, Headmaster's wife, did not fall. She was staggering, breathing heavily like a sow about to give birth. She took a step. The women cheered. It was a miracle.

They sat Headmaster's wife back in her chair, popped the Bible on her lap and patted the lemony blanket around her. She was breathing so heavily her body shuddered under it. The clouds scooted over us. My heart bang, banged. We had seen an actual miracle. Hark we said, then slithered silently down the bank with our secret.

Sarah Lushan

THE TRUNKS CAME OUT OF THE NISSEN HUT. THEY WERE CLEANED AND the spiders banged out. Into Sarah's trunk went her school dresses, Sunday best dress, dressing gown, jumpers, knickers and vests. They were packed by Aunty Muriel in a great flurry, Sarah's cupboard emptied and her little china monkey and piglet ornaments wrapped in her underwear. Except for three socks and a jumper donated to the S.P.A.L.C. fund, in the matter of an afternoon all of Sarah's things were gone. Her hook with the name 'Sarah' carried no dressing gown, towel, or flannels. There was no toothbrush at her basin named 'Sarah', no Sarah Charleston-labelled linen on her bed. Tonight on Lushan there would be no Sarah.

We waved the Charlestons off by the Great Steps at lunchtime. Mrs Charleston hugged us and told us not to worry about the soldiers. Sarah waved at us as the mountain chair was hoisted up on to the men's shoulders. 'Goodbye,' she said. 'I will never forget you.' She looked about the school, the peaks, the pagoda, the Girls' Building, and her face was full of terror. And so we held her finger, her dress, her arm, her ankle, and ran alongside the mountain chair all the way to the top of the Great Steps. We stood and watched as the mountain chairs were carried, tilting, teetering with trunks, holiday suitcases and Freddie's violin, then returned to the empty dormitory. It happened so quickly. Sarah hadn't even had time to be baptised. She was the first of us to leave Lushan.

As the winter descended upon the mountain, the sky filling with clouds the size of battleships, the paths flurried with blood-red leaves crisped in a sparkling frost, so too we felt the approach of the war. There were many signs that showed us no longer to rely on the mountain's protection. Above in the temple, firecrackers were let off at all times of day in intricate rituals to keep the soldiers away. Our pile of breakfast toast shrunk to just a slice each and one day the jam ran out, never to appear on the breakfast table again for the merchant's route from Shanghai to Lushan was now closed. Beyond Woosung village, on a path off the Eastern Trail, lay the blood of three Chinese soldiers, shot, a mark that would not be scrubbed from the earth, a mark that sunk deep into our dreams, and woke us up, cold with sweat. And then there were letters from parents telling us of the war beyond Lushan. Mrs Pinder's lavender-scented letterhead signed off with a careless twenty kisses was replaced with a quickly scrawled note from the Cathay Hotel, where she was staying as a safety precaution, for her house was near the edge of the French concession and the Cathay was better protected in the heart of Shanghai. Other parents told of air raids over their towns, and bombs dropped just outside mission compounds. And then there was Ruth Bridgewater, a brainy girl with copper-wire hair, who had been called from her class and to the staff room of Teachers' House, where she was sat on Miss Preedy's lap and told her father had been captured by the Japanese as a spy, and that he had not survived the interrogation.

The next lunch break it was Miss Kingsley's turn to leave. She was being escorted by Mr Dalrymple, whose main job at the moment seemed to be climbing up and down the mountain protecting women and children, and on each return, his face was more haggard, and the less he flurried across Drill Court with his clipboard. The war was making its way south to Changsha, and Agape House was in its path. Miss Kingsley had received a note carried in a bamboo pole by one of her converts. Miss Tippet had been rounded up by soldiers at the Lung Po mission home where she'd been visiting and was under house arrest. Miss Kingsley needed to get back to the children of Agape House.

But not before we could get her autograph. We'd given her our autograph books that morning and we received them back that lunch by the arbour just before she was hoisted on to a mountain chair. Also waiting by the arbour was Headmaster's wife. She'd been carried down the East Steps by Headmaster. She was sitting on the wooden benches, pale with the exertion of having stood to say goodbye to Miss Kingsley. After Miss Kingsley and Headmaster exchanged goodbyes, Miss Kingsley said goodbye to us, and with a heave-ho of the mountain-chair men, she was carried off into the cavernous passage of the Great Steps.

We watched Headmaster and his wife go back up the East Steps, then opened our autograph books. To our great disappointment, Miss Kingsley had written the same Bible verse in everyone's book: '"Surely I have behaved and quieted myself, as a child that is weaned of his mother: my soul is even as a weaned child." Psalm 131, verse 2.' We sighed for it meant no one was special, not even the baptism girls, who were sad that Miss Kingsley had left just before the conclusion of her course. There was also Miss Kingsley's address in English and Chinese. There was the character for 'love', the one where you can imagine Mary looking over the manger. Agape House in Huichow village. Walking back, I noticed at the top of her message Miss Kingsley hadn't written Etta but Ming-Mei. She'd remembered that I was Ming-Mei! 'Agape House, Huichow village,' – as we wandered back to the Girls' Building, I studied that address until I could recite it.

That night, as I lay in bed I rubbed my feet together and hugged myself for it was cold. Winter was coming. I thought of our daughter. She would be shivering in her temple hut. But we now had a spare bed. Had I been standing, I'd have been on tip-toes, for I'd had an excellent idea. I would bring Twelve home, to the dormitory.

Oh, daughter, I am coming to get you. Coming! Aunty Muriel will let you be our dormitory daughter. You'll sleep in Sarah's bed. You'll wear a gingham dress, a duck-down jacket and we'll give you some proper shoes. Maybe Aunty Muriel will let your chicken live in the bathroom. We could put it in the bath. It might lay eggs in the bath. We could count them together. Oh, daughter!

We Must Obey

IT WAS AFTER SCHOOL ON FRIDAY AFTERNOON, AND IN PREPARATION for the baptism the next day, the girls had laid their best dresses on the beds and were checking buttons and hems. Shoes had been scrubbed, and each girl's knapsack packed with a towel and dry set of clothing, for the trek up towards the waterfall. Flo, Kathryn and I did not feel left out for we had made secret preparations of our own. That afternoon, we'd decided to go to the tunnel and we were sat on my bed, swinging our legs, our supplies laid out. It was the same bag of things that we'd taken on the last two visits. The comb (if we ever succeeded in untangling her hair, Twelve would look more acceptable to Aunty Muriel), the gospel glove (to try once more with the conversion) and, because Edith had had another bad dream of soldiers, we'd wrapped in a sock, just in case, the knife.

'Do you think she'll like sleeping in Sarah's old bed?' asked Edith. 'It's a top bunk.'

'I'm sure Aunty Muriel will get someone to swap with her if she doesn't,' I said. I spoke with confidence, as I did on all matters to do with our daughter. 'But anyway, before we bring her back, we have to perform our ministry.'

'What if it doesn't work?'

'It will work. Remember, we've been shown. Just us three. The Lord didn't call any of the others to see it.' I looked around the room.

On the other side of the dormitory Big Bum Eileen was trying on her baptism dress. 'I barely fit into it,' she said, sticking her chest out and gesturing at it. The girls made consoling sounds.

I leant over my bunk. 'Eileen, when they dip you under, do you think you'll float?' I called. Big Bum Eileen gave a look, black as medicine. 'You might just bob back up. Imagine that. If they couldn't baptise you because you kept bobbing up.'

'You can think what you like, Etta,' said Eileen, in a floaty voice, made to skim over me.

'People of all sizes can be baptised,' said Hilary. Then she lifted up her Sunday best dress to her face and smothered her laugh with it. I looked about the dormitory and saw the others were tittering too.

'That's true,' I said, 'I'm sure Headmaster will be able to capsize her. Don't worry, Eileen Big Bob.' To my surprise all the girls lifted their dresses to their faces and sniggered into a hem, a pocket, a collar of stiff lace. Everyone except Big Bum Eileen, who stood busty and mean as a double-crossed Delilah.

Aunty Muriel strode into the room, her arms outstretched. 'Dresses checked? Knapsacks packed and placed by the door? No? Well, hurry to it, chop chop. I want you in the dormitory garden in three minutes.'

Kathryn, Edith and I groaned.

'You three, you will be disappointed if you're not there. I've arranged a treat to mark the girls' baptism. Chop chop.'

*

154

So there we had to wait, sat under The Beard. I did not want to hang around like a harpist in the court of David. I wanted us to get to the tunnel like we'd planned. We had ministry to do.

Aunty Muriel walked through the rose garden carrying a tray with eight mugs of frothy hot chocolate. She was pleased with herself: 'Behold, how good and how pleasant it is for brethren to dwell together in unity.' She handed each girl a mug, wafting chocolatey steam. Then she left to do an errand up at the laundry. The baptism girls drank from their mugs, fingers cocked, slowly sipping. Edith, Kathryn and I blew hard then gulped. Quick, quick.

'Where are you three in such a hurry to go to?' asked Flo, stretching out her legs.

'Nowhere,' said Edith, meaning 'somewhere'. She made her next slurp a loud one.

'Come on, Edith,' I said. I needed to hurry her away.

Kathryn placed her cup back on the tray, then leant down to take the knapsack. Big Bum Eileen's big foot was on it. 'What's in here?'

'Nothing!' said Edith, meaning 'something'.

'Leave that alone,' I said.

Big Bum Eileen edged the knapsack towards herself. 'Are you keeping a secret?'

'No!' said Edith, in a tone that said 'yes!' And for the first time I wished I had chosen to do this mission myself.

Big Bum Eileen said, 'Should I look in here, girls?' as if it was a moral duty.

'If you look in there, Big Bob,' I said – I realised that if I got pink and anxious she'd have the upper hand, so I made my voice floaty as she'd done earlier – 'you shall find only the humble tools of the Prophetess Club. They'd hardly be of interest to a woman like you.'

Big Bum Eileen's big head tipped over the knapsack. She drew out the glove by its forefinger.

'It's our gospel glove. Etta made it,' said Kathryn.

'We've been using it! For a conversion!' said Edith. I thought everyone would laugh at the painted paper glove, with its colours that ran together, its wonky fingers and roughly glued sides, but as it was passed around a sort of sadness flurried amongst the girls.

Hilary said, 'My mother has a gospel glove.'

'My mother does, too,' said Flo.

'All mothers have one,' said Isobel.

'Mine doesn't,' said Fiona Pinder, whose mother drinks gin and tonic at the Shanghai British Club.

'Well, she would if she was a missionary,' said Edith. We all felt sorry for Mrs Pinder, especially Fiona, who was now nearly baptised. We did daily pray for the conversion of Mrs Pinder and especially that she would not be so fashionable.

Big Bum Eileen took the glove by the heaven-coloured finger. She twirled it around, like when you hold an autumn leaf by its tail. Then she tried to put it on, but the glove did not fit. Hilary took it but it did not fit her, nor Flo, Isobel, or Fiona. 'It only fits me,' I said, for of the dormitory I was the smallest. I put it back in the knapsack and stood to go.

'So have you actually converted anyone?' said Big Bum.

'We're trying but it's not as easy as you'd think,' said Edith.

The clouds darted over the sun. The sky dimmed. 'It's getting cold,' I said, rubbing my arms. 'We'd better hurry or it will be too late.'

Kathryn raised her mug. 'To the tunnel for the healing,' she said. I nearly kicked her. She had told them where we were going and what we were going to do.

The girls stared aghast. The hot chocolate went unsipped. 'You've been going to the tunnel?' said Big Bum Eileen.

'We're going to heal Twelve,' said Edith, leaning forward.

'We found out how. We saw Miss Kingsley heal Headmaster's wife,' said Kathryn. 'They healed her with their prayer.'

I tried not to panic. Feeling the solidity of The Beard behind me, I took the glove out of the bag once more and explained, as wistfully as possible, 'I tried to convert Twelve, told her the stories, led by example, but I just haven't been able to get through to her.' I put the glove on and I leant back. 'We've got to heal her first, of those extra fingers.' With the glove on my upraised hand, I said, 'So, girls, you can stay here drinking hot chocolate, or you can leave these comforts and come with us.' I stood up. 'Edith, Kathryn, drinks finished? Knapsack ready? Let us march.' I beckoned to them with the glove and we disappeared behind The Beard.

When the others made no sign that they would follow, I reappeared by that great gnarled trunk. 'Would you like to see how to heal a child?' I stared at each one in the eye, taking my time just as Eileen does when she's naked. 'Who knows who the gift of healing will be given to? It might be one of you.'

A few moments later the garden was empty and when Aunty Muriel came back to check how we were getting along, all that remained of our party was a tray of empty mugs.

On the steps we burst into a run; like lovely gazelles we bounded down the West Steps, down by the stream, past the Sons of Thunder building dams, who looked up and watched, shielding their eyes from the afternoon sun. We ran past Mr

Wu's hut to the tunnel's lip, took our shoes and socks off and leapt inside.

We came out of the tunnel, and there, as I knew she would be, was Twelve. She was making mud pies by the bank, placing them in the roots of the tree where we had made our imaginary house, putting them where we kept our cups and saucers.

Before we went to greet her, we paused by the tunnel to check for soldiers. With my knife at the ready, I practised slicing the air. The forest was silent. Nothing moved or sounded, except for the stream flowing from the Pool of Mothers into the tunnel, and Twelve, who was running back through the long grasses to the pool, where she squatted, scooped up some mud and thumped it into a ball.

I gestured for the other girls to put their plimsolls on, for it is dangerous to be in long grasses barefoot. I placed the knife on the rock and slipped my shoes on, right, then left.

'Hello, daughter,' I called as I went towards our child. She ran to me and hid by my legs, tugging at my dress. Then the girls, who all know about shy daughters, knelt down by her. At the water's edge, Hilary and Flo began to make mud pies, Kathryn skimmed a stone on the pool, Edith hummed a song, and in time, Twelve picked up her stick and played beside us.

'We're going to heal you of your extra finger,' said Edith to the girl in a singsong voice, rocking her head from side to side. Twelve handed her a mud pie for she knew and liked Edith.

'What is it exactly that we'll do again?' asked Big Bum Eileen, pressing her thumb into a knob of mud.

'We'll stand around her in a prophetess circle and speak in

tongues,' I replied. 'It's a special language. I shall show you how.'

'Someone needs to keep watch for the Japanese,' said Fiona, looking at the thick forest.

'Flo, you keep a look out,' I said.

'But I'm not good with knives,' said Flo, looking at the blade on the stone. It was waiting to be picked up.

'I am,' said Hilary, who has big brothers and knows about these things. She picked up the knife from the rock and jabbed it into the air a couple of times. Then she ran her finger along the cutting edge. 'It's sharp,' she said. Hilary placed the knife back on the rock, rubbing her finger, as if imagining again the knife's touch.

I took charge. 'Okay, Flo is on guard, Hilary is in charge of the knife, now let us set to work.'

We rinsed our hands in the pool and when everyone's hands were clean we surrounded Twelve, who was crouching by the water's edge. She stopped digging and stood up. She thought it was a game. She tried to push her way out of the circle. We guided her back to the centre. No, stay there, dear daughter. That's it. Just there. She looked worried. We placed our hands on her, held them firm.

'Look at it, the finger,' I said. 'Can't you see that it's evil?' We watched it. A tiny, delicate thing, perfectly formed growing out of her pinkie. The finger twitched. It was the only one whose nails were not jammed with dirt.

Big Bum Eileen stood up. 'Let's heal her,' she said.

'How?' said Fiona.

'We rest our hands on her,' I said with new-found certainty. 'Then, you just let the language into you,' I said. 'You're not in charge of it, it comes to you. Your tongue is its guest.'

It was Edith who began, 'Shah ta kapa lak tama.'

We picked up the chant. 'Shah ta kapa lak tama,' we said. The strange words entered our mouths. They took hold of us. They spoke through us fast and slow. We carried on for some minutes. Sometimes speaking all at once, sometimes just one of us. Then we found it. Our rhythm. We got louder and louder, our eyes closed, all saying the same phrase, paka tika ke wawa. When Twelve again tried to push out of the circle, we grabbed her little arms hard, held her little wrists tight. 'No, naughty,' I said, cross as a mother with a child at her skirts, and on we went with the healing. The voices, which I can't even say were our voices, throbbed and sped, everyone on the same beat.

It was Kathryn who broke the chant. 'I thought I heard the bell.'

We listened. The mountain was silent. All we could hear was the rhythm pumping inside us. We looked at Twelve's hands. Kathryn said, 'This isn't working like how it did for Miss Kingsley.' Her whining voice made me cross.

'Maybe it's because they had their eyes open,' said Edith.

'Everyone, eyes open,' I said, pointing them back to face Twelve. Soon we were chanting over the sound of the stream. Everyone was doing it. Everyone was as one. Again the rhythm quickened. The voices whirled within us; they wanted to rise higher, they wanted to wail.

'Ssh,' said Flo. 'Something moved.'

Hilary leant down and took the knife. We held Twelve firm and watched the forest. All was silent except for the beat of our hearts and the snivels of Twelve. Nothing moved.

'It was probably just a leaf,' said Big Bum Eileen, and it could have been so, for the leaves on the trees were the size of dinner plates.

'Back to the healing, girls. I think we are getting

somewhere.' We returned to the circle and once again fixed our eyes upon Twelve, who had given up her fight and was now sat in the mud, snot running down her chin, crying.

'Etta, it's not working,' said Kathryn.

Big Bum crossed her arms and began to tap her foot.

Suddenly I knew what would work. 'Give that to me,' I said to Hilary, and took the knife from her. My palm tightened around the handle. I listened to the mountain. The trees were chattering with light-tongued spirits, the pool was dark with whispering cold. The black song was stronger than ever. I felt giddy with a sense of tumbling, of a strange flight out over the waterfall, but this time I would fly. The blackness in me; it was speaking.

'We must use the knife,' I said.

Flo gasped.

'We must cut the finger off.'

'I don't want to,' said Fiona.

'This is wicked. I'm going back,' said Flo, and she began to walk towards the tunnel.

I summoned my biggest voice. 'As Abraham was willing to hold the knife to Isaac, we must, too. We've been brought here for a reason. We must obey,' I said. I motioned with the knife for Flo to get back into the circle. Then I handed the knife to Big Bum Eileen. 'Isn't that right, Eileen?' I asked. I looked into her slidy green eyes. A knowing look passed between us. It made me bold.

'Each girl must hold the knife,' I said. 'Each girl must feel its power. Light. Sharp. Fast. And so we are a tool in his hand.'

We made the girl place her hand on the big rock by the pool. 'It's okay.' I smiled. Twelve watched me carefully. The finger was very still. 'It's okay, we're going to help you,' I said again. We began to chant as Big Bum Eileen held the knife over Twelve's hand, then gave it to Hilary, who gave it to Flo, and so on. Everyone felt that knife in her hand, gleaming, sharp, until it returned to me. The wooden handle was warm. I lowered the knife close to Twelve's finger. She pulled her hand away. Kathryn pushed it back into place. Twelve squirmed. Kathryn gripped her hard.

Now each of the girls put a hand on Twelve, their hands and forearms pushing her down. The chanting became louder, urging me on. I pressed the knife down on that little finger. Felt the blade run across her skin. Softly, gently. Twelve screamed, her cry shrill, her muscles clenching.

'Hold her still,' I said, angry.

'Etta, this is horrible,' cried Flo. 'You must stop.' She pulled her hand away and sat by the water's edge. Fiona, too.

'It is right that we heal her,' I said. I looked back at the extra finger. A small, crooked thing. The knife was touching it. All it would take was a push, a little push down. But Twelve began to kick. She got me in the shin. The voices roused once more. My head was full of pumping blood. Everything was bright. On the next beat I'd cut. Yes, now.

Then out of the forest came a running, squawking thing. A chicken. White feathered, red throated. Distracted, the hands released Twelve. She pushed past us, and ran after the chicken.

'The chicken, the sacrificial chicken,' someone yelled. I dropped the knife. My throat was dry, my eyes unblinking. A wave of horror spread up my body as the chant released me. I wanted to crouch down and spew out the blackness. But the girls were off. They were following Twelve's path through the long grasses, up the bank where the roots of the trees were home to our imaginary things. I followed them as fast as I could, desperate to be away from the knife.

Twelve was climbing the bank where the roots grew out of the ground. She climbed on her hands and feet, the chicken squawking ahead.

Then she stopped. She let out a cry. Her right hand was pulled in close at her chest. The chicken fled into the forest. We hushed around her.

'Little one.' I put my hand on her shoulder. 'What is wrong?'

She pulled away, frightened of me, and would not unfold herself.

It was Flo who got her to open up her hand. There was the extra finger. Then I saw, on her thumb, two small pricks of blood.

'She's been bitten,' said Flo.

'Something jabbed her,' said Isobel.

Tear marks, wet eyelashes, her mouth open, her baby teeth showing. I put my arm around her. She didn't want comforting, like you might think. She pulled away from me.

'What happened?'

'A snake?'

'A snake.'

'Look there, by the roots!'

'What snake, where?'

'Green . . . snake, there.'

'There in the roots.'

There, by the imaginary shelves where I'd stored the precious things for our house, I watched as a green tail slid into a hole in the bank.

'Let's get away from here,' said Big Bum Eileen. She began to walk back to the tunnel, kicking the long-grasses before stepping on them. The others followed her trail.

Twelve's hand was red and swelling. Flo and Hilary lifted

her up. She began to scream. They carried her towards the Pool of Mothers and placed her on the rock.

'We should get help,' said Flo.

'Hilary should go, she's fastest,' I said.

'If they know you've been out of bounds, they'll definitely stop the baptism,' said Edith.

The baptism girls froze.

'We can't tell Nurse Margaret,' said Fiona, turning to Big Bum Eileen.

The school bell rang.

'My big brother once got bitten,' said Hilary. Her teeth had begun to chatter. 'Nurse Margaret tied an elastic band around his thumb and it was fine after a couple of days.'

'Tie something around it,' said Big Bum at last. The bell for dinner called again. 'Do it quickly.'

'We need something to tie around her hand,' said Hilary.

I took the belt from my dress. 'This.' It was a lovely fabric of pink roses with green stems. Flo wound the belt around Twelve's wrist while Big Bum gripped Twelve's shoulders to keep her still.

'Yes, that's what Nurse Margaret did, but very tight,' said Hilary.

Flo tied the end in a tight knot.

'Good girl, now go home,' said Big Bum. She waved goodbye at Twelve. Twelve breathed in, her nostrils flared. She watched Big Bum waving, but because she wasn't used to doing what Big Bum commanded, she did not move.

Edith tried. 'Home, home,' she said. 'Bye-bye.' Twelve stared, not understanding.

'Go home,' I said. I pointed up the path. 'Go home. To Granny and your chickens.' She was now as afraid of me as of the others, for I had held a knife over her hand. She stepped backwards and stumbled into the pool.

Hilary shouted, 'Last bell, hurry,' from the tunnel. The girls took their plimsolls off, ready for the wade back to the school.

'She doesn't understand that she should go home,' I said, then called after her, 'Daughter, daughter, come back.' Twelve had splashed away to the other side of the pool. With her good hand she clung to a vine, and she wouldn't come out.

'Go,' said Big Bum Eileen from the tunnel. 'Bring her out and get her to go home.'

I felt so sad that Twelve would not come to me from across the pool, that she was frightened of me, that she cried for what I had done. It was horrible. I pushed myself forward across the pool, water splashed up, cold. The dragonflies raced. I was scared, the pool was deep and dark and I couldn't feel the bottom. I kept swimming forward until I reached the other side. I clung to the root that our daughter clung to. I spluttered out water and she screamed.

The girls were leaving, they were slipping into the tunnel. 'Flo,' I called. She looked at me for a second, examined my face, then turned her head away. She too slipped into the tunnel.

'That was the dinner bell, we've got to go back,' said Hilary, the last girl, as she climbed on to the tunnel's ledge.

'Don't leave me,' I called out. But Hilary had already disappeared and I was alone with the child. I looked at that hand. It had puffed up now. All the fingers including the extra one. She was screaming, screaming. I moved to touch her. She scratched my arm as she pushed me away. She would not let me near her.

I swam back and pulled myself out of the pool. I stood

shivering and soaked. 'Please go. Go home.' I pointed her in the direction of the path that led up the hill, towards the temple on whose grounds the Old Lady lived. 'Go. Go,' I said. I made my fingers like a man's legs and ran them quickly in the direction of the path.

Then I stepped into the tunnel. With my hands pressed on the tunnel's mossy sides, I turned for a last look. The girl clung to the roots at the other side of the pool, black hair soaked, silently sobbing now. About my feet, the water flowed into the tunnel, carrying her snot and tears. 'Go home,' I said one last time. 'Home, home,' echoed the tunnel.

The school was white buildings. I had never realised they were so beautiful, so far-away looking. Like lovely white ships at sea. That evening, on the other side of the tunnel, I had never felt such a stranger. As I came to the bridge, the sun began to set, sending the buildings pink. A soft and beautiful world. There, by the edge of the stream, I leant on my hands and knees. I vomited.

I walked up the steps and thought about the last letter from my parents, the one that said they were staying with their Church, not deserting them as the Japanese came closer, on foot, in the sky, in reconnaissance ships up the Huang Ho. I thought about the dead people I knew: my brother and sister in tin suitcases buried on the hill outside our village, the Chinese soldier we'd seen on the mountain path, his bandaged head brown with old blood. I thought of Bertie Ducat, another child to have been called to Teachers' House and the lap of Miss Preedy where he was told of his mother who had gone to help three women of her congregation, ladies with bound feet, but was not fast enough to escape the bombing of Hequ village square. As I thought of all these dead people, I became frightened and, running up the steps in the dusk, I was filled with a violent terror.

I rushed into the empty dormitory, quickly changed out of my wet dress and then joined the last of the children filing into the dining hall, their faces red from play, red as warrior gods. The sunset filled the room, serving spoons shone. I stood behind my chair as Miss Preedy rang the brass dinner bell, calling us all to the quiet with which all prayers should start. Aunty Muriel gave me her wide-eyed look of disapproval for my lateness. I mouthed sorry. Then grace was sung, 'The Lord Is Good to Me', chairs scraped the floor, serviettes tugged from their holders and the lid of the stew lifted. A smell like damp laundry billowed from the pot. On the blackboard someone had chalked S.O.S. for 'same old stew', which Miss Preedy was rubbing out with her serviette.

The dining-room hubbub loudened but our table was yet to break into chatter. I leant over to spoon some cabbage on to my plate. Twelve's scratches stung as they neared the steam. 'And where have you been?' said Aunty Muriel, placing her elbows on the table, her hands clasped before her.

Big Bum Eileen gave me a warning glare then turned her head away, sharp like a haughty puppet. 'I was playing by Livingstone Stream, and when I looked up, everyone had gone.'

'Well, I shall have to get you a bigger pair of ears so you can hear the dinner bell, Henrietta Robertson.'

The girls laughed even though they knew why I was late. 'No, thank you, Aunty Muriel, I'll remember,' I said.

A cautious quiet settled over the table, but Aunty Muriel did not notice for she was deep in a stream of thoughts, just stepping out of them now and then to remind us to chew, finish the cabbage, rest our knives and forks with grace.

Flo, getting changed on the bunk below, would not talk to me. I climbed on to my bunk. Felt black as ash.

I lay face down in my white nightdress, holding my doll. Boom, boom, said my heart into the blankets. Twelve's face came to me. The feel of her wrist, so narrow, in my hand, the warmth of the knife. How quickly the snake had appeared, how quickly everything had happened. In the pool, she had not wanted me to touch her. I rubbed my face in my pillow to try to smooth the afternoon away.

'Etta,' said Aunty Muriel, 'did I not tell you to get down and brush your hair? I'll be making you some cardboard ears for your eleventh birthday.'

I climbed down and leant against the bunk. The counting started and Aunty Muriel busied herself with the stove. Yards of hair, brown, golden, reddish, the brushes ripping through as we counted, one, two, three. We were not far off a hundred when Aunty Muriel left the room, and the counting slowed as the girls gathered around me, seventy-eight, seventy-nine.

'What happened after we left? Did you get her to go home?' said Hilary. The counting stopped.

I checked to see Aunty Muriel wasn't at the door. 'She wouldn't get out of the pool, she wouldn't let me help her and she scratched me.' I showed them my arm. 'Anyway, I couldn't stay much longer without missing the dinner queue, so I left her not long after you.'

There was a silence while the girls took in my information. Then Big Bum Eileen said, 'You mean you just left her in the pool alone?' Her mouth was open as if I'd done something stupid.

'Yes,' I said. 'Well, no, we all left her.'

'We didn't leave her alone,' said Hilary. 'We left her with you.'

'And you left her alone,' said Big Bum Eileen. 'With the snake.'

Aunty Muriel stepped into the room with a top-up of coal. The counting leapt forward, ninety-five, ninety-six while she clattered it into the stove.

'We must tell Aunty Muriel,' whispered Flo.

Ninety-seven.

'If anyone tells, we'll all be in trouble. There'll be no baptism,' said Hilary.

Ninety-eight.

'But what if she's still in the pool?' said Edith.

Ninety-nine.

'No one will tell Aunty Muriel anything,' said Big Bum Eileen.

One hundred.

When the lights went out, I lay listening to Flo crying on the bunk below.

I rubbed my feet together, for the night was cold. I pulled my doll close to me and worried for Twelve. I imagined what she did after I left. How she'd get bored, hungry, then come out of the pool, how she'd walk up the path and show her granny her hand, how her granny would take her in her arms, how in a couple of days the swelling would go down as it had for Hilary's brother and how the next time we'd see each other to play at the pool, I'd be so very kind.

The next morning, the girls were strange with me. Flo rushed from her bed to the bathroom without saying good morning. When I asked Fiona if I could borrow one of the ribbons sent in a parcel of things bought by Mrs Pinder in the Cathay Department Store, she passed it to me without a word. They talked to each other as if in a play, with voices careful to pronounce each word correctly, with a sense that every word was being overheard. No one mentioned the healing, or the snake. It was as if they were doing their best to try to pretend it hadn't happened, that it had all been a dream.

Aunty Muriel was far away in her thoughts over breakfast – eggs, marmalade, toast – then class, which was scripture and arithmetic. Just after break, Mary, the eldest Gable sister, knocked at the door. 'Yes,' said Miss Otis, as if expecting her. 'A letter, Miss,' she said, and handed over an envelope. Miss Otis read it while Mary stood there looking out of the window.

'Henrietta, please head to Teachers' House. Miss Preedy has asked to see you. Mary will accompany you.'

I laid down my pen and stood up from my desk. My shoes squeaked on the floor. I could feel the girls watch me, pious eyes, as I followed Mary from the classroom. Out in the corridor, I wanted to stop, place my hands on my knees and pant for breath. But I could not for Mary Gable was there. We crossed Drill Court, feet in time, and my world was shrieking inside me.

'Mary . . .' I could not finish the sentence.

'Come on now,' she said. 'I'm sure it's nothing to worry about.' I knew she was lying. We both knew what being asked to see Miss Preedy was for. Mother and Father.

I stopped outside the wooden door of Teachers' House. I couldn't step inside. I wanted to run the other way. Sprint back across Drill Court, race to my bed, hurl myself on it and scream.

'Come on,' she said. 'Chin up.' She slid her hand around my waist. I wished she hadn't. I wished she'd been strict and bossy.

I sat in the staff room waiting for Miss Preedy. Pine logs chopped by Gardener Chen were piled high around a European-style fireplace. Instead of high-back glossy wood chairs like the Chinese have, the staff had comfortable sofas, covered in a pattern of chrysanthemums the colour of marmalade, with craters in the cushions where they'd sat, given reports and prayed. My hands glistened with sweat as if left out on the grass overnight. I rubbed them on my dress and got up. The fire had not yet been lit and the room was cold. I went to the window and I breathed on to the glass. My breath spread out like a fan.

The door opened. There was Miss Preedy in an orange dress. She looked like a ginger nut. She closed the door, and came towards me with a smile. 'Etta,' she said as if I was a little niece she had not seen for some years. 'Etta.' Her arms were wide, coaxing me into her orange chest. I did not go to her. I stood by the window. Miss Preedy sat down on one of the sofas and patted the cushion for me to sit next to her. 'How are you feeling today, Etta? It's getting cold, isn't it?'

I nodded.

'That's a nice hair ribbon,' she said.

I nodded and moved towards her. 'That's it, let's have a nice sit-down together.'

I sat down.

'Where did you get the ribbon from?' she asked, touching my hair.

'Fiona lent it to me.'

'Fiona's a kind girl, isn't she?'

I nodded.

Miss Preedy put her hand on my knee. I went all tight. I wondered if she'd ask me to sit on her lap, as she did when she told brainy Ruth Bridgewater about her father dying. But Miss Preedy didn't like me; she'd prefer it if I was sat here.

'Etta, there's something we need to talk about. A very sad thing has happened.' She looked away at the empty fireplace. I saw words shaping in her jaw. I got myself ready for them. She began softly. 'This morning,' I coiled ready, ready, 'Gardener Chen found a little girl, a Chinese girl.'

I almost didn't hear her. I watched her lips as she said again, the words 'a little Chinese girl'. I nodded. Yes, a Chinese girl. I knew I had to be careful of Miss Preedy, as if walking through long grass, minding each step, in case, of what I just wasn't yet sure.

Miss Preedy's hand pressed down on to mine, 'Is she your friend?'

A terrible dread opened up. It must have shown on my face for Miss Preedy, encouraged, went on. 'Did you play games with this little friend?'

'She isn't my friend,' I said.

'So you do know her?' The smile was still there but the eyes were pushing, winning.

'I don't know,' I said.

'You don't know if you know her?' Miss Preedy gave a laugh that spun on itself. 'I think you do know who I am talking about.' She called to the door. 'Muriel.'

The door opened and there was Aunty Muriel as I'd never seen her before. Her eyes were pink from crying. In her hands was my dress belt.

*

They led me down through the starchy mist, down the steps to the Nissen hut. Nurse Margaret was waiting for us on the steps. Gardener Chen opened the door and stepped aside. I followed Aunty Muriel down the aisle passageway, jars of pickled snakes on either side, sleeping, tongues out, necks pressed to the glass. At the end of the hut was a table with a sheet stretched out over it. Nurse Margaret drew the sheet back. There she was. A little girl, asleep.

But she was not sleeping. She was dead. I must keep telling myself this. She is dead. This is her body dressed in rags. This is her head flung back, mouth open. This is her hair, beginning to dry. These her arms, legs, pressed with bright bruises. This her hand, swollen, yellow, as if ripe. And these are her fingernails, jammed with black.

I am not sure if I screamed or how long I screamed but I know they were carrying me quickly out. Miss Preedy was shouting, 'Get hold of yourself,' and when I would not get hold of myself, she slapped me. I put my hand to my cheek and she watched herself a moment, frightened.

While Mr Dalrymple and Headmaster went to the village to report the death, there were many questions. First Miss Preedy spoke to the girls in the classroom and then she joined Nurse Margaret, Aunty Muriel and me in the staff room of Teachers' House.

'What were you thinking? The girl was bitten – why did you not call for Nurse Margaret?'

'I thought she was going to be okay.'

'But what of the snake? You know that Gardener Chen must be called immediately to kill them. And how could you think of going out of bounds? On your own?'

'The others were with me.'

'No, Etta, Gardener Chen saw you come out of the tunnel, alone. You arrived late for dinner, alone.'

'But they were there. The belt was Hilary's idea.'

'It was your belt, Etta.' Miss Preedy, Aunty Muriel, Nurse Margaret all stared at me as if I was talking lies, as if a cockroach had run from my mouth. 'The girls all testify to this. They told us about your knife, which Mr Dalrymple found at the pool on the other side of the tunnel.

'Now, who is she and what is her name? Enough of this Twelve nonsense. We need to find her parents.'

'She doesn't have parents,' I said. 'She has an old lady, her grandmother.'

'Where?'

'Up on the ridge.'

I was shuttered up in our dormitory, while they made investigations and decided what to do with me. Outside all was grey and the neighbouring peaks vanished. I walked up and down the dormitory. It was always so strange to be there alone, without the girls moving through. But today it was almost unbearable. Surrounded by our things, my doll with her broken eyelid, Flo's teddy with felt pupils. Ears sucked, seams split, tongues stitched, precious things all, and all without breath.

I sat by the wardrobes. I could not eat the bread and soup they'd left on a tray for lunch. The lunch break brought wave upon wave of horror. I shook in its presence, but I could not escape, for it was everywhere like the spit of firecrackers on New Year's Night.

Daughter, daughter, where are you? That cannot be you in the Snake Hut.

Something tapped on the window. I ran across the room and pressed my face against the pane. Nigel Pinsent stood below flicking stones. 'Hello,' he said. 'Hear you're in for some trouble at Evening Prayers.' I withdrew back into the room where I could not be seen.

'Oh, come back, Etta. Etta.'

The mist thickened and the bell rang for children to continue their lunch break inside. As it tolled across the valley, I put on my goose-feather jacket, put the bread in my pocket, filled a dormitory water-bottle, then slipped down the stairs, and stepped into the mist. I walked between the other children, invisible, silent. It was as if the mist herself had given me passage. Across Drill Court I went, past the Arbour and into the gut of the Great Steps. I was running away.

The Monks

As I came out on to the mountain path all I could hear was my breath and the echo of my footsteps. The trees were pale green silhouettes, the mist curling her fingers around their branches, drifting in between their trunks. I listened for footsteps or the call of my name, but no sound came. Perhaps it was too soon for the staff to have noticed I'd gone. I will keep walking until I get to Ink Pot pine, I thought. And when I got to Ink Pot pine and the footsteps of Aunty Muriel or Mr Dalrymple could not be heard, I walked to the next strange pine, and then till the next twist of the path and on through the mist I walked without being stopped.

I will go back, I said to myself as I approached Monkey Pine, the last of the pines before the path curved downwards. Then I remembered the cold morning silence of the girls, I remembered the horror with which Aunty Muriel looked at me, as if evil scuttled from my eyes, my mouth. Hot angry tears came, and I chanted my anger until my pace picked up. You stupid boob. You boulder on legs. Faster and faster I walked, and then I realised I was doing it, I was running away. My legs were carrying me, away from Aunty Muriel, the girls, from Miss Preedy and from that body that lay there, bruised, swollen and empty.

Scab face Pinsent. Fish breath Preedy. The pimple, Dalrymple. I pressed on, lost in mean thoughts until a noise stopped me in my tracks. I listened to the forest. It came again. Just the cautious melody of a bird testing the mist. I felt a squeeze of disappointment. I continued along the path, noticing everything, a branch crack, the snap of a leaf, for all about me I could feel a creeping. But every time I looked around there was no one. I bent down and pretended to tie my shoelace, and I felt it again. The creeping of a child, a giggle behind a tree. Perhaps this was the immortal soul of the mountain. A child hiding amongst the mist, calling.

At Woosung hamlet, I ran past the village gate, for I was frightened of the yellow dogs that sometimes gathered there, then fast over a curved bridge, through the rubbish heap and back into the forest. Here the path took me to the edge of the cliff, where it became a bamboo staircase that clung to the side of the mountain. This was the path that led down Lushan.

I had now gone too far for anyone from the school to reach me. All was silent except for the crows. I was afraid, but the view was covered in mist, so I could not see the steep drop. I gripped the bamboo railing, testing each footstep before putting my weight fully down. My boldness frightened me almost as much as the fear of falling.

At the bottom of the forty steps, I ran along the path until I came to a boulder. I climbed on to it, and rested in a small cup in the rock. For the first time in my two hours as a runaway, I began to cry and as I did so, the mist lifted to show a canyon of pines. This was the West Sea Canyon. I gathered my knees to my chest and gripped the rock. It was late afternoon. The clouds were pink as if roses had loosened their petals across the sky. *Oh, Mother and Father, I long to be in the courtyard of your house, together, smelling the peony blooms and looking up at the old moon.*

The wind spread up the gully with a howl. She shook petals from the azaleas, she raked my dress and jacket, she ran her hand over my face. I sat there, arms out, at the mercy of this wild touch. When she left for the far side of the canyon, I brushed the pine needles from my dress and jumped down from the rock. *Yes, I shall soon be in the courtyard of your house, for I am coming home.*

The sky was softening into apricot light and soon the reds and purples would follow. I quickly crossed Fairy Glen Bridge, a wood and rope bridge that swung above a ravine, the sharp tap of my footsteps echoing over the abyss. Night was not far off. I wanted to reach the Boiling House while there was still light. I would ask the lady if I could spend the night there, curled up on one of the benches, watching steam rise from the pot.

But first there was Baboon Corner. As I approached I saw one in the path, picking up a seed with his black, shiny fingers. He lifted his baboon head and his look said, as all baboons do, I hate you. He showed his yellow teeth.

In the forest behind me, I heard the crack of a branch.

Then, a gunshot.

It powered through the peaks. The crows, the baboon, everything called to the heavens. I fell to the ground. Eyes closed, hands gripping soil. More gunshots were going off. I couldn't tell if they were near or far, for the sound flung itself from peak to peak.

Then, a plane.

A buzz, the size of a pine-cone that grew and grew. A flash of metal sunlight. Then gone. The baboon had gone, too.

But a hand shook my shoulder. A monk was pulling my tunic. He was stealing me towards the forest. I pushed and kicked, but the monk was stronger. He put his arm around my waist and covered my screams with his robe, as the roar of a second plane came.

The air shook. The world went many bright colours. We were flung down with a sound that ripped through our ears. I looked down the path I'd just climbed. Fairy Glen bridge was smoke, was ash spiralling into the apricot heavens.

The monk and I stared at each other. He had a trimmed beard, a headscarf and inky black eyes. He got on all fours, motioned for me to follow, and together we crawled like babies into the forest. Here, he put his fingers in his mouth, letting out a strange whistle, and from behind the trees, appeared more monks. There were about twenty of them; all wore grey robes and black cloth shoes.

The monk who grabbed me was talking to the men about what had happened. I understood a few words. Girl, bridge, fire. They pointed to the sky, and looked at each other uneasily as they tried to locate this new smoky world. Then they examined me as if I'd fallen from the heavens.

'*Wo jiao Ming-Mei*,' I said, and pointed to my heart.

'*Wo jiao Lu*,' said the monk who'd saved me as he pointed to his heart. A monk with a frizzy beard plucked three tiny tomatoes from a fold in his robe.

'*Xie xie*,' I said. Thank you. I ate them while they began a discussion. It was the second time today that adults had been wondering what to do with me.

I wondered how they might help me get home. I would have to go down the Yangtze, through the East China Sea, then inland along the Huang Ho. For the first time I began to doubt that it was possible to make it alone. Perhaps they would send me back to school. But the Eastern Pass was now closed.

The monks made a sound of agreement amongst themselves, then began to gather up their things. Where were they planning to take me? If I didn't do something right now, I didn't know where I would end up. Chonqing, Shanghai, Quingdao. I began to panic. I flicked through my mind for ideas. I stepped towards Lu and tugged his robe. 'Agape House,' I said. The monks' faces were clouded with unknowing. 'Foreign devils on the river,' I said in Chinese. Still, they did not know. To better explain, I rubbed a patch in the ground with my fist and drew the sign of Agape House.

At this, the older monk's eyes brightened. 'Foreign devil women,' he said in Chinese. 'River.'

I nodded. When they agreed their plan, Lu brought me into their line. We walked along the old priest trails, silently winding our way through the trees. Sometimes the path became old steps, like the spine of a sea-serpent, rising up above the water. They did not sing hymns as we did with Aunty Muriel. The only clue they were moving through the forest was the slow shifting of grey robes, draped like mist.

At one point, we passed a mountain azalea, white as snow. Lu turned to me and said, 'Ming-Mei.'

'Ming-Mei,' I said, gratefully.

At the bottom of one hundred steps was an ancestral hall, surrounded by autumnal maples, blood red, as if they'd been shot. We stepped inside. Paper lanterns were strung along the roof; a stone trough held the ash of a thousand incense sticks. This was where we would spend the night.

As dusk fell, in crept the fleeing villagers. After speaking to the monks, who had taken charge, each group found themselves some floor space sheltering under the ancestral hall's great curved eaves. One lady came over to me and touched my blond hair, which scared an old man. He warned everyone not to touch my light skin, for he sincerely believed I was a ghost.

People readied themselves for bed, pulling blankets and coats around their bodies, and rolled-up tunics as pillows under their heads. I crept to the far wall and sat down. In a day, the whole world had changed. I had awoken in my bed, in a dormitory of girls to the sound of Aunty Muriel's bell and now I lay in an ancestral hall, no doors, no windows, wondering how to find my way home.

It was a cold night. In the darkness, people spat and crunched on shreds of cured meat. I stared at the shadows that the trees cast against the walls. I could not sleep, for every time I closed my eyes, I saw her, the child we called daughter. Her small twisted body on the trestle table, her fingernails dirty and torn. I thought about her passage through the tunnel. She had been dragged towards the school, her body banging on the rocks. Had she tried to follow me, had she lost her footing and then been swept away? I wondered if she called out, the water, cold and dashing all about her, and if she had struggled against the current, her hands reaching out of the torrent to grab rocks, trailing roots, anything. And when she finally had been drawn into the darkness, what lay there for her?

Dead, dead. That child we call daughter is dead.

There was no way to return to Lushan, to the days when Twelve and I made mud pies by the pool, or roamed the rooms of our imaginary house. That life was cut off, as black and burnt as the bridge over Fairy Glen. I was now alone. I lay back down and listened to the cockroaches scuttle.

Exhausted, I eventually fell into a slumber and rolled about in a bad dream, an awful, starry, skin-tingling dream.

Our daughter turning in the water. We are together, drowning. Down, down into the pool we go, water in our eyes, in our nose, in our throat.

I woke up, gasping for air, calling out 'Mother, Mother' into the curved ceilings of the ancestral hall.

From the darkness a muttering began. The villagers complained about the noise the child with white hair was making. Lu came and sat by my side. I wondered if he'd recoil from me as Aunty Muriel had earlier. But he did not go. He had a bowl of tea that he put into my trembling hands. The tea was sweet. I hadn't realised how thirsty I was. I gave Lu back the bowl, then covered myself up as much as possible and pulled my jacket tight. Lu watched me for a moment then gently and with something like amusement, he took a piece of rice paper, and a pencil very like our ones from school, and there under the moonlight drew, in a few strokes, a woman sitting by a mountain pool. She was a European woman, straight-backed, looking into the water. She looked like Aunty Muriel. He gave me the piece of paper. Holding it in my hand, I wondered if I'd ever see her again. I gazed at the woman looking at the water, and there in the moonlit hall, its lanterns swaying in the breeze of ancestral spirits, finally found some sleep.

Muriel's Diary

29 November 1941

I HAD HOPED SHE WOULD QUICKLY BE FOUND IN THE PLACES LISTED by the girls, these little hideaways you'd pass without note. The tree house, the rock, the stream. Each I ran to, again and again. They were covered with curling mist. I called out her name, but there was no answer. And it was with a rising dread that I realised she was not hiding in these places, that she'd gone out on to the mountain.

This afternoon I discovered there are many ways to watch a forest. You can watch it and see the pines, gummy barked, their red needles scattered over moss. You can watch your spirit in it, the alarmed thrum of a woodcock. You can look for what you long to see. Her stepping softly back.

Bird, Tree, Stream

THE NEXT MORNING, THE MONKS WOKE EARLY. WE CONTINUED down the path, the mountain hidden in cloud behind us. There were no guns, no planes today. Where were the monks taking me, I wondered, but I had no words to ask the question. No words for are you sure this is the way to Agape House or please stop, can't we go back. I had to follow.

On we went for another two hours through the bamboo grove, filled with birdsong. '*Niao*,' said Lu, as he pointed to the birds, then to the bamboo: '*zhu*'. I shyly repeated the words after him and in this way he drew me from the lonely horror of the night into a friendship made out of small words. Bird, tree, stream.

As the sun gained in strength, we left the forest and walked over yellow scrub. At last we came to a bald outcrop of rock. The vast plains spanned to the horizon and there, at anchor on Poyang Lake, was a Japanese gunboat, her bows marked with a red circle, the sign of the Rising Sun.

The monks began their descent into the foothills, where shanty camps of refugees gathered: farmers displaced from their villages, people from the cities, who had run when the soldiers and the shells came, coolies who had been rounded up and ordered by the National Army to dig trenches. People lay at the side of the path, either asleep or dead. Children ran after the monks and their wheelbarrow, calling for food. Beggars thumped their begging boxes, clawing after the monks with their skinny hands.

So that I would not draw too much attention, Lu scooped me up and placed me in a wheelbarrow that one of the monks had found, then covered me with a grey robe. I was wheeled along empty paddies and gates of cobbled villages where the wheelbarrow stuttered until it came to a stop and the robe was whisked off. Before me was a brown river, curled like a dragon's tail.

Was this the Women's River? It was much narrower than I'd expected, more muddy. On the river were broad junks. Chinese boats have eyes painted on each side. This is so they can see and avoid the spirits of the water. The spirits suck you under and choke you.

Lu led me along a slippery wooden pier and pointed to one of the boats, which was being filled with trays of dried fish. The boat had an eye painted on its prow. There were a few people sitting inside. Lu spoke to the boatman, gesturing at me, and I realised the monks were not coming with me.

I didn't know how to say goodbye. I could not take their address to write to them, for they did not know where they were going. I bowed.

'Ming-Mei,' the monk said. He held my shoulders, his eyes watching me with much life. Then his brow furrowed and he gave my shoulders a squeeze. It was time to leave. Lu took me over to Thin Yang, the boatman, and told him to look after me. I climbed into the boat and then we pushed off. The junk creaked, its great yellow sail flickering in the wind. I could feel the river underneath us, full of weeds and spirits swimming.

A granny sat down alongside me, chewing betel-nut. Her face opened and closed like a baby's fist. The woman who had stacked the fish joined us. She had a long pole with a cormorant on it. The cormorant was black and slippery and chained to the pole. It shook out its wings like an old umbrella, stretched its yellow beak, then settled to watch the water.

I thought of the baptism on the mountain, how the girls would be lowered into the stream and arise as new people. And I thought of my own soul, and how it was the colour of this river, and full of wicked spirits.

The cormorant lady began telling a story to the old granny. It reminded me of sitting in the kitchen at home, listening to the ladies of Pingxia village tell me stories about peepers, wicked ladies who poked holes in the paper windows of their neighbours to spy on them, and about the travels of Monkey and Pigsy. But now, listening to the cormorant lady, I could not understand the meaning, just enjoy the rhythm, the rise and fall of her words repeated, like a lullaby.

Rocked by the river, I was so exhausted that even though it was early afternoon, I fell into another drowning dream, in which the cormorant watched me, then with a black stretch of wing, down it came into the water and all was dark.

The lady with the cormorant shook me. 'Ming-Mei, Huichow,' she said, 'Huichow.' I slowly raised myself up. It was night. My arms and legs were stiff from the hours asleep on the hard floor. Thin Yang called to someone on the bank. A lantern on the land bobbed and a man yelled back. The junk banged against the jetty. Go, go, go, Yang's hands said to me in the light of the lantern. Go, quickly. I squeezed past the cormorant and the granny, who were both still sleeping.

The man on the pier spoke to a group of men playing cards in a riverside shack. They put their cards down and stared out at me. When the man repeated the name of Agape House, they shook their heads, they did not want to take me there. Instead, they called to a boy who was smoking a cigarette and made him take me. Standing on the jetty in the drizzle, I waved goodbye to thin Yang and the cormorant lady. The junk sailed into the dark.

I was scared. Scared as a baby in the reign of Herod. I followed the boy for some way in the drizzle, along a path that curved around the corners of the white stone houses and over a small stream. We were walking out of the village, the river glinting to our left. The frogs and crickets sang, the night twitched with noise. Then the boy stopped. Here he pointed to a compound set with a crumbling stone wall that was overgrown with vines, then left.

I moved slowly down the path. The building seemed abandoned. The paving stones were cracked. Big cabbages lined a vegetable patch and green beans shone in the fine rain. I stood at the door and knocked. I waited. There was no reply. I waited and knocked again. As I did, I heard footsteps. Slow, dragging. The door creaked open and there stood a man with no face.

It was hard to see if he was shocked to see me for there was so little of his face left. A maul of skin. An eye. No nose. He was part corpse. More terrifying than the dead, he stood in the doorway, breathing and dying all at once.

'*Guimei*,' he said, moving back into the shadows. All I could see now were his hands, which were stumps.

'No, no,' I said. I was not a ghost girl. I stepped towards him into the corridor, and shouted out for Miss Kingsley.

A girl came to the door. '*Baba*,' she said to the man. Father. She led him away. When she came back she didn't invite me in, but stepped out into the rain-speckled night. She was barefoot. She wouldn't let me walk next to her. Her hand said no. Her father was a leper and there was to be a gap between us. I followed ten paces behind.

I followed her, the leper's daughter, along the paddy fields, her plait swinging as she stepped on the narrow ridge that parted one farmer's wealth from another's. About us the night was busy with frogs and cicadas. Fireflies flew like drunks. After an hour or so, we climbed the bank that led on to a main road. Suddenly the girl stopped and flung herself down on the road. Her pretty face was scrunched with fear. She lifted her head and spoke fast in Chinese. A terrible thing was happening. She pulled me back to the side of the bank. There, I heard it: marching. The drumming of boots on earth. We lay there while the procession of soldiers passed. On and on they went. Thud, thud. I thought of the dragon dances I'd seen as a child, the noisy procession, red lanterns, dragon's head, where all the gods and villagers come out to celebrate.

After ten minutes or so, I peered over the edge of the bank and saw them, Chinese soldiers, khaki, caps, bayonets. Faces set stiff as carvings, all with the same look. Even though they were not Japanese, it would be dangerous to be discovered. I remembered what Miss Kingsley had said to Aunty Muriel about them, that they chased girls, had them, then shot them if they were ugly. Now I knew that these stories of war had faces, had legs, marched, that the threat Miss Kingsley feared was on the move.

We stayed still until the soldiers had gone and the humpbacked hills had become silhouettes against the rising dawn. Later, as we waited in case more men came, we fell asleep. When I awoke, the girl was squatting in the grasses a few feet along, catching a cricket. She showed it to me. It flashed like scissors as it sprang out of her hand. She told me her name was Bao and we sat there a while, looking for crickets. As I caught one, feeling each jump tickle, I noticed white pock marks across Bao's face, the beginning of her own leprosy. We stayed there at the edge of the field, as the sun came up, catching crickets. Soon the sun was spreading warmth all over the earth, saying wake up, get up, walk.

All the villagers from these plains had fled or been commandeered to dig trenches, save a few farmers, who, in triangle hats, tilled their land with buffalos. We continued through the fields until we came to a cluster of trees above a river. Bao pointed to a hamlet on the banks, a cluster of three or four whitewashed buildings surrounded by a wall. Bao took three steps back and would not lead me any further. As the daughter of lepers, this was not a place she could enter and she was telling me to go through the gates on my own.

At the gate of the village, I turned to wave goodbye, but Bao was already a figure in ragged clothes running to the hump of the hill. As I walked through the gate, the first building I saw was whitewashed with gleaming roof tiles. Painted above its door on a red sign was a lady looking over a manger. I had arrived at Agape House.

Finding Miss Kingsley

THE WOODEN GATE TO AGAPE HOUSE WAS NOT LOCKED BUT, AS I knocked, inched open. I stepped inside the courtyard. A golden scholar tree grew in the centre, and all around the courtyard was a series of rooms, each with its door flung open. No one came running out to greet me. Stepping over a hoe, I walked further in. A broken chair lay under the tree. Lines of washing hung, tunic arms and trouser legs flailing in the wind. A cat mewed and ran out on to the street.

'Miss Kingsley,' I called. 'Miss Kingsley?' From room to room I went. Head cocked, leaning into the shadowy cool. 'Miss Kingsley? Are you here?' But she did not answer and the rooms were empty of the commotion of girls living and learning together. There was no clatter of spoons and forks, no squabbles over combs, nor bubble of lunch in the kitchen pot. There was no one there.

I walked to the far end of the courtyard where I found a kitchen. Pots lay everywhere. Grain spilt out of an upturned jar. The ashes of the fire were cold. One pot still had a scrape or two of rice gruel, which I scooped into a gluey ball and ate. I lifted a kettle, also cool, and poured the water into my mouth. A rat slunk across the doorway, its soft belly rubbing the ground.

Looking into the courtyard, I saw that many tracts had spilt from a box and fell about the threshold of a small room across the courtyard. I went inside. Instruments of faith, tracts, posters, flags, lay strewn across the floor. A trunk with the initials 'R. K.' on it had been opened and rustled about with. Inside was a photograph of a man and a woman, and on its corner was written 'T. & D. Kingsley. Bradford 1923'. These must be parents from a long time ago. Under the photograph was a 'Prayer Diary', which I picked up and held as I began to wander about the room.

Pinned to the wall was a sheet with a map of China painted on it. This map was just like the one in Mother and Father's dining room. There was the Yangtze, blue and winding. There was Shanghai with a yellow dot for the mission home on Sinza Road. I ran my finger along the higgledy-piggledy blue lines. This map was useful. You could plot the Japanese invasion, put in pins for battalions, camps and warships. You could plot a journey home. I measured the gap between Agape House and Lushan. I had travelled the length of a finger. I measured the gap between Agape House and Shanxi Province. Mother and Father were six hands away. I wondered where on the map Miss Kingsley was.

It began to rain. Rain spat off the courtyard, pummelled pots, spanked the tiles. In the wind, the boughs of the golden scholar tree bent and curled. The earth began to smell rusty and green. I wondered if there was rain on Lushan, if it was cold, and if the girls had been baptised yet, but I realised I had lost track of the days.

While the rain danced on the courtyard, I sat by the trunk, the Prayer Diary in my lap. I pressed my fingernail along the gold imprint of 'R. K.' in the bottom corner. I leafed to the back page of the diary. Here under a page titled prayer list, were names written in a tiny, black script. Mother, Father, Dr Wang, Eleanor Pak, Miss Fu . . . 'Mother' was crossed out. 'Miss Fu', too. I thought about the woman in the trunk, gazing out from 1923. It seemed there was no longer a need to pray for her.

Then I heard a noise at the door and looked up. An old peasant woman was there, and when our eyes met she screamed and fled as if she'd seen a stinking Lazarus, only to return seconds later armed with a broom. She came charging at me, the broom thrust to my throat.

'My name is Ming-Mei,' I said in Chinese. The tip pressed hard. I'd never imagined I might die by broom before.

I tried again. 'Miss Kingsley. My friend,' I said, and this time, the woman's large cheekbones were seized with a smile. She laughed and shook her head, then led me to the kitchen. There she told me she was Mrs Zhu, the cook. She rinsed a pan and began to make a soup with a little pork and some noodles. As she lit the fire, and added some spices, she told me what had happened.

Chinese soldiers had come in the night, banging on the gates, bang, bang like a ladle on a wok, calling, 'Mother, Mother', full of want to touch pretty girls. This had happened before, and Miss Kingsley did not like them nor the Japanese bombers that rat-tatted like a lady's knuckles on a pot. They'd left at dawn. Nearby, farmers had heard of this departure with cupped ears, and taken what they could. Most of the raiding had happened in the kitchen, for you cannot eat a tract. The cook and her husband had hid in a house across the street, making themselves tiny as dough balls.

Mrs Zhu was old but she told me this with fluid hands and much exclamation. When she was done, Mrs Zhu ladled out the soup. The steam curled. I chewed the fatty pork, which she encouraged me to slurp and suck, which I did, loudly, much to her satisfaction.

Later that morning I sat on Old Zhu's mule in search of Miss Kingsley. I was dressed in an indigo tunic and trousers, black cloth shoes on my feet and hair scooped out of the way into a straw hat. Carrying a pitchfork, Old Zhu, Mrs Zhu's husband, walked alongside.

We followed the twisting river. There were few people on the boats today. The river fled over itself, fast and full. The day was mute. Colours were pressed to the earth. Orange, rust, brown. Winter was coming.

After five or six hours, in the late afternoon, we went up a hillock. I leant forward on the mule. At the top we had a view of the plains, wide and yellow, a ribbon of rivers and, in the distance, the blur of a walled town. I imagined making a map of all I saw, I imagined spooling a thread around little pins and marking the journey towards the Huang Ho and into the loess caves of Pingxia. But looking out over the endless *li* of land, I knew finding my way home would not be so easy.

We began our descent. At the bottom of the hill was a banyan tree, sacred and squat. Its boughs fluttered with paper prayers, tied carefully by villagers. Under the tree a group of peasants rested, flopping next to their rolled-up mattresses. I hoped they would not be trouble and I checked my blond hair was safely tucked away. The mule began to stagger down the hill in a puff of grit and dust. One of the peasants stood, put up a hand to shield their eyes and watched us approach down the steep path. Then they stepped out of the banyan's shade. It was Miss Kingsley.

She squinted. I waved. 'It's me, Etta.' At the bottom of the hill, I swung my legs off the mule and ran the last yards, cloth shoes padding on the soft, dusty earth. I stood panting before her, then flung my arms around her neck.

She tipped my hat back. My blond hair fell down my face. 'Henrietta, what is this?' She looked to Old Zhu, then back at me. 'What are you doing here?'

'I'm trying to get home.'

Miss Kingsley paused for a moment, and watched my face carefully before saying, 'home, Etta?'

Then a child called '*Mama*' and both Miss Kingsley and I turned to look. Under the tree there was a group of girls sitting next to their rolled-up mats, chopsticks and bowl in their lap. They wore indigo shirts and trousers, each with the embroidered character of Agape House on their chests. Their lack of curiosity was strange. I'd have thought they'd be calling me a ghost or at least have pointed at my blond hair. Instead, one called out in Chinese, '*Mama*, can we go yet?'

Miss Kingsley spoke to them in Chinese and I understood a few words; river, wait, the rope. Then she pushed me towards them. The girls' faces turned to the spot where I now stood, still and poised, as if they were breathing with their skin. It was then that I realised the girls of Agape House did not see the river, nor the banyan, for they were blind.

Miss Kingsley paused a moment as she considered how to introduce me. 'Girls, please welcome Ming-Mei.' The girls repeated 'Ming-Mei' in their high singsong; and my name soared and flew into the tree.

They could not see me to be afraid of me. The girls came towards my voice and soon they had their hands all over my face, petting me, reading me with their fingers. I shrank back. I was afraid of myself, of the wicked thing I had done, of how my hand held the knife over Twelve, how I had left her at the pool.

But still they moved towards me, chattering, laughing, trying to be my friend. One girl shook my shoulder. Another tugged my wrist. They wanted a reply. While Miss Kingsley and Old Zhu made a fire and heated water for the noodles, I began to whisper my collection of words. Bamboo, boat, bird. They laughed and felt my fingertips, wrists, face. I could not hide from them.

Miss Kingsley called for the girls, who made a queue with their bowls. I held hands with Mei-Mei and Ling-Ling, two of the smallest girls. They leant on me, slipped their arms into the crook of my arm. It was not like the children of Lushan, who had learnt to go from breakfast to bed without reaching out to be held. After filling their bowls, I led them around the edge of the tree to the blankets, which had been laid out for us to sit on. There, I helped them to eat their noodles.

After everyone had been fed and Old Zhu began to make his way back to Mrs Zhu, Miss Kingsley took me down to the river's edge. Between this bank and the other, the rope rose out of the water here and there. Miss Kingsley explained that it was by this rope that the party, walking in single file over the submerged stone path, would make the crossing to the other side, then on to the city of Luzhou, where they would find safety.

Miss Kingsley then turned to me, gravely. 'Now Etta, I don't know the full story but one thing is clear, this is a dangerous time to leave Lushan. There was terrible fighting a few days ago in the foothills. There are troops, refugee camps, bandits. The church at Poyang has been burnt down.'

'I'm trying to get home,' I said. 'My parents are waiting for me in the caves outside the village. Miss Kingsley, I thought maybe you'd know how to get there. Pingxia village is in Shanxi, not far from the Huang Ho.'

She let out a tired laugh. 'Shanxi is in Free China; you'd have to trek through several battlegrounds, a flooded Yellow River basin, and escape three sets of armies, the Reds, the Nationals and the Japanese. Etta, now will you tell me what happened to make you run away?'

Miss Kingsley knew I'd run away. What else did she know? The horror of Twelve came back, sharp. Her dirty fingernails, her bruised face. I did not speak.

'Etta, there's no point pretending you didn't run away. Come now, you can tell me. Were people unkind to you?'

I shook my head. 'No, Miss Kingsley, I was the unkind one. I was going to go back, but a Japanese plane came and the bridge at Fairy Glen went up in smoke. I couldn't return the way I'd come.'

'Oh, now that is worrying,' said Miss Kingsley. 'Usually the Lushan mists keep the planes away. We shall have to warn the Watsons. They are the missionaries whose church was burnt down and who hoped to go to Lushan where they might rest a while.'

'And what about you, Miss Kingsley?'

'The magistrate has given us free passage on his junks, south into the next province. There we will be safe, at least for a while.'

'And Miss Tippet?' I asked.

Miss Kingsley sighed. 'Miss Tippet is still under house arrest along with the other missionaries in Lung Po. We shall have to wait and see about Miss Tippet.'

Dusk was falling. Miss Kingsley and I watched fireflies, weighted pricks of light, fly along the bank. 'Is this war worse than the Boxers?' I asked.

And Miss Kingsley, who along with Miss Tippet had been captured and held ransom by the Boxers for twenty days in 1919, said, 'It is a different enemy, but our God is still the same God. He will provide.'

Sitting there watching the rope over the water, it became clear to me that if I couldn't get home to Shanxi, I could belong here, at the children's side, instead. Seeing for them, caring for them. Miss Kingsley would need the extra help, with Miss Tippet under house arrest.

I was about to tell Miss Kingsley that God had provided me, when she spoke. 'I have been blest with thirty years on this river and now I must go.' I looked at Miss Kingsley's river, its brown waters full of rags and lost possessions and then, to my astonishment, Miss Kingsley began to cry.

I put my hand into hers. She held it back tight, and I knew *this* was the right moment. 'Miss Kingsley, may I go with you?' I asked. 'I could look after the girls as Miss Tippet did, help feed them, teach them Bible stories.'

'Miss Tippet is a grown woman, you're still a child. You've been kind to Ling-Ling and Mei-Mei, helping them eat this evening, but it is on Lushan that you belong.'

'There really is no way back,' I said, meaning not just the bombing of the bridge.

She turned directly to me. Her face was heavily lined, her hair greyer than even two weeks ago. She was looking more and more like the mother from Bradford, 1923.

'When you're back at Lushan, you must tell Muriel everything. I'm sure she will be able to sort it out. She is a very capable young woman. I will speak to the Watsons when we arrive at Luichow. I am sure we can return you safe and sound. There are many paths up and down Lushan.'

That night, I curled up under the banyan tree, looking up at its prayers – strands of fabric the villagers tied to the branches, where they stayed until they faded and fell, like prayer leaves, gathered back to the earth. I listened to the river, its wicked spirits chattering by and prayed that something would change in me.

Muriel's Diary

1 December 1941

YESTERDAY, I HELPED BURY A CHINESE CHILD. MARGARET DRESSED her in white, a hand-me-down dress, something one of our girls would go to church in, for white is the Chinese colour of mourning. I combed the little girl's hair, pulled and tugged until the knots were out. I expected her to squirm, to whine, but of course she was silent, still.

Oh, Margaret, I searched the gardens but there are no flowers to press into her hands, so let us place paper flowers as the Chinese do. Gardener Chen, Mr Dalrymple, when you let her coffin down into that black hole, please do so gently. Do not disturb her. And Headmaster, when you lift your arms in prayer, pray a prayer of eternal compassion. Let your hands stretch out wide, wide as the eagle's wings and let the prayer carry her . . . Where will she go? A little girl of four or five, where will she go?

After it was done we walked along the stream. A mist swooped down. The world quite vanished, apart from our children's voices chanting out of the classrooms. I went to my own room, and wanting to put some colour back, took out my brushes, my squares of blue, green, yellow, and began to paint. My own childhood was pewter loch, dreich hills, puddles and a hard, slanting rain. Even here, on the other side of this earth, I cannot escape it. There it is in my paintings of Lushan, these Chinese waterfalls and peaks, painted in a palette of heather and gorse.

Don't Let Go

'MING-MEI, MING-MEI, THE ROPE, THE ROPE?' I WAS AWOKEN EARLY by the two girls.

I went to the riverbank. The rope was showing, a muddy brown twist over the muddy brown river, just as Miss Kingsley had hoped. Watching the water, I thought again of Lushan. I couldn't bear to think about the consequences of my return. Surely there was some other way.

I went back with the news. 'I see the rope.'

'She sees the rope, she sees the rope!' the girls said. Then, at Miss Kingsley's say-so, they felt for the ends of the mattress and took strings from their pockets. I helped them tie up their bedding, then we got up and walked to the river. The sky was red and a mist floated up from the land. It was early and Miss Kingsley promised that we'd have breakfast when we had escaped to the other side.

Near the water's edge, Ling-Ling and Mei-Mei held my hands while Miss Kingsley explained to the girls what would happen to them, how they would step into the water. How the water would tilt them, swirl around their legs. How they need not be worried for Miss Kingsley and Ming-Mei would help them. How on the other side they'd hang their trousers by the fire to dry.

As Miss Kingsley talked, I thought of Lushan. I thought of the baptism on the mountain, how the girls would have crossed their arms over their chests, and be lowered in to the pool. How their sins would be made clean, how they would arise out of the water as new people. And I thought of my own soul, and how it was the colour of this river, brown and full of weeds.

Then along the river floated two men standing on a sampan. Cigarettes and straw hats. Miss Kingsley waved at them. There was a buzzing in the sky. It got louder and louder. Ling-Ling gripped my hand. The buzzing became a plane with a red circle on its tail. Miss Kingsley yelled out and we flung ourselves on the ground. The plane swooped low and the river-boat men ducked. Their boat swayed from side to side. How angry was the brown water, all ribboned with waves. In the great bluster of air, the leaves and prayers of the banyan tree tilted wildly.

'What is it?' said Mei-Mei as the plane flew away. But how to explain this terror to them?

When Miss Kingsley had calmed everyone, we were again to try to wade through the angry water. All in a line, deeper and deeper, ankle then knee. I watched Pei, the first girl, as she listened to the river, easing her foot in, sensitive hands on the rope, tugging the distance between herself and safety, feet feeling the sandy bank, the pebbles, the path of rock. She felt the water's gasping cold and stepped on.

I watched with growing terror as the other girls went in. What if one fell? What if one lost her grip, spread her arms and was swept away over the rapids? A terrible dread spun through me.

'Your turn,' called Miss Kingsley from the other side.

I looked at Ling-Ling. Her face was frightened but not her eyes, they were open and calm.

Then Ling-Ling took the rope. Mei-Mei took the rope. I took the rope.

'With both hands,' called Miss Kingsley.

I felt for Ling-Ling's free hand. I guided it to the rope. 'Two,' I said, in Chinese.

'Two,' said Ling-Ling, for she had understood both hands must hold on.

Into the water we stepped. Cold, murky water, full of the torrents of the mountains, perhaps even the streams and pools of Lushan.

Do not get swept away, was all I could think as I watched the two girls begin to wade into the muddy river, for rivers and streams do that: they carry you off. They batter you against stones, fling you up and down, cram your nails with clods of dirt. This I now knew. I gripped the rope hard.

Water sprayed up. The girls stepped on until they were up to their waists in wet noise. Mei-Mei stopped. She did not know where she was. She did not know how much further she had to go. Miss Kingsley shouted us on from the other bank. With new courage, Mei-Mei started again, hands gripping, trusting that soon the distance would be closed. Ling-Ling and I followed.

There was another buzzing in the sky and once again, a plane swooped overhead, but this time very low, and directly above. I could see its metal underbelly. Miss Kingsley yelled. There was nowhere to hide from the propellers, the engine, the guns. The propeller's gust of air blew waves, and the waves gulped over the girls' faces. The girls spluttered the brown water. Wave after wave came. Somewhere in this,

Ling-Ling let go of the rope. The current sucked her forward. I grabbed her tunic sleeve, and tried to pull her back. The current was strong; it wanted to whisk her away. I could feel my feet slipping on the stone walkway.

'Hold her, don't let her go,' Miss Kingsley yelled from the bank. Ling-Ling's body lurched forward again out of my grasp. I reached out, grabbed her wrist with one hand and with the other held to the rope tight. Ling-Ling's hand was in mine. I would not let go.

I pulled Ling-Ling back and placed her hand on the rope. I held her tight, so she knew that she was safe, that she would not float away. The water stilled. Then on we went, feeling for the way with our feet, gripping the rope hard, step by step until we made it out of the rushing torrent and on to the bank where the first the two girls knew of the other side was Miss Kingsley lifting them by their soaked waists out of the water, and on to the dusty earth.

I clambered out on my own; lay on the bank, my chest rising and falling with the effort of the crossing. I had not let her go. I looked back at the far bank, where the banyan stood bound in prayers, and spat out the last of the dirty water.

Luichow was not far but the going was slow. The girls walked in lines of four or five, holding on to the shoulder of the girl ahead, the girl at the front tapping a stick. That afternoon we reached Luichow harbour. Luichow itself was behind us, a busy town enclosed in a wall, at least ten men thick. Miss Kingsley went into the town to speak to the mandarin and to find the Watsons. She returned an hour later, the two junior missionaries at her side.

'And this is Henrietta Robertson,' said Miss Kingsley.

'She's not a bad girl, just sometimes unruly. Sunday is her birthday. She will turn eleven and, I believe, from today's events, infinitely more sensible.'

The Watsons and I stared at each other. They were still pale from England. Or perhaps it was the shock of losing their home. They each wore an armband with a 'B' on it, to say they were British. They'd been made to wear these when they'd been rounded up by the Japanese at Poyang Lake.

While the boatmen stacked Old Zhu's provisions, Miss Kingsley put her hand out and I shook it. Then she gave me a packet of birthday moon cakes from the mandarin. 'Happy Birthday, Etta,' she said. 'Try hard, everything will get better.'

A few minutes later, Miss Kingsley and the girls boarded a junk with painted eyes and white sails. The girls sat watching the brown river with eyes that could not see. I stood on the pier and waved, though not one of them waved back. Then, as the boatmen pushed the junk away from the jetty with long wooden poles, the girls began to call from the boat, 'Bamboo, bird, rope.'

And I called back, 'Chopsticks, flower, tree,' as the junk glided south.

On the day of my eleventh birthday, I rode on that Luichow mule, dressed like a blind girl, up into the mists of Lushan. I had left little more than a week ago and I was returning a year older with eleven moon cakes.

Mrs Watson's wedding ring was loose on her finger and her fingers patted her face over and over, as if searching for a Braille that read comfort. Mr Watson was small, with a small head and small teeth. He sniffed all food, suspicious.

They had not been in China long, and their Chinese was terrible and so was their use of chopsticks.

On the foothills, where you can see both down into the plains and up towards Lushan, we stopped for a picnic. Mr and Mrs Watson sang 'Happy Birthday' and below I could see the burnt-out villages dotted along the paddy fields. The fighting had moved north and villagers were slowly coming home. I could see them going out into the fields.

On we went, until we found the crumbling old path, the one like the serpent's tail. Up its spine we climbed, bone by bone.

At the Boiling House near where the Fairy Glen bridge had once hung, I knocked on the door. After I'd given the woman the last of my moon cakes, the kettle was put on the fire.

While Mr Watson discussed the new route with the mountain-chair men outside, I sat next to Mrs Watson and the Boiling House lady in the kitchen. Sipping tea from a bowl, I watched Mrs Watson trying to get the right pronunciation for things in the room. Tea, stove, kettle, stove god.

I felt sleepy. My back slouched down the wall, my eyelashes drooped. Then I noticed Mrs Watson bring out her gospel glove. It was new. She put it on her hand and began to tell her gospel. The yellow, the black, the white, the red. A life of faith is so many colours. Mrs Watson began to tell the gospel story, starting first with the monkey finger. She waggled it about.

The Boiling House woman looked unsure.

'It's black, for sin,' I told her. 'You said monkey.'

'Goodness,' said Mrs Watson. She stopped waving the black finger.

'It's *hei*, not *ho*.'

'Right,' said Mrs Watson. 'Got it.' Her face set with resolve. She took the woman's hand and peered earnestly at her. 'This finger,' she said, 'is the howling finger.'

The Boiling House woman stared at that glove with something like suspicion.

And on Mrs Watson went; the exhausted finger, the sad finger, the fish finger. How easy it was to get a gospel wrong. Mrs Watson took the glove off and rubbed her face. She'd given up. She laid it by her side and began to answer the lady's questions, which were not about the gospel but about Mrs Watson, how old she was and, most importantly, how many sons she had.

'Why don't you have children, Mrs Watson?' I asked as the Boiling House woman tended the stove.

'Well, Henrietta, the thing is, we're waiting for the Lord to bless us.'

I watched Mrs Watson drink her tea, the gospel glove lifeless in her lap, and wondered when the Lord would do that.

Let me tell you how to get a baby. Niang-niang has a headdress of birds. She is the god to pray to when a lady wants a baby. This is what you do. Set the paper god in your home and petition it. If the baby does not come, buy three long lengths of coloured threads and take these to the paper god each day and show the threads to her saying, 'If you do not give me a child, I will take these threads and go to your temple and steal one.'

Then go to the temple where the goddess sits beside her husband, who holds little porcelain babies on his lap and on his shoulders. While burning incense, pass the little packet of threads three times around the baby you like best. Tie the threads around its neck and quickly break the threads. Then put the packet in your trousers, and do not remove them until a baby arrives.

Later put the packet in the *tou-tou*, the apron that is worn by all children. *Tou-tou* means wrap carefully so the child will not be lost.

After the baby has arrived, take a paper picture of a baby with the child's name on it to the temple so that Niang-Niang will not be lonely and miss the child that she has given you.

If the baby grows nice and fat, give to Niang-Niang your thanks. Take a gift to the temple, maybe paper shoes or a paper hat.

Later, as we trekked the new route up the Western Pass, I imagined Twelve and being a mother to her. If she were here now, struggling on just this step, and if she stumbled, would my hand keep her from falling? And say if her lashes were heavy with sleep, would I lift her in my arms and carry her? Yes, I would do all these things, yes, yes.

Then I said to myself, 'No, Henrietta. She has gone because of you. You left her when she needed you.' Then everything became hopeless and confusing, and Mrs Watson, who was now ahead of me said, 'Henrietta, dear, do come along.'

I marched to catch up. I was growing up. I was now eleven. I tried to remember what Miss Kingsley said, that if I tried hard and was kind, then little by little things would change.

Higher still we went until we crossed Pu-dang bridge and then up and out on to the temple grounds. There had been a misunderstanding between Mr Watson and the men. We came to rest at the top of White Pagoda. Dusk was fast falling, and cats – brown, white, and black – ran mewing out of the shadows. There was no one here. No monks. The people in the shacks outside the temple had gone too. Ashes overflowed from the altar. An empty bowl had gathered rain.

While they discussed the route, I leant back on the pagoda, which, close up, was not the glistening white it appeared from the school, but stained, as if tears had trickled down her for centuries.

'There's Daoshan, darling. I don't think we'll make it before curfew,' said Mr Watson.

'We must make it, else the watchman won't let us in.' Mrs Watson fiddled with her wedding ring.

Mr Watson said, 'Henrietta, I shall take you to the school now,' and then to his wife, 'I shan't be long.'

While Mrs Watson sat by the pagoda, Mr Watson and I followed the stone steps that led from the temple to the laundry, guided by the dragon-tail railing. At the dragon's head, on the last step, I said goodbye and back up to the temple Mr Watson went.

All around was blackness, night and forest coiled about the school like a tail. I came out of the path and into the laundry, the rushing wind covering up my footsteps. There was no washing on the lines and, stepping on to Drill Court, I could see the school was empty of children and full of shadows. It was Sunday night and everyone was at Evening Prayers. Across Drill Court I ran towards Memorial Hall, her lights flickering like a tambourine.

An Evening Prayer

ELECTRIC LIGHT FILTERED THROUGH THE SHUTTERS OF MEMORIAL Hall. I could hear Miss Preedy say, 'Adoration,' followed by a thick silence putt, putted with coughs and a squeak of a chair. ACTS was Miss Preedy's favourite prayer, A for adoration, C for confession, T for thanksgiving and S for supplication, each followed by a silence, in which we were to privately adore, confess, thank or plead, always with the longest pause given to confession.

I walked around the edges of the hall until I found a window where the shutter was not fully closed. I pressed my fingers to the glass. There, in the warmth, were rows of children in dressing gowns. Brown dressing gowns, blue dressing gowns, pale green, a Paisley print and an orange padded silk gown, which belonged to Elspeth West from Peking. They were kneeling on the floor, facing the chair in front of them, hands cupped in prayer. A chair squeaked.

With my elbows on the windowsill and chin in hands, I watched them pray. The children of Memorial Hall could not feel the wind, nor hear the call of the trees. I found I could not pray. I was almost at Evening Prayers, almost a schoolgirl on a wooden chair, I was almost there but not, for I was part of the night, looking in.

'Supplication,' said Miss Preedy, and the chair squeaked again. Miss Preedy responded with a sharp 'Amen'. The school rose to sing hymn number 312: 'How Lovely Are Thy Dwellings', accompanied by Aunt Neb, who thumped *allegrissimo* at the shiny black piano. From the darkness, I mouthed the words, my breath almost in song.

As the children filed out, I noticed a group of the youngest boys huddle around something. One boy went to Miss Preedy, who was at the other end of the hall where she had been overseeing the big boys put away the wooden chairs. As she came over, the group of little boys parted and I could see what they had been watching. There, still at his prayer was a boy. His head was caught in between the two slats of wood in the back of a chair. He had popped his head through during prayers and was stuck.

The little boys looked at the stuck boy, then Miss Preedy, then back to the stuck boy again. The stuck boy's face was red, his ears throbbing. He was jerking his head to wrench himself free from the two slats in the chair back, jamming his ears over and over. The chair was stamping, forward and back.

Miss Preedy stood over the boy. Her hands, on her hips, were purple, so different a colour from the rest of her skin they didn't look like they belonged to her at all, as if she might say one thing and do another. 'You've done it again, have you?' she said. 'Well, you're on your knees, that's a start. Now pray. Pray that the Lord will release you.'

The chair was still for a moment. The boy scrunched his eyes closed, his lips moved quickly. Then the stamping of the chair started again. The chair legs screeched on the wooden floor. The boy was breathing hard, his nostrils flaring, his eyes were open now, big with alarm. He'll scrape his ears off, I thought. Someone must stop him, someone must get him out. The legs of the wooden chair pounded the floor, making a terrible screeching noise.

'Come on then, pray,' Miss Preedy was saying to the boy. Her eyes sparked.

I went around the side of the building and from its shadow watched as the children began to drift across Drill Court in their dressing gowns. The Dormitory A girls were talking about the boy in the chair. They were trying to remember his name.

'He looked like a sort of Peter type,' said Edith.

'I thought he was more of a Bertie. Or a Tom,' said Fiona.

Neville. Erasmus. The names continued. Moses. Winston.

'I know who he is,' said Flo. 'He's the boy who kicked Aunt Neb.'

A few minutes later came Aunty Muriel, walking briskly. She was on her own and this was my chance to hand myself over. But then Miss Preedy called, 'Muriel. A moment, please.' From the shadows, I watched Aunty Muriel walk back towards Memorial Hall, her face alight with its electrical glow.

'Muriel, please mind the state of the girls. The hem of Hilary's dressing gown is coming down.'

'Yes, Miss Preedy.'

'Muriel, it is a lack of vigilance that I am concerned about. If these small things are not weeded out they will lead to a greater wrongdoing, as you can attest to.'

'It is my greatest concern that the girls of Dormitory A are presentable and that they learn how to become good Christian women.'

'I hope, Muriel, that they will not be learning pride from their elders. Instruct the laundry ladies tomorrow and for breakfast I shall be expecting a reformed Dormitory A line.' Miss Preedy returned to the hall and Aunty Muriel once again began her walk across Drill Court, clutching her arms, her head down into the wind.

I watched Aunty Muriel's figure fade into the shadow of the Girls' Building. I had missed my chance to hand myself in. How many days could I live walking along the secret paths, washing my face at the laundry, slipping into the kitchen when the cooks weren't looking, sleeping in the boughs of The Beard? I might stay for ever in this almost place. I ran out of the dark and across Drill Court after her.

At the sound of my footsteps, Aunty Muriel spun on her heel, her hand went to her heart. 'Etta!' She spoke my name like a gasp. When I reached her, she put her arms around my shoulders and drew me in. My teeth started chattering and she held me still.

I began to talk, spilling out my words fast and frantic. 'You were all at Evening Prayers. I watched you from the window. Aunty Muriel, did you see the boy, the boy stuck in the chair?' Aunty Muriel loosened her hold, then put both hands on my shoulder. Her eyes scanned my face. 'Etta, where have you been?'

'I've been with Miss Kingsley. She sent me back with the Watsons. Have you heard of them? They have terrible Chinese. Aunty Muriel, we've got to do something about the boy, because he is really stuck,' I said.

'Miss Preedy will do what is best. Now, Henrietta, tomorrow there will be much explaining to do but for the present it will be something warm to drink and straight to bed.'

We went up the front steps of the Girls' Building and into the stairwell. The building was full of light and the sounds of girls' voices. It smelt of evening, of green vines and cold weather.

Aunty Muriel opened her bedroom door and we stepped inside. She put on a lamp, the flame fizzled and then steadied. Aunty Muriel told me to stand near the stove. She put a little more wood on. 'Now keep an eye on that pan of milk while I go and explain things to the girls.'

When Aunty Muriel left, I stepped closer to the watercolours that were pegged up to dry. It was like a diary for the days I had been away. There was the baptism. A pool with light coming down through the trees and a trio of girls in their straw hats singing. There was another one of Headmaster in the pool and a girl rising up out of it, her arms crossed at her chest. It was Big Bum Eileen. At the end of the hanging paintings, there was another one, a face. It was Twelve.

The door opened. Aunty Muriel had my shawl, hairbrush and toothbrush. She stood in the doorway for a moment, watching me look at the painting, then said, 'Get ready for bed; the girls are just saying bedtime prayers. Here's a nightdress. Wash your face at the sink.' She carefully pronounced each word and moved slowly around me. She treated me as if I was a porcelain doll or a glass ornament. As if I was dropped and broken on the floor and she might cut herself if she touched me. I realised that I was now different to Aunty Muriel and she did not quite know how to look at me. I dare not remind her it was my birthday.

I went to the sink. There I washed my face with a small nub of Aunty Muriel's soap. There was a long line of her hair in the basin. It looked like a crack.

In the little mirror above the sink, I watched Aunty Muriel.

She was shaking out my indigo tunic and trousers. Her face was puffy and tired. She paused for a moment and slid the curtain open with her long thin fingers. She peered out at the blackness. Something was on her mind. Then she turned back to the room. Our eyes met in the mirror's reflection. I gulped. For a moment I had seen Aunty Muriel's other face, not the one that she wore for us dormitory children, but the face she didn't show. Just for a moment, I had seen Aunty Muriel not knowing.

Aunty Muriel walked me through the dormitory to my bed. The girls were in their bunks. They pulled down bedspreads from their eyes and stared.

'Now, girls,' said Aunty Muriel as she helped me on to the top bunk, 'Etta has had a very long journey and is too tired to speak. Finish off your prayers and off to sleep.' Then to me, as she tucked the blanket in, 'If I hear so much as a peep from you . . .'

The girls went back to their prayers. It was for the stuck boy. Voices floated up from the bunk beds.

'Dear Lord Jesus, please help them get Philip Hill out of the chair. Amen,' said Kathryn.

'Dear Heavenly Father, please help shrink his head . . .' said Eileen.

'. . . or, Lord, you could try soap,' said Edith.

'Dear God, please help him and those who are helping him. Amen,' said Flo.

Then everyone, except me, said, 'Night-night.'

Muriel's Diary

7 December 1941

SHE APPEARED ON HER BIRTHDAY, AND STOOD IN MY ROOM, A MARVEL of coldness and wet, dressed in the indigo of a peasant, her hair swept up in a straw hat, her feet in black cloth shoes, leaves about her clothes, part peasant, part forest, part ghost. I had never seen the like. There was little point telling her off. We had to start again. She washed her face at my basin; I poured some hot water from the stove. She waited. Her body was thin, all elbows, shoulder blades. She was frightened that I did not love her, I could see that. I gave her one of my nightdresses. For the past week, I had lived in this lightning fork of futures, one if Etta turned up alive and one if she did not. And now here she is, and I am so angry.

The Flag of the Rising Sun

I COULD NOT SLEEP. I TWISTED AND TURNED IN MY HAND-ME-DOWN sheets. I sighed and turned. I turned and sighed. I finally drifted into a light sleep. The mountain flashed before me, I was falling down the Great Steps, I was slipping into a ravine. I was showing everyone the way to go so that the Japanese would not get us. Up the secret monk's paths. Along our Saturday outing trails. They were coming, the Japanese were coming! I had to tell Aunty Muriel.

I sat up. Breathing fast, heart thump-thump. Scared.

I got out of the covers and climbed down. My feet touched the cold floor. I couldn't find my dressing gown, so I pulled my shawl around me. There was a ladder of light coming through Edith's open curtain, the place where her parents would slip down from the moon. I looked at Flo. The twist of her plait spiralling across the pillow like an escaped dream.

I stepped inside the bathroom. A candle was lit in the far corner of the room, and stood at a sink, with her back to me was Big Bum Eileen. She turned and gave me a glare.

'Eileen,' I moved towards her. She was scrubbing something

in the basin, her hands plunged in and out of the water. 'Are you okay?'

'Don't look,' she said.

'Oh,' I said. 'Sorry. Should I get Aunty Muriel?'

'Just go away. Don't interfere with anything.'

'What are you washing? Have you wet yourself?'

'Get your evil spirit away from me,' she said. 'Go on, run away.'

I was hot, burning sad. No one, not even Aunty Muriel, had remembered my birthday. I would run away then, I would. If they didn't want me, I'd leave. I now knew how. I passed Aunty Muriel's room and went down the staircase and out of the Girls' Building. The door clicked shut behind me and I stood there for a moment. Circling the school was a black shadow. It was the forest, sleeping. But the moon made everything inside the school bright and shiny. The playground and playing field, the tiled roof of Teachers' House were all gleaming. Taking a breath of cold air, I stepped away from the Girls' Building. Now I, too, gleamed. My arms and legs were milky white. My nightie was the colour of rice pudding. The tassels of my shawl were as pale as feathers. The wind shook through my shawl making my shadow look like a girl with wings.

I walked like a winged creature, past Teachers' House with her clock seven minutes fast, in whose upper rooms Miss Otis slept next to a bedside table stacked with pictures of her nieces and nephews. I walked past the kennel where Sun lay chasing fleas in his sleep, past the flagpole that fluttered her Chinese and British flags and the playing field where even at night the grass grew.

I walked on and on, down the bank where Edith once fell

into Livingstone Stream. Here the moon was bright on the shining water. I followed the stream to the mouth of the tunnel. I sat there for a while and looked down the stream towards the Snake Hut. Its corrugated iron roof was all stripes in the moonlight. I thought of Twelve asleep inside.

Then I noticed that the tunnel was not dark as you might expect. There was a light coming from it. Warm, golden light. I took off my shoes. The plinking droplets shone, the feathery water shone. I climbed on to the sill and walked into the mouth of the mountain.

I waded towards the light. The dark tunnel was warmed by the glow. I did not feel afraid for I felt I once again belonged to the mountain, to the world that lay around the school. The smell of the tunnel, moss and rust, the light on the darting waters, it pulled me towards the pool. My legs were moving against my will. I should not go, I should stay by the school. But the light called me towards itself.

On I went, the water, smooth and fast around my ankles until I reached the mouth of the tunnel. With the mountain sloping up behind her and the tall, bowed trees, the Pool of Mothers was sheltered from the wind. There by the boulder was a fire, sending flickers and woody smells across the Pool of Mothers. Around it were small stones to keep the fire in, and around the fire were four sleeping men. I stood there and watched them, while above the trees whispered tree secrets, and the pool shone silver. They all wore the same uniforms, caps and boots. It was then I realised they were soldiers. They were in the shelter of our pool, and sleeping like little boys.

One of the soldiers called out in his sleep. Dreams darted under his eyelids like fish. The soldier turned over. On his sleeve there was a badge. It had the flag of the Rising Sun. Next to him was a gun. My mouth dried, my skin prickled. I turned and ran through the grass, pulled myself up on to the ledge and disappeared into the cool, dark, dank of the tunnel. I waded back to the school as quickly as I could, staggering, for my legs shook with shock. I had to get help.

Lowering myself down from the lip of the tunnel at the other side, I listened for soldiers, their calls, their feet wading through the water. All was silent. There might be just enough time to get help.

The wind began in strong gusts, burrowing into the trees, spiralling around the buildings. Across Drill Court I ran, towards Teachers' House. I banged on the door. It was locked. No one answered. The Girls' Building was locked. I ran back across Drill Court to the bell, which shook and tinkled. I had to raise the alarm. I grabbed its cord, and like the girl in the prospectus, pulled. I felt as if I was ringing the bell from the rafters of the world. I pulled it again and again but no one came for the wind whisked the ring into the ravines. The trees, the streams, the monastery bells above, the mountain – all was sound, ringing into the billowing night. I felt scared being so close to the ridge, my dress and shawl whipping around me. Perhaps I'd woken the soldiers; I had to hide. I shook the handles of the classrooms, they were locked too. I ran to Memorial Hall and the door pushed open.

I stalked past the flags, the batons and props boxes and walked into the centre of the stage, where I stood staring out at the blank, dark space ahead of me, then went to the window where the moon shone through. By the piano I sat and listened to the dark around me. Nothing stirred. The hymn book was propped up on the piano ready to be played. It was still open at last night's hymn.

How lovely are Thy dwellings, O Eternal Lord of hosts!
My soul is longing, fainting, for Thee, O living God.
Yea, the bird has found its home, built a nest to lay
her young;
O that I may find Thine altars, my Lord, my King, my God!

I turned the page and as I did so, my elbow played F sharp. 'Ssh,' I said. Then I heard a squeak. I spun on the piano stool. The sound came again.

'What's that?' I said into the darkness.

'Philip,' a small voice replied.

'Philip?' I said.

'Philip Hill,' the voice said. I could make out a shape a few paces ahead of me.

'Are you an angel?' he said.

'No, I'm not an angel,' I said, pulling my shawl around me. I walked towards the voice. My eyes began to get used to the dark. I felt for the top of the chair. My hand brushed against his head. His hair was soft and thin. I kneeled down beside him.

'But you have come to get me?' he said.

'I've come to . . .' I couldn't 'get' him. Where would I take him to? '. . . I've come to be with you,' I said. I decided not to tell him about the soldiers as it would be hard for him to run away with the chair. I put my hand on his head.

'If you're not an angel, what are you?'

'I'm just a child,' I said. 'Like you.' The boy started crying. His sobs were nearly silent. Every so often his back would buckle. I went to wipe his face with the edge of my shawl, but he turned his head away from me. 'There, there,' I said helplessly. Then I started to cry too. Silently. That is how you cry if you've ever been to Lushan School, and if you've ever run away from it. His teeth started chattering. He was cold under my touch. I got up and went to the stage. The boy shifted anxiously. 'Don't worry. I'm coming straight back.' I rummaged around at the back of the stage and found an enormous flag that was used for drill. It was as big as me.

Then, like an electric shock, the fear of soldiers flashed. I dashed to the main door where Memorial Hall's main light switch was. My heart was racing. I prayed a very fast prayer, 'DearGodPleasedon'tletmegetelectrifiedthankyouamen', and lowered the metal lever. The light fizzed on. There in the middle of the room was the boy stuck in the chair from Evening Prayers.

We stared at each other.

He was kneeling at his chair in a blue dressing gown, with blue pyjama bottoms showing underneath, just as in Evening Prayers. He was trapped around the neck, just as in Evening Prayers. His eyes were puffed up, his lip was a bluey-purple and his ears, which were splayed out because of the chair behind him, were bright red. Under his nose, there was clotted blood. His eyes blinked in the brightness of the light.

Then the light sizzled and went out. This sometimes happened when the wind was strong. We were in darkness once again.

'Are you still there?' Philip asked.

'I'm here,' I said, and went towards his voice. 'You're cold,' I said. I wrapped the flag around him. It was the Chinese flag, red with a blue corner. As I tucked it under his legs, I felt his knees. There was a little blood from scraping his knees on the floorboards. 'There, just like being tucked into bed. Just rest a while. I will stay with you.' I covered my legs in a bit of spare flag. We were quiet.

'I know who you are. They say you're very bad,' he said.

'Oh dear, do they?' I said.

'You ran away.'

'I didn't mean to. Would you like me to sing my happy song? The song I sing when I'm sad?'

'I don't think that I should.'

'I made it up all by myself and you'd be the fourth person in the world to hear it.'

'Um, no, thank you,' said the boy. We were silent for a while. I could feel his breath and his worry, then his head was heavy on my shoulder. He had fallen asleep.

So because I was sad at finding myself a bad girl, I whispered the song to myself anyway.

I shake my bum, shake-shake, wobble-wobble, just for fun,
Then I shake out my hair, shake-shake, like a snake,
And I stick out my tongue, poo-poo, to you,
And I shake my bum and my hair and my arms all at once,
And I kick my legs, left then right,
And I jump up and down with all my might,
Shake-shake, happy-happy, wobble-wobble goes my bum.

I sighed and bowed my head, curling my feet nearer to me. The song didn't work. It couldn't make you happy if you weren't jumping around, wobbling your bottom. Or maybe I was growing up. Maybe songs like that couldn't shake away a war, couldn't bring a mother close, couldn't wake a dead girl.

I awoke to the early morning birdsong and Miss Otis singing from the upper rooms of Teachers' House surrounded by her nieces and nephews. She sang the song of last night: '. . . How lovely are Thy dwellings, O Eternal Lord of hosts! My soul is longing, fainting, for Thee, O living God. Yea, the bird has found its home, built a nest to lay her young . . .' I looked around me. Memorial Hall was shuttered and empty. The boy and I were huddled under the big Chinese flag. He breathed raggedly by my side.

When I awoke again, I was shivering and stiff. My teeth began to chatter. The light was flooding in through the edges of the shutters. The big bell clanged three times, which meant the girls would be heading from their dormitories to the dining hall, where they would line up and sing 'Jehovah-Jireh is His name, He will provide', and they would eat porridge and bread and boiled eggs, and milky moustaches would be around their mouths and crumbs would be about the floor.

I sat with the boy. I would stay with him until God came to get us.

Then the door opened. I looked up. The lights buzzed on, crack, pop, sizzle, and there he was. Not God, but a Japanese soldier. He wore khaki, he had a gun, and when he saw me and Philip Hill he said, 'OOOOAAHHEE', at which another soldier, a thin man with a high-kneed run, burst through the door.

They marched over. The first one picked up the flag. To confiscate it, I think. But then – oh, China – he split it in two with one strong rip. The first soldier kneeled down to Philip. He made a soft growl at the back of his throat. Then he stood up and said something in Japanese.

'*Hai,*' said the thin one and ran off with more high-kneed steps. A few minutes later he came back with a saw. The first soldier took it, and sawed Philip Hill free. Once freed, Philip stayed exactly where he was. Only his eyes moved, looking right, looking left as though about to cross a busy Shanghai Street.

The soldier bent down, stern and close. 'Name?'

'Philip Hill,' said Philip.

'Phirrip Hirr. Stand up.'

Philip stood.

The soldier pointed at himself, 'Name: Nomata.'

I stood in front of Philip and curtsied. 'My name is Henrietta S. Robertson,' I said to Sergeant Nomata. 'Henrietta S. Robertson, at your service.'

'Henrietta S., go study,' said Sergeant Nomata, pointing to the door, his eyebrows stern. Then he strode over to the piano, opened the glossy lid and, still standing up, began to play 'Home Sweet Home'.

I grabbed Philip's hand and out of Memorial Hall we went. 'Home Sweet Home' plinked behind us. The air was laced with the smell of burnt toast from the dining room. It was a bright day, the sky blue and cloudless, one of Aunty Muriel's glorious days, but the glory had been interrupted. There were soldiers everywhere. Soldiers investigated drains, soldiers pulled cricket bats and quoits out of the games cupboard, soldiers armed with a glue-pot and brush stuck long labels to the back door of Teachers' House. Soldiers stood at the edge of the playing field, taking down the Chinese and British flags and hoisting in their place the red and white of the Rising Sun. A soldier rang the bell. It sounded out over the peaks, loud and clear, for the wind was calm today.

'Is it lunch?' asked Philip.

'No, Philip, the soldiers just wanted to hear the sound of our bell.' I tried to sound matter of fact but all the facts were changing. The flags, the time, who was in charge. There were Japanese labels everywhere, on the doors of the classrooms, on the bell, on a tea-chest that came out of Teachers' House. I was sure that, in a few minutes, there'd be one on the piano.

Where were all the adults? Where was Aunt Neb, Miss Preedy and Headmaster? Shouldn't they be doing something, putting the soldiers into place, telling them what was what? Then we saw Miss Otis. She was toddling across Drill Court in her moss-green dress.

'Let's find out where everyone is. Miss Otis will know,' I said, and tugged Philip after me, but we soon stopped when one of the men who'd been investigating the games cupboard yelled across Drill Court to Miss Otis. She went all frantic, all arms and legs, all mouth opening and eyes blinking. Then she stumbled and fell. While she patted the ground, trying to find her glasses, one of the soldiers came over. He put his foot on her glasses and flicked them out of her grasp. Miss Otis tried to reach her glasses. With a sharp, easy move, the soldier kicked them further away. She went after the glasses again, crawling on her hands and knees. It was like how you play with a dog. When the soldier had had enough, he pushed the glasses towards her, and walked off. Miss Otis put her glasses on, then went limping towards Teachers' House, two scuff marks on the front of her green dress.

The soldiers were all about. They did not talk, they shouted. They did not dally, nor look at the clouds, but ran in straight lines with eyes fixed straight ahead. These men, their boots drumming Drill Court, their weapons strapped to their sides. All this metal, all this *man* in the corners and corridors of our school. Our dorm aunties in their flimsy dresses, Mr Dalrymple and his flopping moustache, Headmaster in his tan brogues, these did not feel like protection.

I was about to turn back to the sort of safety of Memorial Hall when Latin verbs marched out of a classroom window. Then from another class, as if in reply, came French conjugations, and then from another the nine times table. The voices were bright and bold and they gave me the courage to pull Philip along.

'Come on, Philip,' I said. He was slow and sleepy in his pyjamas. I squeezed his hand, then pressed my fingernails into his palm, gently, for he had to be more awake. We mustn't toddle, we must march.

We passed along the windows of Teachers' House. Inside a group of the staff were stood in a line. They were being inspected by someone whom I could not see. There was Aunty Muriel, standing ten out of ten with her chin up. She shifted her gaze and saw me. I waved and pointed to Philip. She whitened and turned to face the person who was now shouting.

We walked around the edge of Teachers' House, and standing there at the bottom of the steps up to the laundry was a guard. I bowed my head like how I'd seen the soldier do to Sergeant Nomata.

I kept still. The soldier let us pass.

We climbed the steps to the laundry, and round the back to where the school was almost dug into the mountain, then up more stairs to the back entrance that led to the door with the sign 'Sick Bay' on it. I pushed the door open and we went inside. The cream curtains were closed and the bright day pressed through them. The room smelt sharply clean. It was white, with white beds and a green tiled floor.

All the beds were empty except for one. It was occupied by a big mound under the bed sheets, over which lay a fat pigtail of blond hair. I knew straight away who it was. It was Big Bum Eileen. As if the day could get any worse. Might as well run back down the stairs to the soldiers. But no, we were so tired, Philip and I. We'd go to sleep, we'd ignore her, we'd wait until Nurse Margaret came and told us what was going on.

'Get into bed,' I said to the boy, and I turned over the quilt of a bed in the far corner. Philip climbed up and slipped under the sheets. He made such a small mound, his head resting on the pillow, a little white face between two red ears. I stroked his hair three times, then I got into a bed next to him. The bed smelt of the laundry bubbles rising up, drifting into dreams. My eyes closed, a little puff of breath went through my lips. I was sliding into sleep.

I sat straight up. Philip was leaning over my pillow and tapping my cheek. 'She's been shot. That girl.' I looked over to where he pointed. Big Bum was on the move. She was going to the bathroom. There was blood on her nightdress.

'Get back into bed,' I said, and followed Big Bum. I didn't think she'd really been shot, but I could see it was serious.

I closed the bathroom door behind me. Now it was just the two of us, me and Big Bum Eileen who had a towel around her. 'Big Bum,' I said.

'Oh, it's you,' she said.

'What's happened?' I asked.

'Etta, go away. Leave me alone. For once and for all,' she said. She opened the door and shoo'd me out. I stood in Sick Bay a moment, shocked amongst the white beds, white walls. Then I felt the anger of a monster. You stupid bum. No. I would not be pushed away. I shoved the bathroom door and went back in.

'Have you been shot?' I asked loudly. I stared mean at her as she hunched over the sink, plunging her chapped hands in and out of the brown, soapy water.

'If you insist on coming in, close the door and grow up.'

I closed the door and snarled thoughts behind her.

She let out a sigh. 'I've become a woman,' she said.

I gasped. 'Oh, Eileen, how awful,' I said. And it was awful, not to be a girl any more. I didn't know how to console her. I moved by her side, and patted her bare shoulder. 'I'm so sorry.' Then I looked at Eileen to see how she'd changed. Woman Eileen's face was lumpy with crying, the skin under her eyes was the indigo shadow of a wide-awake night. She looked bad. I patted her bare shoulder again.

'You mustn't tell anyone.' She turned to me, fierce, and I could see that although I knew her secret that did not make us friends.

'Promise.'

Eileen put on a fresh nightdress with frilly collars and frilly cuffs, then settled on the small wooden cupboard. 'Aunty Muriel sent me here to get used to it. She thought it might be easier than being in school today. There were so many soldiers poking around.'

'They're everywhere.'

'Headmaster said at breakfast that we're not to worry, for they're not at war with us, just the Chinese. Although, they're saying the school building and all its property is the emperor's. Everything, every pot, every soap dish.'

'I saw them last night, sleeping at the Pool of Mothers,' I said.

Big Bum Eileen held my gaze. 'She's dead, Etta.'

'I know,' I said.

'They went looking for you for three days. Aunty Muriel was crying and crying.' I looked at her as she did up each of the tiny pearl buttons right up to the frilly collar. 'We're surprised they've let you back.' Eileen got up from the cupboard and went to the sink. She prodded the nightdress.

'Eileen, it wasn't fair for you to tell Aunty Muriel that it was just me that went to the tunnel.'

'We didn't tell anyone that.'

'Well, why didn't you all get into trouble then?'

'When they asked us if you'd ever talked about a tunnel, we said yes. And when they asked if you had talked about a Chinese friend, we said yes. And when they asked if this was your knife, we had to say, yes. You didn't expect us to lie, did you?'

'No,' I said. Then I imagined them in Teachers' House, standing in a line, nodding and giving Miss Preedy and the staff the story they already believed. 'But they think it was all me, and it wasn't,' I said.

'In a sense it was all you. I mean, if it hadn't been for you, none of this would have happened. You were the one that took us there, that tricked us into going to find mothers.'

'I saw the paintings of you all baptised.'

'So?'

'I think that's why you didn't say anything.'

'Why should we get into trouble when it was all your fault? It would never have happened without you.' The cleverest thing about Big Bum Eileen is how she makes you believe her even when it comes to matters of your own heart. I looked into my heart at that moment and I didn't know what to think of it. I felt bad for taking the girls there, and couldn't bear to think about Twelve. I didn't know what to do about it.

'You *are* a bit evil,' said Big Bum Eileen almost sadly as she prodded the nightdress under the soapy water. 'Not all of you, but there is a part that is. We've all been praying for you, and for the evil in you at Evening Prayers. Miss Preedy says it's girls like you that lead a flock astray.'

'All of you wanted to push the knife. I felt your hands pushing my hand down. If I'm evil, you're evil too,' I said.

The door edged open.

'Go away,' said Big Bum and I in unison. We carried on, Eileen speaking fast and first. 'That poor girl, and now Aunty Muriel. You should have seen Miss Preedy this morning. I don't think they want Aunty Muriel to look after our dormitory any more.'

Big Bum Eileen saw me sag a little, then she put her arm around me. 'Aunty Muriel's always found you exasperating,' she said. 'And now that you've shamed her, it's as if she hates you.' She spoke so gently, she stroked my hair.

I pictured Aunty Muriel's hands and words, from the night before, so careful, as though she feared she might cut herself on me. The whole world was falling apart. There was nowhere to put myself. Not in Memorial Hall, not in Sick Bay, not with the monks, not at the Pool of Mothers, not with Miss Kingsley, not under the gaze of Aunty Muriel. I felt like the sound of the bell ringing out over the peaks, chased by the wind from peak to gully to gorge, until I became no sound at all, just a small memory of sound, caught in the whorl of something much bigger, as it sped and dispersed itself across the mountain range.

'Etta,' said Philip, from the other side. 'There's a soldier here. I think he wants to count the bathroom.'

Big Bum and I looked at our shocked reflections in a mirror that was now Japanese, and then at Eileen's bloody nightdress soaking in the emperor's new ceramic sink.

A Visitor

THREE DAYS LATER AND I HAD RECOVERED FROM THE JOURNEY, but it seemed as if it was more convenient for the staff to keep me in Sick Bay. Other than Nurse Margaret, who opened and closed the curtains, and Amah Liu, who brought the food trays, shaking her head with the words, 'Naughty girl', there were no visitors until my third day.

My visitor did not come through the door, but up the drainpipe. The first thing I saw was a hand and then an arm, with an armband over a blue blazer, which hauled Nigel Pinsent into view. His hair was messy and his face was grinning. I got out of bed and opened the window. Nigel fell in a heap on the floor, then sprung to standing, hung his head out the window and gave a thumbs up. I looked down; there were the Sons of Thunder.

'Hello,' they called up.

'Hello,' I called down. They stared at me with a sort of wonder.

'Aren't you meant to be in class?' I said to Nigel, who was having a look around Sick Bay, opening cupboards, flicking through a book from the small bookcase before seeing my half-eaten breakfast on the tray at the end of my bed.

'No class this morning, just a big old Assembly. We're at war with Japan.' He took a bread crust from my breakfast plate. 'Staff are having a meeting. Aren't you going to eat this lot?' he asked.

I stood shy in my nightie and shook my head. Then, because my feet were cold on the green tiles, I sat on the bed and tucked them under the covers.

'You sick?' He sat down and began to eat the crusts.

'No, I'm feeling much better but they're keeping me in.'

'Well, it is infectious you know, bad influence,' he said, and leaning his head back laughed, his mouth full of crusts.

'I'm not infectious,' I said, arms crossed. I could push my legs down the bed and flip that tray on to the floor.

He quickly changed tone. 'You were away for over a week,' he said. 'Pretty impressive.'

'It wasn't all by choice. Fairy Glen bridge was blown up and I couldn't get back.'

'See any soldiers?' he asked.

'Oh, thousands of them,' I replied. 'Thousands of Japanese soldiers and thousands of Chinese too, marching along the plains. Everyone is on the run down there. Farmhouses all burnt. People living in makeshift camps.'

'I reckon we'll be put into a camp soon,' he said. 'Now that we're enemies.'

'Enemies?' I asked.

He continued, 'The Japs bombed Pearl Harbor, in Hawaii, then they sunk an American ship near Shanghai. Boom. It went down in one. So Americans and Brits are officially at war.' 'Officially at war' – I could see he and the boys had relished the phrase and repeated it over and over to each

233

other. 'Officially at war,' he said again, licking marmalade off his lips.

'Pearl Harbor,' I said. 'It sounds so beautiful.'

'Well, it wasn't after the Japs had been there. A surprise ambush last Sunday. That's why those Japs arrived at the beginning of the week. To keep an eye on us in case we're spies. You're not the only one being held captive.' He gestured to my Sick Bay cell. 'We're all prisoners now.'

He leant back on the bedstead. 'Reckon they'll want to round us all up with the other captives. Reckon they're going to use this place for their soldiers to recuperate.'

'But this is our school,' I said. 'They can't do that.'

'They're our new leaders. That's what Mr Dalrymple called them.' He sat forward. 'We can't play on Drill Court in the afternoons because that's where they do bayonet practice. Have you seen their swords? They've got sting-ray skin on their handles. First rate. I think the Japs will win.'

'Not against the Americans,' I said, and I thought of Mrs Charleston and Sarah in that beautiful land.

'The Japs are strong. They've got persistence.'

'I saw some sleeping, at the Pool of Mothers.'

'Where?'

'Oh, by the tunnel, there's a pool.'

'Where that girl died?'

I shifted uncomfortably.

'I saw her,' he said. 'Was on an errand for Mr Dalrymple, when he sent me over. Gardener Chen lets me in, you know, to see the snakes, help with things. He's not as fussy as the staff. People die, children die, every day in China. It's a fact of life, but the staff want to hide all of that from us. Just like they won't talk about what will happen now we're at war.' He stopped eating and began on a story. 'I was once bitten by a snake. My whole arm puffed up. Thought I'd die.'

'What happened?'

'Mother got some anti-venom and I went to the clinic and it was all okay. This was back home in Yunnan last summer. I think I'm going to be a doctor when I grow up. Or a vet.'

'Where is she now, the girl?' I asked.

'Well, none of us were allowed to play down there for a few days. We were all to stay on the Playing Field or Drill Court. In case anyone got ideas about running off, I guess, and to keep us from looking at what was happening down there. But we boys climbed one of the trees and we had a good view of things. We saw Gardener Chen digging a big hole.'

Then the bell rang and Nigel stood, stared at me giddily, shoved a crust in his mouth and disappeared down the drainpipe.

I sat there looking at the empty breakfast tray. There were so many new thoughts to take in. That we were officially at war with the Japanese, that Nigel, fast-crunching crusts, was, unofficially, my first visitor, and of the big hole being dug by Gardener Chen.

To Headmaster's Cottage

NOT LONG AFTER NIGEL HAD DISAPPEARED DOWN THE DRAINPIPE, Nurse Margaret arrived. Over her brown dress and brown cardigan, she wore an armband. It said B149. In her hand she had another armband with B243 on it, and one of my Sunday dresses. It was not a Sunday so I knew I was not going to church but rather that I was being led somewhere nearly as important as church and that I had to look presentable. I dressed in the bathroom and brushed my hair. For a moment, I thought Mother and Father might be here; perhaps that is why I had to look smart. Then I put the armband on and remembered that the world had changed and we were at war, officially.

The B and 2 and 4 and 3 were sewn to the black fabric in tiny, neat stitches. I imagined a Japanese mother leaning over it and stitching very carefully, so that her nation would be well represented, a bit like how our mothers did their best to have our name tags neat as possible, to give us a good start at school. I told this to Nurse Margaret when she came back, and she told me it was most likely sewn by a machine. It made me feel sad, not that it was sewn by a machine, but that

Nurse Margaret had not heard what I was really saying, which is what kindness there is in the things our mothers do.

Then Nurse Margaret led me out of Sick Bay, through the laundry and along Drill Court, where, as Nigel had said, a group of thirty Japanese soldiers practised bayonets, which involved wearing faceguards, running sideways towards each other and thrusting sharpened sticks. Their shouting echoed among the peaks and you could not hear the lessons from the school rooms.

Nurse Margaret led me across the school and up the steps to Headmaster's Cottage. From here Headmaster had a very good view. I looked at what he could see: a group of boys playing cricket in their sporting whites, watched by two resting soldiers; the Dormitory A girls under The Beard digging up worms and weeds as a soldier strode around the garden. Edith standing to attention as he examined her trowel.

Nurse Margaret called from a few steps above. 'Hurry up now, Etta. Stop dallying.'

I climbed up slowly. I dreaded what was coming. 'Will Big Bum Eileen be okay?' I asked.

'She'll be fine. And anyway, it's not nice to say the word "bum".'

Through the gate we went and up the stone-paved path. I'd never been inside the garden before, just watched Headmaster's wife from the rose bushes. Nurse Margaret rang the bell. It had a bright ping. The door opened. I wished I had someone's hand to hold. We went in.

The living room was small with a fire and brown corduroy-covered chairs. A woman stood by the fireplace. For a moment I thought it was Mother. Then the woman turned. It was Aunty Muriel, her shoulders curved forward, her face red with crying. She saw me, took a breath and looked away. Nurse Margaret left and Miss Preedy and Headmaster came in. He was a tall, gingery man who had a way of tapping all the furniture, as if he was ever listening to a brass band.

Headmaster closed the door, then crossed the room to stand by the mantelpiece. 'You've caused a lot of trouble.'

'It wasn't all me,' I said straight out.

'Henrietta, you broke the rules. You played out of bounds.' He tapped the mantelpiece.

'The others came too.'

'You ran away alone,' he said, drumming harder.

'Yes, but they were there with me at the tunnel, it's where we all went to play.'

'Henrietta, that is enough of your deceit,' said Headmaster. 'Have you considered the seriousness of what you have done? Playing out of bounds is always going to end in trouble. In this instance, it ended in a death.'

'It wasn't out of bounds for her,' I said.

'Don't answer back,' said Miss Preedy.

Headmaster continued, 'Being your friend meant that she strayed from the protection of her grandmother. And then to run away. Do you know the trouble you've caused? How selfish you've been?' He stepped towards me. 'Consider the others in your dormitory, consider the feelings of Aunty Muriel. The younger ones know a child died just yards from where they sleep. They had nightmares, because they knew that you were out there, hiding on the mountain. We have sent a letter to your parents telling them you are lost. We are hoping to have it intercepted before it leaves the Zhujiang mission home.' He glowered. 'And of course there is the matter of Mr Dalrymple.' He took the switch reed from the mantelpiece and handed it to Miss Preedy.

'Is there anything you want to say?' Miss Preedy asked.

'Sorry, Aunty Muriel,' I said.

Aunty Muriel turned her face to the window. Headmaster touched her shoulder and they left the room.

'Are you ready?' Miss Preedy asked.

'Yes, Miss Preedy.'

The beating began.

After a glass of water, Nurse Margaret then led me to the staff room at Teachers' House. 'The commandant said he'd like to see you. Don't worry. I'm standing here waiting for you.' I was not sure what protection Nurse Margaret would be. The guard outside the door let me in and there, standing behind the slouchy, comfortable chairs, sat the commandant. His shirt was crisp white and his cap had a star on it. The room was full of the smell of burning pines, and it was warm, for the fire was stacked with logs. There was a desk with two chairs and a lamp. Looking at them reminded me of the last time that I'd been in here, when I'd been interrogated by Miss Preedy.

A sergeant came in. He exchanged a few sentences with the commandant, who was taking long inhales of a cigarette. Then the sergeant spoke to me.

'What is your name?' he asked.

'Henrietta S. Robertson,' I said. I looked at the commandant and bowed my head. He flicked ash on to a dining-room plate.

Then the sergeant asked in Chinese, 'What is your name?'

'Ming-Mei,' I said in Chinese and, when he gave a dark look from his heavy eyebrows to the commandant, I explained in Chinese, 'Ming-Mei is my Chinese name. I do not have a Japanese name.'

'You speak Chinese,' the sergeant said. 'Do you have many Chinese friends?'

'I don't have any Chinese friends now.'

'Where were you on the twenty-ninth of November?'

'I was here,' I said. 'Then I left.'

'Why did you leave?'

'I did not like being at school.' The sergeant wrote that down.

'Do you know Mr Dalrymple?'

'Yes.'

'He is your friend?'

'He is my teacher.'

The commandant told the sergeant to ask me to sit down. I tried to sit at the chair but it was too painful. I got up again.

'Is there a problem?' he asked.

'I've been punished.' I replied in English for I did not know the Chinese for it.

'She's been punished,' the sergeant said to the commandant. The commandant wrinkled his face and snorted.

'You have done a bad thing?' asked the translator. The commandant watched me behind a cloud of smoke.

'I was punished because I ran away.'

The sergeant wrote that down in his notepad. He and the commandant seemed satisfied with my answer and I was asked to leave. I bowed to the translator, I bowed to the commandant, then hobbled out of the room.

Waiting outside the door was Nurse Margaret just as she'd promised. She did not take me back to Sick Bay but back to the dormitory. Drill Court was empty now, just the two of us walking along, slowly, for each step hurt.

'They asked me lots of questions,' I said as we went up the steps to the Girls' Building. 'I think they thought I was a spy.'

'They thought Mr Dalrymple was a spy because he was wandering all around the mountain. But he wasn't spying, he was looking for you. That's why they wanted to know your story, to see if you'd really run away.'

'I think they believed me when I couldn't sit down. Will they let him free now, Nurse Margaret?'

'Oh, I do hope so, Etta. We're all praying for it.'

When we were in the dormitory, Nurse Margaret said, 'Behave now, Etta, won't you?'

'Yes, Nurse Margaret,' I replied.

'Good. Miss Preedy will be here shortly.'

'What about Aunty Muriel?'

'She's busy with lots of organising. Miss Preedy will be looking after your dormitory for a while.'

I lay down and fell asleep to the cries of children at afternoon play. When I woke up, I went in the bathroom and there they all were, the girls, in a tight circle whispering. It looked like a measurement was going on, although no one was naked.

'You're back,' said Flo.

'Yes, I'm back.' I edged towards them. I wanted to walk confidently but I couldn't for I was so very sore. I winced. They were cautious around me, gentle even, but they kept their distance. They asked to hear my story, what had happened, and I told them about the bridge, the river, the girls' escape, though when I finished they were silent. A bigger drama was in the air.

'Aunty Muriel's gone,' said Edith. 'We're not sure where.'

'I think she's not allowed to look after us,' said Fiona.

'It's your fault, you and your running away,' said Kathryn.

'Miss Preedy thinks she can't keep us in control when you go off and do things like that.'

'Now they've taken her away.'

'Listen, everyone, don't get in a panic,' said Flo. 'I think it's as Miss Preedy says, that she's just helping with the housekeeping, which must be more difficult now there are Japanese soldiers around. They've taken over Teachers' House, and apparently they expect all their laundry to be done.'

It did sound plausible.

'And anyway, remember, Etta can't help behaving like that sometimes. She's got problems, an evil spirit or something.'

'We should try to forgive her,' said Hilary.

The girls made a circle around me. 'We forgive you for making Aunty Muriel leave,' they said. And by accepting their forgiveness, which I did by saying, 'Thank you,' I accepted that the blame was mine.

As we crossed Drill Court to the dining hall, the winter sky pleated with light, Philip Hill came running after me.

'Would you like this leaf? It's shaped like a half-moon.'

'Thank you,' I said, and turned my face away in case it cried, then hobbled after the others towards the light of the dining hall, where sitting in Aunty Muriel's place was Miss Preedy.

Although Aunty Muriel slept in the room next to ours, we were woken and sent to bed each night by Miss Preedy. We did see Aunty Muriel around the school, going up to the laundry, organising the games cupboard and making lists in the kitchen. She would always wave but then she moved on to her next task. Miss Preedy made less fine company, but when she talked about the Second Coming each night, it struck me that this might not be a result of her religious fervour, but because she was a bore. It made me a little sad even to see how Big Bum Eileen rolled her eyes as Miss Preedy sat in Aunty Muriel's chair, her cardigan sleeves draped over her shoulder, talking about the different ways Jesus might appear. I did my best to keep out of her way, to nod and laugh when the other girls did. They did not speak to me, not even Flo, and I was swept up in my own thoughts. I wanted to know what happened to Twelve, to say goodbye to her in some way, but I dared not ask. I thought about it all day, where she might be and if there were any ways to return her. I read the bit where Jesus heals the girl with the words, 'Arise and walk.' I longed to say it over her grave, but I had the feeling it might work no better than singing my happy song, and that frightened me. I preferred a world where Jesus parted the sea, opened blind eyes or, as Miss Preedy nightly suggested, might at any moment appear angel-thronged over Lushan.

The Portrait

A WEEK AFTER MY PUNISHMENT, DURING PLAYTIME, I WAS SITTING alone in the garden, by The Beard, pulling dead roses from the bushes and thinking about these things, when I felt someone stand behind me. I turned around sharp. It was Aunty Muriel. She had her jacket and walking boots on and around her shoulder was a bag.

'I thought I might find you here,' she said. Her eyes were bright. 'How are you getting on?' she asked as she knelt beside me.

'All right.' I rubbed the old petals in my hands. There was not much more to say.

'Etta, I promised that I'd paint your portrait and I'd very much like to do that before we leave. Shall we do that this afternoon?'

'What was the game you played here?'

'Looking for mothers,' I replied.

Aunty Muriel stood barefoot on the bank, her feet white as alabaster from the cold water wade through the tunnel. She looked up to the trees that surrounded the Pool of Mothers. Leaves were beginning to fall. The ground was russet with pine needles.

'We always put our plimsolls on here, Aunty Muriel,' I said.

'Yes,' she said, almost to herself. Then she fixed her eyes on me. 'Sit there, on that rock. Sit very still.' I did what Aunty Muriel said while she put on her plimsolls and undid the clasp of her satchel. She brought out her watercolours, her paper and a little jam jar which she filled with water from the pool. She dipped her paintbrush into the jar and swirled it over a square of colour. Then she watched me. She saw me breathe, she saw me blink, she saw my gaze wander to the surface of the pool and back to my hands clenched in my lap. I felt a funny feeling open up in me. That her gaze held me. That I was not a ghost, but seen. She began to paint my portrait.

We did not see Aunty Muriel for another few days until the Saturday afternoon when we returned to the dormitory to do chores and there she was, inspecting our beds. 'Heavens above, Edith, this barely constitutes a hospital corner. Four out of ten.'

We ran around her. 'Are you back, Aunty Muriel?'

She did not answer but tugged the sheet on Hilary's bed, 'Hilary, that's three out of ten for you.' She kept her chin high and walked around the bunks, tutting and tugging. We were full of thrill. When she'd finished the inspection, for which I received four and a half, she said, 'You girls look pallid. Boots on, please. Hats and gloves.'

We put on our winter boots, hats and gloves and followed along the balcony after her.

She was walking fast across Drill Court and white clouds of steam were coming out of her mouth when Miss Preedy came over. 'Muriel.'

'Yes, Miss Preedy,' said Aunty Muriel, spinning round.

'Where are you all off to?' Miss Preedy was smiling her teeth at us.

'We are going on a brisk walk. I think these girls have spent too much time indoors. It's not healthy.'

'Do you think that's wise, Muriel, with the soldiers?'

'I've spoken with the commandant and he's arranged for a guard to come with us.' And there we saw at the other end of Drill Court, by the flagpole, a young soldier, with a bayonet and rifle, a kitbag, a canteen, a holster and a cigarette.

'Well, I do think I might come on this walk with you,' said Miss Preedy.

'It's going to be a steep walk,' Aunty Muriel replied. 'But you are welcome if you don't mind the exercise.'

We followed this new Aunty Muriel up through the forest. The Japanese guard followed us, rifle slung around his shoulder, watching the trees carefully. We climbed up the bank at the back of the laundry, up towards the temple. There we walked around the pagoda and along a row of shacks.

'I've been on several walks to this temple,' said Aunty Muriel, stopping outside the last shack. 'The monks, some of whom I got to know, have gone, and the few lay people who lived here returned to their villages. But at one point many people lived here.' I sensed that Aunty Muriel's walk was not just for the benefit of our pallid faces but a walk for the burnishing of our souls. The girls looked worried.

'I'm getting cold,' said Big Bum Eileen.

'Well, if that's the case perhaps Miss Preedy will take you back,' said Aunty Muriel.

'Shouldn't we all return?' said Miss Preedy.

'No, it's all right,' said Big Bum Eileen. 'I'd rather we stayed together.'

'In this hut lived an old lady, and her granddaughter,' Aunty Muriel said. She lowered her head and stepped through the small doorway. We followed, each one in turn, putting our head in, smelling, looking. This was our daughter's home. We all knew it. It was a small, low room, perhaps even smaller than a tree house. There were pots and a kettle, a scythe and in the corner a paper stove god to watch the lives of the family, noting the good and the bad for his yearly report to Heaven. Aunty Muriel watched our faces. There was no knot in her forehead, for this was a different kind of watching. Everyone kept their feelings close as a breath.

Then Aunty Muriel took us along a path that led out of the temple grounds and into the forest. Many smaller paths led from it, down either side of the slope, and I was suddenly worried that Aunty Muriel might choose one that led us down to the Pool of Mothers. I could see the girls were afraid of that, too, for they were looking sideways at each other, their eyes saying, 'Keep quiet.' But Aunty Muriel did not take that turning, and instead we walked on through the forest, which crunched underneath our feet, tiny crystals on grass, the brown and red leaves, the grey, leafless branches above.

On we went. 'Stay next to me,' said Aunty Muriel, taking my hand. The girls all had to stop in the clearing, and wait for me to catch up. I was slower than even Miss Preedy. 'This way, girls,' said Aunty Muriel. We headed down the hill to the school by a new path, and when we came out in the school grounds, we were down by the stream. It bubbled with white cold water.

'Muriel, do you think this wise?' asked Miss Preedy as she huffed and puffed out of the forest and on to school grounds.

'I do,' said Aunty Muriel firmly.

We walked along the stream, towards the tunnel for a minute or so. And there we paused.

There was fresh soil heaped over in a barrel-shaped mound. We were at a grave. There was no headstone, just a small brown bush.

A mist drifted down over the trees. This wasn't a normal Saturday outing. We had come to visit our daughter's grave. They'd buried her outside the boundaries of the school. I thought of her down there, all alone, deep in the soil, far away.

'This, girls, is the grave of Twelve, or as her grandmother called her, Shi'Er. They lived in a little hut in the temple grounds. The girl's grandmother left along with the people of the temple and the villages. We do not know where she is now. What we do know is that she was not able to take Shi'Er with her.'

The girls looked at each other, moving from foot to foot with cold and unease.

'It's terribly chilly, Muriel. I think the girls and this poor chap would be happier indoors, with a cup of tea,' said Miss Preedy.

'I think they might like to spend a moment with her in prayer, wouldn't you, girls?'

'Yes, Aunty Muriel,' the girls said, for you cannot refuse a moment of prayer, no matter how inconvenient to the spirit.

Aunty Muriel began to pray, her arms lifted up towards the mist-shrouded trees. We closed our eyes. 'Lord God on High, you know our hearts, you have searched us and know our ways.' She paused. I opened my eyes. Aunty Muriel was watching Big Bum Eileen. I closed my eyes. 'We pray for this child, Shi'Er, a little girl who liked to play by the stream. We ask that you protect her soul as it passes through into the

248

next life. We know that in the Father's house there is room for many souls. We pray for her grandmother, who has lost her dear grandchild.'

I heard the gasps and sobs of the girls, and opened my eyes. I watched their snot and sadness and saw that Aunty Muriel was also watching them. We both looked at each other. Aunty Muriel knew that the girls had all known Twelve, and had played their part in what had happened to her. She was as clever as Solomon.

Miss Preedy picked up the prayer. 'These young Christians are in our custody. Grant wisdom and the knowledge of how best to administer your authority. And I pray in particular for your servant Muriel. Amen.' It was a prayer that she'd hoped would put her back in charge but it was too late for that.

'Amen,' said Aunty Muriel and the girls of Dormitory A.

When everyone had raised their heads, Aunty Muriel spoke. 'Girls, do you see that brown bush?' The girls dabbed their eyes with their tissues and stepped closer to look at the few twigs over the grave. 'Well it's an azalea bush and it will grow and, in Spring, it will flower white.' The mist swooped around us, holy and fast, and we were hidden from ourselves, from each other, and from the grave. The bank by the stream had become another of the mountain's thin places.

There is a wound up on the mountain. But still the stream flows, still the mists come. Vines grow. Azaleas bud. There is a wound upon the mountain. You can see it in the shapes of pines, of rocks. It is a voice saying, Little Girl Rise Up. A voice unanswered but by the sound of the stream, the call of a mountain bird.

Leaving Lushan

THE SECOND COMING HADN'T QUITE COME, BUT THE JAPANESE HAD. All of that week our school was folded away with the briskness of laundry ladies at the end of the drying day. Stripping the beds gave our leaving that end-of-term feeling. But it wasn't to our parents that we travelled. We were going to an internment camp in the direction of Shanghai. This was communicated to us first in whispers from oldest to youngest, then in assembly. Holiday suitcases came out. There were only two days to pack. 'Just the necessities, girls,' called Aunty Muriel as she sailed through the dormitory with a pile of towels. After the trip to the temple and the grave, Aunty Muriel was fully returned to us, as Miss Preedy was now very busy with preparing for our departure. We had to put what we could into our suitcases, making sure to include a nightdress, a handkerchief and a change of clothes. We left many things. Blankets, jackets, stamp collections, precious buttons, summer hats. I pressed two flowers from the Girls' Building among the Psalms. Philip Hill's half-moon leaf I placed safely inside an epistle.

On the last evening, I slipped down West Steps, across the

bridge towards the stream but it was not possible to run across the bridge, for the Japanese had cordoned this area off for military exercise. I was not able to go to her grave, to say goodbye, to look at the azalea bush of which Aunty Muriel had said, 'It will bloom.'

That night, I lay in bed and smelt the hand-me-down smell of the children before me. I wondered when we'd come back, how long we would be away. When next I would see the stripe of moon through Edith's open curtain, the pagoda pointing into the night. I lay listening to the wind fling herself at the peaks. Then it began to rain and the smell of the forest came inside. The pines, the ferns, the earth. I lay there and imagined myself walking amongst the swaying trees. Then down towards the rushing stream, to the grave, where I sat for a while with the child buried there.

Muriel's Diary

22 December 1941

THIS MORNING WE WILL LEAVE LUSHAN. EVERYTHING HAS BEEN packed and while we wait for orders to go, I wanted to sit for a moment in my little room. The bed is stripped, the paintings unpegged from the string across the wall, all that is left to place in my knapsack is this, my diary. The gold embossed 'Missionary's Diary' is nearly faded now. We are told that the keeping of diaries will not be permitted in the camp. It may be that I do not write for a while. I might leave my diary here. We all have to leave things behind. I passed some of Aunt Neb's boys, who'd started a small fire and were burning their letters from home. Perhaps I shall put this on their fire too. I am tempted. To watch the flames lick up the pages, to watch words blacken, crisp and disappear, for I leave Lushan feeling I have failed somewhat.

Looking out for the last time, I can see the balcony of our building and beyond that the fractured peaks, the gullies awash with shadow. The mountain, the monks say, is where you may glimpse your immortal self. The part of you that lives beyond time, that was you before you were made in your mother's womb. 'The mountain is you,' the monk said to me, all those months ago when we met at the waterfall. I walked these peaks on my searches for Etta, sending prayers out into the ravines that she might be returned. And after she was and I fully felt my failure, I weaved endlessly through the forest, trying to find a path back to myself. Still, I cannot say I have seen my soul. But in the act of listening, of waiting amongst the rocks and mist, I felt my insignificance. I felt witnessed by something I could not name.

Packing everything yesterday, I looked again at my sketches and watercolours, choosing what to keep, what to leave here. All these hours of looking. Trying to see things as they are, not as I so easily suppose them to be. When painting Etta's portrait, what I saw was a child who thought she was very bad, even wicked. But when she sat there, I painted a sad girl, lost and desperately searching. After I finished I asked her if she would like to see the portrait. She shook her head for she could not look at herself, and back through the tunnel we went.

Today is a bright, clear day. Today there is no mist. The peaks are sparkling in this pale winter sun. That is the bell. It is time to go.

Exodus

Accompanied by Japanese guards, all the children and teachers filed past the Girls' Building, past The Beard and our dormitory garden, past the foundation stone, 'Lushan School, To the Glory of God, 1892', across Drill Court and past the flagpole that now waved a great red sun.

Each of us older girls were to help the little ones. I held hands with Elspeth West from Peking. She had red plaits and skipped. But we had to walk in a straight line, and a soldier soon reprimanded her. They were stricter than dorm aunties, although a dorm aunty could get you to shift-along-chop-chop without a pistol.

Headmaster and Miss Preedy were at the front. Headmaster's wife had suffered a setback. The Japanese had come and she had stopped her morning strolls down the steps and along Drill Court. Instead she had retreated to the cottage. We weren't sure what it was, perhaps the shock of seeing soldiers marching all over the school. The Japanese allowed her to be carried by a group of the older boys on a makeshift mountain chair.

Lining the path at the bottom of the Great Steps were

mountain-chair men, some of our laundry ladies and even Gardener Chen, all of whom had been rounded up to jeer and to spit. The Japanese guards urged them on with bayonets. We were to leave humiliated.

As they booed and hissed, Elspeth West skipped no more but clung to my arm, afraid, as we all were. Sensing this fear, Aunt Neb made up a song of praise on the spot, and it fed down the line until all were singing it. We walked singing, past the pines, Ink Pot, Monkey, past the Boiling House, and Baboon Corner. Every so often, as I paused to wait for Elspeth I would listen to the mountain, for the strange creeping of its immortal soul, that child hiding behind the trees. But this time, I heard no such being.

On we went. Over the slippery rocks. Over the newly strung bridge at Fairy Glen drop. At Three Falls there was a man dead in a hammock, flies buzzing about his open mouth. 'Don't look,' I said to Elspeth. We kept on walking and I thought of the line of ants across the map of China at my parents' house. We were a pilgrim people with small suitcases. Above us, over the Western Canyon, clouds as big as palaces swayed past. The wind swirled through the pines. Shadows galloped through the gullies. Everything was in migration.

For three days we travelled. First, in a parade down the mountain, then on an old livestock boat where we were packed into the gut of the ship, windowless and with rats that ran over our hair as we slept, a whole school head to toe, in the groaning wooden hold. There, we lay, ate sandwiches and learnt to count in Japanese. 'No point lying about like sardines,' said Mr Dalrymple, and he wrote the numbers on the wooden sides of the hold with the lump of chalk he carried in his pocket. '*Ich, ni, san, chi,*' we counted as a tug pulled the boat east. China floated outside; paddy fields, bombed bridges, burnt towns, though we could only hear her as a series of underwater groans. At Luichow we disembarked and got into a convoy of Japanese army trucks for a day-long journey along potholed roads.

It was late afternoon when the truck rattled to a stop. There was a whine of brakes, a hiss of carburettor and much steam. The door of the front cab slammed shut and the tailgate clattered open. There stood a soldier with rifle and bayonet. We watched as the bayonet motioned at us to dismount, the blade pointing first at us, then to the road. When we did not move, the bayonet motioned again, accompanied by shrieks in Japanese. We looked to Nurse Margaret and Aunty Muriel, who had now stood, and at their say-so we scrambled out and down on to the yellow clay road. The soldier stopped screaming and we huddled there at the roadside. Before us was a vast sprawl of brown fields, empty except for clusters of white gravestones, and behind us a grey brick wall with a great black gate. The gate was the size of a Lushan pine, and bore two signs, one in English and Chinese that read 'The American Presbyterian HQ' and one in English and Japanese that said 'Tsitao Civilian Centre'. The wall was topped with rolls of barbed wire and a bamboo watchtower in which a soldier sat with a rifle trained upon us.

The remaining four lorries lurched to a halt, and the staff and children came spilling out. Headmaster's wife was carried out last on a stretcher. Petrol dripped from one of the engines and the stench made me retch. There was a howl of metal. The gates were pushed open. We peered through the entrance to see our new home. There were lines of huts, and a large stone building in a European style in the middle with an exercise yard in front.

Now more soldiers began to shout in Japanese, their bayonets pointing us forward. Through the towering gateway we walked. From the shadows of their wooden huts, other prisoners watched as we dragged our suitcases and bedrolls into the courtyard. I wondered what they'd think of us. Dirt on our skirts and under our fingernails, stockings drooping, our mouths agape, the adults with their greasy hair and sweat patches. I noticed, however, that despite her exhaustion, Aunty Muriel stood straight as a flagpole.

Six guards ordered us to line up. Although they spoke in Japanese this time we understood. When they shouted, it was as if they wished to shatter us with sound. The crackle stayed in the air long after they'd spoken. Standing in line, our bundles at our feet, we looked up for the first time at the Commandant's Quarters, a building of grey stone. It was a solid building, impressive in contrast to the ramshackle huts that clustered around it.

My legs ached. My tummy cramped with hunger. And I was not the only one. After ten minutes, the line fidgeted, shifted, turned and in some cases sat.

'Stand straight!' a guard shouted again.

After we were counted in Japanese, a guard ran up and down the line to make sure everyone was standing properly to attention. Suddenly a door on the balcony swung open, and the commandant, a short man with a crisp white shirt and a black uniform, stepped lightly out and on to a crate. Through a translator, he welcomed us to Tsitao Civilian Centre. He was a man of many words, but the translator was not. We were crisply told that the Tsitao Civilian Centre was to be our home and that if we were polite and respectful of the rules and cordial to each other we would be happy. The commandant gave a nod of the head. The translator pointed to the gates that were still open and informed us that should we attempt to escape we would be shot. Then he and the commandant returned into the shuttered room and the balcony was once again empty.

An English man with a full beard, shorts and clogs came over to the staff, shook each by the hand and unrolled a scroll of paper. The staff watched as his hand pointed to different parts of the paper, then at huts, the outhouses, the exercise yard. While this was going on we children were taken over to Kitchen One to be given a cup of tea, led by a woman called Gladys Wicks. She had platinum-blond hair and eyebrows so thin, they looked like they'd been drawn on with a pencil. 'They have,' said Big Bum Eileen who had gone close up. 'Just like a film star.'

We watched her for other signs of glamour but I was surprised when this Gladys Wicks stood behind an urn and ladled tea into metal cups herself.

We sipped the watery tea, looking at the *ko*, the great iron cauldrons from which all our meals would come, each the size of a paddling pool, filled with rice gruel. Then there was an almighty shriek of metal. We all turned round to see the great black gates of the Tsitao Civilian Centre screech closed. I watched China, her brown fields dotted with gravestones, narrow until all I could see was gate and a distance cut short.

Part III

The Camp

Six Months Later

IT WAS LATE AFTERNOON AND WE WERE SAT IN THE DOORWAY OF Hut 221. 'Now what?' said Big Bum Eileen. Because the girls thought that I'd been tending Headmaster's wife for some days now, I had to pretend I'd done this before. 'After I've sat here, I usually go inside the hut, and sing to her or feed her, or just hold her hand. But before we go in, someone needs to volunteer to keep look out. Headmaster might come back early from the Camp Committee meeting.'

Hilary went to the corner of the alley and Main Street. When she gave a thumbs up, I dipped inside the hut. There on the camp bed lay Headmaster's wife covered in her lemony blanket. Her skin was the lightest yellow and her lips tea-cup white.

'Come in,' I said with a wave of my hand. One by one Flo, Big Bum Eileen, Edith, Isobel, Fiona and Kathryn entered the room.

'You sit on that side of the bed and I'll sit in my usual old spot, here.' We knelt on the floor and sat in silence, noting the stale air, the window covered with a patchwork of tea towels, Headmaster's jacket hanging from a nail on the wall, the upturned crate with the two tin plates, two tin mugs, two tin spoons, and family photograph that showed Mabel and Vincent as children next to a mother that could walk.

What could we do next? I wanted the girls to feel visiting Headmaster's wife was worth the risk.

'They call her Jenny,' I said. It was a quiet name for someone whom we had placed in the realms of Gabriel. We watched Jenny. She looked very different from the Headmaster's wife who had prayed for our safety on the hillside. Her skin was yellow, her throat was arched and her jaw hung wide open. I wondered if she still prayed for us. I leant close to hear her breath and see if any prayers were upon it. Her grey-pink tongue flicked out on to her lips. So near, this tongue was meaty and alive. I felt a creeping revulsion and sat back. Then I realised: Jenny was thirsty.

We had to help. I looked around for water, but I could see none. I'd remember that next time. 'Let's plump her pillow a bit,' I said, trying to sound as if this was my daily duty. Afraid to wake her, but wanting to lessen the awkward angle of her pale neck, I carefully reached for the pillow, which was really just some rags in a pillow case and began to move it. When she looked more comfortable, I felt a flash of accomplishment, and stayed close until I was sure she breathed more easily.

'Does she still sing?' asked Edith.

'Sometimes. But her throat is too dry today,' I said. 'In fact, it's probably better that today, we sing for her.

'Flo, you've got the nicest voice, so you start,' I said. 'But not too loud.'

'Do "Great is thy faithfulness",' said Edith, and I nodded in agreement because this was the hymn that had drawn me to that hut on the day I discovered her.

Flo rolled her eyes but began, her once-soaring voice now crackled with exhaustion. '"Great is thy faithfulness—"'

Headmaster's wife's eyelids twitched.

'Keep singing!' said Big Bum Eileen.

'"All I have needed, thy hand hath provided . . ."'

Headmaster's wife opened her eyes. 'Mabel,' she said, reaching her hand towards Flo's face, 'oh, Mabel, you're here.'

'Yes,' I said. 'It's Mabel.'

'No, it's not,' Flo hissed over the mattress but it was too late.

'My darling girl,' said Headmaster's wife.

'Say hello back,' said Kathryn.

'Hello, Mum,' said Flo.

Headmaster's wife stroked Flo's face, her fingers holy white, 'Mabel, my sweet girl, I've been praying and now you're here.'

Hilary appeared at the door, breathless. 'He's here, Headmaster!' She tipped her head out of the room for another look. 'Quick! He's coming down the alley ever so fast in those clogs.'

'Etta, if we get caught, I will never go along with your silly ideas again,' said Big Bum Eileen.

'Through the window,' I said. 'Quick.'

'Just getting some water,' we whispered as we climbed out, leaving pale Jenny behind, her hand raised, touching not the face of a girl, but air. And there in the alley, among the old bricks and scorched stoves we crouched, in case our running down the alley drew any more attention.

The room echoed with wooden footsteps and there was a drumming of fingers on the back of the chair. Both confirmed it was Headmaster. Then he spoke. 'Jenny, darling, whatever is the matter? Here, I've brought some water.'

'Don't worry, Mabel's just gone to get me a drink.'

'Darling, Mabel is in London, doing the typist course. She's staying in Wimbledon with Uncle Wally. Don't you remember?'

'She was here, Edward, then she slipped out the window.'

'Oh, darling, no one slipped out the window. See.' At the sound of Headmaster's approaching clogs, we ran from Hut 221, pumping our arms and legs, kicking up dust, toppling over a pile of bricks, ducking under rows of sun-baked laundry, crying, 'Run, run!'

A Year Later, 20 August 1943

Everyone had a chore. Philip cleaned pots while squatting inside them, Elspeth unpegged sheets she could barely reach, Nigel got taut and stringy from stoking the fire for water boiling. It was mid-afternoon and I was returning from scrubbing in the laundry. The sky sat close above the camp, a dusty yellow sky, scuffed with raggy clouds. From the wall the barbed wire cast long shadows that scored the ground with vast hoops. I leapt across them.

Skip, skip, do not touch the black lines.

As I skipped, I played a food game, announcing a favourite dish on each step – Custard! Dumplings! – and soon found myself, breathless, at the end of the wall. Here I reached out to touch the brick. It was dusty and surprisingly warm, like a mule's flank. I heard the thwack of a soldier's boots, and stepped back on to the cinder path. Why was I playing so stupidly close to the wall? What if they thought I was a black-market trader, waiting for a peasant to lower eggs over the wall? I put my head down and went steadily along the path, a rhythm I'd learnt did not attract the attention of the soldiers. Brisk spurts, sudden stops, these were what made them come and investigate, but the steady tramp of my boys' brogues caused no alarm. At the top of Main Street, I turned to see which of the guards was behind me. It was Private Tanaka, dressed in khaki, his sword tapping the cinder track. He stopped at the gate in the wall that led to the Japanese quarters, checking with a kick to see if it was locked. I ducked into Main Street and hoped he had not seen me wandering aimlessly once again.

Main Street was wide and led down the centre of the camp. On each side were huts where families lived, two to a hut, White Russians, diplomats and East India Company executives separated only by a sheet. Between the huts, washing hung from twine. Today there was a green tea dress, a dinner jacket and a cassock.

The camp was such a different place from Lushan. You could wander the perimeters in twenty minutes. There were few trees, no streams and, except for the sparrows, the rats and the bedbugs that nightly sucked our blood, the camp was without wildlife. But it was wonderful and mysterious to me, for the camp was full of adults, and not just the sort of adults that I was used to. There were business ladies that smoked, a Bulgarian crook, Shanghai wives asleep under fox furs, and Father Pilson, the Dutch priest who ran the black market, gathering up contraband in his cassock. But best of all, there was Gladys.

I waved at old Mr Kennedy, with his white linen suit and long, soft ears. He was sitting outside his hut, chessboard set up, kings, queens, pawns, waiting for someone to sit down and talk. Often that person would be me, but today I had to get to Gladys, so when he called out, 'Good for a game, Etta?' I said, 'Tomorrow, Mr Kennedy,' gave him a queenly wave and kept walking, thump, thumping my boys' brogues down Main Street towards the Ladies' Building.

I shouldn't have been wandering there. Chores were over and it was prep time, and I should have been on the other side of the camp, in the dormitory writing out algebra equations or in the Recreation Hut practising Mozart under the despairing gaze of Miss Otis, or attending Mr Dalrymple's Bible class, preparing for a life of mission grounded in the journeys of Paul. The staff had been quick to recreate the school at camp. We did a class in the morning and a class in the afternoon, with further lessons delivered by members of camp, who were mostly rounded up by Aunty Muriel, whose poise and rolling rr's made them feel called to the task: 'You read History at Cambridge, Mr Briscoe? Well, we'd certainly like you to come and share your research . . .' We wrote our answers on can labels and waxy toilet paper, x = sugar, plums and setting agent, the woes of Job shall never be wiped away. Our dormitory buildings were on the other side of camp, and sometimes I wondered if our classes were partly a way to organise time, and partly to keep us Christian. Most children did stay away from the more worldly internees, but I could not, for I wanted to know all about them.

I arrived at the Ladies' Building, a drab block, and the highest in the camp. I went up the three flights of stairs and hopped into the top-floor dormitory. Here were curlers, mascara and women on their beds fanning themselves with copies of *Reader's Digest*. Stockings hung from the low rafters, the tan feet waltzing in a breeze from a window.

A fight was going on between Moira Budd and Mrs

Mullory. The Welsh lady, Nan Brown, leapt in saying, 'She's right, shut the window, or else it will be another night of mosquitoes,' while another called out, 'Fight! Fight.' This didn't interest me; what did was at the far end of the dormitory, where, under the dormitory's only mosquito net lay Miss Gladys Wicks, like a princess about to be drowned.

Her bed smelt of orange blossom and sweat. She lay there in exquisite stillness, her blond hair plaited and oiled, each eye covered by a slice of withering cucumber. I wasn't sure if I should talk to her when she had the cucumbers on, so I sat there for a while. Although there was a cucumber on each eye, I knew that she wasn't asleep, for when I sat down, she drew her lips into a pout. I also knew she wouldn't mind being looked at, for Gladys had been a singer in Shanghai and she liked an audience. 'Singing is also a visual art,' she said once, raising her plucked eyebrows, and although she wore a pink silk scarf around her neck to protect her vocal cords, I never once heard her sing.

I watched the cucumbers, the dark green skin, the pale green middle, the fleshy seeds. I hadn't seen fresh vegetables for a few months now. We'd tried to make a dormitory garden and grow tomatoes but they'd kept being stolen, and then water became sparse and our garden was no longer a necessity. Perhaps the cucumber came from the black market. Or perhaps from one of her admirers. Then it happened again: I began to cough, bent over, an ugly rasp in my throat.

Gladys took the cucumbers off and propped herself on to her elbows. 'Hey, kiddo, don't go coughing on me. You better get your aunt to see to that. And to that skirt. It's halfway up your knickers; you'll be wolf-whistled all around this camp.'

'Yes, Miss,' I said. The dress was one that Aunty Muriel

had stitched for me in the early months of camp. She'd made it from an old curtain and there was plenty of what she called 'grow' in the hem. I wasn't sure what wolf-whistled meant, but it sounded tiresome, judging by the way Gladys rolled her eyes. I felt into my pocket for the soft, squidgy lump I'd brought for Gladys. I knew she wouldn't part with the *Reader's Digest*, but perhaps she'd reward me with something else, a hairpin, or a few moments with the nurse's watch, one of the few watches never found and confiscated, pinned to my dress.

I brought out the ball of soap.

'Good girl,' she said. The uncucumbered eyes of Gladys Wicks narrowed with pleasure, for soap was precious as gold. We only got one bar the size of a matchbox each month for our clothes and one for our bodies. My job in the laundry meant that I could sometimes make soap balls by sifting around in the honking, cloudy water for little lumps of the stuff, which, over a couple of weeks, I'd squeeze into the ball the size of an imperial ruby for Gladys.

Gladys took the jewel of soap in her pink fingers, fiddled down her brassiere for a bit and then brought out a tiny, silver key. Swinging over the camp bed, she slid out a red tin box from underneath, and opened its lock with a smooth click. The soap was put in and out came a *Reader's Digest*. Even though Aunty Muriel had dismissed its educational value, saying, 'It is unfortunate that the *Reader's Digest* only calls on a vocabulary of six hundred words,' I had gorged on each edition. The cover of this *Reader's Digest* was glossy, bright, with corners crisp and uncurled. 'It's new!' I said.

Gladys opened the mosquito net and I climbed in. 'Sure is!' she replied as I began to flick through the adverts. Nescafé, Tate & Lyle. Gladys stroked the cover of it with a fingernail.

'Tom Briscoe brought it for me.' Her voice went oozy as Bournville.

'Tom Briscoe,' I replied with the zeal I mostly used for imagining food. Tom Briscoe, according to the women of the Ladies' Building, was the most handsome man in camp. And he'd been here to visit Gladys!

I leant forward. 'And, Miss Wicks, what did you give him?'

'Give him? Give him?' Every time she said 'Give him' Gladys's laugh got louder, and she said it many times. Soon she was howling. The women came towards the bed for Gladys was flat out on it, laughing so hard, I worried she might tear the mosquito net. 'She wants to know what I gave him.'

The women made ooos and aahs, swapping smirks, clucks and flashes of dimple. Here was a joke I knew had a whiff of something worldly, more than a whiff, in fact. I was sure Aunty Muriel would not laugh. I was sure she'd make them clean their mouths out with a month's worth of soap.

I got out of the bed. 'I tell you what I'd like to have given him,' I heard her say behind me. Whatever it was, was impossible to make out from the laughter of the women.

I imagined the things in Miss Wicks's box and which of them she'd like Tom Briscoe to have. The coconut oil for his lovely dark hair. The nurse's watch to measure his pulse. But perhaps it wasn't in her box, perhaps it was something else, the thing married people do. And after trying to imagine that, I wasn't sure if I should be there at all. I loved the top floor for I was learning how to become a woman, but the woman I was becoming was a worldly one.

I went to the open window. The top floor of the Ladies' Building was the only place in the camp where you could see out over the barbed wire, the guard houses, the electric fence, and into the fields.

A large black bird, a cormorant, stood on one foot, deep in a patch of swampy water. Then it shook out its umbrella wings and flew. The freedom over which it soared went on for miles until it was bleached out by the distance itself. I thought of my parents out there, far west, and wondered if they were safely hidden in the loess hills.

Then I felt Gladys's arm around my waist. 'Hey, kiddo, that's the bell. Time for roll call.' The women had put dresses over their slips, buttoned their low-heeled lawn shoes and stubbed out their cigarettes. I thought they looked marvellous in their dresses, all copies from the photo-shoots of *Vogue*, made by their Shanghai tailors and delivered the next day by rickshaw.

'Take this to your aunt,' said Gladys, handing me a folded-over tin-can label.

'Yes, Miss Wicks.'

'I don't want you to read it. Promise?'

'Promise.' I put the note in my dress pocket. Then, because I knew it would be some time before I had a ball of soap worthy of another visit, I took one last look at the world beyond the wall, at the yellow gash road that had carried us here, that carried trucks with sacks of food, along which the coolies came to empty the cesspit, the road that never took anyone away.

We each had our own plate that we kept next to our mattresses by our Bible and precious things. My plate was a frying pan. When I was asleep I dreamt of food. When I was awake I thought of it. I lay on my bed and imagined all sorts of food in my frying pan. I imagined noodle soup even more than I imagined Mother and Father. Sometimes, when going on an errand between huts, I stopped dead in my tracks, because I'd imagined a pink wobbly jelly, or a potato slobbed in butter, and I'd stand still and feel smothered with joy. Like the rapture.

Tate & Lyle! Nestlé! With these words on my tongue, I took my place in the exercise yard behind Edith and Flo for roll call.

'Candied crab apples,' said Edith, and Flo said, 'Rich Tea biscuits' and Edith said, 'Fruit scones.' I jumped in with a juicy 'pork cutlets'. Then Big Bum Eileen joined the line. Edith and Flo stopped saying foods, turned their backs and began to talk to Big Bum Eileen. I went on tiptoe behind them, trying to entice them with an exotic 'Nestlé Milk!' but the game had moved on. I stood behind them muttering, 'Bournville', 'sugar cube' but the game had lost its sweetness.

Private Tanaka arrived, Big Bum Eileen took her place in front of me, and the roll call began. We were counted each morning and each afternoon, all of us, embassy men, casino girls, Dutch priests in clogs. It didn't matter who you were, you were counted, all equal in the eyes of His Imperial Majesty. We stood in snow, in dust, in heat, in fainting and in health.

Private Tanaka counted us children, as he did in all weathers, his face clenched, spit sailing, voice threatening to stop our enemy blood. This was his duty. My duty was to say my number. Two, four, three. My number said, I have not escaped in the night, I have not gone to the hospital suffering from beriberi or blood poisoning, I have not gone to the grave leaving one more portion of gruel for others to share. I am here. I am captured and counted.

Yes, Mother. I am alive and counting. I count the hours

until the next meal, I count the weevils in my gruel, I count the shirts scrubbed in the laundry, I count the twenty-five words on my Red Cross letters home.

When roll call finished, as the girls left for the dormitory chanting food words to each other, as the Sons of Thunder mobbed Private Tanaka with questions about his sword while he unsheathed the blade, as Gladys lifted her cigarette to Tom Briscoe's flame, I turned and went the other direction, stomping through the camp's alleyways.

Now that she'd volunteered for the Welfare Committee, tending the ill in their huts and at the camp hospital, a shack in the far corner of the compound, Aunty Muriel was not so easy to find. I searched through the huts but she was not walking through any of the alleys. I asked Miss Preedy if she'd seen her, for they shared a room. Miss Preedy's chin wobbled, then she mumbled no, turned her gaze to the ground and stepped back into the quiet room. Everything about Miss Preedy wobbled, and after a year of the camp's bad food, several of her teeth had wobbled right out of her mouth. The more teeth she lost, the more she left us alone, preferring instead to lie in the shade of the room praying for the Second Coming and dentures.

Perhaps Mr Kennedy would know. He was putting his chess set away. 'Mr Kennedy . . .' I was out of breath. 'Have you seen Aunty Muriel? I've got an important note for her.'

'Best if I read it,' he said. I'd never told an adult that they couldn't do something before. I gave him the note. He tugged his soft, long earlobe and said, 'No, I have not seen her.'

This afternoon's vanishing made me worry. Perhaps Aunty

Muriel was in trouble. I remembered my words on the twentieth step. *Aunty Muriel, Aunty Muriel, we must rescue her from her funeral.* Ever since saying them, I had always wondered if one day she might need our help.

I walked back down Main Street, passing a group of little girls, including Elspeth West and also Philip, flicking marbles in the dirt. They looked up at me, striding fast with the importance of my errand. 'Can we come?'

'Scram,' I said, 'scram!' I ran into the exercise yard and there was Tom Briscoe having another cigarette. He had curly, dark hair and a broad chest, and he was staring at me! I stood on tiptoe and waved, but when he didn't wave back, I realised he was looking beyond me. I turned. There at the far end of Main Street was Aunty Muriel striding in her grey dress. I raced between the huts, hopping over Elspeth and Philip, sending marbles scattering, then beyond the latrines and the cesspit, where I saw her at the end of Cook's Alley. She was walking hurriedly towards the laundry shed. I was within calling distance but had to stop while a trail of cesspit coolies took vats of stinking muck away. When I next looked up, she'd disappeared.

I sat outside the laundry shed, feeling a bit cross. Aunty Muriel didn't need rescuing, she was now just one of those adults who was hard to find when you needed them. I stared at the grey wall. The crickets hissed, a magpie cackled. I wiped my sweaty face, and opened the note.

Arrangements made. Tom will bring to you tonight. Before curfew. Wicks.

Then I heard her voice. I put the note behind my back and pressed myself close to the laundry hut wall.

'Mr Dalrymple.'

'Please, call me Reginald.'

'Well, Reginald, I will have to consider this carefully.'

'I think we share a certain love,' said Reginald, 'for this country.'

There was a silence, in which I imagined Aunty Muriel, wishing to see China, found herself instead gazing at a ten-foot wall.

'May I call you Muriel?' said Reginald. I imagined Mr Dalrymple right up close to her, his moustache tickling her ear.

The next thing I heard Muriel say was, 'What in heaven's name are you doing here?' And there she was, standing above me, cross and flushed.

'I hope you're not planning another escape,' said Mr Dalrymple, appearing at her side. Aunty Muriel gave him a firm look, then he coughed and stepped into the laundry. There he began a complex whistling.

'Back to the dormitory this instant,' said Aunty Muriel.

'This is from Miss Wicks,' I said, and gave her the note.

She tucked it up her sleeve. 'Well, be off with you,' she said.

Mr Dalrymple was wearing a cedarwood scent and it was wafting. I wanted to wait around a bit to see if he'd waft out, too.

'Well?' she said.

I went back, kicking the cinder track with my brogues. There was something about Mr Dalrymple that I didn't like. I didn't like the shape of his head. It irritated me. The funny bald patch that kept growing. And his moustache; after a year in camp it had bred a beard. I wondered if he wolf-whistled before he became a Christian.

I passed the family huts. Usually, I loved to watch them, the mothers and fathers and little ones. Sometimes, I'd play with the children, sometimes I just gazed into the rooms until the mothers tired of me and suggested I should go back to my friends. But today, I kept walking, today I wouldn't stop for the stupid families.

In our dormitory, with its blossoms of mould, its rows of mattresses facing each other, where the bedbugs awaited night's arrival, I was alone. The others hadn't come back from their evening activities yet. I checked through my things, making sure all was in order. My cardboard box with the Bible, Philip's half-moon leaf and the monk's picture tucked inside, my frying pan and my tin spoon. Everything was there. Then, I lay on my bed and worried. I worried Mr Dalrymple might take Aunty Muriel away.

Then Flo came in, Edith came in, Hilary, Fiona, Isobel, Kathryn, nearly everyone was there. Clogs, plimsolls, brogues were pulled off. Girls began busying themselves for bed. Flannels, nightdresses, the clatter as they put away plate and spoon. The room was too small for all of us. We were so close. Could feel their heat. Smell them. Flo's musty waft, Kathryn's underarm pong, Hilary's feet. Everyone's vinegary breath puffing at you as they spoke. You couldn't take off a vest without barging someone with your elbows. Even when you had a thought, there was barely enough room for it.

Big Bum Eileen came in last and sat down on her mattress and began rummaging in her suitcase. There would certainly be more room without her. But guess what, even though Big Bum Eileen was still mine enemy, I could no longer call her that. It would have been lying, for she no longer had a big bum. She was now Thin Bum Eileen.

'What are you doing?' Hilary asked.

'I am preparing my trousseau,' she said.

'You mean your bottom drawer?' said Edith.

'I mean a trousseau,' she said firmly, for there were to be no more jokes about bottoms. And she went on to explain how Miss Preedy had suggested the task to some of the older girls and Eileen had decided to take it up. She was going to use the pocket of the suitcase to hold these things that she might need if she got married. In it was her sewing kit and, curled up tight, the dormitory measuring tape. She was going to embroider serviettes first. Then there would be a lace doily, which, for those of us who didn't know, was something that you put under a vase. Everything would be coordinated so that when it was laid out in her new home, it would all look – and here she cast her eyes around our cluttered, mouldy room – as charming as at the mission headquarters on Sinza Road.

In the hush that followed, Thin Bum Eileen settled down on her bed and began ferociously to embroider the words 'Love is patient, love is kind', the verses of the First Epistle to the Corinthians 13, on to a serviette.

So, how did it start, the fight? Eileen needed to concentrate on her serviette, Edith needed to practise her clarinet. Flo hated the way my bedspread drooped over the floor, I scowled each time Fiona turned a page of her Hebrew primer, Kathryn huffed and puffed as she solved an equilateral equation while holding her nose from the rotting rice stink of Hilary's feet, and Hilary, leafing through Aunt Neb's recipe book, covered her ears not just to block out the tune that came from Edith's clarinet but also, the drip of spit.

I began to list some of the food I'd seen, Nescafé, Bournville, Tate & Lyle.

No one spoke.

'I was up with Gladys,' I said, 'and she showed me the new *Reader's Digest*.'

'Stop showing off,' someone said. 'You're just trying to get attention.'

'If I was doing that, I'd tell you about the discovery I made this afternoon,' I said. 'A terrible one that will affect us all.'

The girls eyed me cautiously.

'You better keep your discoveries to yourself,' said Hilary. They nodded at each other knowingly, and carefully sharpened a pencil, turned a page, poked a thread through a needle.

'How terrible?' asked Flo, putting her books down at last.

'Mr Dalrymple wants to marry Aunty Muriel.'

'She wouldn't!'

'She said she'd think about it.'

'You're gossiping,' said Isobel, fresh from Bible class.

'I'm just telling you what I heard.'

'That's still gossiping,' said Kathryn.

There was a tight silence while we hated each other. Then Flo got up and stoked the fire. 'Why didn't you start the night-fire, you were here first?' she asked. She took out a heap of ash from under the stove and swept it into a pan with a straw brush. I got up to give her a hand. 'It's too late now, I've done it,' she said.

'Oh, for God's sake,' I said, 'you never let me help.'

'For God's sake?' said Hilary.

'For goodness' sake, then.'

'So that's how you and your new friends speak, is it?'

'There's nothing wrong with Gladys. She's kind and generous.'

'What did you get this time?'

'Well, nothing.'

'Miss Preedy said people like her spread deceit.'

'Will you all shut up!' Eileen stood. The needle was in one hand, love and patience trembled in the other. 'I can't bear this any more, all this moaning and bitching.'

'Bitching?'

'Doily!'

'Bitch!'

Someone grabbed my hair. I turned and pushed the person away. It was Hilary. I hit out at her but infuriatingly missed. We were all bright with anger. The air was tight, as though something, someone might burst at any point.

Then I grabbed some ash and threw it to the ceiling. It travelled down in a talcy cloud.

Hilary jumped in and threw the next plume. It fell about her, her dark hair made grey.

Flo threw some. We all did. Eileen hid her sewing, then threw some. Kathryn took a spadeful of ash and threw it all over the dorm. We were covered in dust. There was ash everywhere. Our faces, our clothes, our beds, greyed out. And there was no water until tomorrow to wash it off.

Then the door opened, and there stood Aunty Muriel. She was bright and clean, and held above her head a candle on a plate. Each girl froze, still as a corpse. Aunty Muriel paused. Her foot made a rainbow-shaped arc through the ash. It went back and forth a few times, while she thought. Then she lifted her head. 'Dear me, it looks like a room full of ghosts.' Aunty Muriel began to walk, her light footsteps printed along the length of the dormitory, the candle flickering.

'I've arranged a treat,' said Aunty Muriel. She'd decided to ignore the ash and instead lowered the plate. There was such a wonderful sight. A scattering of boiled sweets. Berry reds, purples, buttercup yellow, marigold orange, stripy ones, toffee ones. We burst into a round of 'Aunty Muriel!' and 'Where did you get these?' and 'You must have swapped something very good for these.' Aunty Muriel laughed and instructed Flo to choose a sweet and share the plate round.

'Now, girls, you can save them until later or you may eat them now.' The brides-to-be, the missionaries-to-be, the Mozart-to-be, and I sucked those sweets as long as we could. The syrupy flavour ribboned around our mouths, we closed our eyes, let the sweetness mingle with our spit until we could gargle pools of gloop over every single tastebud. As we sucked, each in her private thoughts while the sweets became glassy and fragile, I began to feel troubled. Where had the sweets come from? Aunty Muriel must have got them from Gladys. We were licking black-market sweets. Not only was this sinful, it was an act that could put Aunty Muriel in danger.

Then Edith, who had the misfortune to crunch first, asked, 'Aunty Muriel, do you have a wedding trousseau, because Eileen has.'

'Well, that's quite a sensible thing for you to work towards, Eileen,' said Aunty Muriel to Thin Bum, whose tongue was black.

'But do you have one?' said Edith.

'I did have one, as all the girls of my village did,' she said. 'Mine had a white tablecloth with matching serviettes, a quilt of light blue pieces that spiralled out into a dark blue sea. There were many lovely things in my bottom drawer.'

'Where are they now?' I asked, for I too had crunched.

'I gave them to a friend at my village church.'

'Didn't you want to get married?' That was Hilary, her tongue an alarming orange.

'Don't you ever want to get married?' We all stared, as one in ashen horror, a many-headed beast with many coloured tongues.

Aunty Muriel's gaze spiralled to somewhere far away. 'Goodness me, marriage. Everyone today wants to talk about marriage.'

'Who, Aunty Muriel, who else?' The light flickered, setting her red hair aglow. Her hands were neatly cupped in her lap and she looked at them. She wore no rings.

'Girls,' she said, raising her head and looking upwards, as once she had in the forests of Lushan, her hair shimmering in the flame, 'should a man feel called by God to marry you, that doesn't mean that God has called you to marry him. Sometimes God calls a woman to marriage, sometimes God does not. There are rewards for the single life.' Her voice faltered. We curled around her. Her lip trembled. Big Bum Eileen passed her her trousseau serviette, the only fabric that had escaped the ash. Aunty Muriel took it. 'Now, absolutely enough of this nonsense,' she said to herself, in the voice that she'd once used to scold us with. When she'd dabbed her tears and given a good blow of her nose on the cross-stitched word 'Lo', Aunty Muriel added quietly, 'Sometimes, even good kind men, you are not called to marry.' Then lo and behold, she stood up abruptly and rushed from the room, her footprints a flurry in the ash.

'She's not getting married,' said Eileen, taking back her serviette.

'But in any case, she's not really ours any more,' said Kathryn. It was true. Even though she wasn't going to marry Mr Dalrymple, Aunty Muriel had left us. She had not told us to clean up the ash, or to go and scrub our faces at the wash house. We were to look after ourselves.

The mood was sad as a vegetable patch in winter. The girls brushed their hair, one to a hundred in silence. The candle stub was blown out. Lying there, I felt the first pinches of the bedbugs. I scratched my legs, cracking the shells between my fingers. As the unknowable dark came, I listened to the camp's jazz band, three Negroes from a Shanghai nightclub, ease over the crease between day and night. The silhouettes of our imprisonment, the barbed wire, the watchtowers, black against a blood red sky, while 'Honeysuckle Rose' floated out into the sunset of the world beyond.

A Year Later, June 1944

The hair of Gladys Wicks was going green. I sat behind her on her bed and brushed it. It was green as a cucumber, although no black-market vegetables had been seen for months. Chunks of her hair came off in my hands. I put them in my dress pocket so she wouldn't see.

From the bed along, Mrs Mullroy and Mrs Brown sat on greasy sheets, giving each other detailed bulletins about the thing the whole camp was talking about, the captured radio. It had been found the night before in the hut by the cook house, hidden, as Mr Kennedy had told me, behind a loose brick. We had all been made to attend roll call during the night, standing in our dressing gowns, while the guard dogs growled, and a Mauser was pointed at each of our heads while our number was ticked off. The next morning the Japanese announced that as a reprisal, mealtime rations would be halved to a fist of gruel.

'Everyone made to suffer for one person's stupidity,' said Stacey Mullroy, hoisting her swelling legs up on the bed.

'We all want to know what's going on in the war, we all benefited from the information,' said Gladys. 'That radio probably saved lives. It gave us hope.'

'Punishing all of us is clever of the Japs,' said Nan Brown. 'Sending everyone hungry for a week is a sure way for one internee to make a thousand enemies.'

'What about Tom Briscoe's escape plan?' whispered Nan Brown to Gladys. When Gladys didn't answer, she carried on to Mrs Mullroy, 'Speaks fluent Chinese, you know.'

Mrs Mullroy nodded. 'Have you seen him? Dressing like a Chinese, too. He's shaved his head and don't you notice he's spending a lot of time with his tunic off, standing about in the sun.'

'Lucky us,' said Nan. 'My bet is he'll go with the cesspit coolies. What do you reckon, Gladys? You'd know.'

'I reckon you should mind your business, Nan. No one's escaping,' said Gladys with a surprising nip in her voice. And then to me, 'People squeal, you have to be careful who you tell things to,' she said. 'Who would have squealed about the radio? Someone must have. Someone who's suddenly got extra rations.' She began to neaten a torn nail with her teeth.

I lowered my voice. 'It won't be long now,' I said to Gladys. 'I'm sure we'll be out soon.' When I couldn't bring soap, I liked to bring her good news. 'I think that you'll be able to get back to Shanghai soon, and I'll go back to Shanxi. I played chess with Mr Kennedy earlier and he says that the last report from the radio said the Japanese had lost Burma and Guinea too. He doesn't think China will be long.'

'Is that so, Etta?' she said. 'Well, I think you should be careful about being seen talking to your Mr Kennedy. There's more going on with that man than chess . . .' She opened a small tin. In it was some coconut oil for her hair.

'I'll be careful, Gladys,' I said as I rubbed the oil into her ratty ends. 'But just think, all the salons in Shanghai will be open,' I said as I began to weave her hair into a French plait.

'Well, I don't care if all the salons are open, what a woman needs is for Madame Choo's salon to be open. One salon is not like another.'

'No,' I said, and took great care as I brought the plait to its scrawny completion. 'There,' I said. Gladys reached her hands behind her head and she felt the plait. 'Good,' she said. Then she gave me a small jar filled with the oil. 'You can put some of this on your hair, keep it nice, you know, now you're growing up into a woman.'

Then the midday gong went, and Gladys took the nurse's watch from her metal box and noted down the time on a tin label. 'They rang the midday gong at 11.43 yesterday, then 12.24 today,' she said. 'They want to keep us on our toes, to stop us making any plans.' Then she yawned. 'I'm tired.' She messed up my hair. 'Kiddo, it's time to fuck off.'

I did fuck off, a little shocked and then gaining speed until I was skipping in my boys' brogues, whispering, 'Fuck off, fuck off, fuck off,' past Mr Kennedy, who was talking to a man over the chess board, past the huts and down Main Street. I passed Tom Briscoe and his friend, Peter Hammond, taking a rest from pushing a cart of bricks. They lounged back on the cart, chests shining with sweat, and then Peter Hammond whistled at me. I gave him a vile glare. He whistled again. 'Fuck off,' I said, and marched high and mighty away. They both laughed.

I turned left into the maze of huts and leant against the wall of one. I was out of breath from the running. It happened so quickly these days. I bent over. Put my hands on my face. The world was bright and giddy. Then I stood up. I saw my reflection in one of the windows. I put my hands back on my face. Around my hair. I looked down at my body. I was growing and growing. My shins were long. How my legs had lengthened. My feet butted the ends of my brogues.

I walked then through the huts holding the oil, catching my reflection as I went. 'Fuck off!' I mouthed to the pale face to see what she would think.

I came to the edge of the exercise ground where a group of Sons of Thunder practised drill, but quickly turned away, and stepped sideways towards the huts. I felt too ugly and strange to be seen by Nigel Pinsent and his friends. I kept walking, leaning into the shade, hoping to lose myself in the maze of huts. Then I looked up. There was Aunty Muriel passing through with a bucket. She walked briskly, her grey dress loose about her waist. I followed her as I did on some afternoons, watching her carefree walk. It was as if she might be whistling, although I was not close enough to hear. She knocked on the door of a hut, and went inside. I followed after and sat in the hut's shade.

She came out, 'Henrietta Robertson, why do you insist on following me?' I didn't answer, just looked at my long shins. The furrow in her brow deepened. 'Henrietta, you should be in your dormitory studying. Off you go, chop chop.' I felt cross that she spent all her afternoons on the Welfare Committee. I wondered if it made her feel like being a proper missionary, more than looking after us. She began to close the hut's door. 'Why do you want to look after sick people?' I asked.

The door stopped. Aunty Muriel's brow furrowed deeper. 'Etta, in all works, whether that be caring for the children of Lushan or the women of Tsitao Camp, we are called to be Christ's hands. Now back to your dormitory. There's Greek,

Hebrew, Geography and Algebra to learn.'

'I don't feel called to sitting about.' I looked at the dusty huts, ramshackle with washing. 'I'd rather help properly,' I said.

'Well, I think I know something of that feeling myself,' she said. 'But on you go, think of Flo, Edith, Eileen and the others, and think how you can be Christ's hands in your dormitory, for your dormitory is where you're meant to be.'

Up I stood, and walked away without even turning to say goodbye.

That evening as we readied ourselves for bed, Eileen froze. She held her hairbrush out to us. It was full of long blond hair. 'Please God, get me out of here,' she said. The wildly flickering candle showed her crumple forward. She began to sob.

'It will grow back,' said Hilary, 'when we get better food. That's what my brother says.'

'When will that be?' said Eileen. She lifted her red face; she did not hide her tears. 'Who would want me now?' Eileen slumped forward on her mattress and let out a tiny cry.

I went over to her bed, and sat beside her sobbing body. 'Would you like to use this?' I asked.

Thin Bum Eileen took the jar in her hands.

'You just use a bit, warm it up in your hands. It will condition your hair.'

Eileen opened the lid and smelt the coconutty smell. 'Where did you get it?'

'Bet she stole it.'

'Gladys gave it to me.'

'I don't think you should use it,' said Flo to Eileen, who'd scooped some on to her forefinger.

Hilary joined in. 'You know what kind of woman she is.'
'You should be careful.'

Eileen began smoothing the oil between her finger and thumb, slowly as if thinking, then put her hand in and scooped a great palmful out. She rubbed it quickly into her hair.

'It smells good enough to eat,' she said, and passed me back the jar.

I looked inside. There was none left. 'You're welcome,' I said.

We woke up to screaming. 'What is it, what is it?' someone shouted.

The screamer screamed again.

Then we heard hard boots pounding the stairs, the charge of a guard. The door was flung open and a torch sent frantic light across the room. Searching for the scream, it shone on the mouldy ceiling, a pistol in a halter, our alarmed faces, the cold stove, a hand holding a pistol, then finally on to the soldier's face. It was Private Tanaka but his face was gone before we could see his intent.

At last he found Thin Bum Eileen. For a terrible moment I thought he was going to shoot her to stop the noise. Instead, he kneeled on her bed and shone his torch directly at her. Her blond hair had been turned black. And that black was moving. Her head was covered with ants. They'd come for the sweet coconut oil. They were pricking and biting her face. Private Tanaka put his gun back in its holster, undid her plait and picked off the ants one by one. Eileen lay in his arms and cried as his hands tended her.

The next morning, her face was blotchy with bites, and her eyelids swollen. She looked an unlikely fiancée. 'Poor

Eileen,' said the girls, and to me, 'You just bring trouble.' In stinging silence we girls walked towards the kitchens, our spoons clattering in our empty bowls.

That afternoon the diamond heat of the planes was upon the camp. It was one of those days sweat clings to the backs of your knees, when going inside fills your vision with colliding suns. It wasn't a day for wandering outside but I wanted to avoid the company of the girls as long as possible, and knowing that the company of Gladys brought disaster, I chose a winding route back from my chores at the laundry. I was walking along the cinder track when I saw sitting in the shade of the wall Private Tanaka smoking a cigarette.

He asked, 'Girl okay? No ants?' I sat near him on the ground, which was scoured with barbed wire shadows. Private Tanaka leant over and gave me a radish from his jacket pocket. It was rumoured – and I now saw that it was true – that the soldiers had their own gardens, and the water to water them.

'Thank you,' I said in Japanese. I bit into the radish then and there, taking tiny nibbles of the peppery crunch. He nodded approval and smoked as I ate. When Private Tanaka finished his cigarette, he stubbed it in the cinder track, and took from his wallet a picture of his wife and daughter.

'Okami,' he said, pointing to the woman. 'Osanago,' he said, pointing to the baby.

I repeated the words after him. We both watched his family for a moment, Okami with her dark bob and Osanago's plump arms and serious stare. Then Private Tanaka slipped his family back in his wallet and looked at me. He stood and without another word, continued his round.

I walked on, too, but I would not go to the Ladies' Building as normal. I kept walking, sticking to the edge of the street where I might find some shade. Then I saw her, Aunty Muriel, tall and light-footed. She'd disappeared around the back of Hut 23 on Main Street. Even though I knew I shouldn't, I followed her through the maze of huts, and stopped sharp when I heard her call, 'Etta. Quick.' And when she said 'I've been looking for you,' I ran to her. 'Here, take this bucket.' The contents of the bucket sloshing, we walked along the dazzling cinder track that wound its way through the maze of bamboo huts, all the way to Hut 221.

There, in the stiff heat, lay the shivering Headmaster's wife on her canvas camp bed, her lemony blanket about her. A fly sat on her face and cleaned its fingers. 'Jenny,' said Aunty Muriel. She put her hand on Jenny's forehead. The fly flew away.

'Give me a hand, will you, Etta?' said Aunty Muriel. We held Headmaster's wife by her shoulders and sat her up. Aunty Muriel began to hum a little and gently stroke Jenny's hand. It felt very lonely in that hut. I remembered how Aunty Muriel had been in the beautiful rose garden with the other ladies. Aunt Neb and Miss Otis were now busy doing all the school's teaching, Mrs Charleston was in America and Miss Kingsley had sailed south.

'You prayed over her once,' I said. 'I saw you in the garden with Miss Kingsley and Mrs Charleston. You spoke in tongues over her, and then she stood. Was that a miracle?'

Aunty Muriel tipped a little more water into Jenny's mouth, then said, 'Sometimes he gives a miracle to encourage us on our journey. But sometimes we are to be his hands and feet.'

'That is so, that is so,' said Headmaster's wife, her eyes

closed, her skin so thin you could pierce it with a fork, and I wondered whose hands and feet she could be now.

'That's why we tried it on Twelve, after seeing you speaking in tongues.'

Aunty Muriel gave me a horrified look.

Then Headmaster came in, his clogs clunking, his hipbones jutting above his shorts. This time I did not have to escape out of the window. 'Miss MacKay,' he said, tapping his fingers on the wooden chair, 'I see you have an assistant.'

And that is how I began to help Aunty Muriel. Each afternoon after scrubbing a legion of dresses in the laundry, I'd meet her at the corner of Main Street and Cook's Alley and together we'd visit the huts. And though at first these visits made my flesh creep, I liked having a job to do and I liked watching people get better. We'd turn the old ladies fusting in their beds, we'd clean out old wounds, letting the yellow pus drain, trying not to retch at the sweet rot stench. We'd scrape the milky white boils that grew on legs, burrowing down to the bone. The dysentery patients were the worst, bent over double with cramp, humiliated by the reek of their own excrement. The best we could do for them was to clean the filthy mess around their beds. We sat by feeble malaria patients, spooning gruel into their dry mouths, careful that they did not choke. In all things, I worked as Aunty Muriel taught me. This is how you do it. You take the cloth. The water is to be hot. Add a little salt. Gently clean the wound. Ease the knife in. Good, that does it. Now, let out the pus . . .

Some days on a round I'd see Gladys, her hair tucked up under a trilby hat, her pink scarf around her neck, walking up and down the street with Tom Briscoe, who despite the rumours still had not escaped. Gladys would always wave and one day she called me over. She wanted to give me a sweet.

'Sorry, Gladys,' I said. 'I can't.'

Her thin eyebrows were raised, 'Not even a sweet?' and I knew that I'd hurt her.

After the round, I would go to the small hospital at the far corner of the compound. It was a small wooden Nissen hut, with twenty or so beds, an empty dispensary and a mosquito net for those nearest death. Here worked Dr Durrell, a retired doctor with the Northern Christian Alliance, and Nurse Margaret. Together, they tended the worst cases of malaria, dysentery and malnutrition with the Red Cross supplies of saline, sulfadiazine and quinine. As we approached our second year of internment the Red Cross packages stopped. It was rumoured they had been taken by the soldiers who sold the quinine over the wall, and if it couldn't be bought or bartered back from the peasants for a sufficient price, there was little the medical team could do but keep wounds cleaned and drained, turn the bodies, light as husks, help them eat, drink and then wash them clean again.

I helped in small ways. Mopping the floor, emptying bed pans. Dr Durrell tried to make ointments from the plants that grew in the fields; I'd grind them in a pestle and mortar. Sometimes, I just sat by patients and held their hand. Once, they took out the appendix of a White Russian boy without an anaesthetic. Everyone was called to hold him down, and because he was especially strong for a ten-year-old, the Bulgarian burglar, one of the few internees who'd kept his bulk, had to be called to help. In the end, Dr Durrell gagged him. My job was to walk with his mother, Mrs Litviak, to the other end of the camp, slipping my arm in hers and steering her towards the Sons of Thunder while they practised their hymns. There Mrs Litviak and I stood for an hour, the boys' tooting and parping covering her son's screams, while we looked at the jays and sparrows that flitted over the wall.

As the war went on, things became worse. Internees were too tired to do their chores; there was very little water for there were not enough people to keep the fire going to boil and purify it. The effort to keep the camp going, all that scrubbing, pumping, scraping, cutting, stirring, lifting, pouring, counted for nothing against the Japanese power to feed or withhold food. Desolation spread over the camp. Rations were cut again, and still more people fell ill from malnutrition.

There were also more beatings. Some days Dr Durrell and Nurse Margaret had to stitch gashes caused by the butt of a rifle, even bayonet stabs that bore down to the shoulder bone. The frequency of these beatings rose with the reports of Allied progress on the last camp radio. Italy's capitulation. Allied progress across the Pacific. This information brought new fears. What would happen if the Japanese lost the war? The Ladies' Dormitory was full of answers. 'The Japanese might desert us to the warlords who'd kidnap us for ransom.' 'If they commit suicide rather than admit defeat, we'll all be killed first.' There were many ways to die and these thoughts plagued us like the bugs and boils.

Summer 1945

As we entered the sweltering summer of 1945 and the third year of internment, people lay listless on their beds, too frail to move. Some days it was so hot, I could not get up; just sitting made my head reel. The queue for the pump stretched for an hour and many fainted before they reached the fountain of tepid water. In our dormitory, Hilary lay in bed for two weeks unable to walk because of a large boil. Each morning I cleaned and drained it. Without vitamins and calcium, Fiona's night vision began to worsen. Soon she was blind from six o'clock until dawn. We were all thin. I could lie in bed and name many of my bones.

On the night of 14 July Norman Trapper and Tom Briscoe escaped. They'd left on a full moon (the moon cast a large shadow from the Ladies' Building over the wall), during a change in the guard that took place at ten o'clock, a moment that had been perfectly calculated by Gladys, one of the last people in camp with a watch. While soldiers and their dogs searched the fields, seven men and Gladys Wicks were taken to the guard house for questioning. The local paper had been notified with a report that said nine prisoners had escaped, of whom seven were captured, allowing the commandant to save face.

The following day one of the black-market coolies was shot. It was not until we left our dormitory that we saw him. There he was, as if floating over the wall, blood clotting on his indigo jacket, his jaw agape, his wide eyes a jelly treat for a crow. Three packets of flour had exploded to the ground, leaving dust marks like travelling stars. The coolie's death was a reprisal. There he would stay, a warning, and sure enough the black market stopped. No more medicines, eggs or cigarettes.

That afternoon, returning from the guard house, Gladys came across Philip Hill. He was by the latrines, stumbling. She knelt down beside him and tried to speak with him. He was very confused about where he was. Gladys took him up to her rooms, where he lay down under the mosquito net.

'Etta, over here,' she called as I came into the room to help drain Stacey Mullroy's leg. I was hesitant at first; I wasn't sure what it was on her bed and I knew I shouldn't talk to her. Then I saw the mound shivering under a sheet was Philip. He barely recognised me. I stroked his fine hair, his face all bone. He was hot to touch. After a few minutes of my questions, he pushed me grumpily away and said he had a headache. I continued to sit beside him, resting my hand on his shoulder. Then he flipped over on his back, his eyelids half closed, his eyeballs upturned in their sockets. He began to shake. I tried to hold him down, Gladys joined me, and he shook, arms, legs, head, kicking out at us in a violent fit. Then he stilled, his body floppy as an old tea towel. A strange snoring sound gargled from his throat, then his eyes pinged open. He blinked. I thought he'd died. But he was alive.

'Let's get him to the hospital,' said Gladys. Between us we tried to carry him down the stairs, and although he was a very thin, nearly naked nine-year-old, he was too heavy. In the exercise ground, I saw the Sons of Thunder taking a rest from their band practice in the shade of a hut. I waved at Nigel, and he came over, slow but smiling in the fierce heat. Together, the three of us took Philip through the maze of huts, out along the Cinder Track and up to the hospital hut at the far end of the camp.

'Malaria,' said Dr Durrell, rising from the hospital bed. 'Possibly cerebral malaria, the worst kind. Nurse Margaret, please bring what you can of the quinine.' I looked at Philip, watching his still body for flinches, twitches, any signs he might fit again. 'And what about you?' Dr Durrell said to Gladys.

'Bit of bother in the guard house,' she said, readying

herself to go. There was some blood on her dress, and stripes where she'd been hit across the back of her legs.

'Well, let's see to that before you go,' said Dr Durrell. And there on the edge of the dispensary desk, much to the surprise of the returning Nurse Margaret, Gladys reclined like a goddess while old Dr Durrell wound a bandage round and round her thigh.

As Gladys stood up from the dispensary desk, Aunty Muriel came in. Nurse Margaret told her about Philip, adding, 'We've given him the last of the quinine. There's only one vial left.'

'Well, something must be done,' she said, taking off her sunhat.

'There's always something, someway,' said Gladys, walking stiffly towards us.

'Indeed,' said Aunty Muriel, giving Gladys a brisk nod. 'What about the black market?'

'No one will risk selling anything to us after that peasant was shot,' said Nurse Margaret.

'We'll think of something,' said Gladys, and I noticed she wasn't wearing her scarf. There was a little line of pale flesh, the markings of a scar across her throat. Not a new scar, an old one. She saw me look at it and quickly put her hand to her neck.

That afternoon, I stayed by Philip. I was glad to sit with him for I had no energy to walk about the huts. I watched him in that place that is deeper than sleep but not death. I watched his silent battle. I stroked his hair, brushed away the flies, cleaned each bowel movement away.

As evening fell, I went outside to stretch my legs. The hospital was surrounded by what had been, in the first days of camp, a garden. I sat among the dead tomato plants for a moment. There on the ground amongst the dried out stalks and parched clods of earth, was a little dried leaf, shaped like a half-moon. As I stood to go back in, a group of the younger girls arrived at the fence. 'Nigel told us about Philip. How is he?' they asked.

'At the moment, he's having a good sleep,' I replied. 'And when he wakes up, I'll tell him you were asking for him.' They gave me the bag of his marbles for when he awoke. As they walked away, I felt sorry about my little lie. None of us knew what battle Philip fought and if he would return.

When I went back inside, Muriel and Nurse Margaret were standing by the dispensary desk, deep in conversation with Mr Dalrymple, who'd come to check how Philip was. 'That's the last of the quinine, there's nothing else.'

I stepped closer.

'He needs more, ideally another week of it, to navigate his way out of the fever, and he needs it now, tomorrow at the latest. These couple of vials have stilled some of it, but if he doesn't begin to take a turn for the better in the next day, it will mean . . .' Nurse Margaret did not finish her sentence but simply said again, 'We need more quinine.'

'I know where to get quinine,' said a voice behind me. It was Nigel Pinsent. He'd slipped in after me. We all stared at him. 'The boys and I do band practice by the wall sometimes because it's a good ruse. One of us gives another a leg up the wall. Then we go and explore. If the person on lookout sees a guard, they strike up a tune. All the tunes mean something, like a code. Beware, guard to right, is "Jesus Thy Robe of Righteousness". We've had a look around the Jap quarters. We've seen their storeroom and where they put the Red Cross parcels. There's a shed in their garden. Got loads of supplies. Three weeks ago we found a stack of beer bottles outside it, which we took and bartered with the jazz band for custard powder. Didn't you notice the way "Honeysuckle Rose" was played out of tune all night?'

'Nigel Pinsent, firstly, I forbid this mindlessly dangerous behaviour,' said Mr Dalrymple. 'And secondly, I congratulate you on your daring, and risking punishment to share it with us this evening. I think this could prove useful. Wouldn't you agree, Muriel?'

'I do, Reginald.'

There was an awkward silence. Mr Dalrymple cleared his throat and said, 'Well, that's settled. We shall make the necessary plans,' then hurried into the night.

This was the plan that was hatched by Muriel, Margaret and Mr Dalrymple with some help from the Sons of Thunder and Gladys. It was agreed that Nigel should not go, for he was a child, and nor should any of the women, but that Mr Dalrymple should take the risk. Nigel drew a map of where he'd seen the Red Cross boxes, in a hut within a garden in the Japanese compound. Gladys would give the time when the guards changed, at about three o'clock. The Sons of Thunder would play 'Jesus, Thy Robe of Righteousness', if guards came from the right and 'I Left My Burdens at the Cross', should they come from the opposite direction.

But the next day did not start as planned, for roll call was called an hour early. We had not even time to get in the queue for breakfast. Towards the centre of the camp we interns walked, uneasy. After we were counted, two soldiers brought a bound and gagged man to the front. A young man, his hands tied behind his back. It was Tom Briscoe's friend, Peter Hammond, who'd been taken in for questioning the day before. Peter Hammond was bare-chested. His head and sunken torso glistened with sweat. The soldier pointed a pistol at Peter Hammond's head. He jerked his head back and whacked it with the handle of the gun. The crowd gasped. Peter Hammond swayed to and fro and when he settled, the soldier hit him again. He kept hitting Peter Hammond, until urine ran down his trouser legs and on to the dusty ground. The soldier shoved him in the back. He fell forward, landing with his face in his piss. The three soldiers then walked through the crowd leaving Peter Hammond with trickles of blood down his face, gasping into the wet earth. During the beating, no one went to him. It was not wise to be friends with those who deceived our captors.

Back at the hospital, while Dr Durrell stitched Peter's bloodied face, Headmaster stood in his worn-out clogs, tapping the dispensary desk. The Japanese were too unpredictable. Even before breakfast one had been seen stumbling drunk along the cinder track singing a Christmas carol. After much discussion amongst the adults it was decided that the plan was too dangerous. Not today. It could mean death for Mr Dalrymple if caught. Better wait until the guards' mood shifted.

I sat beside Philip, as his seizures gave way to a deep sleep. He might wake up changed, Nurse Margaret had warned me; he might not wake up at all.

'Come on, Etta,' said Aunty Muriel, 'didn't you hear the gong? You need to go to lunch, you need all the strength you can get. I'll sit with him a while.'

When I returned from the kitchens, a crowd of internees was gathered under the commandant's office. Was it true that the war was over, they wanted to know? After ignoring the chanting prisoners for over an hour, the commandant came out on to the balcony, stepped on to his pallet box and, speaking through the interpreter, gave a reply that avoided saying yes or no. The commandant returned to his shuttered office and the people returned to their huts and dormitories, to lie on their beds, to speculate and grumble.

I went through the alleys and was about to turn up Main Street towards the hospital when I saw Aunty Muriel walking down the street, her basket under her arm, covered with an old tea towel. At the cinder path, she turned the corner. With her out of my vision, I reflected on how small she'd become. Those spindly legs within that billowing grey dress. How a mountain wind, or perhaps even a mist could spirit her away. Then a giddy feeling came over me, that old palpitating dread. I followed her.

But when I turned on to the cinder path that ran the circumference of our camp, Aunty Muriel had vanished. I couldn't see her anywhere. It was nearly midday and the internees and Japanese were all sheltering in the huts. All was silent except for a noisy jackdaw. The dread drew me on and I continued walking down the empty path but without seeing anyone. Then I noticed that a wooden gate in the wall between us and the Japanese compound was ajar. I crossed over the verge and pushed the gate wider open.

I whispered, 'Aunty Muriel.'

There was no answer, so I stepped inside. Here was a small garden. There were rows of manure, buzzing with flies in the heat. Upon them grew radishes, bright lettuce and tomatoes. They were sparse, tiny but vividly coloured. The possibility of crunch, of sweetness, of sharpness. My mouth began to water.

I heard boots marching on the path outside. I pressed myself against the wall. The marching passed. Then I saw her. She was peering into the window of a shed at the far end of the garden. She went to its door and shook the handle. It was locked. She tried again, harder. It made a loud rattle but remained closed. She covered a rock with the tea towel and threw it at the glass. It splintered open. The sound of shattering glass pierced the quiet afternoon and the jackdaw called again. Aunty Muriel hid herself behind the shed. After a few moments, she went back to the window, slipped her hand between the cracked glass but a big box prevented her from reaching further. With a look of resolve, she gave the box several hard shoves but it wouldn't budge. Again she tried the hut door, shaking the handle hard. When the jackdaw called once more, Aunty Muriel passed in a billow of grey dress, through the gate and back in bounds.

I followed her and stepped into the gateway. There I stopped, for a soldier ran past. It was Private Tanaka, and though I saw his face, he did not see me. But he'd seen Aunty Muriel. He began to yell. Her back stiffened. She stopped. He came up behind her and yelled at the nape of her neck. She slowly turned, there was a stiff pause, then he slapped her. Aunty Muriel raised her head up high and gave him her haughty look. Then he bashed her with his fist. Right in her tummy. She buckled forward, then stood up. He slapped her again. She was taller than he so he kicked a pallet towards her and stood on it.

Two internees passed with their wheelbarrow. They did nothing to stop Private Tanaka but looked on blankly as he began to pummel Aunty Muriel in the chest, the face, the head. She did not raise her hands, but took the beating, her fists gripped at her sides as his fists smashed into her. Why was no one stopping this? I looked to the men but they fixed their gaze on the ground. Three more people came from the huts. After each punch, she steadied herself, and swung her head to face Private Tanaka. It was like turning the other cheek, but with vast defiance. And still he beat her. I had thought Private Tanaka was our friend. Someone must help. I found myself praying, God, please help your servant Muriel. Make Tanaka stop. But nothing happened. I prayed again. A crowd of internees had gathered now, mostly men, but not a single voice called out to Tanaka, no one stepped forward. My head drummed with blood, my fingers shook, I was afraid and I prayed harder. Still nothing. Then I turned madder than a dragon. One of those great wild dragons doing their New Year dances, a body made of many paper lanterns, a writhing tail of light. My whole body beating with one thought: 'No.' Then I found I was running at Private Tanaka.

'Stop, stop, Private Tanaka! Stop!' I flung myself at his feet. 'Please, please,' I said in Japanese. He unsheathed his sword. I saw it above me. A slice of light in the sky. How stupid I had been. I closed my eyes. 'Okami. Osanago,' I made myself small and humble and grabbed Tanaka's boots. He did not use the blade, instead he kicked me away first in the shoulder, then a sharp kick to my skull.

I could taste blood. I put my hand up to my head and felt the soft gash. My fingers were red and wet. Above me, Private Tanaka still towered, the orange sun behind him. He stood panting from all the punching, but it was over now. He kicked the pallet and yelled at us in Japanese, his words a spitting rage. He sheathed his sword and walked off mid-sentence, the tip of his scabbard tapping the cinder track.

Aunty Muriel dropped to the ground. I pulled myself towards her. Her face was spattered with blood. Her breath was jagged, and blood and spittle bubbled in her mouth. I crawled closer, blew cool air on her face and stroked her hair. She turned to her side and coughed blood. Her nostrils flared with the pain.

The crowd began to shuffle and murmur. What was she thinking? Breaking into the garden. Stealing brings reprisals. Less food, just you wait. Someone spat.

I lay there and watched Aunty Muriel. Her pinkish eyelids, her neck scabbed with little insect bites, the mosquito bite that would not heal – I saw all the lines on her face, so close was I. This was a new Aunty Muriel, slumped, unable to stand. Just lying there, unable to lift her head up high, with no choice but to wait for help.

Then Gladys broke through the crowd. She was quickly followed by Mr Dalrymple. He helped Aunty Muriel to her feet. The man she would not love, the man she would not marry, though he was gentle, he was kind. With his ragged clothes and sandals, he looked like a prophet.

Gladys held me by the shoulders. 'You're in a right mess, love,' she said. I gripped her arm.

When I stood the world was a wonky one for I had sprained my ankle. I leant on Gladys. I could feel her shoulder bones. I tried to bear more of my weight.

She spoke firmly. 'Let's get you to the wash house, that's it.'

I will never forget the way Aunty Muriel hunched over a bucket to wash, how she scooped the water over her face, her arms. How the water trickled down her dusty, blood-streaked body. How she would not stop cleaning herself. The water was brown, bloody. It flowed away into the ditch.

Gladys came back with a fist full of salt for us to wash with, the soap having run out long ago. 'Been saving this,' she said, 'for a rainy day.' Aunty Muriel rubbed her face again; it was swelling before our eyes. She gasped with the sting of the salt. Then rinsed her face. The water would not run clean.

After our cuts had been carefully cleaned by Nurse Margaret, the single women nursed Aunty Muriel in her hut, while I lay on my mattress in our dormitory, with a puffed-up cheek and a swollen eye. The girls looked after me, feeding me watered-down gruel from my frying pan.

I came in and out of sleep. I'd wake, gasping, to a bone-dry world, then sink again. In time, the fever went and I lay there thinking about our home. I opened my Bible. I remembered how I used to fly on it, slipped between the Psalms. I tried to imagine Mother and Father. But their faces were lost to me. All I could see was the shape of Mother, bent over the trunk, like the lady over the manger. I remembered tugging at her skirts, nuzzling into her hip, trying to become part of her every movement. When you have lost something, think of when you last had it, is Aunty Muriel's advice. I tried again. I imagined Mother and Father as I last saw them, on the pier, waving at me, but the red string had long since snapped and all I could see were the coolies, the fish stalls, the churning water of the Huang Ho.

The following morning the girls marvelled at my bruises, the shape and colour of them. They asked again and again about the moment that I stepped out and flung myself at Private Tanaka's feet. I asked about Philip. 'He's woken up,' said Flo. 'He's doing better.' Then they took turns with feeding me from the frying pan and I noticed how heavy it was, and how they struggled to hold it up.

Just after roll call, Gladys came to visit me. 'That's a mighty good bruise you've got brewing,' she said. 'The gals are on their way,' she added, 'they wanted to see you.' Gladys was wearing a scarf, a scruffy peach one made of some old rag. She saw me looking at it. 'Got to protect my throat, Etta,' she said.

'What happened?'

'A man I once knew, a nasty piece of work. I was nineteen, living in Rome, hoping to train for the opera. Sometimes you get into situations. So, what do you do? You stand up for yourself, you fight, and then you move on.'

Nan and Stacey came in, Stacey's legs still swollen. They were quickly followed by the girls returning from roll call. The room was suddenly full and after teasing me about my admirer, whom Nan had seen standing outside the dormitory, the women got up to leave.

'To thine own self be true,' said Gladys as she stood at the door.

Nan Brown nodded, 'Wise man, that Churchill.'

In the afternoon, I got up and went to visit Aunty Muriel. She lay in the quiet of the hut, facing the wall. I approached slowly, looking at the back of her head. Her scalp was striped with pink cuts. Her hair was shorn off the better to clean the cuts. Her beautiful hair. The hair through which the Lushan light had shimmered, so fiery, wonderful.

She turned her head slowly to look at me. The balloon of her face smiled. 'Aunty Muriel, I found this, I've been keeping it in my Bible,' I said. I pushed the picture towards her. There in ink on rice paper was a lady with long hair, sitting by a waterfall.

Her split lip twitched. I wanted to explain that the monk

who had helped me down the mountain drew it for me so I wouldn't be afraid of the night. I wanted to explain how, that night when I had found myself on the other side of the mountain, far from everything I knew, I had looked at it and found that I was no longer scared. I wanted to say all these things, but instead all I could say was, 'I think it's you, Aunty Muriel.'

As she looked at the picture, I saw that she recognised both the woman sitting by the waterfall, and the hand that drew her there.

And I left Aunty Muriel, looking at herself, beautifully and wonderfully seen.

Later that evening, as we washed up our plates and spoons, we found out that Headmaster's wife had been called home. Although I hadn't been able to return to the hospital since the incident, it came as no surprise, for the last time I sat by Jenny Lammemuir's side, her skin was papery with dehydration, her breathing was fast, then slow, as it is when death is close, and when I squeezed her hand she did not open her eyes. The next morning they had her funeral, burying her in the graveyard, which lay beyond the hospital hut. She was laid to rest surrounded by the internees who had succumbed to sickness and malnutrition, who now lay in shallow graves, their names carved into wooden crosses.

It was a hot scorching day. Mr Dalrymple and the senior boys dug her grave. The school band played, a tribe of Sons of Thunder on trumpets, cornet, trombones. They laid the coffin in. Prayers were said, hymns were sung, Headmaster, barefoot and blinking, bowed his head. Jenny Lammemuir. The woman who once lay in her lemony blanket above Lushan School, her hands pressed together, lacing the air with prayers for the mountain's children, now lay in the hard soil of the Tsitao Camp, over which we stood.

Jenny Lammemuir had escaped; she had left internment. I had examined the walls of the Tsitao Civilian Centre so many times, knew the curve of the barbed wire, the shadows it cast at different hours. This is existence, I thought, as we trudged past the gate, rusted and closed. My gums ached, a jawful of pain. I had a clear sense of my skeleton in a way I'd never had before. We stepped towards our hut. We walked like ghosts, frail beings in faded clothes. Dust in our hair and earth under our nails. Our eyes dulled with exhaustion.

Back in our dormitory, we sat on our beds and did nothing. The trousseau was not opened, nor the Greek Primer, nor the clarinet case. No one did anything. We stared at the ceiling, at the light through the high-up windows. We sat as if waiting. Some of us had Red Cross news of parents to think about, some of us, including me, did not. I touched the sores on the sides of my face. One began to bleed. I looked at our room, the suitcases, musical instruments. We'd tried to put up little partitions but in time had needed the fabric for clothes. We had looked at each other so often. The stove, the shelf along which the rats ran. The bedbug jar, which was filled with thousands of the little red enemies.

'Our future. That's what's been taken from us,' said Kathryn.

'Mr Dalrymple said the first ten years of camp are the hardest,' said Hilary, 'and that it will get easier after that.'

'So when we're twenty-one camp will be easier?' said Edith, doing the sums.

'Twenty-one!' I said from my bed.

'Our life is over,' said Kathryn. 'We'll be old by the time we get out.'

'I had always thought I might get married,' said Fiona, smoothing down her blanket. 'To think that now I probably won't.'

'I still intend to get married,' said Thin Bum Eileen. But I could not imagine her thin bum, thin hair wedding.

Flo balanced things out. Her faith could. 'God wants us here. It's part of his plan. Four years or forty years, his timing is perfect.'

'So do you think we'll die in here?' Hilary asked us. 'As part of his plan?'

'Remember the Prophetess Club?' said Edith.

'Well, none of us foresaw that we'd be captured,' said Hilary.

'And kept captured for years and years,' said Kathryn.

Then someone stood up and walked towards my mattress. It was Thin Bum. She shook my leg with her hand and sat down. 'Tell us a prophecy,' she said. One by one the girls sat on my mattress.

'Prophecies hurt my eyes too much,' I said.

'Go on,' said Eileen.

'That was just a silly game from years ago. And it didn't lead to anything good,' I said.

'Well, if you won't make a prophecy, I will,' said Thin Bum. 'I prophesy we are captured and will remain captured until we're thirty.'

'Captured till we're thirty?' said Kathryn.

'That's as old as Aunty Muriel,' said Edith. I thought of Aunty Muriel and her wedding trousseau, her embroidered quilt and napkins and sheets, those dreams briskly given away.

A holiday haunting came to me, of watching Mother's sheet pinned to the wall, with its carefully drawn map of

306

China, with mission stations, rivers and cities, the one that the ants crossed endlessly. 'Captured?' I said. 'No, it's the opposite. We are a pilgrim people. We are forever travelling. Forever free. That's . . . that's the problem,' I said. 'We never arrive, we never find home.' Then, I remembered the ghost-girls. The ghost-girl the women of our village said I'd become. Beyond the city wall. And it came to me then that we children, pale as ghosts, would forever wander outside the city wall.

I propped myself up on my elbows. 'We float beyond the wall,' I said. 'That's my prophecy.' Then, I lay back down and staring at the ceiling, began a chant.

'Kathryn, whose mother and father who are safe in faraway Mongolia, you are called, your ghost floats beyond the wall.' *She floats beyond the wall*, replied the girls.

'Flo, whose mother and father are teaching divinity in Johannesburg, you are called. Your ghost floats beyond the wall.' *She floats beyond the wall.*

'Eileen, whose mother and father preach near the Tibetan border, you are called. Your ghost floats beyond the wall.' *She floats beyond the wall.*

'Fiona, whose mother and father are in a Hong Kong camp, you are called. Your ghost floats beyond the wall.' *She floats beyond the wall.*

'Hilary, whose parents await you and your brothers from Lunghua Camp, your ghost floats beyond the wall.' *She floats beyond the wall.*

'Isobel, whose mother lives with her grandparents on Prince Edward Island, whose father is in Yangchow Camp, your ghost floats beyond the wall.' *She floats beyond the wall.*

'And I, Henrietta, whose mother and father are waiting in

a cave in Shanxi Province, I am called, my ghost floats beyond the wall.' *She floats beyond the wall.*

'Do you think that prophecy will come true?' said Edith.

'I don't know. Anyway, it's not a prophecy, it's just a silly story.'

Then a sound ripped through the air. A mighty engine above the camp. It shook the corrugated roof with such force, you'd think it would blow your scalp off.

We went outside and shielding our eyes from the sun, we looked into the sky. Three planes circled above. They were not Japanese Zeroes.

'Look at their markings. It's American,' yelled a Son of Thunder, 'a B-24!'

Round and round the compound the plane circled. All the internees ran out of their huts, waving rags, dresses, a *Reader's Digest* at the sky. We are here. Do not forsake us. Save us.

Then over a nearby field something dropped. Six black bombs. The bombs became parachutes became legs became men. These sailing saviours floated to the field in parachutes like falling rainbows.

The gates, which had been opened for the cesspit coolies, were stormed by a wave of running internees. Through the gates we came, motherless children, shirtless businessmen, Shanghai ladies without furs, toothless missionaries and the Bulgarian burglar flying in a cassock.

Thank the Lord the fence was not electrified that day. The Japanese soldiers watched this escape from the parapet. They did nothing. We ran to freedom. But this was such a thin running. Skeletons with arms outstretched, necks tipped back, our weak lungs breathing knives of air.

Together we girls stumbled into the bright, free fields of

China. With Flo and Edith at either side of me, through the dust, through the muddy field, we ran. Our stomachs were empty, there were thorns in our feet, but we were free, free.

We reached the GI Joes, who were armed with guns, grenades and fists full of chocolate. They were setting up machine guns and radio equipment on the Chinese graves. 'Where are the Japs?' they asked.

'We will take you to them,' said a ragged Peter Hammond, and the soldiers were raised up on internee shoulders. Carried by a wave of joy, they were greeted at the camp gates not by bayonets but by the out-of-breath 'God Bless America' played by the Sons of Thunder, now thin as trombones.

Major Jackson handed out chocolate all the way to the commandant's office. When the commandant came out on to the veranda, he did not request roll call. Major Jackson ran up the steps to the veranda and the two men disappeared into the shuttered room. Twenty minutes later, they came out and the commandant rolled out a scroll. It was a decree from the emperor. He read it to Major Jackson, then handed over his samurai sword in its black lacquer sheath and his gun.

Then Major Jackson gave an address, his gestures wide and generous. We were to stay at the camp until the Allies had found a safe way of transporting us through the country-side, which was now roamed by warlords. The Japanese guards were to be kept on, to keep the Chinese out. And finally, there in the courtyard, we were set free.

While interns found Union Jacks to fly and the band began a medley of national anthems, I staggered back to my mattress. Free as a bird, sick as a dog, I lay down and vomited chocolate into my frying pan.

For six days planes dropped parachutes of food parcels. Explosions of spaghetti, beans, pork and peaches. Internees now roamed all over the camp. Lessons stopped, much to the disappointment of Miss Preedy, for although the Second Coming hadn't arrived, Red Cross dentures had and she was ready to resume her role.

I lay unwell in my bed. Late one afternoon out of the falling dusk there was a visitor at our dormitory. It was Philip. He was thin and somehow shy. I wanted to hug him but he was nearly ten and I didn't want to make him more embarrassed. 'Thank you for looking after me,' he said quietly, his eyes on the ground. In his hand was a note. He gave it to me, and waved goodbye.

'Thank you, Philip,' I said as I anxiously watched him walk back down the alley. A frail, shuffling boy. As he turned on to Main Street, a GI Joe came up to him. 'Hey, Phil, how's it going? Do you want to try on my cap, little buddy?' Philip took the cap. He would be okay, I thought. He had his own ways of making it through.

I opened the note. It was from Nigel Pinsent. He asked me to meet him at seven o'clock.

I joined him under the eaves of Kitchen One. The first rain in months began to patter on the corrugated iron roof.

'Hello.'

'Hello.'

Nigel Pinsent stared strangely at me, right into my eyes. He took a step closer. There was a raindrop down his face. His green eyes were blinking. His face was fading but oh, such nice eyelashes! He puffed out his cheeks, which were paler than ever, furrowed his eyebrows and stared. He had a look on him like he was about to leap the electric fence. Then he kissed me. I was somewhat astonished but then we kissed again, our feet sinking into the squishy mud.

We walked along the cinder track, glancing sidelong at each other. We went through the wooden gate and into the garden where the Red Cross medicines were stored, and also it was discovered, several large sacks, each containing bundles and bundles of our Red Cross letters, which hadn't been sent for more than two years. As we stepped over the gnarled twigs, covered in raindrops, I realised that without news from those monthly Red Cross letters, Mother and Father must think I was dead. I remembered Miss Kingsley's prayer list at the back of her missionary's diary and imagined Mother praying over her own list, stopping in silence for a moment when it came to my name, before continuing her prayers. As we left the garden that had once been out of bounds, with its weeds and brown stalks, Nigel put his hand in mine, and I thought, but Mother, I am alive, very much alive.

Then there were the goodbyes. We were all to leave in convoys over two weeks in early September. The old dust road had become so potholed lorries could no longer make the jolting journey. Instead, internees were to walk a mile to a small village, where they would be taken in trucks to Shanghai, where ships would travel to Australia, Canada, America, South Africa. Just a few wanted to stay in China, mostly missionaries keen to get back to their posts.

Gladys was in the first group to leave. She'd managed to arrange a lift for her and the gals. She stood in the back of an open-top Jeep wearing a khaki dress made from an American uniform, her green hair swept under a US Army cap. She leant across to kiss me on the cheek.

'I'm going to live with my sister in Calgary,' she said. 'And

I want you to visit.' She gave me the address, then Tommy, the American soldier leading the convoy, switched the engine on. Gladys tried to say something over the noise and fumes, but I couldn't catch it. The Jeep jerked, Gladys flew forward. She regained her balance and blew kisses as they bumped over the potholes, Nan Brown and Stacey Mullroy in a battered Jeep behind.

We were the last group to leave, our date set for a week's time. On the last Monday in camp, Aunty Muriel appeared in the doorway of our dormitory.

'Good morning, Dormitory A,' she said, as radiant as a Lushan afternoon. Her arms were full of parachutes. Red, yellow, green.

'Aunty Muriel.' We got up to greet her. The bruise on her face was now yellowish and the swelling around her mouth had gone down, so that she spoke with only a slight lisp.

'Now, girls, first things first. I want you to stop calling me Aunty Muriel. Instead, I'd like you to call me Muriel.' Then she went on to explain that earlier that day she had taken her first walk into the fields and gathered up the parachutes. 'Now, girls, what I need is the dormitory measuring tape.' We all looked to Eileen, who brought it out from her suitcase.

Muriel took the measuring tape – 'Thank you, Eileen' – and unwound it. Then she told us to form an orderly queue and she measured each one of us, shoulders, waist, hips, bust, the length of a girl from clavicle to knee. She stretched out the fabric and cut it to fit these measurements. And then she said that we would each sew our own dress. 'This you will do yourselves. As a mark of your growing up.'

During the next days, we did exactly that: slow sewing with a needle – pockets, collars, hems – each girl in the silence of her soul, which is memory, which is hope. For myself, I thought of home, of Pingxia village, our courtyard dotted with pot plants, and inside, my parents at the dining table, waiting.

This is how, on 4 September, we girls of Dormitory A left Tsitao Civilian Centre. Through the great iron gates we went, out on to the yellow dust road. Towards wide-open fields, dotted with white gravestones, and cormorants readying themselves to soar, we stepped, dressed in parachutes. Flying, floating beings, in garments of red and green and yellow, so thin that surely if there were a gust of air we too would float. Barefoot we walked, each holding a holiday suitcase that rattled with our few belongings: a family photograph, a Bible, a needle and a thread. Young women, dressed in flying fabric, for the journey home.

Part IV

Aboard a White Ship

The South China Sea, 1945

I AM WRITING THIS TO YOU ON THE P&O *POONA*, A WHITE SHIP that floats across the sea, from Shanghai to Southampton and all the latitudes in between. I am fifteen years old. I wonder if I might be heartbroken. I am lying in my bed, which is an army hammock in the Women's Partition. All about there is a strange bunting of stockings and brassieres. The women hang heavy in their swaying beds. Miss Preedy, Miss Otis, Mrs Leopold. We are being repatriated. The war has come to an end, the camp dismantled, our school for ever closed. Churches burn all the way up the Western Coast. The Reds have come and the missionaries must go. 'Ah, ruins, they are a call to faith,' sighs Miss Otis over her knitting. I have never seen Aunt Neb so still. There are no lines of children to organise, no Evening Prayer to prepare. Miss Preedy has gone a whole day without saying 'Chop chop'. There is nothing to do but to lie down in a hammock and think of what has gone, of what will come. We are in between places. A pilgrim people. Just as Ruth left Moab and Sarah left Haran, and Noah's wife found herself in a zoo, afloat.

I have decided to write down my story. I swapped the cigarettes given to me by an American soldier with Mrs Pinder, and got this Red Cross paper. Miss Otis donated some old sheets of Mozart music that the orchestra played in camp. Miss Preedy, who has asked me to call her Janet, let me use her pencil. Thank you, Janet.

This is a list of what I own. A green, a blue, and a parachute dress, four pairs of Red Cross knickers, a pair of Red Cross glasses, my Bible with its pressed leaves, a sewing kit and half of Nigel Pinsent's stamp collection received with a last kiss outside the Cathay Pacific Hotel. They are all in my holiday suitcase. I lack a brassiere.

I also lack China and parents. It has been four days since we sailed out past the junks and the fishing boats to where the Shanghai Bund became a flat line. I write from the waves, where there are no flies, there are no birds. If you were to stand on the shore and look out to sea, my ship would not be on your horizon.

China, land of my birth, through Red Cross glasses I watched you disappear, my chest pressed against the railing, my hair blustering this way and that. I cried and cried and no one came. There is no Muriel, Kathryn, or Eileen, for last month they were shipped to Australia. Isobel, Hilary and Philip Hill have travelled to Vancouver. Edith and Flo sit with Nigel and the other half of his stamp collection, in the Shanghai mission home waiting to set sail to Johannesburg. Apart from Elspeth West and Fiona Pinder, who, having been reunited with their parents, live in the *Poona*'s family cabins, and the clutch of staff in the Women's Partition, I am alone. I stood on the deck past lunch and teatime and no one made me go in, for I am no longer a schoolgirl, and until I am delivered to the pier at Southampton, I am not yet a daughter.

Land of my birth, how can the women settle so quickly into their hammocks to knit and repair their socks? I stood steadfast until the stars came out, until the only sound was engine and ocean and my own voice, listing the things I love: watermelon pips, red bean buns, the strange twists of your mountain pines. I am listing you so that I never forget. Could you hear me chanting into the wind?

Once a cruiser, the P&O *Poona* was requisitioned by the Ministry of War Transport and converted to a troop carrier, and here we lie in a barrack-like room, where soldiers once lay as they travelled to war, watching the pewter sea through the portholes, remembering home.

Home. It's all they ever talk about in the Women's Partition. Each day the accent of Miss Otis gets more Yorkshire. 'It'll be nice, dear, to be at home,' she keeps saying over the clack of her needles. Yunnan, Hunan, Zhenjiang, Jiujiang. We were girls from all over China. And now we have been sent to Canada, South Africa, Australia. To places we have never been.

On the day our camp convoy arrived at the Shanghai mission headquarters, I was told by the superintendent that Mother and Father were alive but no longer in China. They had fled the marching Reds, escaping west through Tibet, then flying over Everest before sailing from Calcutta to settle in a place called Hull. They have been told of my return and will be there to watch the white ship sail in from the ocean.

Oh, Mother and Father, what if they walk right past me on Southampton pier? Their eyes searching but unseeing, shouting to the crowd, 'Where is our daughter, where is our daughter?'

I lack the daughter-words to answer them.

Last night I was so sick of hearing of this England that I swung in my hammock, Red Cross glasses off, singing 'China is home' with all the howl of a Chinese opera. The Women's Partition stiffened and tutted. When Miss Preedy appeared at the end of my hammock with new Red Cross teeth, and asked if I thought I might need a wee prayer, I shook my head. No, thank you, Janet.

Instead, I rolled over and thought of my mountain. I lift mine eyes up to the mountain, where does my help come from. Oh, beautiful mountain, remembering you is prayer. I trace you with my fingers. Up, up the Great Steps, across Drill Court, by the Girls' Building all rambled over with flowers, over the arched bridge where Livingstone and Carey Stream bubble into each other. Leaf by leaf of our dormitory garden, step by step to the door of the Girls' Building, bud by bud of the graveside azalea.

Miss Tippet. Everyone knows she is dying. Something in her stomach and it isn't sea-sickness. 'A Psalm, dear,' she said, as I sat by her bed. There in the Sick Bay, under a brass-rimmed porthole, I took her Bible in my hands. It was light as a bird. Written inside the front cover was, 'Georgia Tippet 1877'. Miss Tippet didn't say please or thank you and I didn't mind for she's an old missionary who escaped the Boxers, survived two Yellow River shipwrecks and was the other half of Miss Kingsley's famous Duo. Being read Psalms is her right.

'Psalm Eighty-four,' she said, and closed her eyes. *My heart and my flesh crieth out for the living God.* I held the Bible close to my eyes. Today was a good reading day; my eyes were not so sore today. The waves crested and ploughed. I let my voice get softer, a dusk falling, until Miss Tippet's eyes came to stillness under her eyelids, and her breath slid easy under her Red Cross blanket. *Yea, the sparrow hath found an house.*

This afternoon I was lying on my tummy, writing, when Elspeth West came to my hammock again. She stood there swinging me without even saying hello. I turned to glare when I noticed her goldy eyelashes were damp with tears, and her nose pink. I invited her aboard. She got in, curled up and shook like a squall.

The problem is this: Elspeth West is simply the wrong size for her parents. She and her brother, Frank, were reunited with them in Shanghai two weeks ago. They are busy trying to be a family in Family Cabins. Elspeth West is now twelve and, despite the lack of food in camp, is taller than me. Huge. Now that she's a daughter again, she is trying to be little, just like the girl her parents once knew. But Elspeth West is so big and grown that her parents don't know what to do.

I leant over Elspeth. 'Would you like me to pray for you?' She nodded. I prayed a pretty prayer of rainbows and eagles then, like the storm on the Sea of Galilee, the tears of Elspeth West stopped. Sometimes prayer is the Lord running his hands through your hair, saying ssh, there, there, be still.

'Elspeth, a question. How to speak to mothers and fathers? How to be in a Family Cabin?' Elspeth can only shrug her big, soft shoulders.

There is a mirror in the ladies' bathroom. While the Women's Partition is having its afternoon nap, I went to visit my face. Hello, face. You are blue eyes behind metal-rimmed Red Cross glasses, pointy chin, sharp cheeks, limp blond hair. You are what they will see when we arrive in England. Are you Bright? Are you Beautiful?

The face blinked. She looked sad. I couldn't see her future.

Tomorrow, I will take Elspeth to visit the mirror. We must practise our smiles.

Entering Sick Bay, with its smell of bitter bleach, I went to the furthest corner and gave Miss Tippet a smile so big, it almost split the dry cracks of my lips. It was the last day of travel and was a bad day for both of us so we were talking not reading. Miss Tippet told me of her plans to stay for a while with a cousin in Eastbourne. I wanted to know what had happened to Miss Kingsley. 'Oh, Miss Kingsley,' she said. 'She will not be found by the Mission. If they found her, they'd make her leave and she will not leave for it is in China she wishes to be buried.'

Later that afternoon, as I sat on the deck and wrote, I thought of Miss Kingsley upon her junk sailing south to the Karst Mountains, of Gladys waving from the GI's Jeep, of Muriel setting off in the rickshaw towards the Bund, her russet tufts tucked under a woollen hat. Every now and then I'd look up at the sky stretching far away to the horizon where it became a bandage of yellow haze. We were by the toe of Portugal. Tomorrow we'd arrive.

For that last goodbye there had been the business of luggage, of getting the Australia party into the rickshaws that waited outside the mission compound on Sinza Road, of hugs to cover the pain, to avoid the tears, a celebration almost, of new beginnings. That Muriel had chosen to go to Sydney was, some said, a mystery. But I knew that the mission headquarters would be based there until things settled in China. Aunty Muriel would type letters and keep files up to date. Then she would return to China but this time to work as a proper missionary. I remembered how she had stood above Twelve's grave. That white azaelea, she had said, it will bloom. I knew that she wanted to return to China to try again.

It began to rain. Eileen and Kathryn climbed into their rickshaw, practising an Australian accent as they said goodbye. Then it was Muriel's turn. She gave me a quick hug, her hair poking from under the woollen hat, which hid her scars. 'How long has it been since you've seen your parents?' she asked as people brushed past in a jostle of holiday suitcases, trunks and bundles.

'Five years,' I said.

'You do remember what they look like, don't you?'

'Yes,' I said, 'Mother is . . .' I searched for the image to describe. A woman stood on the pier, a man by her side. Their hands were waving, that was all I could see, that and the snapped red thread. Muriel saw me falter over the image. Stutter over the gap.

'But you'll see them soon,' she said, looking at me firmly, as if wishing to pass on her own strength and resolve. 'Do you remember that night you returned to Lushan when you came running to me out of the dark? I thought you were lost for ever. But here you are, a brave young woman. Just think, you'll be in England before the end of the year. Etta, as I travel to Australia I will think of you, especially your help in the camp. Thank you.'

The rain spattered on our faces, on the road. The suitcases were now packed into the wooden rickshaws. The Australia party was waiting. It was time.

'Goodbye, Etta.'

'Goodbye, Muriel.'

Pretending to be more grown up and self-sufficient than I am, I waved like the rest, but when the rickshaw's canvas cover was drawn up and the wheels began to move, I watched, watched, so that if she turned, she would see that I was there, that I was always there. The crack of thunder, then more raindrops, fat plops, spattering, clattering, we were soaked, goodbye Big Bum, goodbye Kathryn, goodbye Muriel, how quickly they disappeared into the stream of rickshaws on Sinza Road, their canvas covers darkened by rain.

Two white uniformed stewards passed, saying, 'Okay, Miss?' I nodded and continued, trying to keep the pages still in the wind, pressing the corners down, pressing down on my pencil, so that my fingers throbbed, so that my pages were dented with the weight of my thoughts. I wanted to record everything, to order it, to make something I could hold, could put in my suitcase and carry ashore.

I tried to capture Aunty Muriel. And dear Twelve. And Big Bum. And that danger that burrowed, that lay in the skin of the earth. I scribbled and thought, but I couldn't make things bright and simple as a tract. Couldn't set down a life on a page with clear, black outlines.

I sank back. Exhausted. My eyes were straining. My fingers pulsed red. I took off my glasses. I looked up. There in the sky was a fish. A cloud fish. I had seen such a fish once before. As I watched the sky, one of my holiday hauntings came. It arrived like a fish tipping a ship, and I sat for some time, keeling, unable to find the horizon.

Nearly five years ago, my parents and I joined a group of missionary families at the mission's guesthouse in Zhefu. It was our only ever seaside holiday, for my parents' post in Pingxia village was several weeks west from the ocean. On our last evening of the holiday, we walked out from the guesthouse and on to the yellow sands. Which way to go for our evening stroll? Heads turned left and heads turned right.

To the hubbub of the harbour with its fish-stink stalls, where black eels flipped in tiny tin buckets? Or to the headland where the golden pagoda rose?

I didn't look to the left and to right as the adults did. I gazed straight ahead, out towards the China Sea where in the sky amongst blobs of fluff, I saw a cloud in the shape of a fish.

'This is the way to go,' I said, raising my finger to the pink sky. 'This is the way for fishers of men.' The adults looked to the sky and laughed. Why, yes, what a good idea, they would follow the nose of the fish.

I liked being the girl with a cloud-fish, but most of all I wanted to be a daughter. I watched the other boys and girls. The Braziers, Johnsons and Dewarts danced in and around their mothers and fathers without even thinking, oh now I am waving at a mummy, oh now I am talking to a daddy. They didn't seem nervous or excited about having parents. They were too young to have been to Lushan School, where you learn to forget such things.

I made do with looking at our footprints. I twisted round to see them. Father's heels pressed a deep and clear mark in the ground. My footprints were light and small. I wondered if I could get so light, that no mark of me would be left, so I made my footsteps as light as possible. When I peered back, I could barely see them at all. It looked like Father had walked along the beach alone. I didn't want to be invisible so I stomped with all my might.

I ran in fretful circles around the mothers and fathers and children. There was a great danger but the adults did not know. They laughed and talked about a Chinese pastor's new wife and the price of rice. I ran out beyond them, behind them, to the sea, to the bank. I chased crabs. I zigged and I zagged across the sand. I picked up a shell. It was creature-less. I followed a squiggle of seaweed. It twisted and snaked. I prodded the washed-up jellyfish, dead but still munching its lunch. I had tried to be a daughter but I wasn't one. I was a soothsayer, a seer of signs on the shore and messages in the sky.

How can I warn you? What can I say?

They do not know. They have not seen what I have seen.

I crouched by the ocean to wash my hands that were dirty from examining death. The children came to the water's edge. 'What are you doing?' they asked. One of the Dewart boys tapped a jellyfish with his stick. I yanked his arm away. 'Be careful.' The jellyfish could sting us, the crab could tweak our toes. We could be sucked away by the ocean. 'Come on, come on! It is not safe here.' I began to pull the children up towards the bank.

'Henrietta, what are you doing? What a disturbance. Don't drag Stephen and James like that. Let them go.' Mother scolded me for pulling the children away. We never made it to the harbour. We never saw the eels thrashing in their tiny tin buckets. My cloud-fish disappeared in the black sky. We had to return to the slanting-eaved guesthouse for night had come. There, lying under my blanket, I could hear the ocean, hushing in and out. I listened as it ate my footsteps.

Once upon a time, Mother and Father crept out into the night and, with fingers as straight as pencils, they wrote my name upon the shore. But by morning the tide had come in and the waves had lapped away my name. I had vanished into the big, grey ocean.

*

We look for our daughter upon the shore. We trace the shapes of seaweed for secret words. We walk up and down, up and down, collecting chipped shells in our pockets, checking footprints.

I am her mother yet she does not know me. I bent to kiss my daughter but she retreated as a wave sucked back into the ocean. My daughter, like a droplet in the ocean. I stand upon the shore and call out her name.

One of the stewards came back along the deck clutching his cap. He told me to go inside. Another battened down a swaying lifeboat. There was a storm before we entered the Channel. I gathered my papers, stepped into the small side door, down the narrow, steep steps, and down more to the lower levels, where the air was still musty with the sweat of soldiers, and along the corridors, feeling the ocean rise and roll, until I came to the Women's Partition. There the women were readying themselves for dinner. Although converted to carrying troops, the P&O *Poona* still had a long dining room with round tables and chandeliers. Each night, dinner was a grand affair, and although we'd dined in this way for six weeks, I was still shocked to see the leftovers, chicken carcasses and vegetable peelings flying overboard the next day.

Tonight was to be our final dinner under those bright and beautiful lights, and the women rushed around rubbing talc under their arms, neatening their collars, tucking hair behind their ears. I felt a ball of worry in my tummy. The ocean tipped and buckled underneath us. Time was slipping away. Soon we would be ashore.

Up in the dining room, where the air was briny and you

could hear the waves crash, the white-clad stewards dampened tablecloths so none of the plates slipped off. It was seven o'clock and a wintry night. Our reflections were all we could see of the wild ocean.

I was sat at a table with Mr and Mrs Watson, the West family, Janet Preedy and a canon from Shanghai Cathedral. I hadn't seen Mrs Watson on the six-week journey for she had lain in her cabin, sick. They had survived the war and, to their great surprise, Mrs Watson was pregnant, her belly a firm bump.

While Mrs Watson quietly sliced meat off a chicken thigh, Mr West and Mr Watson spoke of their plans to return to China. As soon as things settled.

The canon gestured his fork at Mrs Watson's belly. 'What will you do with the child now that Lushan has been closed?'

'Oh, I am sure the mission will quickly make provisions for a new school. And if not, then no doubt it will be the usual arrangement: boarding school in England,' Mr Watson replied.

'A new Lushan will open, of course!' said Miss Preedy, plunging her fork into a potato. She was so delighted to be dining near the canon her lips could barely contain her Red Cross teeth. 'Missionary parents need somewhere to send their children so that they might continue their work.'

The canon turned to Elspeth and me. 'A missionary's sacrifice,' he said, and winked. Mrs Watson put her hand on her belly and I thought of the child there, swimming, eyes closed in the dark.

Then Mr West, father of Elspeth, patted his mouth with a napkin and, carefully folding the napkin up again, began to quote Mark's gospel: 'As Jesus said to Peter, "Truly, I say to you, there is no one who has left house or brothers or sisters or mother or father or children or lands, for my sake and for the gospel, who will not receive a hundredfold."'

'God will bless us for these sacrifices,' said Mr Watson, patting his wife's belly. The adults nodded and murmured.

I felt furiously sick. The table was like a round world and everyone was oceans away from me. I glanced at poor, over-grown Elspeth. She was staring at her chicken bones. I couldn't eat another disgusting bite. The dazzle of lights made me dizzy. Without saying excuse me, I got up and ran through the room with its bright laughs, glinting lights and plates of sinew and bone. I staggered into the dark outside.

I climbed through the small door, down the narrow staircase, and lurched along the stuffy corridor where the lights flickered, on and off, all the way to the Women's Partition. The room was empty. I kneeled down, opened my suitcase and took out my Bible. I felt its weight in my palm. The ship began to groan. I put my fingertips inside my Bible's leather cover, stroked the ribbon bookmark, the bent-over corners. I felt the thin pages, pages that were weaker than me. I began to tear them. Genesis, Exodus, Leviticus. I tore book after book. Psalms were severed, the Israelites forever wandered in the desert, separated from the Promised Land, the descendants of David fell scattered.

I looked around the women's cabin, shocked. There were scraps of Bible on the floor, in my suitcase. I waited for an Almighty bash on the head.

Nothing came.

I gathered the pieces into my arms and, cradling them, ran from the Women's Partition, up the corridor, the steep stairs, through the small door and along the slippery walkway to the ship's stern.

What a blustery night. The waves towered like black

peaks, then crashed. The davits screeched in the gale. The lifeboats swung out over the ship's edge. Night was so dark and there was no horizon. It was difficult to stay upright, for everything – the railings, the deck, the rivets – was slippy. The spray was light as mist and my lips tasted of salt.

I walked along the deck, towards the angry, angry ocean. A man yelled. I looked around. It was one of the stewards. 'Don't stand outside, Miss. Too dangerous.' I ignored him and ran towards the railings. And there, like breadcrumbs for the seagulls, I threw out the scraps of God's word. The wind sucked and spun them high. Some blustered back to deck, then were snatched out over the sea again. The spray dampened them, and they were made heavy and were dragged into the water. I gripped the rails, watching the ocean through which we had come. Somewhere in the great in-between, was God drowning.

Back in the Women's Partition, I hurled myself into bed, fully dressed. As the ship moved through the gale towards land, I lay in the dark, clutching the sides of my hammock.

Have you seen Lot's wife? She lives inside you. A salty lady, looking back. She is the trickle down your face.

When I woke up in the morning, my heart and the sea were still. But all was bustle in the Women's Partition; it was the day of our arrival. Suitcases scraped on the floor, trunk locks clicked open and shut. After six weeks at sea, we were coming home.

'Time to pop on your arriving frock,' said Miss Preedy, appearing at my hammock. I took the green dress from the suitcase. It had been given by the Red Cross. Miss Preedy had advised me to keep it for good, for the day I arrived so that I'd make a pretty impression. It was beautiful, a green pleated skirt with a green velvet bolero top. Great green puff sleeves. Oh, but the wool stockings and cardigan were itchy, itchy. I put them on, then went to the ladies' toilets to a choir of compliments: 'Oh, quite the lady, Henrietta; it's nice to see you scrub up.' 'Very nice, but do remember to give your hair a good brush.'

In the washroom, I looked in the mirror. First I practised my smile. Then, I slid a hair clip above my ear. It had three little red apples on it. I imagined Muriel saying, 'Very good, Etta.' I set my glasses straight. There, I felt more ready to see England. Now, my list of daughter words:

Hello. Very pleased to meet you. (Extend hand, smile.)

It was a good trip, thank you. I particularly enjoyed passing through the Red Sea. From the boat we saw Mount Sinai. Have you seen Mount Sinai?

And yourselves? Are you well? Mother?

Mother. I could barely mouth the word.

Mummy?

Mrs Robertson?

The daughter words disappeared. I stared at the girl with the list in her hand. Her mouth was open and a tear was coming down her cheek.

The sea carries me to England, a pale woman with long yellow hair, weeping. I have always been afraid of ghosts. Of being haunted by one. Of becoming one. A ghost is what you become if you are tethered to nothing. No place, no person, no deity, not even yourself.

A crowd was crammed on to the prow. A man played the trumpet. Mrs Pinder wore red lipstick. She held Fiona tight by her wrist. Next to them a lady with a dead fox about her shoulders stood on a chair, held up by a dozen cheery men.

The lady with the fox began to sing, 'God save our gracious King'. Everyone turned to each other and joined in, 'Long live our noble King'.

I pushed through the crowd towards the railing. A man nearby said, 'On a good day you can see the Isle of Wight.' But today was not a good day. Today was a grey day.

Then a man somewhere shouted, 'Land!' and the crowd cheered. The men with the trumpets started up again. I peered over the rail. There it was. England. A grey ridge between grey sea and grey sky. It smelt of wet earth. I couldn't imagine ever arriving. I wanted to stay on the ocean. Waves foamed. The sky was heavy with dark clouds.

I stood in my new clothes, with my itchy arms and my itchy legs. I watched England get bigger and bigger. Then a white flake drifted down. And another. And another. It was snowing. The snow brushed my face. It was white snow, little snow, here-then-gone melting snow. There was snow on my eyelashes, on my cheeks, on my tongue. Snow, light as kisses. Snow that tickled.

Behind us, was China. We were separated by nights and days of ocean. The snow fell and fell.

Acknowledgements

I'd like to thank the many gifted people who have helped bring this book into being. To my literary agent Judith Murray for great heart and enthusiasm, to my amazing editor Mary-Anne Harrington for her enlivening perception and the occasional hark, and to the wider Tinder Press team, in particular Yvonne Holland for an eagle eye and Big Bum Eileen's skipping rope, Yeti Lambregts for so beautifully translating the world of Lushan into paper mist, pines and peaks, Amy Perkins for compiling with grace, Tom Noble for having his finger on the pulse, and to the wonderfully cosmic Ella Bowman; thank you.

Big gratitude too to the many people who helped with my research. I'd like to thank Susannah Raynor at the SOAS Special Collections, the staff at the British Library, and OMF International for permission to publish a photograph from their archives and Chinese character artwork. Thank you to those who shared memories of their missionary childhoods in war-time China, in particular, Eleanor Pen Itehn who showed me her photograph albums, Peter Bazire, Chefoosian and trumpeter in the Weihsien Internment Camp Salvation Army band, and Fleur Griffiths, child psychologist and missionary kid for wise counsel about girls and childhood separation. I'd also like to thank the pre-eminent Alice Huntley for helping with the novel's Pinyin and place names. And to the many Chinese people who offered kindness, stories and assistance as I journeyed from Jiangxi to Shanxi, in search of Etta's childhood landscapes, *xie xie*.

For encouragement, inspiration and laughter, there are many people I'd like to thank: Kirsti Abernethy, Seke Chimutengwende, Sophie Coleman, Susanna Jones, Susie Maguire, Andrew Motion, Jo Shapcott, Matthew Simpson, Dr Jenny Stevens, Mairi Taylor and Honga Wright. I'm very grateful for my friendship with Helen Stedeford and our conversations about third culture childhoods. Special thanks to Jane Anderson (the paper dogs will not be forgotten), to Sally Jacobs for faith, and to Jess Swift for home while I wrote.

Thank you to my family. To my parents for their support and love. To Mimi for listening to my earliest stories.

And last and most of all, I'd like to thank Joanna Mackenzie for her medical acumen, vigorous reading and eternal sunshine. Jojo, you are truly bright and beautiful.

Author's Note

This book is a work of fiction inspired by the history of missionaries in China. The first Protestant missionaries came to China in 1807 and remained there until the Communists closed the country to mission work in 1953. During this time, missionaries founded hospitals, preached from tracts and gospel gloves, ran schools for blind children, and evangelised up and down the fabled Women's River. As the missionaries pursued their calling, mission boarding schools were set up to educate their children. One such school was the China Inland Mission's Chefoo School, situated in the treaty port Chefoo (now Yantai) and overlooking the Yellow Sea. With many parents working far inland, it was not uncommon for pupils, some as young as six or seven, to have a 3,000 mile trip home for their yearly holiday. The onset of war meant these journeys became more perilous, and so the separation between parent and child lengthened.

The novel's school is set on a fictional mountain, a landscape inspired by Wang Wusheng's photographs of Huangshan in his book *Celestial Realm: The Yellow Mountains of China*. Captivated by the granite peaks and pouring mists of his photographs, I travelled to China to climb Huangshan for myself. As I walked the ancient paths that criss-crossed the mountain, I searched for the places where Etta would have played, feeling my way for an Etta-like absence as I went. I also spent time on a mountain called Lushan, which was situated further east in Jiangxi Province. A strong missionary community once lived there, including, at certain periods of its history, a missionary school. During the Second World War the Japanese invaded and sent the missionaries to internment camps near Shanghai. I used the historical detail of this invasion, combining it with the mystical landscape of Huangshan along with much imagination to create a fictional 'Lushan'.

One of the novel's key events was inspired by a moment in the history of Chefoo School. The port of Chefoo was occupied by the Japanese and after Pearl Harbor in December 1941, the whole school was interned, first at Temple Hill Camp and then Weihsien Civilian Assembly Centre. The imagined camp of the novel is a darker place than the one experienced by Chefoo School children, with a tougher regime, perhaps something more akin to that experienced by children in the other Japanese camps. Nicola Tyrer's book *Stolen Childhoods* was helpful here. However, one shared event between the Weihsien camp and the fictional camp was the liberation by American airmen who parachuted from their plane into a nearby field and were carried atop prisoners' shoulders on a victory march through the gates to the accompaniment of the camp band.

After the war ended, the children were repatriated to their home countries and reunited with their parents. One ship, the SS *Arawa*, set sail from Shanghai with a group of missionary children on board, docking in Southampton in last days of 1945. Some of the children had not seen their parents for more than seven years. Some did not recognise the faces waiting on the pier. But it is on the ocean that I chose to end Etta's story, a young woman in-between places.